THE LAST SHADOW

THE LAST SHADOW

J.D. ROBINSON

This is a work of fiction. Names, characters, places, and incidents are either the product of the author's imagination or are used fictitiously. Any resemblance to actual persons, living or dead, or events, or locales, is entirely coincidental.

Copyright © 2019 by J.D. Robinson

All rights reserved. No part of this book may be reproduced or used in any manner without written permission of the copyright owner except for the use of quotations in a book review.

Book design by J.D. Robinson
Cover artwork by Bastien Lecouffe Deharme

No generative artificial intelligence (AI) was used in the production of this work. The author expressly prohibits the use of this publication as training data for AI technologies or large language models (LLMs) for generative purposes. The author reserves all rights to license uses of this work for generative AI training and the development of LLMs.

DEDICATION

For my family, both real and imagined.

JOIN MY NEWSLETTER

The J.D. Robinson newsletter offers news, sneak previews from upcoming releases, plus oddments and ephemera.

See the back of the book for details on how to sign up.

PART 1

1

FRIDAY, APRIL 12, 1991

BAS MILIUS FAILED to dodge the uppercut to his jaw as Tom Petty was *"Learning To Fly"* on the jukebox upstairs. As the kid's knuckles found their mark, the musical accompaniment seemed almost fitting.

"*Told* ya this wasn't gonna go your way, gramps."

Bas hardly heard his opponent's taunt; he was too focused on the pain settling somewhere behind his molars, too busy trying to figure out what had just happened. How had this kid landed that blow? Bas was a foot taller than the shark-faced punk bouncing around across from him like a marionette, and the kid telegraphed his every move. But none of that mattered. Because in that moment, the one thing Bas knew for certain was that the sleight of fist he had just witnessed was not physically possible.

Maybe it had been a trick of the light. The bulb dangling overhead was barely bright enough to illuminate the gathered crowd, let alone the mostly empty shelves lining the Red Bell Tavern's storage cellar.

Bas replayed what had just happened. The stranger had bent his knees to prepare his throw—a rookie mistake—but before Bas could make his move, his face was already contorting around an incoming fist. The kid's arm had never even moved from his side. The blow had been instantaneous, as though Bas had lost a second of time.

Bas shook off the humiliation and filled his lungs with loamy funk as he got his guard back up. The kid might be half his age, but it would only take one shot to shut that ego down for the night.

And all of this over a misshapen old wedding band.

Bas read the kid's next move before it came—a left jab, easily avoided with a two-point slip. He ducked outside the punch, feinted with his left hand, then pivoted as he threw a devastating right at his opponent.

At least it *would* have been devastating—if the kid were still there.

The sympathetic murmur of the onlookers crescendoed as Bas's opponent used a bony shoulder to dig into Bas's ribs. Sweeping his infuriatingly long blond hair out of his face, the kid whispered through gritted teeth, "I'll spank you so hard you'll forget your name."

Bas almost had time to laugh before he was besieged by a hail of blows to his gut. That was when it finally registered: the kid was fighting with more than two arms.

How?

Spooked as much as staggered, Bas pulled away from the kid's sour exhaust and was forced to square up just to regain his balance. He knew that was a mistake even before the kid's next blow stabbed into the meat where neck met jaw, launching a constellation of stars behind Bas's eyes.

There was no way this kid was good enough to induce hallucination. He had no balance. His form was all over the place. He wasn't even in shape. Bas should have sent him packing two minutes ago, despite his aching joints and bad eyesight.

But Bas had never stood a chance.

This kid, whoever he was, was pulling some serious supernatural mind games, and Bas was the only one who saw it.

Ten minutes ago Bas had been staring down at a bottle of some nutty craft malt Griffin had stocked, likely another of his efforts to ward off the townie contingent. It wasn't bad, just over-engineered—more complicated than nuanced.

Slouched over the bar, Bas patted his breast pocket and fished out a misshapen ring. Lana's ring was the last thing he had left of his wife. The third garnet had long since gone missing, and in the smoke-yellowed light the rose gold looked even more misshapen. There was only one fix for that.

Bas stood the keepsake up between his forefinger and the counter, then gave it a flick. In that moment, as the ring whirled in a gentle circle, it was perfect: a flickering sphere with no indication of the stresses it had endured.

As Bas watched the gold band dance, he decided he had worked his last case. He swirled another sip of the bitter beer in his mouth, and the idea of retirement finally tasted true.

He was done.

It wasn't a new idea, of course. It had first occurred to him eight years ago, only minutes after the Commonwealth of Massachusetts issued his private investigator's license. But at this moment, the thought of taking on even one more infidelity or missing persons case, or camping in his Monza Spyder on a stakeout, made his chest feel tight.

"That's gotta mean something to you."

Bas looked over at the stranger loitering next to him. He automatically sized up the man. A kid, really. Scrawny, with sharp eyes and sharper features. And a fading orbital laceration that suggested he had recently walked face-first into something.

At the moment he was looking down at Lana's ring, which was just gyrating to a gradual stop beneath the yellow track lights.

Bas cleared his throat. "'Scuse me?"

The stranger needed no more of an invitation than that, and

made himself comfortable on the next stool. He reached over and snatched the ring from the counter.

Bas's muscles tensed. "Hey, pal."

"Easy," the thin man said. But he did a double-take as he took in Bas for the first time. "Jesus, look at you. Were you cross-bred with a grizzly bear?"

His tone was anything but intimidated.

"Let's go. Hand it over," Bas said, wiping his hand across his pant leg.

"I just want a look."

Boundary issues, low inhibition, lacking discretion when approaching strangers. Bas was all too familiar with the type. Once a man caught the eye of someone like this, it was difficult to disengage without some sort of escalation.

"This is really something, you know," the man said, assessing the jewelry like some street appraiser. "I could see that much from across the room. Name's Wallace, by the way. This is *really* warped, isn't it? Like, melted."

"Yeah, well I'd appreciate it if you could give me back my ring."

"*Your* ring?" The man's smirk carved a hollow beneath his cheekbone. Bas's face grew warm, but the ring was back in his palm before he could speak. The man chuckled. "Man, I don't know if you've seen your fingers lately, but no way you're getting *that* thing on."

Bas grunted and looked in the mirror behind the bar. He stared past himself, out through the window behind him. Maybe it was the shitty spring weather, but the atmosphere in the Red Bell had grown salty early. Once he finished this beer substitute, he would head home to find something to wash away the flavor.

"She leave you?"

Bas blinked. "What?"

The jukebox in the corner clacked as it swapped out records, and Bas's voice was too loud during the momentary lull.

The thin man was still there, working a handful of nuts like they were dice.

"I'm just wondering about this sad-sack routine of yours," he said, tossing a nut into his mouth and chewing with his mouth open. "I mean, you're better than that, right? If she left you, why waste your time crying over it?"

"You need anything, Bas?" Harriet asked from around a mostly ash cigarette hanging from the corner of her mouth. The Red Bell's proprietress had materialized behind the bar and was giving Bas a loaded look. She stood up for her regulars.

"I'm good," he said, more tired than annoyed.

She shrugged and moved away while the scrawny stranger tracked her with interest. He was enjoying this, like a moth who had found the only bulb in the alley. His amusement only fed into Bas's feeling of fatigue.

"Buddy, look," Bas said, rolling his glass between his fingers, "I'm just not feeling sociable at the moment, okay?"

The kid shook his head. "Way I figure, I'd be doing you a favor if I took that ring *off* you."

"Yeah, well…" Bas shook his head. "Not interested."

The kid grabbed another fistful of nuts. "You *say* no, but you didn't see your face a minute ago. That thing's no good for you—the ring, I mean. And I think you know it."

Bas's thoughts drifted to his apartment. In that moment he could think of no other place he wanted to be—despite the fact that he didn't have the place to himself. Mo had been camping there for the past few days, calling in favors as she meandered through Boston.

"How 'bout we go a few rounds?"

Bas found it impossible to stifle a laugh. "Unbelievable," he said, almost to himself.

"First man down gives up any claim," the kid said. He was serious.

"You *have* no claim, buddy," Bas said, turning on his stool to face the other man, locking eyes with him. "I'm not *fighting* you for my own ring, got it?"

They had drawn glances from the other patrons at the bar.

Who was this kid? Bas had never seen him in the Red Bell before, and the transients and tourists tended to stay away from the regulars. It was a natural social dynamic that maintained the civic balance.

"She couldn't have been all that," said the stranger, pushing his blond hair out of his eyes.

"Jesus Christ."

"What?" A defensive tone, as if Bas was being unreasonable. "I mean, if she left you, right? What does it say about her? Either that, or you have a lower opinion of yourself than I do. Is that it? Is this like a wallowing shtick, a boo-hoo kinda thing?"

"It's a go-away-and-leave-me-the-fuck-alone kinda thing, okay? Whatever your game is, I'm not interested."

"Fine, but I promise you every time you see that thing it's only gonna remind you of the jamoke she's fuck—"

Before Bas was aware of what he was doing, he had stood and pinned the thin man up against the bar.

―――

Now, in the cellar, as the scrawny man's fist dug into Bas's jaw, the bare overhead bulb flared once, then went dark.

Only, no, it wasn't the bulb at all. For a moment Bas's eyes just stopped working.

The grit of the Red Bell's basement floor caked in his mouth and his heart thrummed in his ears, nearly masking the crowd's collective groan. It took four sets of hands to prop Bas upright, and by then the man with the ghost arms had plucked Lana's ring from its perch on the light switch and was heading back upstairs to the bar with his entourage.

Bas was still trying to piece together what had happened as he balanced himself over his legs, waiting for the wave of dizziness to pass. Pats of encouragement from the dispersing onlookers offered little consolation.

What was that?

He had gotten taken, that's what. He should have cleaned that guy's clock, but the guy had cheated somehow. He had baited Bas into a basement scrap because he knew the game was rigged.

But how?

"You should have ignored Wallace Thaw."

Bas jumped.

Harriet was dabbing at his jaw with a dishrag.

How had he gotten upstairs to the bar? He must have faded out again. Maybe something in his skull had been knocked loose.

By now the Red Bell had mostly cleared out. Bas should have been home by now himself—seeing a place shut down was never a good scene.

A flash of panic washed over him, and his hand shot to his shirt pocket.

Lana's ring was gone.

Really gone.

"God *fuck* it."

He had squared off against some random asshole, and now said asshole was probably bragging to his schoolmates that he'd beaten up an old drunk.

"He's scrawny, but he's always been a pugilist," Harriet said. She pressed something cold against his jaw, making him wince. "Hold."

"Always?" Bas asked out of the corner of his mouth.

Harriet puffed on her cigarette. "Drifted in about a month ago. I take it you hadn't met."

"Not before tonight."

Harriet took a step back to assess her work.

Bas shook his head. "No *way* that kid could have won."

She tutted. "You lost soon as you two made for the cellar, don't you figure?"

Pulling away the ice pack, Bas tested his jaw, probing its tender flesh with his left hand. His bottom left canine was loose, and for what?

"Fucking idiot."

2

FRIDAY, APRIL 12, 1991

DEE KHALAJI WATCHED the mailman through Junmo's eyes. It felt almost like standing there on the porch herself.

Almost.

"Look at that weather, Hector," Junmo said, peering out from beneath the awning. "You got to love it." His eyes traced the fringes of the clouds as if looking for a pattern there.

"It's a nice day," the mail carrier agreed, hiking up the pouch slung across his back.

Junmo's laugh was like a bark. "Well you would know, since you're outside all day. Almost all day, I mean."

The man smiled and held out a short stack of envelopes, and Junmo's left hand reached out for the mail. Dee found the precision and fluidity of the boy's movements strange, though not unpleasant. That was how head-hopping always was—familiar but foreign, tactile but detached.

"Thank you, I appreciate it," Junmo said, raising a hand as Hector moved away down the walk. "Rain or shine, Hector!"

Their traditional salutation.

"Rain or shine, Junmo."

The young man remained on the porch for a moment. He would flip through the envelopes three times, of course, counting under his breath. Dee distracted herself with the classification system for her favorite flower.

Plantae, Tracheobionta, Spermatophyta, Magnoliophyta, Magnoliopsida, Dilleniidae, Dilleniales, Paeoniaceae, Paeonia.

Junmo's obsession with counting was too compelling, and Dee couldn't risk falling into it, particularly not while her foster brother's senses were so close to hers. It served her right for hitching a ride while her friend was making his rounds, but she had felt confined in her own body today. Anyway, there was no harm in it—Junmo would never notice Dee's little head-hopping stint.

"Almost time for dinner, Junmo." Brenda joined him on the porch, letting the screen door clap shut behind her. "Would you run upstairs and tell Walter and Dee, please?"

"Yes, I can do that as soon as you take this mail off my hands. There's seven envelopes and one postcard and one magazine."

When she smiled, a dimple always formed in her left cheek, never the right. As much as Dee loved symmetry, her foster mother's smile always made her feel warm inside.

"Thank you for helping," she said.

The boy headed inside. In less than a minute he would be standing in Dee's doorway.

Letting her mind drift, Dee braced herself for the inevitable jolt as she hopped back to her own head.

Only... something interrupted her before she could return.

―――

Junmo was gone, and so was she.

Or maybe not gone. Just... not where she should be. Something had happened. Something was *still* happening. It was there, in front of her.

Dark room.

TV screen.

The blue-gray glow from the tube was bright enough to obscure the details of the rest of the room.

She was somewhere else.

Where?

She tried to push away from it, to pull back into herself. But whatever had stolen her away from Junmo was not letting go.

Don't panic.

That would only make things worse.

It's like before.

Was it? She had occasionally caught fleeting glimpses of foreign settings, almost too briefly to make out—grocery store aisles, a park bench, a construction site. She had always dismissed them as a mere side effect of her head-hopping, like a touch of vertigo after an elevator ride.

But such moments had never threatened to pull her out of herself.

Not like now.

She had come fully detached.

As Dee's eyes adjusted to the glare, two figures came into view, both peering toward the TV screen. The person Dee inhabited was standing several feet away, looking down at them, passive.

Only that felt different, too. Dee knew it even as she had the thought. She had seen the world through the eyes of others hundreds of times, and there had always been sensory cues to keep the experiences grounded in reality: the temperature of the air, a sense of gravity and weight, breath filling lungs.

She felt none of those things now. She was suspended in the air... bodiless.

There were only two people in that room.

Dee tried to quiet her thoughts. This wouldn't go well if she lost her calm. There had to be an explanation. But for now she could only watch.

"Well, it's multiplexed, so that's the problem."

A woman's voice.

"That's why it looked scrambled. I can demux the video, but you'll probably lose the timecode."

Not just any voice. The woman sounded familiar. But this was so out of context that Dee couldn't place it—and her calm was already on the verge of slipping away.

Trapped.

She felt nothing.

She was not in control.

She couldn't find herself.

"If I adjust this... yeah, there you go."

The woman was making some sort of adjustment on a panel. Tiny lights like an ordered constellation dotted the table before her. The screen flickered, and the picture on it resolved into a stuttering black-and-white image.

A solitary figure, huddled in an alleyway.

"*There!* That's her." A man's voice. Not familiar. "Whatever you just did, can you make it stay like this?"

"Uh-uh," came the familiar voice, "but I can dupe this out for you so you can watch it."

The man was inches from the screen. He couldn't get close enough. "Where is she?" His voice held the slightest quaver.

"Hey, I told you, I'm happy to help, but—"

"I know—this isn't your case. Look, I just appreciate you helping me out. It's just... seeing this now? Seeing my daughter? It's a lot to take in. A *whole* lot."

―――

"*Dee!*"

For a moment Dee saw herself through Junmo's eyes. He looked down at her on her bed, legs dangling, body still, eyes somewhere far away. His hand was on her shoulder. All it had taken was a shake, and the darkened room was gone, just as suddenly as it had first appeared.

"Dee, dinner," Junmo said, his voice insistent, as if he had tried to rouse her several times already. "*Dinner, Dee.*"

Before anything decided to snatch her away again, Dee hopped back to her own head.

Diesel engine rumbling by, ventilation system, plates clinking against a table, clock ticking, Junmo breathing.

When she stayed out too long, the return always caused a rush. A flood of tense urgency was the price she paid for being still for too long.

But it wasn't her fault this time.

Dee sighed involuntarily, and her hands fluttered around her ears, but thankfully the electricity of the moment was already fading, leaving in its wake the questions she had brought back with her.

Her foster brother had backed away a few paces, maybe to give her space.

"Are you okay now?" he asked, his eyes scrutinizing her. "Because I can never really tell with you."

I'm okay, she thought. It was just as well the lie would never pass her lips.

Her eyes flicked up, and she managed to hold his gaze. He seemed to understand.

"Okay, Dee."

With a curt nod, he disappeared down the hall.

Dee's fingers found the wisps of hair by her neck, and the softness of those strands provided some comfort. But questions loomed. What had just happened? She'd been head-hopping since she was seven, an ability she had accepted long ago. But she had only ever hopped into the heads of people in close proximity. If they walked down the block, she would lose them like a distant radio station.

This time, something had pulled her much farther away.

And even more unsettling—into something that wasn't another person.

And there had been that familiar voice.

"*Dee!*"

Walter this time, calling from the foot of the stairs.

Dee's legs were full of pins and needles from sitting in the same position for nearly an hour. Her hands were already slapping at the mattress to drown out the painful signal, and she scooted to the edge of the bed before the sensation grew overwhelming.

She tried to push away thoughts of the remote episode.

It was a one-time thing, that was all.

It was only a fluke.

3

SUNDAY, APRIL 14, 1991

ZELDA JACKS PEERED over the rim of her jeweler's glasses as the electronic bell above the door chimed.

"Well hey, I wasn't expecting to see you on a Sunday, baby."

Bas's cheeks grew warm as he crossed the floor of the Hawley Hill Trade Center. He had to tell Zelda about his decision to retire—he couldn't just start clearing out his office. He owed her an explanation.

But he had more pressing things on his mind at the moment.

"I'm not here for work."

Zelda frowned and set down the oboe she'd been inspecting. Removing her glasses, she gawked at him.

"Bas, what the hell?"

"What?"

With an exasperated hiss, she touched her cheek.

"Oh," Bas said. "I... got into a scrape."

"You?" She blinked, looking confused. "Was he standing on a stepladder?"

"Zelda, is there any chance someone brought in Lana's ring?"

Her eyes widened and her jaw dropped. "Oh, Bas. You've got to be *kidding* me."

"I know," he said quickly. "Just, don't start in with me, okay?"

"Bas, honey, if you lost that ring in a fight, you surely *deserve* to lose it." She shook her head. "If I'd seen it, I would have told you. You know that."

"Yeah."

"Anyway, I don't peddle in stolen merch. Come on now, I've been at this too long."

Bas shook his head. "Had to ask."

She let out an exasperated sigh and took the instrument from the display counter. "I will call around for you, okay? But you are one ridiculous human being, you know that?"

"I do, yes."

Bas breathed deep and gave the glass case a friendly rap. Now that he was here he might as well grab some of his things.

He retreated to the back of the pawn shop, realizing his hand was up at his breast pocket only when his fingers closed on empty fabric. For ten years the ring had been there, as much an accessory as his watch. Now it was gone, and he might as well be flicking the light switch during a power outage.

Idiot.

His office was the size of a walk-in closet, made even smaller by the filing cabinets and computer equipment. He had long thought about paying someone to move all his old investigation reports to a software database, but that would never happen now. He regarded a decade of stacked records scattered into piles, as if he had happened upon an archaeological site. That was what it was. A museum exhibit.

And he'd have to do something with the equipment. Some of it he had borrowed from the front of the shop. Those things he could return piecemeal. The rest he would have to sell.

"Hey, babe." Zelda rapped on his open door. "I need to run

downtown for an hour. Vernon's out this week, and since you're already here... will you be here?"

Bas settled back in his old swivel chair. "Sure, I'll be here for a little bit."

It would give him time to get things straightened up.

Zelda had already disappeared from the doorway. "Just an hour or so," she called as she scuffed out. She was ten years older than he was, nearly seventy, but she showed no signs of slowing down.

"I'll be here," Bas repeated.

Bas probed the raw spot inside his lip and winced just as the doorbell at the front of the shop chimed. Bottom left canine was definitely a little loose. He rubbed his jaw as he went out front to tell Zelda he was heading home. She was right: he was ridiculous.

A man stood with one foot inside the shop and the other out, his hand still on the door handle. He looked dubiously at the shelves of merchandise.

"Oh," Bas said. "Can I help you?"

"This a detective office?" the man asked.

A sign in the window advertised Bas's services, but running a private investigation business at the back of a pawn shop always threw people off. Still, the location had had its benefits, cheap rent chief among them.

The man's timing couldn't be worse. He should turn the guy away, that much was a no-brainer. Instead Bas found himself holding the door open for him. "In back," he said, hitching a thumb over his shoulder.

The man let the door shut behind him. He was giving Bas that familiar look of uncertainty, as if he'd come face to face with a yeti.

"So you're Sebastos Milius?" the man said.

Who had told him that?

"Bas. That's right. Did you call?"

"No, sir. I'm Mordell Bolden. I was... referred to you. Sorry, did I need to make an appointment?"

"It's just, I usually..."

Bas bit his lip. A walk-in meant no time for a criminal background check. Not that that mattered, since Bas wasn't going to take the case. On the other hand, this was a referral. Who had referred him? It couldn't hurt to find out that much at least.

Bas led the man to his office. "Have a seat," he said, shutting the door behind him. "Pardon the mess, I'm in the middle of... stuff."

His visitor's goatee was white as beer foam, though the hair on his head was still black. He had a trepidatious air about him—not uncommon for a prospective client—as if he was afraid he might break something more than it already was. As he settled into his seat, Bas tried to clear some of the crap off his desk, moving his camera and tape recorder to the side.

Mr. Bolden still had a good grip on his armrests as he spoke.

"I sure hope you can help me, Mr. Milius." He patted his jacket pocket, then produced a card and slid it across Bas's desk. It was worn, like it had found its way back to its owner more than once.

Mordell Bolden
L&M Auto Works

At the bottom was the shop's phone number, and on the back of the card the man had scribbled his home phone number.

When Bas looked up, the man's eyes were fixed on him.

"Hey, you okay, man?" Bolden asked. "Looks like you had a rough night out."

"I'm fine. What brings you here, Mr. Bolden?" Bas would figure out the nature of the man's situation, then refer him to someone who could handle the work.

"I hear you're good with surveillance."

"From where?"

"An old friend of yours?"

Friends had been hard to come by lately. It must have been a really old friend. What was the statute of limitations on friendship?

"I need you to find my daughter, Cynda."

"Cynthia?"

"Cynda, C-Y-N-D-A. Cynda Bolden."

Judging by the man's age, the woman probably wasn't a minor. "You already file a missing persons report?"

"For sure, I tried that a year back, when she left. But she's an adult, and she left willingly—fact she announced it like she just got herself a record contract. Anyway, so the police said wasn't much they could do. Not missing, the guy said, just... *missed*, you know?"

"You married?"

"My wife passed."

Bas adjusted in his chair and played with the cover of his timesheet binder. If this were a real job, he should be keeping track of the minutes. But this wasn't a job. He nudged the notebook to the edge of his desk and crossed his arms.

"After Cynda left she really was *gone* gone. Like she fell off the map. Asked her friends, and no one knew where she went. But then four days ago..." Bolden reached into his other jacket pocket and brought out a padded envelope. "Someone sent me a video with her name on it. No return address."

Bas watched, impassive, as Bolden placed the parcel on the desk between them and gave it a pat.

"It's a security tape," Bolden continued. "It was in some weird format, but I found someone who could get it translated, or whatever. It's my Cynda, alone in an alleyway. Someone tagged a Boston phone number on a dumpster, so it's got to be somewhere around here."

Bas nodded. This was how an actual case might start. Except he felt outside of the conversation, as if he were observing it from a distance.

"It's my *daughter*, man," Bolden said, this time with a note of urgency. "She's there on the street, and then... she's gone. I mean, the video cuts, and then it's just the empty alleyway. I don't know what to make of it, except someone wants me to know she been around, nearby."

Bas's eyes flicked from the tape back to the man sitting across from him. "Who referred you?"

Bolden pursed his lips. Then, "Gisela Andie. Said you guys used to work—"

"I know who she is," Bas said, too abruptly. He put up a finger and grimaced. "Sorry, man. It's been a long day."

He had fallen out of touch with Gisela after leaving the BPD. She and Lana had been friends before Bas had met his future wife. And of course Gisela had been there at the end, too.

"Mr. Bolden... I hate to say it, but Gisela's info is a little out of date. Fact is, I'm retiring. Already got another gig lined up."

That was a lie. Maybe Mitch had held the museum position open for him, maybe not. It had been a few months since he'd made the offer. And it was a cushy job, by the sound of it, the kind that was sure to draw a lot of applicants.

"Retired since when?"

Bas snorted. Was the guy challenging him? "What time is it?"

Bolden wasn't buying it. "Mr. Milius, now, you led me all the way back here for a reason, I assume. The lights are on and you're listening to me. Are you wasting my time on purpose?"

"No, Mr. Bolden, that's not..." But the man had a point. Bas's vacillation was coming off as cruel now, since he'd already let the guy get this far. He sighed. If he at least heard Bolden out, he might be able to come up with a colleague to refer him to. "You don't know where the tape came from?"

"No. No return address. I got the original at home. I could bring it to you, but like I said, it's in some... multi-something format."

Multiplexed, most likely. Meaning it had come from a multi-camera security rig.

"Getting back to your daughter's social scene, you said you already talked to her friends. How about other acquaintances? Coworkers, partners, anyone she may have come into contact with?"

"Yeah, I asked around. She always kept to herself, pretty much. And especially later on. All I got back was a lot of shrugs and gossip. People think they got her back, even when I try to tell them the difference between gone and missing. Telling them I was her pop didn't get me nowhere, to be honest."

It was seldom easy for someone with skin in the game to make the reticent talk, especially when strained family dynamics were a factor. Bas had seen misplaced loyalties gum up even a proper investigation.

"I hate to ask," he said, "but what about hospitals and mortuaries?"

Bolden crossed himself before answering, clearly unsettled by the thought. "I surely did check. If I found anything there, I would have told you so. But... excuse me if I'm out of line, but isn't all this kind of your scene? If you're about to take this on for real, I got to know you're all in."

Bas nodded as he sat forward and wiped his eyes. *Was* he all in? Could he really throw himself into this, or was he leading himself on? "Maybe you're right."

"About what now?"

"Look, any good investigator will ask you the same questions I'm asking. I'm sorry Gisela got your hopes up with me, but you're right: if you're going to find the right investigator for this, it should be someone who is all in."

"Unreal, man."

"I'm trying to do right by you now rather than later, you understand? It's got nothing to do with you, I promise. I was packing up the office when you showed up."

The man's lips tightened as he looked around Bas's office, but some of the fire went out of his eyes. "You all done helping folk then?"

"I've been at it a long time. When I started, my hair wasn't gray."

Bolden regarded him levelly. "You ever lost anyone, Mr. Milius?"

Bas almost laughed. He'd not only lost Lana, he'd never really *stopped* losing her. Every missing persons case brought that feeling back.

Bolden didn't wait for a response. "Okay," he said, pushing himself out of his chair. "Well, I'm going to leave this here with you, case you reconsider." His eyes were on the envelope.

Bas grabbed it and held it out. "No, Mr. Bolden, please take your tape."

But the man was already moving for the door. "Ain't no good to me, sir."

"Mordell." Bas stood and followed him. "There are other investigators, ones who aren't retiring."

The chime rang as Bolden pushed the shop door open. Outside, the rain sounded like distant applause on the pavement. "You do what you need to with the tape," he said, then ducked out into the night.

Bas slid the cassette from the bubble wrap–lined envelope. On the label, a name had been written in black ink: *CYNDA*.

Poor guy. Bolden couldn't have known what he was walking into when he entered this shop, the last embers of hope still glowing behind his dark eyes. It wasn't his fault Bas had gotten better at losing things than finding them. After ten years, he had even managed to lose Lana's ring. What could he lose in another ten?

The chime rang out from the front of the shop. "Bas? I'm back."

Bas heard Zelda tap her umbrella against the floor, then slide it into the stand.

He pulled his coat from over the chair and flicked off the lights in his office. Maybe tomorrow he would tell Zelda he was finished, for good. Tonight he just didn't have the energy.

She gave him a smile as she moved behind the counter and opened up her little note minder. "That took me longer than I thought, baby," she said, scribbling something down.

"No trouble. Hey, I'm clocking out, boss."

She laughed. "Roger that, you old gumshoe." She slid her pencil into the spine of the notebook and folded it away.

"This is for you," he said, placing the cassette spine-up on the display counter.

"*Cynda*," she said, squinting down at it. "Porn?"

Bas chuckled. "Ah, no. You can erase it."

"Ain't worth the shelf space then."

"Use it for your security system."

Zelda rolled her eyes and went to the register to zero it out for the evening. "Oh, Bas, honey?"

Bas raised his eyebrows as he pulled his arm through his jacket sleeve.

"No more brawling with hooligans, okay?"

―――――

Finding a spot near Eshe's apartment, Bas waited for the Monza's engine to sputter to silence. It reminded him of their relationship. They had been an improbable match, and her youth was the least of it. On the one hand, Eshe saw the world with a refreshing, matter-of-fact creativity that continually kept him on his toes. She was the first person after Lana who made him play down his enduring contemplation of things lost. But on the other... as much as he tried to hide that part of himself, he knew he wasn't fooling her. The truth was, he'd always been afraid to ask her what she saw in him, and that was even more true lately.

Now, as he stared through the rain-slicked windshield, the car key cool in his palm, it occurred to him that he had meant to drive home, only he had gone into autopilot somewhere along the way. He pictured starting the car and driving off, but that seemed less likely with each passing moment. He was here now, so might as well stop in. It had been days since he'd talked to Eshe, let alone seen her.

As he walked up to her apartment, the last thing he was thinking about was the condition of his face. But he was instantly reminded of it when she opened the door and he saw her expression.

"Bas, what's this?" She reached up to trace her fingers along his cheekbone.

"It was..." The words didn't come.

"Come in," she said, tugging his jacket. "I'm already paying enough for heat."

The warmth inside made his eyes water. As he shrugged out of his jacket, he surveyed the series of oversized black-and-white prints strung up around the cozy space. Most of them were double-exposed portraits of solemn-faced women, framed tight enough that he could make out the fuzz on their cheeks, like the faint atmospheric haze around photos of Earth.

"These are something," he said, taking them in.

"I'm serious," Eshe said, still fixated on his face. "Were you on a case? What happened here?"

She had stopped him at the edge of her living room, as if his answer would determine whether he could proceed. "It's nothing, really," he said, feeling his empty pocket again.

No ring.

"I got into a... a scrap."

A wave of revulsion crossed her face. "What's that supposed to mean?"

Bas put his hands out. "Some jerk at the Red Bell was goading me, and—"

"Are you twelve?"

"What?"

"Are you a child?"

"He took my ring!"

Eshe's face dulled. "That answers that."

She left him at the edge of the carpet and headed into the kitchen.

"It was nothing," Bas said, tagging behind.

She poured something into a tumbler, and as he took a seat at the kitchen table, she put the glass in front of him. He could tell by the smell, it was her ginger beer—ginger root, lime, and a little ground pepper in sparkling water. Something from her childhood, she'd once told him.

"You knew how I would react to your scrap, didn't you? You make me feel like a parent sometimes. So, okay, why are you getting into scraps? And don't tell me about Lana's ring. Tell me the *real* reason."

Bas wished she would go back to doing whatever she had been doing before he barged in. Even better, they could just sit next to each other in silence for a while.

"Well it's not what I set out to do when I woke up this morning. I wasn't even thinking of it when I came over. Honestly, I'd rather not talk about it now. I came over because I thought we could—"

"Not a good idea."

"Spend *time* together, I was going to say. Like we've always done."

"You've got your back up, and I can see something's eating at you." She took the seat across from him. "Get it out now, *then* we can talk about spending time together."

There hadn't been anything eating at him before she started giving him grief about his face. She made it sound like he was using her for some kind of emotional support, which was ridiculous. He could take care of himself. Was it so bad if her pragmatism rubbed off on him when he spent time with her? He could have used something like that earlier today.

She waved a hand at him. "Hey, what have you got on your mind?"

"Work stuff. I got a walk-in today."

"That's good?"

Bas shrugged. "It felt good that he was a referral from an old colleague. This guy wanted someone to investigate his daughter's disappearance. But on the other hand, I've been thinking—"

"Of making a change, yes."

"Right."

"Okay, did you get back to... was it Mitch? About that position at the Gardner?"

The Isabella Stewart Gardner Museum had experienced one of the largest art heists in American history last year, and the case was still open. In the aftermath, management had purged its entire security team, and was now looking to staff up again from scratch. Bas's former colleague was a Senior Security Officer there, and had floated the idea of bringing him on. But the thought of babysitting monitors all day didn't seem like an answer to anything.

"I've thought about it, but I just keep going back and forth. It's hard to call it off after so many years. It feels like I'm quitting."

She wasn't interested in indulging him. "Well the missing persons case will buy you time to decide, at least. Still, you shouldn't put off—"

"I didn't take the case."

She laughed in disbelief.

"I know, but you asked what was on my mind," he said. "Yeah, I have options, but what am I supposed—"

"You say you can't decide, but you didn't have to. This man tracked you down, Bas. Fell into your lap, basically. But it's like you *want* to make things difficult for yourself." She shook her head. "Sometimes I wonder if I can really know someone who has no idea what they want."

Suddenly Bas couldn't read her face. It was like... she was like a stranger. What had changed?

"I want to get out, Eshe," he said. "But investigation was never just a job. I built it up by myself, from *pieces*. I made this for myself, so it feels... like I'm about to leave part of myself behind."

"Pieces." She bit her lip, then stood and moved over to the pot of water on the stove. "I can't tell if you're talking about investigation... or Lana."

"What's that mean?" Bas asked. Lately she had been fixated on this narrative that he was on some self-destructive binge. It was ridiculous. "Sweets, what does any of this have to do with Lana?"

"For goodness' sake, you just got into a *fight* over her." When Eshe turned around, she was stirring a drink of her own. She was less upset and more resigned. Bas didn't know which was worse. "I know that ring you carry around like a safety blanket. But I never say anything, do I?"

"Never? How about right *now*?"

"Bas, I've never heard you so much as admit that Lana is dead."

"Where is this coming from all of a sudden?"

"It's been ten years."

"*Almost* ten years."

"And for the past year I've seen it eating away at you. You know I can actually see you, right?"

Bas grunted dismissively. "You don't just pack away something like that, Eshe. So yeah, it's on my mind lately."

"You've never moved past it is my point. You're getting into bar fights. You're passing up paid work because... missing persons requests somehow remind you of her all over again."

"I never said that."

"What's sad is that you've given up." Her voice was too calm.

"You want me to take the case?"

"I'm not talking about the case!" Her eyes were like embers, but just as quickly they cooled. She joined him at the table again, taking a sip of her drink. "You can't bring Lana back. But maybe you can get out of your own head for a little while, help this man, and get paid for it."

Bas sat back in his chair, not so much relaxing as retreating from her scrutiny. Maybe she was right. Working a straightforward case might be a good distraction. "I can write up the contract tomorrow."

Or maybe he would call Mitch to ask about that rent-a-cop gig.

Eshe nodded and took another sip. Her hand was warm on his. "I don't mind you staying over, Bas. But I think it needs to be on the couch. We're just... You're watching the clock tick, and I'm trying to get my act together. I just wish I could see you doing the same thing."

4

MONDAY, APRIL 15, 1991

BAS PRESSED the handset to his ear. No one was picking up.

In the front of the shop, Zelda was explaining to a prospective customer the difference between sentimental value and street value. She spoke with a confidence tuned to reassure the anxious while preempting the bargain hunter's wrangling.

Bas pressed the switchhook and shifted the receiver to his other ear. Peering down at Mordell Bolden's card, he dialed the number again, more carefully this time. The man's handwriting was neat enough that none of the digits were ambiguous, but Bas's finger might have slipped the first time.

Still no answer.

He hung up, flipped the card over, and called L&M Auto Works, half expecting it to go unanswered, too.

Someone picked up after the first ring.

"L and M Auto."

"Yeah, this is Bas Milius calling for Mordell Bolden."

"Uh, hold on just a sec."

The remote handset thumped, and Bas heard the man talking to someone, but the discussion was drowned out by a series of metallic clanks.

After a moment the same voice returned. "Yeah, he's not in today."

"He has Mondays off, or...?"

"No, he's usually here every day. I haven't seen him today though. Maybe it's a Patriots' Day thing, I'm not sure. I could take a message."

Patriots' Day—that's right. The third Monday in April meant battle re-enactments, baseball, the Boston Marathon, and usually some fucked-up traffic.

"No, that's okay. Do you have another number where I can reach him?"

"Uh, not really. Sorry."

"Not a problem." Bas sucked the inside of his lip. It was still a bit tender, but better than before. "Hey, is this number the garage?"

"Service shop, yeah."

"Can you give me the number for the front desk?"

The man gave Bas the number. "Do you want me to transfer you?"

"No, I'll call back later. Thanks, man."

Bas hung up, then waited for a moment, hand poised on the receiver.

Up front, Zelda had convinced her customer that she was offering the best price for the collateral, and was explaining the terms of the pawn loan.

Bas cleared his throat and dialed.

"L and M Auto Works, this is Wanda, how may I direct your call?"

"Hi, Wanda, I'm Sam, with City Link Courier Service. I'm calling because I have a situation on my hands, and I'm really hoping you can help me." More and more, pretext calling was frowned upon in investigation circles. But in a pinch it beat sifting through court cases, property records, and marriage licenses, let alone the indignity of trash hits.

"Oh, okay, what's the situation?"

"Well, I have a delivery here for a Mr. Mordell Bolden."

"You've got the right place."

"But see, he requested that the package be delivered to his home address, and the only address I have here on the board is his business address, which is why I called you."

"Ohhh."

"And... I'm sorry to trouble you with this, but I'm new here, and I'm just trying not to get in trouble. Thing is, if I can't deliver it where the customer wanted, I have to send it back to the manufacturer, see?"

"Aw, I understand." Sympathetic. "But we don't usually give out that kind of information."

"Oh, that's too bad. So there's no way you can help me out here, Wanda?"

A long pause. That wasn't a good sign.

Bas's next words were out of his mouth before he thought better of it. "The package here says Cynda Bolden. Maybe it's from a relative of his?"

"No *shit*." Pay dirt. "Sorry for my language. Um, just give me one second. You got a pen?"

Mordell Bolden's apartment building was a four-unit walk-up down in Roxbury—the city notable for a mid-eighties referendum that had proposed its secession from Boston and reincorporation as "*Mandela*," after the former political prisoner.

Bas parked his Monza toward the rear of the building, where Unit 2B was, and peered up at Bolden's window. The sky was still somewhat overcast, and the lights were on in the apartment.

Bas would be showing up on the man's doorstep with hat in hand, there was no getting around that. But that's what he got for brushing Bolden off. He could spin his reconsideration as a compliment—a testament to the legitimacy of the case—then launch into his standard spiel.

As he looked up, a blinding flash lit the apartment, bright enough to burn the windowpanes into his retinas. It looked like something had detonated—far stronger than a camera bulb—only there had been no corresponding report.

"*Shit.*"

Bas stepped out into the cool air, still blinking away the bluish afterimage of the flash. He slammed the car door shut and jogged to the building.

A muzzle flash wouldn't have been nearly that bright. So what then?

The doorbell panel at the entrance listed no "Mordell Bolden"—the button for Unit 2B was labeled 2B. Bas gave the button a press anyway.

No response.

He gave the door a shove. It was open.

Bas took the stairs two at a time, expecting the worst, and cursing himself for it. He'd just *had* to go over his notes one last time before coming over.

His heart pounded as he rapped on the door of 2B and gave the doorknob a firm twist.

Locked.

"*Mr. Bolden?*" he called. "It's Bas Milius. Are you home?"

He held his ear by the door and slowed his panting. A television was on inside, blaring the sound of a crowd and a high-pitched referee whistle. Could the flash have been part of the broadcast? No—no screen was that bright.

When Bolden opened his door, Bas's breath caught. The man was fine. Bas suddenly felt self-conscious, and he couldn't help but peer into the apartment, just to be sure.

No smoke billowing. No sign of mayhem.

"Man," Bas said, shaking his head. "I thought..." Didn't matter. Bolden was fine. Which meant that Bas might still have some work, if the man hadn't already found another investigator.

"You thought...?"

Bas put his hands out. "Never mind. Mr. Bolden, I'm prepared to work your case. After you left I got to thinking about it, and I think we can figure out what's going on, but we need to start right away."

Bolden squinted up at him. "Work my case." He repeated the words with no inflection.

"I can find your daughter, is what it comes down to. And I'm ready to start, if that's what you want. As in right now." He patted his jacket pocket. "I brought the contract."

Bolden pointed at the number on his door, dull brass characters stained green with patina. "Sorry man, but you got the wrong apartment."

Bas exhaled. "Look, I know I gave you the brush-off, so you got every reason to tell me to take a hike. But I tried to call you earlier, and your number didn't—"

"Lemme stop you right there," Bolden said. "My phone hasn't rung since last Tuesday. And plus, I got no daughter, man."

Bas's stomach sank. Bolden was cutting him loose before he'd even begun.

"Look, Mordell—"

"And *ain't* no Mordell here, sir, like I been trying to tell you."

Bas stood before the man who had come to him just yesterday. *What does he want me to say? Is he just going to gaslight me until I give up?*

"So you're not Mordell Bolden, that's what you're telling me now." Bas took out the L&M Auto Works card and held it out for Bolden to see.

"*Auto shop.*" He didn't seem impressed. "I ain't got a car."

Bas watched the man's face closely. He saw no trace of recognition. If anything, Bolden looked bemused as he looked Bas up and down. "You a private eye or something?"

Bas squinted. "Yes."

"Better get yourself some more practice then. My name's Alton Griggs, and I been right here since forever."

Bas's hand was up by his pocket again.

Still no ring.

No ring, no client.

"Fine," he said. "That's fine, that's your prerogative. But since I'm here, just let me ask, why did you come to me yesterday? Was that cassette blank? Was it just for a prank?"

"Man, look. Maybe you're one of them thinks we all look the same. I never seen you in my life. I didn't give you no *cassette*, and the only daughter I ever had didn't live long enough to taste her first breath."

Bas rubbed the back of his neck. Something wasn't right.

"You alone?"

The man widened his door. "'Less you count the Sox and the Indians, I'm the onliest one here."

Bolden—or Alton Griggs—was utterly convincing. On instinct, Bas's eyes searched for clues within the apartment. The man spotted Bas eyeing the stack of mail on his hall table, and he chuckled, grabbing up a few pieces. "Here you go," he said, showing Bas the mailing labels.

They said Alton Griggs, each and every one.

"Name my momma gave me."

It wasn't looking good for Mordell Bolden.

"Would you happen to have a brother?" Bas asked.

The man laughed again, amused enough by the lummox on his doorstep to endure the interrogation. "Younger brother. We ain't nothing alike, if that's what you getting at. Man's skinny as a scarecrow right about now. Sick. Terminal, like the rest of them." The smile faded. "Look, I'm sorry. You freaky-deaky for sure, but I don't know what else to tell you, man, except... happy Patriots' Day."

Bas tucked the business card back into his pocket. "Yeah," he managed, and retreated toward the staircase as the man watched.

On his way back to his car, Bas could think of only one explanation for what had just happened. Maybe Wallace the many-armed pugilist had hit him harder than he'd thought. He tried to ignore the sinking feeling in his stomach. Brain damage was a shitty explanation, but what was the alternative?

Well, at least he hadn't yet invested any time into the case. Now he could let the whole thing go.

But several miles down the road, he was still turning their conversation over in his head. There *had* to be an explanation. And he still had the cassette Bolden had brought him. Or Zelda did. If it was blank, as Bas suspected, then he would drop the investigation and move on.

As he drove up the ramp to the turnpike, he heard Wallace's taunt again.

I'll spank you so hard you'll forget your name.

Zelda was switching off the lights of the Hawley Hill Trade Center as Bas pulled up. He left the Monza as it was still sputtering, and ducked under the partially drawn storefront security gate.

Zelda had on her awful fur coat, the one Bas sometimes referred to as "Patches." She'd bought it for herself as a gift years ago.

"Hey, babe, just closing up," she said. "You need something, best grab it now."

"Actually, I wanted to ask you. Did you happen to see the guy who came in to talk with me yesterday? Maybe on your way out?"

She frowned. "Sorry."

"Mm. He's the one who gave me that tape."

"Tape?"

"The one I gave you before I left."

"That's right," she said, pointing at him. "Only, you know, it was an S-VHS. I don't use those."

"You could have used it just fine, Zee. It's basically the same as the VHS tapes you use."

"Oh. Well by now you'd have to check the dumpster out back. The truck usually comes earlier, but Patriots' Day might have thrown everything off."

"Thanks."

"Hey, you coming in tomorrow?"

Bas shrugged. "That depends on a few things."

"Now *that* sounds like someone working a case. You got something cooking?"

"Not sure. I just need to... we'll see."

She gave him a curious look. "Then I guess I'll see you when I see you."

Bas gave her a salute as he ducked back out into the evening.

The dumpster was around the side of the building, down an alleyway that stood yawning and dark under the purple dusk sky. Bas pulled his LED penlight from his pocket and twisted it on. As he rummaged through the garbage he couldn't help but think that a trash hit was doubly undignified when it was your own. But a moment later he found what he was looking for.

5

MONDAY, APRIL 15, 1991

THE MOONLIGHT MADE the flowers look luminescent despite the dusk's lingering gloom. Dee had nearly finished transplanting her peonies to their fresh bed, taking extra care to plant the eyes just two inches below the soil line. The gardening gloves lay clean by the planter box, while Dee's hands were covered in soil. The feel of moist loam between her fingers—the cool grittiness, the crunchy sound—was intoxicating.

Brenda had left the back porch light on, but Dee didn't need it; she could have straightened out her garden by touch alone. People thought peonies were fussy, but Dee had a special understanding with them.

Angry voices erupted in the yard next door, making Dee jump.

"You may have meant that, but that's not what you *said*."

"How would you know? You never *listen* to what I say!"

The neighbors, yelling at each other at the top of their lungs. It happened once every few weeks, but there was no acclimating to it.

Dee had left her brain muffs inside, and the loud words were poking through the fence like thorns. Her hands flew to her ears, despite the wet dirt clinging to her fingers.

Plantae, Tracheobionta, Spermatophyta, Magnoliophyta, Magnoliopsida, Dilleniidae, Dilleniales, Paeoniaceae, Paeonia.

Dee ran through the classification several times, letting the syllables explode into colorful blooms in her mind's eye.

The screamers screamed unabated.

Dee rocked, touching fingers to thumbs in a pattern she fell into automatically.

One, two, three, four, one, three, two, four, one, two, three, four, two, three, one...

The soothing cycle made the words seem farther away. And it made something else happen as well.

Fingerglow.

Thin filaments of light that danced from her fingertips like gossamer threads, catching pink petals in their glow as they were borne on night currents.

Dee had first caught sight of *fingerglow* just after her placement with the first foster family. During a weekend away, her foster parents left her with a babysitter whose boyfriend shut Dee in a room lit only by a bare ultraviolet bulb. The walls were lined with blacklight posters with fluorescent serpents, and Dee's resulting dread sent her into her stim world for so long that her hands eventually ached from the flapping. But in that nightmarish room, in the hour just before dawn, Dee got her first glimpse of what her fingers had conjured. It was so jarring that it halted her flapping immediately.

Which in turn stopped the glow.

Dee wasn't yet ten years old at the time, but that was old enough to know that if something could be repeated, then it must be real. So she waited. And when the itchy restlessness returned, and her hands got back to it, sure enough—the glowing streamers returned as well, more quickly this time.

It gave her an odd sense of reassurance.

Her light trick was a pleasant side effect of her stimming, but there was a method to it. As with most good things, order and timing were key. Then again, it wasn't *just* order and timing. She was sure there must be more to it, or more people would know about it. Yet the trick was hers alone, so far as she could tell.

And she had kept it to herself.

And now Dee sat in her garden long after the screamers next door had taken their show back inside, pulling ribbons of light by her fingertips and tracing delicate arcs like cartoon clouds under the watchful moon.

———

The next moment Dee was no longer in her garden.

And there, once again, was the single TV flickering in the dim room, the same room she had seen last week.

Something had pulled her here, and she was helpless to fight it.

Why is this happening?

Why can't I leave?

Maybe there was something special about this room, something that interfered with Dee's use of her abilities. If so, she had to figure out what it was—or it might just keep happening.

Someone was in the room. Just one person this time. A woman, sitting before that screen.

As Dee watched her from the back of the room, the woman leaned toward the image on the screen. The light cast the woman's face in a spectral silhouette.

Gisela?

That would be some coincidence.

Dee had first met Gisela Andie in 1981.

Gisela had rescued her.

Following the deaths of her parents in the South Station tragedy, Dee had spent the first five months of her eighth year living with Roddy and Teresa Hock, the parents of an older son with autism. However, she soon found herself the victim of myriad creative torments directed at her by the Hocks. While Dee often found a kind of sanctuary in her stims, excess anxiety often led to involuntary vocalizations. These, she discovered, coincided with Roddy's self-described *bad days*. He soon got it into his head that shutting her in a dark room for the night with her wrists bound was a suitable punishment.

One evening, she managed to slip her wrist free and revealed her third ability to Roddy Hock—the first and only time she *whispered* to him.

The man became unhinged, batting at his ears and doing worse to her, while Teresa shouted at them both to shut up, shut up, *shut the fuck up*.

The police arrived at their doorstep soon after, and Gisela Andie was among the responding officers. Dee stayed with her for a few days, until Brenda and Walter Luckie—friends of Gisela—could take Dee in. They were as different from the Hocks as a rose is from its thorns.

Now Dee was spying on Gisela in this dark room. So maybe it wasn't the room that had drawn her from her body at all. It couldn't be coincidence that she was watching one of the few people she knew in the world. Was there something about her connection to Gisela—something specific—that had triggered this long-distance observation?

Maybe I'm supposed to see something.

If there was a reason for all this, maybe she shouldn't be fighting it. That idea settled her mind somewhat. She was here, so why not try to observe all there was to see?

She studied the TV, which depicted the same image Gisela had been staring at the other day: a solitary figure hunched over in some trash-strewn alleyway. The woman swept her arms in various formations, almost like a dance.

The woman clearly held Gisela's interest. Was it her job to watch videos like this?

Then something changed.

The woman in the alley was still pulling and pushing against the air around her, only now trails of light followed behind her arms like streamers. She had triggered a kind of *fingerglow* Dee had never seen before.

As she continued to watch, the image on the screen degraded, until all that remained of the woman was a pulsating silhouette—a continuous swirl of light and dark that looped back on itself.

It was mesmerizing.

A moment later, the image yielded to whatever forces had started the distortion. The center collapsed inward, and dark edges eroded the image from the outside. Soon the TV showed only a seething tunnel of light.

"Dammit," Gisela muttered to the empty room. She reached across the table full of blinking controls to turn a knob. Lines appeared across the image, and color halos seeped from indecipherable contours. The tunnel effect was still there.

And Dee realized—it wasn't a TV she was looking at, it was a monitor. Gisela had been watching a tape the whole time.

"What the hell?"

Gisela hit a button that stopped the video, then Dee heard a mechanized whooshing. Gisela was rewinding. After a moment she tapped another button, and the image returned. Not the woman in the alleyway, but the tunnel. The effect had grown more intense.

Gisela cursed again and played with the controls, but something at the very center of the tunnel drew Dee's eye.

It was faint, but it was there.

Another monitor?

As the blur of intertwined rectangles resolved into a new image, Dee felt that edge of panic again, felt suddenly captive to an unknown force outside of herself.

Something cold and insistent.

On the screen, now, was Gisela's room: Dee's own view, repeated now on the small screen.

And Gisela saw it too.

Saw herself, staring at the back of her own head.

She kicked away from that console so forcefully that she nearly tumbled backward.

Every nerve fired at once, a concussive jolt that tore Dee from the dark room.

Brenda was shaking her shoulder.

Where?

Garden

Night

Back

She had returned from the involuntary head-hop.

Had returned to an all-consuming torrent of sensations fed from every nerve ending at once. It felt like diving into an icy pool, and she was lost in it.

Lost in herself.

She fought the impulse, but the restraint only made her feel tighter, and the pent-up energy had nowhere to go.

She was squeezed.

Pushed closer to meltdown as Brenda fussed over her.

Without thinking, Dee nearly used *whisper* on Brenda, just to reassure her that—

No!

Just hold on.

Until the moment passed.

Just breathe.

That would be bad.

Breathe.

Now, on top of everything else. So bad.

Bad.

The charged buzz moved to Dee's hands, which she wrung as her voice came out in a low moan.

"Dee, it's okay."

It's not.

"Dee, you're *okay*."

Brenda's hands were on her again. Kind hands. Dee's foster mother couldn't know what it was like on the inside. The energy inside Dee had grown wild, like an outbreak of weeds in an untended garden. It had consumed the last of her control, and still it was not sated. The autism wanted to spread.

Dee stood, ignoring the pain that shot down her legs.

She saw that scene again: Gisela watching herself.

Watching herself watching herself, like a mirror pointed at a mirror.

Dee was already halfway across the garden. She felt a compulsion to move, to pace, that was beyond her ability to control. If she didn't move it would hurt, like electricity licking out from every bone. When she reached the far side, she spun on her heel and paced back.

She repeated the route. Back and forth.

"Hey, Dee," Brenda said, staying several paces to the side of Dee's path.

So patient.

No one was more patient.

"I startled you, honeybee. I'm so sorry."

She reached out a hand, but Dee pushed past it. There was more pacing to be done.

"Oh, Dee, your flowers," she said, more quietly this time. "Okay, you get it all out, sweetie. I came to tell you dinner is ready. Lemon piccata. Whenever you feel you can, we'll go inside. But I'll sit out here with you for a little bit, okay? I'll be right here, so you're not alone."

Dee heard the uncertainty in Brenda's voice. Uncertainty about whether her over-excited foster daughter even understood what she was saying. Dee would have liked nothing more than to whisper into Brenda's head, to tell her that she did understand, and that she was sorry her body sometimes needed to unwind, even if it was disruptive. Dee had been tempted to use *whisper* many times over the years, but had resisted. It wasn't worth it. Not after what happened with her first foster parents.

Brenda wasn't like Roddy, of course.

No one was.

The noise coursing through Dee's system diminished with every stride. And in time she slowed, then, finally, stopped.

She was standing up to her ankles in moist soil. She peered down at her feet, wiggled her toes in the dirt. Peonies were long-lived—they could easily live for more than a century.

If no one trampled them.

As for this planter, she would have to start over.

Maybe this weekend.

Brenda was sitting at the edge of the flower box, smiling up at her, saying nothing.

What if I just tell her that I can communicate?

No. Bad idea. Now was definitely not the right time. Her talents didn't even seem to be under her control anymore, and worse, now she was having involuntary out-of-body episodes. In the ten years since she'd learned of her abilities, nothing like that had ever happened.

This isn't happening by chance.

There had to be a reason she was seeing Gisela now. She couldn't just ignore that.

6

MONDAY, APRIL 15, 1991

BAS'S APARTMENT door was blocked. Something squeaked against the linoleum floor as he pressed his shoulder into it. He shifted his bag to his other arm and gave the door a firmer push. When it was wide enough he put his head through.

Mo Keveney, his sometime roommate, had passed out on the hall floor. This left him less than shocked. When she wasn't impersonating a doorstop, Mo was getting fired from day jobs, clubbing with friends, and house-hopping, testing the hospitality of a sizable portion of Boston's denizens. Little had changed for her since Bas had first met her back in his days with the BPD.

"Hey, Mo."

She didn't stir. But her chest rose and fell.

Bas gave the door a hard push and stepped inside. He clanked his keys on the table by the door, put his bag down, and tossed his coat over the hall chair. "Couldn't make it to the couch?" A bit louder this time.

"Fuck you," she said into the floor. "I walked up three flights of stairs."

With a sigh, Bas grabbed his bag and stepped over her on his way to the kitchen. He pulled out a tuna salad sandwich, two somewhat abused bananas, and a six pack of High Life. He set everything on the counter, then pulled out Mordell Bolden's *CYNDA* cassette.

"Sorry," Mo said, appearing on the other side of the breakfast bar, wiping a smear of dirt and spittle from her cheek. "Long night." She grabbed the six-pack and twisted the corner can from its plastic ring. "I can clean up."

Was she just saying the first thing that popped into her head? "Thanks, but I was hoping for some quiet."

"Let me make dinner."

Bas sniffed. "You're *drinking* dinner."

"Hair of the dog," she said, and took a swig. "Fine, I was going to go back out anyway."

Bas glanced at his watch. "You know it's almost Tuesday, right?"

"Shush, Papa. I'm a pro."

Bas tore the plastic front off the sandwich container. "Sure you don't want something more solid?"

"Is that your best line?" Her eyes were on the videotape. "Seriously, I appreciate your concern, but I'm good. I'll leave you to your porn."

"It's not porn. Hey, you got somewhere you can go?"

Now she looked offended. "Shit, I'm not *that* hard up, Bas. Seriously."

"Yeah, okay." He put up a hand. "I'm just..."

But she had already disappeared into the bathroom.

Bas nibbled on his sandwich. It wasn't as bad as it could have been. He wanted to hurry up and watch the tape—but he wanted to be alone.

For all he knew, it *was* porn. What should he expect to find on a tape given to him by a man who didn't exist?

The toilet flushed and Mo reappeared, somewhat straightened out. She breezed back through the kitchen, giving Bas's arm a squeeze. "Thanks for the beer, old man."

"Yeah."

"See you around." She clomped down the stairs with much more energy than she'd had just minutes ago.

Bas balanced the remainder of his sandwich on a beer can, grabbed the tape in his other hand, and headed to the living room. He turned on the TV, nudged the cassette into the VCR, and took a seat on the couch, shoving the rest of the sandwich into his mouth.

The video flickered on with no preamble and no audio. It looked like security camera footage—shot in black-and-white, in time-lapse mode—but without a timecode. If Gisela had demuxed the original tape—isolating the footage of a single camera from the combined signals of many—it could explain the missing date and time.

The scene was of an alley, just empty street and stone walls, and the brightness seemed inconstant—either there had been a problem with the camera light levels, or there had been some sort of ambient variable. But far more curious was the star of the show. A woman in robes—Cynda, presumably—squatted at the center of the alley, facing mostly away from the camera. She was waving her arms in formations—too ordered to be called flailing, but too quick to be caught clearly by the camera. Her hands were little more than blurs from frame to frame. Bas couldn't see much of her face, but her mouth appeared to be moving. Was she talking to herself?

She looked like a panhandler in the midst of a psychic break.

A moment later she picked something up from the ground and began scratching at the asphalt. She was drawing something, using a rock or a piece of chalk. At first Bas thought it might be a face, or maybe a letter of the alphabet. No—it was more like some kind of stylized logo. Whatever it was, she definitely wasn't just doodling: this was something she had practiced.

She then rotated her arm in a protractor-like arc, creating a large circle around her drawing.

At the very moment she completed the outer circle, the video changed. The image switched to full color and went from time-lapse mode to real-time. From the speakers came the murmur of traffic.

Some multi-camera security systems did employ alert modes that would prioritize the footage from a triggered camera when motion was detected, or when an operator intervened. But Bas had never seen such a dramatic leap in video quality. From black-and-white to full color? It had to have been captured with a high-end system. The image was almost cinematic.

The other odd thing was the focal point of the video. Security cameras were supposed to be trained on high-risk targets for crime—entry points, cash registers, or other high-security locations. This camera seemed to be trained on Cynda herself. If she hadn't been in frame, Bas would have been looking at a patch of pavement, a dumpster, and the stone wall behind it.

At least the improved video quality provided a clearer view of the finished symbol: a large circle containing an M-like shape, with a smaller circle carved out of its middle leg. Or maybe it was a stylized lower-case 'i' in front of the 'M'. Whatever it was, it meant nothing to Bas.

It was also now evident that the periodic changes in illumination weren't the result of erratic camera light levels after all, but rather an attribute of the location itself. The ambient brightness had a rhythmic quality, flashing in a fixed pattern, as if cast by nearby marquee lights.

As Bas studied the symbol, Cynda returned to her ritualistic arm-waving. Despite the improved video quality, her gesticulations were still so rapid that the video couldn't keep up. It looked like she had more than two arms. That had to be an artifact of a video shot in a poorly lit environment, but the thought of Wallace in the Red Bell Tavern's cellar fluttered around the back of his mind like a moth.

"What the hell are you up to?" Bas asked the screen, then took a sip of his beer.

A second later the entire frame filled with white, and Bas sat back hard into the couch as though he had been pushed.

When the picture returned, the alley was intact, but there was no sign of Cynda.

Bas grabbed the remote and rewound the tape, then watched those few moments several times.

Flash.

Gone.

Though he wasn't an expert in video forensics, he had seen a few examples of video tampering while working cases, and he could spot the signs. But here, he saw no evidence of missing footage. There was no jump, no change in the quality of the video.

The woman seemed to have vanished within the space of several frames.

Bas paused the tape just as the flash started to fade, at the moment the alley came back into view. He saw now that the flash of light wasn't the result of a bad edit—it had been there, in the alley. It was clear in the shadows—cast beneath the dumpster, and within the mortar of the stonework.

It's not the first flash I've seen today.

Mordell Bolden.

The burst of light he had spied through the man's apartment window.

Was that a coincidence?

The video continued for only a few more seconds before cutting to black.

Bas rewound to a spot that gave him a clear view of Cynda's completed symbol. He fetched a pencil and notebook from his desk, then reproduced the figure as faithfully as possible.

As he sketched, his hair stood on end. Something about the video was off, something that had started bothering him soon after he had begun to watch. What wasn't he seeing?

Returning to the couch, Bas switched off the TV and listened to the static crackle across the glass tube. Things made less sense now than they had at the start of the day. Mordell Bolden might be calling himself Alton Griggs these days, but then how did this Cynda fit into it?

Bas scowled. What he ought to do is drop this case. No one would care. In fact, he wouldn't have to drop it, because he wasn't on the case.

There *was* no case.

Even Eshe wouldn't want him to pursue this any further. There was no case, no client, no payment.

So why couldn't he let it go?

That itch from earlier had returned, only it had begun to travel.

"Stupid."

He was forcing a connection among a handful of unconnected events. Wallace, Mordell/Griggs, Cynda. Eshe would tear him a new one—and with great enthusiasm—for wasting time that he could be spending more profitably.

And she would be right.

It was time to do the responsible thing and end this spooky deep dive into silliness.

7

TUESDAY, APRIL 16, 1991

BAS PULLED up to the open drive-in window and put his car in park. He snatched his wallet from his jacket pocket, sending the L&M Auto Works card twirling like a helicopter seed. It landed face down on the passenger seat.

"Egg McMuffin, hash browns, and large orange juice," said the woman at the window. "That's three forty-nine, please."

After paying, Bas sat idling in a free parking spot, sipping his juice and flicking the edge of Bolden's business card with his finger. By now he should have tossed the thing out, told Zelda he was done, and started stuffing a decade's worth of investigative notes into his fast food-scented car.

He put his drink down and pulled the phone from its console holster. If he had any sense, he would call Mitch at the Gardner and tell him he was ready to spend his twilight years waving security wands at art nerds. But that wasn't the number he dialed.

"L and M Auto, this is Taye."

"Yeah, I'm calling for a Mordell Bolden."

"Uhhh. Sorry, there's no... Morton?"

Bas felt his arm hairs prickling inside his sleeves. He tried again, speaking more slowly. "The name is Mordell. Bolden. I have his L and M Auto Works card here."

"Oh. Well, there's no Mordell here. But did you have an appointment?"

"No."

"Well this is Service. I can connect you with Parts or... what were you calling about?"

That was a good question. He massaged his temple. "Would you by chance have an Alton Griggs there?"

"Sorry, no Alton."

Bas looked at the card again. An orphaned artifact. "One last question and I'll leave you alone. What does the L and M stand for?"

"Uh, that's the owners' names. The founders. Lavon and Medgar. But like, they're not around here no more."

"No, that's fine," Bas said. "I was just curious."

A muffled series of clicks sounded on the line.

"I'll let you go, Taye. Thanks for your help."

"Yuh."

The line went dead.

Bas removed his muffin from the bag, pulled the paper to the side, and took a bite. It seemed that no one had any memory of a Mordell Bolden. Maybe no one but Bas. The business card was all that remained to suggest he had ever existed. That and the videotape.

Bas patted his pocket and pulled out another artifact from the case that never was. In the light of day, with the smell of junk food filling his nostrils, the symbol he had sketched from the *Cynda* tape looked far less sinister. It could be a band insignia or a corporate logo.

Bas remembered a legal case he'd read about in the *Globe* last year. A local bagel restaurant had done a promotion, and the art they used for that promotion was deemed too similar to the label art of a donut produced by a national food conglomerate. The conglomerate sued for trademark infringement, and as part of the legal proceedings, the local Patent and Trademark Office supplied a trademark expert to testify on behalf of the local business.

If Cynda's symbol was a logo, there was one easy way to find out.

He wrapped up his food, stowed it in the bag, and placed it on the passenger seat. The Patent and Trademark Depository was at the Boston Public Library, which was on the way to Hawley Hill. A visit should take less than an hour. Then this whole thing would be out of his system.

"Do it and get it over with," he said to himself.

Whether that was encouragement or resignation, he didn't know.

"I wanted to see if there's a trademark associated with this symbol."

After giving up on signage and asking a passing group of students if they knew where he could find the Patent and Trademark Depository, Bas had finally discovered the Washington Room at the rear of the second floor of the McKim Building. Now he produced his sketch and slid it across to Eamon Nunn, the curator at the Science Reference Department.

He felt his face growing warm. Was he really embarrassed about his drawing ability?

If this man in thick glasses thought ill of the sketch, he didn't show it. "You said you were doing an investigation?" Nunn asked.

"That's right."

"Hm." Nunn held the paper too close to his face. "What else can you tell me about this?"

"Like...?"

"Like context." Nunn placed the drawing back on the table. "It'd have to be something you could run a search on."

Bas shrugged. "This is all I've got. I just want to know if there're any matches with companies or brands."

"I understand. But you can't use a shape as the basis of a search," Nunn said, loosely swirling his finger over the sheet of paper. "You can only search the *properties* of the thing. What we call metadata. That's why I was asking about context."

"So what are the properties of this?"

Nunn traced the lines. "Well, looks like you have an 'M' here, with maybe an 'i' embedded in the middle of it? That's not nothing."

Bas picked up his sketch and considered it for a moment. He hated a dead end, but maybe that was the sign he needed. On the other hand, he was here already. "I'd like to try it out," he said. "I mean your computer search thing."

"No problem. The cluster search room is right through there." He indicated the doors at the other side of the office. "We close at five."

An hour later, Bas was watching search results scroll by without really seeing them. His search terms simply came up with too many results. It would take him forever to review them all.

"Mr. Milius, did you find anything?"

Nunn. Maybe he had seen Bas slouching in front of his terminal.

"Nope." Bas sat up and stretched, evoking a wince from the curator as his joints cracked. "Nothing useful."

"Well, I'm really not surprised," Nunn said, backing up a step as Bas stood. "Eyeballing our visual database, that's arduous, there's just no way around it. I'm sorry we couldn't help you."

"No, this was good," Bas said. "Sometimes not finding anything is still something, you know?" What bullshit. He should write Hallmark cards.

Nunn gave him a grin. "Well, have a good day, Mr. Milius."

As Bas turned to leave, Nunn called over a colleague. "Hey, Ruth, can you make sure the other terminals all have the latest library installed?"

Bas grabbed his jacket from the back of the chair and prepared to leave.

"What's this?" Ruth asked.

Nunn sounded flustered. "Oh, that's..."

Bas turned to see his sketch in the young woman's hand.

"Sorry," he said. "That's mine. I can take that."

Ruth shook her head. "No, I mean, this looks kind of familiar to me."

Bas blinked. "Really?"

"You remember?" she said to Nunn. "In morning review a few weeks back? Nishioka showed that one label, with all the little symbols on it?"

The curator shook his head.

Ruth looked at Bas. "It would be too new to be in our system, but I could pull it up from the meeting notes."

"That would be great," said Bas, suddenly feeling hopeful again.

Nunn pursed his lips, but he motioned them both to a private terminal behind the front desk. "Now you've got *me* curious."

As Ruth logged in, Bas and Nunn watched over her shoulder. She pulled up a list of some kind, mumbling dates under her breath as the rows scrolled by. Finally she highlighted a row and hit a key.

"Okay, I think this is the one. Yes, here it is." She looked back at Bas as she pointed at one of the images on her screen. "This was a proposal for a coffee label."

Bas squinted at the screen. None of the images looked to him much like the one Cynda had etched onto the pavement. "Coffee?"

"It was a mockup, so none of this is actually in circulation yet." She turned to Nunn. "San Antonio got it."

"This was Nishioka's show-and-tell."

"That's his thing." She leaned toward Bas. "Anyway, so the idea with the ethnic symbols is for a kind of United Colors of Benetton concept. Only, you know, for coffee."

Bas's fingers were up by his empty pocket again. No ring there. He forced his hand back by his side.

"It's kind of hard to see..." Nunn said. "But maybe."

Ruth held the sketch up next to the screen. "You don't think there's a resemblance?"

Bas saw only a collection of exotic symbols, none of which looked exactly like the one Cynda had sketched. In any case, he had already taken up too much of their time.

"I appreciate your help, guys."

Ruth wasn't so easily discouraged. "Actually, you know who you might talk to?" She looked to Nunn.

"You're thinking Peabody," he said.

"I mean, maybe, right?"

"What?" Bas asked.

"The Peabody Museum of Archaeology and Ethnology, at Harvard," Nunn explained.

Ruth handed Bas his sketch. "If this is some sort of ethnic symbol —or even if it's not—they may give you some historical context that we couldn't."

———

Back in his Monza, Bas pressed his phone to his ear as he watched the Harvard campus lunch crowd thin out. The day was more than half over, and he was still chasing ghosts. Then again, one extra day wouldn't matter one way or another. It wasn't like he'd face penalties if he happened to miss his own move-out deadline.

"Peabody Museum, this is Iris Quigley."

Bas cleared his throat. "Hi, Iris. My name is Bas Milius, and I'm a private investigator."

"Oh. Okay."

"The reason I'm calling is because I've come across a... a visual symbol in the course of my investigation. An image. And I'd like to find the significance of it. Am I making sense?"

"Sure, I think so. You'd like to see if there may be an anthropological link, or... is that the kind of thing you mean?"

"That's right," Bas said, with relief. "So if I could come in and talk to someone there..."

"Well, yes, but we can't see people on short notice."

"Not even to just take a quick look at the symbol?"

"Unfortunately not. But I can take your name and number and see about scheduling an appointment."

In the background he heard pages riffling. "Like how far out are we talking?"

"Looks like... we could see you in about three weeks. May ninth? That's a Thursday."

Three weeks from now Bas would have his life sorted out, and chasing people who didn't exist would have no place in it.

"Actually," he said, "there's no need. Thank you for your help."

"Are you sure?"

"Yes, thank you."

The handset was warm in his hand. He checked his watch. It was just after one.

Mitch had a Harvard connection, didn't he? Bas had planned to call him anyway, about the job—and if he had an in at Harvard...

It couldn't hurt to ask.

Bas found the note he had made in his notebook, which included Mitch's direct line at the museum, and dialed. At this rate he would need to charge the phone before dinner.

"Mitch Kidd."

His old colleague's voice was familiar, if curt on his private line.

"Yeah, I'm calling for a Mitchell Leighton Kidd?"

"Oh, shit. Bas Millionaire? Is that you, big guy?"

Suddenly Mitch sounded just as he always had.

"Yeah, I thought I'd check in," Bas said, unable to stifle a grin.

"What's that sound? Are you calling from the street?"

"Actually I'm in my car."

"Oh, fancy-pantsy," Mitch said. "Hey, buddy, you know, I wish you'd gotten back to me sooner. We ended up hiring a guy for the spot, you know? I mean, he's actually not great. But he's young, so that always makes up for it."

"I get it," Bas said, trying not to sound too relieved to hear it. "I'm glad you found someone."

"Yeah, well. He's a little green. So I could still, you know, put in the good word. Leave out all the perverted stuff, so you come across like a stand-up kinda fella."

"As usual," Bas said, chuckling. "But look, I'm actually calling about a case."

"You're shitting me. You're *still* out there gumshoeing it?"

"You know me," Bas said.

"Can't keep a good man down."

"It's just one of those cases I can't seem to let go of."

"I hear ya," Mitch said. "Like something stuck between your teeth."

"That's it."

Or maybe he was just watching the clock tick, as Eshe had said. Her words had stuck with him, and if he wasn't careful they might metabolize into resentment. But that was silly. She was looking out for him. If she didn't care, she wouldn't be riding him so hard to pursue work that didn't constantly put him in mind of Lana's unsolved disappearance.

"So what's on your mind, buddy?"

Bas watched two young students kissing before going their separate ways.

"Is this a good time, Mitch?"

"The museum's closed on Tuesdays, which you would know if you were here. So we're a skeleton crew today. I've got all the time in the world."

"Okay, well, do I remember you saying once that you had a brother or something, teaches at Harvard?"

"Me? No... Oh, you're thinking of Tina. Her brother Jimmy—I don't think you've met him—he works in admin down there. Reason we moved back up from the Cape was so she could be closer to Jimmy after their parents died. Shortest retirement ever."

"Is there any chance I could get in touch with him?"

"With Jimmy? Oh sure, he's good people. What's it about? Or is this hush-hush?"

Bas licked his lips. "I'm following up on a lead, and I need to get some face time with someone at the Peabody Museum, about some archaeology questions."

"No shit. Archaeology, huh?"

"It's a stretch. Anyway, when I called them they said they're booked solid for the next few weeks, and... you know, I just don't have that kind of time to chase what's probably a dead end anyway. I want to cross this off my list. So that's why I thought..."

"Say no more. I'll tell Jimmy to expect your call—I can call him first thing tomorrow."

"You sure it's okay?" Bas asked, shifting in his seat.

"Seriously, don't sweat it. You ready to take his number?"

"Yeah, go." Bas wrote Jimmy's full name and phone number as Mitch recited them. "Thanks for this, man. I really appreciate it."

"Any time."

"And I'm sorry for not getting back to you about the job. It was a real generous offer. I've just been... I'm trying to figure some things out."

"Happens to the best of us," Mitch said, sounding sincere. "Don't worry about it."

"Maybe once I've filed this one away."

"Sure, sure. You know where to reach me, here or at home."

Bas nodded. "Thanks again, Mitch."

8

WEDNESDAY, APRIL 17, 1991

MAINTAINING the hedges around the New Chardon Street Office Park wasn't challenging work, but Dee found it satisfying—she took pleasure in the rhythmic snap of the shears as she trimmed wayward branches. Still, the hedges weren't what kept her coming to this particular vocational training program. After the routine pruning duties were complete, Coach Ursula always let her get her hands dirty with her flowers. The other "Kids Kan" kids either weren't interested in botanical pursuits, or weren't physically able to give delicate plants the attention they deserved.

Dee peered around the planter for the dozenth time, unable to suppress her nervous energy. Just across the street, the entrance to the Haymarket subway station beckoned.

She took a deep breath. If she didn't cool it with her leering, she would surely blow her chances. Moving from shrub to shrub, she tried to stay focused, so as not to raise suspicion.

Next branch.
Clip.
Next branch.
Clip.

Dee looked back toward the Kids Kan van, parked in the Haymarket Square driveway. Coach Ursula was helping Benny unload the hose extender. Even from a distance Dee could see that the young man's limbs were stiff with agitation. He often struggled at keeping his emotions in check, though he was always lucid and articulate about his state of mind immediately after a meltdown. And now, Benny's agitated state was the opportunity she'd been waiting for.

As soon as Ursula's attention was fully on Benny, Dee set her shears on the edge of the box planter and joined a small group of people waiting at the crosswalk.

Her presence drew their eyes. Why? Was she vocalizing? Touching someone? Stimming? No, it must be something else. She looked down, and felt a wave of dismay. *Of course.* She wore bright orange overalls emblazoned with the Kids Kan logo. She was hardly inconspicuous among the office workers with their briefcases and sunglasses. If Ursula so much as glanced in this direction, Dee would be spotted immediately.

To keep her visual stimulation to a minimum, Dee stared straight ahead while awaiting the white walking man on the intersection display. As soon as he appeared, she squeezed herself between the people crossing the street. Being pushy was a good way to leave bad impressions, when she shouldn't be leaving any impression at all, but she was anxious, and rushing was always a difficult compulsion to suppress. Still, she would have to learn to be more careful. She might never be able to blend in, but she could at least avoid barreling through people like a bowling ball through pins.

Focusing on her walking, she tried to pace herself as she made it to the other side of the street.

The map for the T, along with the timetable, was posted just beside a row of turnstiles. Dee cast a glance back across the street; the van wasn't in her line of sight. Good. Hopefully Ursula was still occupied with Benny.

Dee turned back to study the route map, to find out what she would be up against. As she found her position on the map, she realized she was still wearing her gardening gloves. She pulled them off and stuffed them in the pockets of her overalls.

Dee had been to Gisela's house in Somerville before. She had even ridden the subway with Brenda and Walter. And Brenda had always pushed her to be more independent; the vocational program had been her idea. But taking public transportation on her own—buying fares, making connections, and not making a scene—would be something new entirely.

She had never contemplated something so foolish. Why take the risk?

Because someone's watching Gisela.

That single thought kept Dee on track. This was not just a frivolous compulsion. Her friend might be in trouble, and the greater risk might come from doing nothing.

She found East Somerville on the map, and worked her way back through the tangled lines until she connected to the *You Are Here* pin. The route was easy enough to grasp, unless she was overlooking some key thing. She parsed it out in her head just to make sure she had it.

Take the Green Line
across the Charles River
to the North Station
in Lechmere.
Then
take the Arlington Center bus
to Medford and Thurston.

From start to finish—if she did exactly those things in exactly that order—the trip would take less than an hour, plus a three-minute walk to Gisela's house.

Relief surged through Dee, and her excitement resulted in a drawn-out hoot as she clapped. This drew more eyes, but it no longer mattered. She would be able to make it to Gisela.

In theory, at least.

She turned back and retraced her steps, running through her mental map as she hurried.

Green Line, Charles River, North Station, Lechmere...

At the crosswalk she stepped into the street. But a strong pair of hands yanked her back before her back foot had left the curb.

"Look out, miss."

She turned to see a man wearing a ragged overcoat, too heavy for the weather. He had already released her arms, and his hands were up by his shoulders to show he had meant her no harm.

"Don't wanna get squished today," he said with a wink.

While Dee was still replaying what had just happened, the man stepped past her into the street, along with the rest of the crowd.

The white walking man was flashing now.

In Dee's excitement, she had forgotten to check.

It could go wrong just like that.

Good intentions alone were no guarantee she could pull this off, even if she planned everything perfectly.

Her enthusiasm dulled, Dee scrambled back to her shrubs, put her gardening gloves back on, and took her shears in hand.

9

WEDNESDAY, APRIL 17, 1991

VERN LOOKED up as Bas entered Hawley Hill Trade Center, but his eyes darted away just as quickly when he saw it wasn't a customer. It wasn't just that, of course. Vern had never much liked Bas, nor the fact that he had set up his office in the back of Zelda's shop. The man was just being protective of his boss, Bas supposed, but it tended to come out in a sour, unproductive way.

"How's it going, man?" Bas said as he made his way toward the back.

"Yup."

That was as good as Bas could expect.

In the back, he found a large box sitting on his desk. Bas knew full well that the box wasn't for him, even before he peered in and saw the pile of digital clock radios inside. Vern again, marking his territory.

He put the box on the floor behind his door, pushing it well into the corner with his foot. In a few days Vern could do whatever he wanted with this dank closet. Until then, it was best just to stay out of his way.

Bas removed his jacket, draped it over the guest chair, then pulled his notebook from the pocket and tossed it on his desk. He slumped into his chair and opened the notebook to the latest page.

At the top left he had written *Peabody, archaeology*, followed by the name *Jimmy Hartnett*, his work phone number, and *Harvard admin*.

He picked up his phone, then paused, eyes on his door. He placed the receiver back in its cradle, pressed the *speaker* button, and dialed.

"Hartnett, Human Resources."

"Hi there, my name is Bas Milius. I spoke with Mitch Kidd yesterday about reaching out to you. I'm a friend of his and Tina's."

"That's right—"

Vern was at Bas's door, a pained expression on his face. He formed his hand into a phone, put it up to his ear, and mouthed, *Come on!*

Oh! Bas mouthed back. He put up a finger, then lifted the handset and clicked off the speaker button. *Sorry.*

Vern rolled his eyes as he pulled the door firmly shut.

Bas grinned as he spoke. "Sorry, Jimmy, I didn't catch that."

"I said, he told me you had some sort of archaeology question for an investigation you were working on. Is that right?"

"That's the gist of it. I tried to get an appointment over at the Peabody Museum, but they were booked or something. So I was wondering if you might be able to help me."

"Well I called over there and talked with them this morning," Jimmy said, "and I was able to get you a slot for tomorrow. Is that okay?"

Bas laughed. "That's perfect. Hey, I really appreciate that."

"It's not a problem at all. I mean, everyone's busy this time of year, is the thing. They get backed up, so they wind up lowering the blinds."

"Yeah, oh, sure. But my question isn't all that involved. I'm just going to be in and out."

"Well you're in good hands over there. Iris Quigley is the literature editor in the anthropology department. She's expecting you tomorrow at noon."

"Got it," Bas said. He decided it was best to not mention that he had already spoken to Iris—just long enough for her to shut him out.

"Mitch didn't really get into the details of your case."

"Yeah?" Bas was used to this kind of comment. The idea of a private investigation sparked people's imaginations—it made them think of espionage and blackmail. The truth of it was, most of the time Bas was writing case reports or sitting in his car with a half-eaten burger in one hand and a pair of binoculars in the other. "I'm just trying to identify an image. Probably nothing."

"Oh, okay," Jimmy said. After a long pause, he added, "Well you're in good hands, like I said. I'm sure they can help you."

"Thank you, Jimmy."

"Yup, good luck."

10

THURSDAY, APRIL 18, 1991

DEE SNATCHED an orange wedge from Junmo's plate and took a bite.

"Dee, *no!*" Junmo said. "You're really starting to bug me."

"We don't raise our voices at the table," said Brenda.

Walter, pouring himself some grapefruit juice, nodded in agreement.

"Dee took a second one of my orange pieces—one, two," said Junmo, his voice marginally more controlled.

Dee looked at the piece of orange in her hand. She hadn't even thought about taking it from his plate—she had seen the wedge, and her hand had done the rest. Her teacher, Mrs. Siméon, referred to this behavior as a "struggle with executive function." That just meant she tended to be impulsive, especially if she wasn't paying attention. Junmo's autism was different; he had never been a snatcher, so he didn't understand Dee's behavior.

Dee plopped the rest of the orange in her mouth, then took one from her own plate and placed it on Junmo's.

"Thank you, Dee," Brenda said, with that coaching tone.

"Thank you, Dee," Junmo repeated under his breath. "Only you touched it."

Dee ignored him. She felt jumpy—had felt jumpy all morning, which made her impulse control even worse. She just couldn't stop thinking about her scheme to get to Gisela's house.

Green Line, Charles River, North Station, Lechmere, Arlington Center bus, Medford and Thurston.

The thought of making such a journey alone flooded her system with adrenaline, and she felt a heaviness at the pit of her stomach. The combination brought a queasiness that made her wonder whether she would be able to keep her grits down.

Grits with honey.

The honey went on almost everything, because it came from flowers, and that made everything better. But sometimes it made her sick.

Only now it wasn't the honey that caused her nausea.

How could she take such a long trip from home? She would be surrounded by strangers. She would have none of her familiar comforts. She would be tossing away her routine like a piece of trash. Most people could handle that, but for her the stress could lead to trouble far worse than snatching orange wedges. What if she had a meltdown? What if she was pulled away by men in uniforms and locked in a room?

She felt Brenda's hand on hers, and her attention snapped back to breakfast. Her free hand was rapping the table. She had forgotten herself again, and her apprehensions had come out through her fingers.

She stopped herself before she summoned the *fingerglow*. That wouldn't help at all.

"*You've* got something on your mind this morning," Brenda said.

There was no hiding it. Already Dee was rocking, as if the energy had moved from her arms to her spine. It had to come out somewhere.

"I think she just needs to channel it," Walter said, smiling as he gathered his silverware. "All finished?" he asked Junmo.

"I guess so."

Brenda started to clear the table. "Did you need anything special from the farmer's market?"

"Oh, I was going to go," Walter said.

"We'll go together. We can take the kids. We could all work off some of this nervous energy."

Dee continued rocking, vocalizing each time her back hit her chair, a rhythmic song that reflected a growing consternation. But rather than feed into it, Walter and Brenda continued to clear the table.

Junmo gave Dee's hand a friendly pat as he stood. "So we're all going for a walk?" he asked Brenda and Walter.

"Yup, we'll go together," Walter said, ferrying a stack of plates to the sink.

"Wash your hands before we go, Junmo," Brenda said.

"Okay, I just need six minutes." Junmo left the kitchen.

Dee looked at her foster parents. It was ridiculous to think she could go along with them. Not the way she was now. She was rocking, out of control, her parents talking to each other over her moaning because they knew it as well as she did.

"You want to stay here with her?" Walter asked his wife. He glanced over at Dee, the apprehension plain on his face.

And that's when Dee hopped into his head.

It was just a whim, as impulsive as any of her physical tics.

And now she was looking back at herself from Walter's eyes. She saw herself grow suddenly still, as if a thought had just occurred to her. Her eyes were open but distant, and her hands came to rest on the table.

Walter looked back at Brenda. Looked down at her. Walter was tall.

"I think we can all go," she said.

Walter nodded. "Yup, okay." He didn't push, though he did cast a glance at Dee once more as he left the room.

He padded down the front hall and grabbed his wallet and keys, which jangled in the quiet house. Jumping into Walter's head had short-circuited Dee's autism, and now she was still.

She felt the cool of the floor under Walter's feet, and the slight pain in his shoulder when he reached into the closet to pull his jacket off the hanger. Of her own senses she felt almost nothing—only a vague sense of connection, a pull much more subtle than gravity.

Dee was only really predictable when she was seeing the world through someone else's eyes. It took her away from the constant stimulation, away from that feeling of being lost in her body.

Junmo joined Walter by the front door.

"Hey, buddy," Walter said.

"We can all go for our walk now," the boy said.

Walter leaned past Junmo. "Guys?"

Brenda emerged from the hall bathroom, the toilet tank still replenishing itself. "I'm ready, just have to get my jacket. Do you have money, or...?"

"Yeah." He looked back toward the kitchen. "Hey, Dee, you ready to go?"

Dee resisted the urge to hop back to herself. She remained where she was, watching from Walter's eyes. At the back of her mind, a thought had occurred to her.

"Maybe you can help her?" Brenda asked him as she pulled on her shoes.

Walter returned to the kitchen, and Dee saw herself again, sitting as still as she had been minutes earlier.

"Hey, Dee?"

Walter looked at her.

Silent Dee.

Predictable, controlled Dee.

For the first time all morning, the feeling of heaviness lifted.

11

THURSDAY, APRIL 18, 1991

"IRIS QUIGLEY?"

The slight woman standing beside the Peabody Museum's admissions desk blinked up at Bas, her momentary surprise masked by a smile.

"Bas Milius," he said. Her hand disappeared into his as they shook. "I wanted to thank you for seeing me on such short notice."

"I hope I can help you," she said, ushering him back toward a staff office. "You'll have to pardon the mess—we're in the middle of transferring artifacts to archival boxes, so it's been hectic."

They entered the office, and Iris shut the door behind them. She motioned for him to sit before taking her own seat behind a desk.

"We spoke yesterday, didn't we?" she asked.

"We did." Bas didn't know what else to say.

"Private investigator."

"That's right."

"Well I have to say, that's a first. This is already the most interesting part of my day."

"And what's your... uh, role here?"

"I am the Peabody Museum Editor for Anthropological Literature."

Bas's face grew warm. He was definitely wasting this woman's time. Well, no need to draw it out. He patted his pockets until he felt the telltale crinkle of paper. "How much did Mr. Hartnett tell you about my visit?"

"Not a whit," she said.

Bas laid the scrap of paper on her desk and smoothed it out for her. She leaned forward for a closer look.

"I was searching for the origin of this symbol at the Patent and Trademark Depository a couple days ago, and... do you know Ruth Hansen?"

Iris shook her head.

"Well, she mentioned that this might be an ethnic symbol of some kind."

Iris's brow furrowed as she reoriented the symbol, looking at it from several angles. Finally she sat back in her chair. "Well I can kind of see what she meant, if she was thinking about adinkras. But ..." She shook her head. "No, this isn't one of those."

Adinkras?

"Is this the best copy you have?" Iris asked. "It's hard to tell from a sketch."

Bas shook his head. "This is actually my sketch of another sketch."

Squinting, Iris reached over again covered part of the symbol with her hand. "If you were to cut this in half..." But instead of finishing her thought, she stood. "Here, let's look together."

She led him from her office, through a small crowd of guests, and down a flight of stairs to the basement. The air temperature dropped as they entered an open area as large as a ballroom, but with an unusually low ceiling. A myriad of painted wooden masks lay on a long table beneath dim lights. A young woman—a student perhaps— looked up as they entered, then returned to her notes. Toward the back of the room, towers of shelves held collected objects of every shape and size, from pottery to skulls. It reminded Bas of the BPD evidence room, only with fewer weapons and cash bundles.

Iris whisked around the shelves to a cabinet of drawers. A sign above them read, *African Ethno. Coll.* Beneath that was a long catalog number.

Iris pulled out the top drawer and consulted an index, tracing her finger down the list. Then she slid the drawer back, scanned the labels next to the drawer pulls, and pulled out another drawer. Inside lay an oversized book. She opened it, revealing thin yellowed pages filled with diagrams and simple geometric forms. They looked hand-drawn.

"Okay, this is what I was thinking of," she said.

"That word you said earlier?" Bas said. "Adinkas?"

"Adinkras. Yes, that's what these are. They originated in West Africa, and were used in a pre-literate context to represent complex concepts."

Bas scanned the symbols. "I'm not seeing a match."

She gestured at him. "Let's see your sketch again?"

He brought out his scrap and handed it to her.

She laid it on the page. "Right, so watch." She put her hand over the base of the sketch. "Now imagine the top part mirrored below."

Bas imagined what she was suggesting. The 'M' became something more like an infinity symbol with a flared nodule at the center. One of the symbols on the adinkras page was almost an exact match.

"It's like this one," Bas said, pointing. "Right? Kind of."

"It's closer than I thought, actually," Iris said. "Yours has a kind of 'i' punched out of the middle bar, but it's similar enough to look intentional."

Bas read the inscription printed just below the symbol. "This is the symbol for hope?"

"Well, yes, but there's more to it." Iris handed the scrap of paper back to Bas and turned to the next page in the book. Smaller versions of the same symbol were laid out in a single column here, with information next to each. "These glyphs aren't just sounds or words.

They're like proverbs. So this one's full meaning..." She pointed to one of the blurbs and leaned back to let Bas read.

"*O God, something is in heaven, let it come into my hand.*" Bas straightened, turning the phrase over in his head. "I guess that would be a kind of hope."

"Or depending on your reading of it, maybe a bit Promethean?"

"Hm." Bas's idle hand pinched his empty pocket. What did stealing from the gods have to do with a woman's hasty drawing in an alleyway?

"Does this help with your investigation?" Iris asked, hands resting on the edge of the drawer.

Bas sighed. "Honestly, I don't know. Is there anything else you can tell me?"

She pursed her lips. "Not without more context, I'm afraid. With a corpus of imagery, we could apply configurational or ethnological analyses, but with just this... you can't rule out that your symbol is a one-off, a doodle with no symbolic meaning at all."

That couldn't be true. Bas thought back to Cynda's ritualistic movements. The symbol wasn't an afterthought—it was part of a ceremony.

Iris was eyeing him curiously. "Can I ask where you saw this symbol?"

As they strolled back toward the basement steps, Bas gave her an overview of the ritual on the security video. He left out the parts about Cynda's father and her apparent disappearance.

"You know," said Iris, who had listened intently, "there's some debate that use of symbols during rituals may even predate *Homo sapiens*." Her voice was quieter now, as if she was speaking off the record. "But it brings to mind a panel I attended at a conference last year, on interpretive anthropology. You wouldn't think... " She laughed, shaking her head.

"What?" Bas was barely following her, but he was desperate for leads, and this symbol was all he had to go on.

"I'm not one to get woo-woo."

"Go for it," Bas said.

"Well, the discussion centered around two schools of thought when it comes to symbols, and what symbols mean. Especially with regard to abstract symbols in magic cultures, like Wicca."

Bas nodded. Was she talking about witchcraft?

"To boil it down," she continued, "you have the symbol-reference view and the symbol-link view. Symbol-reference suggests that a symbol is just a reference to its meaning with no other connection than that."

"So, basically the way we think of any symbol? Like a logo."

"That's right. But the other view, the symbol-link view, sees the symbol as a kind of a gate or window. In that case the sign itself might possess a direct connection to its meaning, and bring about certain actions in the physical world."

Bas hoped she couldn't see his arm hairs standing on end.

"Do you really believe that?" he asked after several seconds. "Because, I have to say, that's *intensely* woo-woo."

Her smile just then was a welcome sight.

"I'm saying that's what that the woman in your video footage may have *believed*." She shrugged. "It may be something to file away."

12

THURSDAY, APRIL 18, 1991

DEE PULLED Junmo into her room and shut the door behind them. The boy was visibly nervous, but not nearly so worked up as Dee was.

She paced her room, as if that might help her to focus.

She could still change her mind. She hadn't yet demonstrated her abilities to anyone; hadn't fully committed herself to the foolish scheme she had hatched. Except she had already made up her mind —that was the truth of it. And that was just as irreversible as what she was about to do.

Dee positioned Junmo before her and squared herself up in front of him. Her hands went back to their wringing as she considered how to proceed.

"I probably should go, Dee, actually." He gave her a shallow smile and turned toward the door.

No, Junmo. Don't go.

The boy froze, then looked back around at Dee.

"Is that..." he said.

Dee made low, guttural sounds. She was too excited to stop. He had heard her, of course, but he had no way of knowing it had been her who had spoken in his mind. She was the same nonverbal sister he had known for almost a decade. Why shouldn't he believe he had experienced some auditory hallucination?

This is me. It's Dee.

She made a barking sound. It would only get worse unless she reset herself. She went to her bed, sat down, then jumped to Junmo's head for a split second. It was just enough to short-circuit her autism.

Junmo's eyes were fixed on her.

You know I can't talk the usual way, Junmo.

"Yes."

Well... this is what I can do.

For a moment Junmo didn't move. If he darted from her room, she wouldn't have blamed him. But instead he came and sat on the bed next to her.

"Okay, so you can talk then," he said, nodding as if this new ability wasn't a big deal at all. "I'm relieved. I always suspected you were inside there somewhere."

She put a hand on his arm.

Please don't tell anyone yet, okay? Not yet.

"I don't think they would believe me if I said you could talk without talking. I would get in trouble if I said that, I suspect."

He was probably right.

"But Dee, why is this the first time you talked to me since we knew each other? We could have said so many things already by now."

Dee rubbed her fingers together as the memories of her prior foster family surfaced.

Do you remember when I first came here?

"Of course. You were seven and I was nine."

I came from a bad place, Junmo. I whispered to someone, like this, and I got in trouble for it.

"Oh, okay," Junmo said. "You didn't want to get into more trouble. That makes sense. But I would never do anything to get you in trouble."

I know that. Thank you for being so understanding.

Junmo sat up straight. "Wow, your voice sounds just like a voice, only I can hear it inside my head. This is such good news." After a moment he added, "*Secret* good news."

Dee stood and grabbed from her table the pen and pad she had taken from downstairs. She'd never had the motor control required to write, but Junmo was always drawing and writing out notes for the rest of them. He would even write two-word poems, which consisted of word pairs that struck him as funny. The last one Dee had found taped to her door was *bubble-beak*.

Can you do me a huge favor?

He looked down at the pen and paper. "Yes, what is it?"

Junmo held the index card out to Dee to inspect. His handwriting was so neat, the letters so tight and uniform on the lines, that it resembled print.

She read the message she had whispered to Junmo.

I Have Autism

I have been medically diagnosed with autistic disorder. Communication with others is difficult for me. I can not respond to your questions. Also my mind does not communicate well with my body. I am extra-sensitive to sounds and sights. I may appear anxious if over-stimulated. If I behave with physical agitation it is not intentional. You may contact my parents if you need to. They can provide you with more information.
Thank you.

Dee.

On the reverse side of the card, Junmo had written Brenda's and

Walter's names and contact information, with Gisela's contact information next to that.

Was his handwriting too small? No, Dee was just fixating now. It wasn't like people would have to read the card from far away. And hopefully she wouldn't need to show it to anyone at all.

She relished how real it made her plan feel. It was really happening. At least it would be, soon enough. Unless Brenda or Walter came in now, in which case her adventure would be over before it started.

Thank you so much, Junmo. This is perfect.

"My hand hurts."

I know it was a lot to write, but I want to be...

She stopped herself. She couldn't alarm him.

"Who is this message for, Dee? Because it sounds like it's for someone who doesn't know you."

He was on to her. He had more years of experience interacting with people, and his instincts were sharper than he let on.

Promise not to tell?

"I know how to keep a secret. I'm asking only because it makes me nervous. Even if you can do magic."

Dee's hands fluttered. She was getting anxious again. But she felt she could finally confide in someone, after all this time. She had seldom been alone, but she had always been isolated. And now that she'd communicated directly with someone... it felt less and less like something she would ever want to stop doing.

I might go visit Gisela.

"Mom's friend, Gisela Andie? The one we had dinner with on Halloween last year?"

Yes. She's my friend, too. She helped me a long time ago. Gisela is the reason I'm here now, with Brenda and Walter, and you. And she may need my help.

Junmo said flatly, "Do you mean special magic help? Is that why you're thinking of this idea?"

I don't know. Maybe.

It was an honest answer. Dee didn't know what Gisela's need

was, or how she might provide it. She didn't even know what she would say to Gisela if she managed to arrive on her doorstep.

One thing at a time.

"It's hard out there for people like us, Dee. And especially you, since your autism is so much better than mine."

His turns of phrase had always tickled Dee. But he was only giving voice to her own concerns.

I know. You're right.

He placed a hand on hers. "But a lot of times people don't give us the credit we deserve. I think if I couldn't talk I would explode. But you can do some things better than most people, I bet. So I won't tell a soul, Dee." He held his hand over his heart.

13

THURSDAY, APRIL 18, 1991

BAS FOUGHT with the cords dangling from his office blinds until he had the slats lowered roughly parallel to the ground. He twisted the adjustment rod to block the orange glow of dusk, then made his way back to his chair by the light of his monitor.

He looked at his sketch once more, and compared it to Cynda Bolden's mark, now paused on his screen. Maybe it *was* an adinkra. Maybe the woman thought it was imbued with some witchy power. But where did any of that get him?

He rolled the tape forward in slow motion and watched as Cynda went about her gesticulations. In a moment there would be a flash of light, and she would be gone. Then some unknown person would send this recording of the incident to her father.

And then her father would cease to exist.

And no one would care.

"Fucking waste of time."

Bas paused the video again, just before the flash. Where was that alley? Bolden had been right about the graffiti on the side of the dumpster: *Call Angie B.* — 617-FUCK-YOU. That was a Boston area code. But that wasn't much to go on.

Bas examined every detail of the location. One the right side of the alley was a brick wall; on the other side the wall was stone. And at the top left corner of the frame was a window with a pointed arch. A church, maybe?

Bas rewound the tape and started it again just after the picture transitioned from black-and-white to color. This time he studied the fluctuation in the light levels. It definitely looked like the glow of a marquee chase sequence, but the pattern was elaborate, more like the multi-sequence marquee of a theater or arcade than the rudimentary strobe of a porn shop or hourly motel.

Bas froze the video just as the ambient light was at its brightest. Were those ticket stubs on the ground?

"Lights off in fifteen," Zelda called from the front of the shop.

"Roger that," Bas said, distracted. It was impossible to glean anything else from the video.

He turned away from the monitor, eyes flicking to the door.

"Uh, hey, Zelda?" He stood and went to his office door. She had already switched off the neon sign in the front window and was closing out the register. "Hey, can you think of a local church that's next to a theater?"

"You know, sometimes I can't tell them apart."

"Seriously."

She looked up from the register, her pencil still poised over the balance book. "A church next to a theater."

"Yeah."

She frowned. "I'd probably need more to go on, baby." She returned her attention to her record-keeping, scribbling figures in her book.

"Sorry, Zee, but could you maybe come into the back?"

She set her pencil down and gave him a look.

"I just want to show you something. Take a second."

"Fine," she said, shuffling over. "But if I'm helping your case, I want a cut of the purse."

That worked for him. A percentage of nothing was nothing. Now he was officially wasting *her* time, too.

In his office, Bas swiveled his chair around for her, then leaned over her shoulder as she peered at the screen.

"I'm trying to figure out where this is." He pointed at the top corner of the display, where the image was the jumpiest. "Does this look like a church to you?"

"Hm," she said, squinting. "You know, it surely does. I think I actually do know that striped voussoir."

"*Voussoir?* Where'd you get that?"

She looked up at him. "Catholic school. We learned all the parts of a church the way some kids memorize all the bones in the body. Voussoir, acanthus, archivolt. The alternating colors here, that's not so common."

"You're saying this is your church?"

"No, sunshine, I grew up in Maine. What I'm saying," she said, tapping at the screen, "is I think I know where this is."

14

FRIDAY, APRIL 19, 1991

DEE ENTERED the Haymarket subway station with the Friday crowd, her backpack secured tightly across her shoulders. She was hurried along like a leaf in a stream, the din and the jostling already eating away at her calm. But at least the hectic surroundings granted her some anonymity. She wouldn't stand out here so much, not as long as she was surrounded by tourists, commuters, and crying children.

She nearly walked right past the token machines.

Vending machine, token, farebox, train.

She could manage complex tasks if she broke them into pieces. Tending to plants through the seasons was difficult work, but she had a natural gift for gardening because she could focus intently on each task, one at a time. And if she stayed focused today, she would make it to Gisela's house.

Extricating herself from the flow of foot traffic, she approached the first token machine, pulling the backpack off one shoulder so she could move it around to the front. She had seen Brenda use the machines several times before. They weren't complicated, and the steps were numbered.

Step one was to read the instructions, which was just a list of prices for the tokens. That was hardly a step at all.

Step two was inserting the coins. The T leg of the trip—to the North Station in Lechmere—was eighty-five cents. Dee unzipped the front pocket of her backpack and found three quarters and a dime, which she fed into the slot.

Step three was a press of the brushed silver button.

The machine issued several guttural clicks before dropping a single gold token into the metal tray.

Dee snatched up the coin and squeezed it in her fist, her arm tensing as relief surged through her. The feeling of triumph cascaded through her body, and she knew, even before it reached her feet, that she was going to run. The impulse was too strong. It didn't matter that she needed to stay; her feet didn't always listen to her. Sometimes they would take her to a different room than the one she had aimed for. Sometimes they would do nothing at all when she needed to take action. It was the most intimate betrayal imaginable, and it had woven uncertainty into the fabric of her daily existence.

Now, only the sight of the passengers amassed behind her stilled her urge. When had the station gotten so busy?

Focus, Dee.

She couldn't forfeit her machine, not until she was done.

She stilled the urge.

As she returned to the front panel, she heard the grumbling of several people behind her.

"I don't think she knows," one of them whispered.

Anger welled up in Dee, but she blocked out the voices of the onlookers.

Focus.

She fished more change from her backpack pocket and tried to get back into the ritual of her task. Following the three steps again, she deposited sixty cents for the Arlington Center bus to Medford and Thurston, then pressed the metal button.

Dee made it to the right platform, but she couldn't relax. Her brain wasn't getting the *mission accomplished* signal. She would have to stay on her guard, in case she got away from herself. Her eyes flicked to the digital sign over the boarding strip every few seconds, as if it might change. Her heart pounded, and her agitation crept up her spine like a blossoming weed. She felt like she was doing something wrong on some level. Brenda and Walter would never have condoned this.

A dozen feet away, a mother sat her son down on a bench and told him to wait there for the train. He reluctantly complied. Dee followed his example, taking a seat on the opposite end. From this position the arrival sign was now out of sight.

Good.

By the time the Green Line train pulled to a stop, Dee's anxiety had settled in her gut, rooting her in place. Her habitual vocalizations had drawn curious eyes, which only made her more anxious.

The doors of the train slid open, and Dee watched commuters spill from the cars. The boy and his mother left Dee behind, joining the rest of the passengers waiting to board. The speakers overhead rang out with some prerecorded message about the Orange Line. Who cared about the Orange Line? Dee cared only about Green.

She needed to get to her feet.

Back at the ticket machine her body had been overactive. Now it wasn't responding at all.

This isn't going to work.

How could she have thought she could get all the way across town without incident? Without assistance?

She pictured Gisela sitting in that dim room, watching her strange video while someone else watched from behind.

Dee fought with her body to stand. She had to keep going.

Rocking in place, she focused every ounce of her will on standing up.

Her body didn't cooperate.

She was about to watch her own train leave.

Inside the nearest train car, just a few dozen feet away, the boy stood with one hand in his mother's and the other clasped around a stanchion.

He was watching Dee.

Without thinking, Dee hopped into his head.

She saw herself the way the boy did: a young woman, alone on a bench, eyes far away.

This might be enough.

She hopped back to her own head and jumped to her feet just as the boarding tone sounded. Her momentary head-hop had been just enough to get her motor started again, and she raced across the platform just as the doors were sliding shut. The edges of the two panels pressed into her—one across her back, the other into her shoulder—and for just a moment she was caught between the doors. Then they retracted, and an urgent-sounding tone played over the speaker, followed by an admonition to clear the doorways.

With her breath still hoarse in her ears, Dee stepped onto the train.

The fabric of her sleeve tugged against her arm, startling her. She wrenched her arm free before she realized that an elderly man seated beside the doors was merely trying to get her attention. Before she could respond, the car lurched, and she was pitched backward. Only the gray-haired man's quick response prevented her from falling over. He grabbed her arm, providing her support and steadying her until her hands found the nearest handrail.

"Have you got it?" he asked with a smile.

Then another voice. Gentle. "Did you want to sit?"

Her heart racing, Dee noticed the elderly woman sitting next to the man. She wore a straw hat with a red flower affixed to the band.

Its eight petals were the deepest crimson, so vibrant that they seemed to leech the color from the rest of the train car.

Plantae, Tracheobionta, Spermatophyta, Magnoliophyta, Magnoliopsida, Asteridae, Asterales, Asteraceae, Dahlia, Dahlia coccinea.

The specimen was as captivating as it was real. The woman must have clipped it that morning.

"Stand up, Stan," the woman said. "Let the young lady sit."

The woman's silver eyes were still on Dee as the old man stood and moved aside.

"Here, next to me," the woman said to Dee, patting the free seat beside her.

Dee let go of the handrail, and her hand immediately got to flapping. She sat hard, jostled by the still-accelerating car. Sitting helped, but it didn't eliminate the newness of the experience. The stress of it all would come out in ways that drew attention. Which would only cause more stress. More risk.

"Do you speak English, dear?" the woman asked slowly.

Dee's eyes fixed on the flower, which swayed back and forth as the train rolled over the tracks.

Dee supposed she *didn't* speak English, though it was the language that formed her thoughts and dreams. Her parents had spoken Persian to each other, and to close friends, but even though Dee understood them, they had only used English with her. It was as if they feared two competing languages might cause her more difficulty than her autism already did. So it remained the whispered language of her parents, exotic and exclusive.

The woman tapped her own ear. "English?" She nodded, perhaps to signal that it was safe to respond. Her husband looked concerned, and his eyes said that he was trying to figure out the strange girl next to them. They saw that she was agitated, but they probably hadn't figured out that autism was involved. They would assume she was mentally handicapped and had wandered away from her family.

Dee managed to break her hand-wringing just long enough to

reach into her breast pocket and remove her traveling info card. She handed it to the woman, then turned and looked down at her feet as the woman read the message Dee had dictated to Junmo.

"Autism, Stan," came the woman's voice.

"What's that?"

"Read this. She's traveling alone." Louder, the woman spoke to Dee as she placed a hand lightly on her shoulder. "You're very brave. You understand me?"

Dee looked at her and managed something like a grin. Her facial expressions were as unreliable as any of her motor functions, but the woman seemed to understand well enough.

"East Dartmouth Avenue in Somerville," said the old man, pointing to the destination address on the back of Dee's card. "So the stop you're looking for is Lechmere. Tell her, Eva."

"We can make sure you get to the North Station safely," she offered. "Lechmere is where we're getting off."

Her husband held the card out for Dee to take. "And from there she'd just take the Arlington Center bus out to Medford, I think."

"That's right."

Dee couldn't have hoped for friendlier travel companions. She only had to worry about scaring them off. Even now, she couldn't seem to coax her hand to take the card back. Instead she nearly stood. That was the last thing she needed—to walk away without her card.

She looked up at the man and hopped into his head. His left eye didn't work at all, but through his right she saw herself. She watched the tension leave her muscles. Her eyes stared straight forward at nothing in particular, as if she had fallen into a trance.

The man turned to his wife, handing the card to her instead. "That must be hard, going through life without any speech."

Eva nodded as she took the card, which she pressed directly into Dee's hand.

Dee hopped back to her own head and slid her card back into its pocket before her hand got other ideas.

15

FRIDAY, APRIL 19, 1991

BAS FORDED his way through the teeming streets around to the alleyway between the First South Church and Newbury Hall, a restored theater. The sun hung directly overhead like an interrogation lamp, setting the rough stone of the church aglow in stark relief and lighting a path all the way to the far end of the alley.

Bas found the symbol—what remained of it—fewer than three yards from the mouth of the back street. The white noise of traffic was hushed to a somber murmur, and the sweet funk of sun-dried refuse warded away the foot traffic choking the sidewalks behind him.

Kneeling, Bas traced over the weathered white lines with a finger. A chill inched across his skin. What had Cynda been thinking as she scratched out her symbol in this desolate alley? Why had she come here? And had she intended to disappear?

Bas pressed his palms into his knees and stood with a grunt. As he waited for the sting in his joints to dissipate, he scanned the alley from front to back, looking up to the tops of the walls on either side.

Not a single CCTV camera was anywhere in sight.

How the hell had that video been captured?

He gave his surroundings one more inspection just to be sure, strolling deeper into the alley then retracing his steps.

There were definitely no cameras.

Bas shut his eyes and pictured the footage from the tape, trying to pinpoint the location from which the images had been captured. Cynda had knelt at a three-quarter angle from the camera, which itself had been pointing straight down the alley.

He moved back out toward the sidewalk. He had assumed the camera had been mounted to a utility pole, but there was no pole, no place for a camera to be mounted.

He did, however, spot some CCTV cameras across the street at a Gulf station. These couldn't have been the source of the video—they were too far away—but one of them was pointing more or less toward the alley, and it was possible it had captured something of use. Then again, if the original video had been captured more than a week ago, it was unlikely any footage from this camera remained. Bas counted himself lucky when a proprietor retained a week of footage before tapes before were reused, and even then, security tapes were often so old that the pictures were incoherent.

Bas trotted across the street and entered the station's chilly mini-market. The proprietor's eyes were on him immediately, and they remained on him even as he rang up a woman with five cartons of Marlboros. Bas picked up some beef jerky and cheese sticks—car provisions—and got in line behind the woman. When she left, Bas placed his items on the counter.

"You are the largest man we have in here all day," the cashier said, sounding impressed. He started to punch keys on the register without waiting for a response.

Bas's eyes flicked down to the man's name tag. "Are you the manager here, Nameed?"

"No," he said, stuffing Bas's items into a plastic bag. "You need something?"

Bas pulled a business card from his wallet and held it out. "My name is Bas Milius. I'm a private investigator."

"Three twenty-nine," said Nameed, his interest in the card already gone.

Bas placed the card on the counter by the bag. "I'm looking for a girl who was last seen in this area, and there's a chance she was captured on one of your security cameras." He handed over the money. "If I could review your tapes, it would be really helpful."

"I don't know about any girl," Nameed said, putting the money in the register and handing Bas his change.

"Right, I know. But your front camera there, it may have seen her in passing. This would have been in the evening hours, about a week ago."

Nameed looked him up and down. "You are not police."

"I'm a private detective."

The man mulled the information over before answering. "Tomorrow." He pushed the plastic bag toward Bas.

"Tomorrow?"

"Come back then, talk to the manager."

16

FRIDAY, APRIL 19, 1991

DEE RAPPED on Gisela's door with a sense of relief that hummed like a current throughout her body. She had made a plan—an absurd, impractical plan—and then she had actually accomplished it. In that moment on Gisela's doorstep it felt every bit as miraculous as glowing fingertips or communication by thought.

When the door pulled open, Dee nearly shrieked.

It was really Gisela.

"Dee? What in...?"

Gisela looked over Dee's shoulder, beyond the front porch, her face a mask of confusion. "Are they coming?" she asked under her breath, though she knew Dee couldn't respond. She joined Dee on the stoop to scan the street.

Dee ushered Gisela back into her apartment and leaned into the door, pushing it shut with her backpack.

"Wait, are Brenda and Walter *coming*?"

Dee gave Gisela a hug. She squeezed her eyes shut and felt the tension drain from her body.

But she couldn't relax, not just yet.

When they separated, Gisela was looking at her as if she had painted her face purple. "You can't be here alone," she said, and reached for the door.

Dee planted herself against it, vocalizing in a way that Gisela understood.

"You *are* here alone." She backed off and studied Dee more closely. "You look okay. But I don't get why..." She shook her head. "Let me call Brenda."

Before things got out of hand, Dee put her hands on Gisela's shoulders. That got her attention. Dee shrugged off her backpack and pulled a second card from its pocket, with another message that Junmo had written for her. She held it out.

Gisela accepted the card, the furrow between her brows growing deeper as she read.

> I am okay! Gisela. Brenda and Walter are okay. My friend Junmo helped me write this note. I will explain how. But there is something I need to show you first. We need to go sit down. I know that does not make sense right now. But trust me.

Gisela flipped the note over, then looked at Dee. "Is there more?"

A new kind of anxiety blossomed in Dee just then, though her vocalization could only hint at it.

"Well let me get that at least," Gisela said. Taking Dee's backpack in one hand and her hand in the other, she led her into the living room. They sat next to each other on a pillow-strewn couch, the backpack between them.

"Did you have something else to show me, Dee?" Gisela patted the open front pocket of the backpack. "Did you bring me something?"

Of course Gisela would be dubious. She didn't know about *whisper*. And if Dee made a misstep now—if she assumed Gisela could handle what she was about to demonstrate—she might just lose Gisela, too.

Dee had several of the couch cushions in hand before she realized she had been stacking them into an unsteady tower. She was acting out again, had dropped into auto-pilot when the nervousness racing through her system made her forget herself. In frustration, she grabbed one of the pillows and hugged it to her chest.

Gisela sat still, giving Dee space to wind down. She had seen this before.

She knew Dee.

The thought loosened Dee's grip. There was no way that reaching out to Gisela would drive her away.

Gisela looked into her eyes. "Hey, Dee, it's okay."

Dee sighed, her wordless voice high and steady. She cooed as she slowly rocked, finding comfort in the steady rhythm.

Gisela reached out over the backpack and stroked her arm. "I know you must have a good reason for being here. Oh, sweetie, are you okay?" But the concern on her face shifted gears. "You know what, let me call them before we get too comfortable."

That was enough of a prompt that, without breaking her rhythm, Dee whispered into her friend's head for the first time.

I can talk, Gisela.

Gisela leapt from the couch as if she'd been shocked. She stumbled back into her coffee table, her hands to her temples, and in that moment it looked as if she had forgotten about her houseguest altogether.

"What... what?"

It's me, Gisela. This is Dee.

Gisela's eyes were on Dee, but she didn't move.

It's really me.

"It's in my head," Gisela said, squeezing her eyes shut. When she opened them a second later, they were somewhat clearer. "If that really is you, how are you talking in my head?"

I'm sorry. I know this is really weird. But this is the only way I can talk. I just... I think what I want to say, and you hear it.

"But... *how?* How is this happening?"

It's weird for me too, I promise. Please don't be scared of me, Gisela. I'm still me. I just found a way out of my silence.

For a moment Dee wasn't sure how her friend would respond. Would she call Brenda and tell her?

Instead, Gisela edged back toward the couch.

"I just want to know what's going on."

Dee squeezed the pillow again, encouraged. *The first time I whispered was by accident.*

"Whispered?"

That's what I call this.

Gisela nodded.

I haven't always been able to do it. But the first time was ten years ago, the day my parents were killed.

"In the South Station Singularity."

Dee nodded. Her rocking slowed to an easy sway.

Gisela sat back down beside her, closer now. Her shoulders were still tense, but she was willing to listen.

April twenty-eighth, nineteen eighty-one. I was eight, and suddenly our apartment was full of people—neighbors and police and Child Protective Services. Molly was there, my aide. But I didn't know anyone else, and I didn't know what was going on until I overheard them talking. They didn't think I could hear because I never look like I'm listening. But I do hear. I heard everything they said. That my parents were presumed dead. My mom had been picking Dad up from the station when it happened.

Dee searched for the words, but she was far away, lost in her stims. Her fingers worked the pillow's fringe until the pattern left indentations in her skin.

I sat on the couch under the light, where Mom used to read stories to me. I tried not to let their words in. Everyone looked at me like I was a broken toy, which I guess is pretty much how I felt. Inside I was a wreck, but my face doesn't show how I feel. My body was even less under my control than usual. My muscles were starting to cramp from all the stimming. More than anything, I just wanted everyone to leave.

I had it in my mind that... that my parents wouldn't come back until everyone was gone. So when the CPS lady tried to take me away, it felt like she was making everything worse. It felt like if I left, my parents would be dead for real.

Gisela reached over and rubbed Dee's hand, her own eyes moist.

There's a difference between thinking words and whispering. I talk a lot in my head. But that day my words went a different direction, and they got out. Not from my mouth, but directly into the CPS lady's head. She let go of me and almost looked like she was going to jump out the window.

"Like I did a minute ago."

Dee squeezed the pillow. *I know this isn't possible. What I can do. I know that. But... I've gotten used to it. I guess it would freak me out more if it didn't feel like me. Do you know what I mean? Like if I could make things explode, then I'd be worried. That wouldn't be me. But this is still me, even if I don't know what it is.*

Gisela laughed. "'What do you see when you turn out the light? I can't tell you, but I know it's mine.'"

What's that from?

"The Beatles."

It sounded familiar.

This is me, Gisela.

Gisela nodded, biting her lip. For a moment her eyes were distant. Then she leaned forward. "Does anyone else know?"

Dee's fingers had worked their way through the knitting, into the cotton filling of the pillow.

Roddy Hock found out. That's when he got scary. When you came, I thought you were saving my life.

"Oh, Dee." Gisela's voice hitched. She moved the backpack aside and put her arm around Dee's shoulder, caressing her with her thumb. "I am so sorry. It's no wonder you've been keeping it to yourself this whole time. But Brenda and Walter?"

I've never whispered to them. I haven't wanted to risk it. It's hard enough getting by without the added scrutiny. But I'm nearly eighteen, so... maybe it's time for me to trust more people. I mean, Brenda knows me so well that I don't really need *to whisper to her.*

Gisela's eyes narrowed. "So why me? Why now?"

It was the question Dee had feared most, the question she could no longer avoid.

Her words darted away like insects after the light is switched on. She hadn't fully thought her plan through. In fact, she had put off planning what she needed to say, for fear of being wrong—or worse yet, being right. She had made it to Gisela, and this felt like the right place to be. But she had come at great risk, and Gisela knew it.

I wanted to visit.

"To visit." Gisela wasn't buying it. "Well that's nice, Dee. You know you're always welcome here. But you're so bad at lying that I can tell just from the voice in my head."

I know. I'm sorry. I'm just... I'm tired. Maybe we can talk tomorrow?

Gisela bit her lip again and looked up toward the stairs before returning her gaze to Dee. "Did you want to sleep over?"

Can I?

Gisela shook her head, and Dee feared the worst. But then Gisela said, "Sure, I think that should be fine, at least for tonight. It's Friday, so..."

Thank you, Gisela.

"But we're going to have to call Brenda. If she's okay with it, I'm okay with it. I've got the spare room, and it's comfortable."

I'll be as quiet as I can. And we can talk more tomorrow.

"Whisper."

Whisper.

"Unbelievable," Gisela said. She took a deep breath and patted Dee's knee. "Stay here, or, you know, feel free to make yourself at home upstairs. If you're hungry... Well, let me call Brenda and Walter first, and we can sort out the rest after."

Dee remained on the couch as Gisela went to the kitchen. A

series of clicks was followed by a few moments of silence. Something dragged across the floor—Gisela pulling a chair out to sit.

As Dee rocked, she listened to her friend's voice.

"Hey, Bren."

Brenda probably already know Dee was missing; Ursula would have phoned her as soon as she noticed Dee's absence from Kids Kan. Brenda would be frantic. If there had been another way for Dee to get to Gisela, a way that didn't worry the people who cared for her, Dee would have done it. But something Walter had once said stuck in Dee's mind. He had just bought several pints of ice cream, flouting Brenda's mandated calorie restriction, and he told her: *Better to ask for forgiveness than permission.*

It had worked out fine that time. Maybe it would this time, too. That had just been part of the risk. Hopefully Brenda would understand that Dee wouldn't have performed such a stunt if she hadn't felt the need to.

"I know. She's here with me."

Dee strained to listen, but heard no yelling.

"Totally fine. I thought the same thing. I did, yeah. You know, I think she just missed me, that's all. And she's more independent now, thanks to you guys."

She was covering for her. Good.

"Well, it seems like she wants to stay over. But you know, I'd be happy to drop her off if you want. I don't know if she has therapy tomorrow, or..."

Please let me stay.

"Oh, okay. I mean... Yeah, totally. But are you *sure* you're sure?"

Brenda had always been the one to encourage Dee to try new things. Maybe it took more to alarm her than a solo venture on public transportation. Walter was another story. He had always been overprotective, to the point of protecting Dee from things she might otherwise have enjoyed. But Brenda had a way of talking him down.

"Yeah, I think it's a good thing. I'm *really* impressed, to be honest." Gisela laughed. "You should have seen the look on my face. She was just there at my door."

Then again, would Dee have been able to accomplish such a thing without using her abilities along the way? Maybe?

She was glad she would never have to find out.

17

SATURDAY, APRIL 20, 1991

"TRY THIS," Griffin said, sliding something pleasantly dark across the bar. In the Red Bell Tavern's dim lighting, the beer's head looked as thick as cotton, but the malt odor hit Bas's nose with a spicy tingle.

Bas sat up on his stool. "What is it?"

Griffin grabbed the bottle from under the bar and set it before Bas, turning the label around.

"*Duckin Cover Brew*," Bas read. The label featured a cartoonish duck eyeing a distant mushroom cloud with what appeared to be profound dismay. "Well that's terrible."

"Yeah, well, don't mind the art. Just tell me what you think."

Bas brought the foam to his lips. The flavor wasn't nearly as bad as he had expected. "Okay, that's interesting. It kinda moves around, doesn't it?"

"See? Yeah, it's subdued at first, but then it really blooms." Griffin slapped the bar. "*I* think we have a winner. You know Harriet, but I'll tell her you gave it a thumbs-up, and maybe that'll convince her to list it."

Harriet had brought Griffin on about a year ago. The details of his life were a mystery to Bas, but he'd brought a level of enthusiasm to his work that the proprietress had never had, and she'd taken an increasingly hands-off attitude toward him. At this point Bas had a feeling that Harriet would be happy to rubber-stamp whatever Griffin recommended.

"Where'd you find it?"

"Local beer brew BBS I dial into. Same place I tracked down the *Satan's Dewclaw* the week before last." His voice balanced pride and shame in equal measure.

Bas blinked. "You don't say."

He had given himself the weekend to waste on his dead-end case. On Monday he would give Mitch another call, or reach out to other former colleagues. The last thing he wanted to do was scan the classifieds.

His hand was back up by his empty pocket. What would Lana have thought about the life he had made for himself? He winced and shook his head.

"Idiot," he said aloud. He forced himself to let go of the loose fabric of his empty pocket.

"Say again?"

He had forgotten about Griffin.

"Nothing," Bas said. "You just gave me an idea, I think."

Sitting at his terminal, Bas dialed into CDB Infotek, then waited as the modem chirped and hissed. Less than a minute later a logo emerged across his screen, rendered line by line, followed by a prompt. Bas entered his credentials and was taken to the index screen.

```
Discovery - Name Search
Date: 4/20/91 Time: 12:54 PM
Reference: PI87
Requestor: MILIUSB
```

If there was anything to be found on a Cynda Bolden, surely he would find it in the online database of several billion records from local, county, and state governments.

He entered Cynda's name in the input box, ignored the other fields, and pressed *enter*. The best place to start was with the broadest search possible. If he got too many hits, he could scope the search with other criteria to narrow down the candidates.

The cursor flashed erratically, spitting out a number of progress dots as the seconds ticked by. Eventually a new menu appeared, with the first option being the best:

```
S) Display a Brief Summary of All Matches
and Detail
```

Bas typed S, and hit enter.

```
A search of our DISCOVERY - Name Search file
on Apr 20, 1991 identified [0] possible
match(es) using the following search
criteria:
"CYNDA BOLDEN"

N) Narrow the Search Area by Modifying
Criteria
E) Exit Search
Please make your Selection and press ENTER:
```

"Damn," Bas said. Either Cynda had never left a single electronic footprint—evading DMV records, court records, tax records, and death certificates alike—or she had followed her father into insubstantiality.

The cursor blinked.

Bas scanned his two options again.

```
N) Narrow the Search Area by Modifying
Criteria
E) Exit Search
```

He attempted another search, this time changing the query to C *Bolden*, which was sure to be too broad. Sure enough, there were hundreds of exact and partial matches, including a good number of entries for *Cynthia Bolden*. But Mordell, before he had disappeared, had insisted his daughter's name was Cynda. And none of the Cynthias listed Cynda as an alias.

Bas exited the service and logged out.

There were times when no information was itself information. But this was one of the times when no information was just no information.

Tapping his nails on the table, Bas stared at the blinking cursor. The expensive professional database had failed him. *Cynda Bolden* was a dead end. But the logo she had drawn might still mean something. Maybe the so-called information superhighway could point him in the right direction.

He paged through his latest notebook. Half the pages were blank still, and at this point in his career they would remain so. His sketch was tucked in after his last page of notes. He set the sketch on his desk and headed to the front of the shop.

Vern was minding the counter today. He was peering into the guts of a clock radio, a series of tools laid out before him. He glanced up as Bas walked by, but said nothing.

"Vernon," Bas said as he made his way over to the shelves labeled *Computers*. He found what he was looking for in the peripherals area: a flatbed scanner that still had its cables.

"Uh, what do you think you're doing?" Vern asked, peering over his jeweler's loupe.

"I just need to borrow it."

"If that's the Microtek MSF-300Z? Yeah, that's two thousand bucks, new."

"Jesus." Suddenly it felt much heavier. "I'll have it back on the shelf in ten minutes, I promise."

Vern's eyes tracked him into the back office.

After figuring out the scanner's SCSI interface and installing the driver—that took more than ten minutes alone—Bas managed to get the thing working. He scanned his sketch and saved it to a file. Consulting the cheat sheet next to his monitor, he then dialed into a bulletin board called *Boston Connection BBS*. It had occasionally yielded leads on cases, especially cases dealing with local lore or social events. Boston Connection had never held any recreational allure for Bas, but keeping up with local matters had become more of a chore with each passing year, so the network filled a gap.

When he was connected, he posted his image to several forums, each time with one simple question: "Anyone familiar with this?"

"Nameed mentioned something about an investigation," the manager of the Gulf said as she led Bas back to the employee office. She had introduced herself as Bruna Armenta, and she was at the accommodating end of the curious-dubious spectrum.

The station's surveillance system consisted of half a dozen cameras trained on the pumps, points of entry and egress, and the register. The video feeds were piped into the manager's office, where, Bas now saw, they were recorded on VHS tapes. The office was cramped with the usual accouterments, from the shift assignment board to shelves of accounting binders.

Bas leaned against the doorframe. "A young woman was spotted in the vicinity about a week ago. I know she was across the street at one point, but I wanted to see if I could get another angle."

"What day? Do you know?"

Bas grimaced, shaking his head.

Bruna sat in the sole chair and rolled over to the shelf, where she retrieved the first tape. "Well, they should mostly be in order. Here's Sunday."

"I appreciate it. I'll start from there and we'll see where that gets me."

She loaded the cassette into the spare machine, then got up and edged around him. "Did you need me to stay, or...?"

"You're welcome to, of course. Otherwise, I'll let you know when I'm done."

There she was.

Bas watched Cynda enter the alleyway between the First South Church and Newbury Hall Theater on Friday, the fifth of April. The timestamp at the bottom of the frame read 8:46 p.m. The picture was black-and-white, with the usual stop-motion effect of time-lapse mode.

The angle of the camera cut off most of the sidewalk, so Cynda was only visible for a moment before she ducked around the corner of the building into the darkness beyond. If this was the moment the *Cynda* tape picked up, she would be performing her ritualistic movements now.

Bas watched for a few minutes, until the picture jumped.

8:50 p.m.

The picture rolled once, then caught itself.

Bas paused the playback, rewound, and watched again. He saw no flash from the alley, but it was still interesting. He couldn't be sure if the Cynda tape began as soon as she entered the alley, but if it did... then the two cameras glitched at right about the same time.

"Two separate cameras, same glitch," he said aloud, as if hearing the words could make it make sense. Could there have been some sort of electromagnetic pulse? Unlikely—something that powerful would have affected everything in the area, and might even have made the nightly news.

Bas rewound the tape further this time, all the way to the moment just before Cynda disappeared into the alley. He paused it there.

What was he doing, besides delaying the inevitable? Sure, more details had come to light. He'd nailed down the time and location of the mysterious Cynda tape. But where did that leave him, besides sitting in the back of a gas station?

You ever lost anyone yourself, Mr. Milius?

Remembering Bolden's question, Bas shook his head.

"Case closed," he said under his breath.

At least he could start packing one day early.

18

SATURDAY, APRIL 20, 1991

THROUGHOUT THE NIGHT Gisela's cat Phoebe had watched Dee from the shadows, too timid to approach. But by morning something had clicked for her, and now the feline—a Persian herself—wouldn't leave Dee alone, and was now curled up in her lap. Dee had never been in a house with a full-time pet, but Phoebe was as easy to appreciate as a warm pillow. Dee's fingers tousled the animal's fur, and her reward was a sonorous purr of approval.

Gisela came into the living room from the kitchen with two steaming mugs in her hand. Phoebe gave her a look, then tucked her head back between her paws.

"Mint tea," Gisela said, coming around the couch and sitting down. "This one has honey. Take whichever one you prefer."

Being careful not to upset her lap mate, Dee reached for the mug with honey.

Gisela smiled as she handed it over. "I thought I remembered you had a sweet tooth."

I like anything that comes from flowers.

"That's right. You're the gardener savant, aren't you?"

Dee stared at her mug. *Well... I prefer not to use that term.*

"Oh no! I'm sorry. That was offensive, wasn't it?"

Dee set her mug on a coaster. *It's just, my interest in gardening has nothing to do with my autism. I just like flowers. I feel like we understand each other.*

"I get it." Gisela smiled. "Well the honey's from the farmer's market."

Phoebe got up and hopped down from Dee's lap. Could she sense Dee was using some special means to communicate? Dogs could smell cancer, or so they said. Maybe cats could hear telepathy. Maybe they didn't like it.

"I talked with Brenda and Walter again this morning." Gisela took a loud sip from her tea, as if to give Dee a moment to respond. When Dee said nothing, she continued. "I wasn't quite sure what to tell them, so... we probably need to come up with a plan."

You're right.

Something bubbled in Dee's stomach.

"How long did you want to stay with me? I mean, you have your school of course, and your work, and your therapy, too."

She was talking about Applied Behavior Analysis, which had been wasting Dee's waking hours for nearly a decade now. In the beginning the program had been somewhat useful, showing Dee ways to keep her focus and escape from her stim world. But eventually the repeated drills and guided coursework got stale; they failed to keep pace with Dee's internal maturation. It was as though the program assumed she simply lacked the ability to make progress beyond these rote exercises. Granted, Dee's outward bearing didn't convey the progress of her inner self, but if her teachers hadn't been so checked out, they might have seen something more in her anyway.

The only person at school Dee respected was her personal aide, Cathy. She always had something snarky to say about her coworkers —a behavior that probably would have been frowned on if anyone other than Dee heard her. But she had always spoken to Dee as if Dee could understand—had spoken to her person to person—and that was a precious rarity.

"I love that you're here, Dee," Gisela said. "I'm flattered. But I'm not really set up here to give you all you need."

Dee slowly rocked on the couch.

"Plus I can see there's something going on."

Dee had put off this moment. She knew couldn't expect her friend to accommodate her forever. She had to explain why she had trekked across town alone.

Gisela squinted at her. "Come on, Dee. I can't help you if you don't level with me."

Dee grabbed the closest pillow. It wasn't as soft as Phoebe, but it also wouldn't be upset if Dee's hands got out of control.

She took a deep breath. *A few days ago you were watching a video.*

After a pause, Gisela nodded. "You know that's part of what I do." But already her face had changed as she tried to work out why Dee had said that.

No. This video was different. I mean, you'd watched it before, but this time it had changed.

Gisela looked shaken, but she recovered quickly. "And you know this how?"

I saw you.

"Saw?" Gisela set her mug on the table. "Is this like the talking?" she asked, her voice steady. "Like your whispering?"

In some ways, yes.

Dee should have planned this conversation ahead of time. How was she going to explain without sounding crazy?

It's kind of like our TV's remote control, where the instructions say it needs line-of-sight to work.

Gisela nodded. "Infrared."

Whispering is like that. To start, the other person has to be nearby. And then... then there's the head-hopping, which starts that way too.

Gisela remained silent.

Head-hopping is when I see from someone else's eyes. I can't interact with them, and my body stays behind, wherever I left it. But for a little while it's like I'm with them, watching what they see, at least to a certain range.

Gisela sat back on the couch, her eyes flicking back and forth as she worked out what Dee had told her. "I guess I shouldn't be surprised at this point," she said quietly. "After all, you're whispering directly into my head. How could I question you?"

I know how weird this all is. But I can't explain what I've seen without telling you how I saw it.

"No, I get it. I think." Gisela squinted. "So you *saw* me reviewing that tape. That's what you're saying? You somehow projected yourself across town, right into my eyes?"

Yes, but—no. See, this was different. Like I said, I've only head-hopped to people near me, when I could see them. I have to be looking at them to make the hop. That's how it's always been. But this time I was at home. And Gisela, I didn't initiate it.

"So like, you're getting better at it, with practice?"

That's not it either. I wasn't seeing through your eyes at all, or anyone else's. This time you were already being watched from behind, and I just tuned in to it. Gisela, there was no one else in the room with you.

Gisela swallowed, her pupils large and dark. "You're scaring me."

Dee looked down at her hands, at her fingers twisting the fabric of the pillow. *It's happened twice now, this sort of remote viewing. And both times you were watching that tape. I don't know how or why, but when I saw it was you—*

"That's why you came."

I didn't have a plan. Just a feeling. Like something was happening, and it wasn't just a fluke.

Gisela nodded slowly.

So what was it then?

"The tape?" Gisela sounded far away, like she was still thinking about what Dee had just told her. "It was only a copy..." She shook her head as if to clear it. "A colleague brought me a tape that was... well, security footage is kind of mixed up sometimes. It's complicated. But I cleared it up and made a copy for him, and I made another for myself. There was something peculiar about the video, and I wanted to have a closer look at it when the guy wasn't hanging over my shoulder."

She picked up her mug and cradled it in her hands.

"You think it's related? Like, somehow... like the tape is triggering... I don't even know what I'm trying to ask. It doesn't make sense to me."

But I was thinking the same thing. Maybe I'm just extra sensitive because of my abilities. So when you play the tape it draws a signal so strong that I can't help but pick up on it.

"What about *his* copy? My client's, I mean. If he plays it back, would that cause your remote viewing, too?"

I don't know. I've only seen you. So there's something about your copy that's... not normal.

"Well, you're right about that. That first time I watched it, I knew there was something odd about it, though I couldn't put my finger on what. And you're right about another thing, too: the video wasn't the same the second time I watched it."

Could you destroy it? Make it unplayable?

Gisela got a curious look on her face, and sipped her tea before answering. "Would it be weird to destroy something without knowing what it was?"

How could she ask that, after everything Dee had just told her? Did she believe her or not?

At least promise me you'll never play it again.

Gisela shook her head. "Okay, yeah. It's just... this is a lot to take in."

I know. And I'm sorry I don't have more answers. But that doesn't mean we can ignore this. Like you said before, something is going on. You asked me why I came. This is why.

19

MONDAY, APRIL 22, 1991

BAS'S OFFICE looked more like a storage closet than it had in a decade, now that he'd packed most of it away into boxes. Zelda had taken the news of his imminent retirement well, but she had been quiet in the hours following. He understood: they were of an age where every goodbye seemed a little more final.

He was boxing his books on forensics and crime scene photography when something caught his eye. He froze, as if the feeling welling up inside him might spill over the sides if he dared move.

There at the back of the shelf was something he thought he'd lost.

Lana's last gift to him.

He dropped the books into the open box, reached to the back of the shelf, and pulled down the Paul Bunyan socks. They must have fallen back behind the books shortly after he'd arranged with Zelda to rent the spare room.

On their first blind date, Lana had done a double-take as he crossed the floor to her table, owing to Bas's size. She would repeat the action over the years, doing parody double-takes whenever he entered any room. Her pet name for him, Bas Bunyan, had become their in-joke.

J.D. ROBINSON

The ridiculous socks—featuring the lumberjack at the top and blue oxen all the way down to the toe—weren't really wearable, since they were nearly the size of air socks. But of course he'd kept them. After all, they were from her.

Holding the novelty gift now, Bas was transported back to a time of shared secrets, of ecstatic glee, and some promise of permanence. The fresh sting of loss surprised him, and he sat down hard in his chair, breathing hard.

He considered throwing the socks away. What did he need of them now? But that thought only made him sadder still. Instead he blinked the moisture from his eyes and tossed the socks into an open box.

Ten years was a long time to mourn. Maybe that was why he had been willing to hear Bolden out in this very office. Maybe he had recognized something on the man's face—the same look Bas had seen on dozens of faces over the years. When a person disappears it's never a clean cut. And sometimes Bas could at least help cauterize the wound.

Only with Bolden, the wound had simply disappeared. That was a new trick.

Bas sat back, and the chair complained under his weight. He rolled over to his desk and dialed up *Boston Connection BBS*, expecting to find no activity. But one of the threads he'd started now had a flag next to it. He tapped the cursor down to the thread and hit enter. The screen refreshed, showing his original query in green text. But beneath it the thread now continued.

Someone posting as *anonBob #74* had written:

```
that symbol relates to something like "me,
myself, and i," some sort of terrorist
group. i'd definitely stay away. they caused
the south station singularity in 1981.
```

Bas chuckled. "What the fuck?"

Shaking his head, he scrolled down to the next response, this one from a deleted member called *it-from-bit*:

```
That's the 'I Mine' logo. They are /not/
terrorists, but they /are/ a cult. I first
heard about them after the South Station
singularity. My aunt died in that, and they
tried to get my uncle interested in their
grief counseling shit. In the mid-80s I had
a friend who ended up totally buying into
them. We were at the Spit every weekend
then, and I Mine actively recruited from
there. I heard they were at clubs a lot, and
anywhere else you can find 'lost souls'.
```

"Holy shit," Bas said, reading both replies several times.

I Mine would explain the symbol: the merging of a small *i* into a capital *M*. And if they were a cult, that might explain why Cynda dropped out of sight a year before her final act. Cutting all ties to the outside world was *Cult 101*.

Could that explain the mystery of Mordell Bolden's sudden identity conversion into Alton Griggs? If he was part of the cult, too... they might have enough control over his mind to make him believe anything.

Bas pushed back from the computer and popped up front. Zelda was taping up a shipping box so thoroughly that the recipient would have to use a blowtorch to get into it.

"Hey, Zee? Do you know if *the Spit* is still around?"

She looked up from her box. "*Spit?*"

"A local club of some kind."

She chuckled. "Baby, I haven't been to a club since Sabby Lewis was at the Morocco Lounge back in Portland, around the time you were discovering your first pubes."

Bas winced and put up a hand. "Okay, that's... that's fine."

He retreated to his office, retrieved his work notebook from the box where he had tossed it not an hour ago, and carefully transcribed the two messages.

Bas left Hawley Hill Trade Center and dashed across the street to the Red Bell Tavern. Proximity had a lot to do with Harriet Bland's establishment being Bas's bar of choice. In fact, in recent years, it had proven to be *over*-convenient.

It was pretty dead inside at this early hour, with just a handful of out-of-towners buzzing around just inside the door. The few old pros had installed themselves farther within, where the light from the windows wouldn't remind them how early it was. They would clear out for parts unknown before the after-work crowd showed.

No one appeared to be minding the bar as Bas took a stool. He retrieved his notebook from his jacket pocket, then draped the jacket over the stool next to him. Flipping to the most recent page, he reviewed his notes.

Both bulletin board messages pointed to some involvement by *I Mine* in the South Station Singularity. It was quite a specific association to make. A secretive organization that counseled survivors in the wake of the 1981 event... that might be a convenient way for a cult to score new blood. But how to draw a line between all that and Cynda Bolden's vanishing in that alleyway a decade later?

"Hey there, Bas."

Bas swiveled around as Griffin waddled by, hefting a sagging box toward the back of the bar.

"Hey, Griffin."

As the man set the box down hard on the floor behind the bar, Bas heard the telltale clink of bottles. The latest sample from Griffin's internet supplier, probably. The barman straightened, arms akimbo, and thrust his shoulders back until something cracked.

"Do you have a moment?" Bas asked, holding his notebook open.

"Uh, sure." He walked over. "It's early for you, isn't it?"

"Yeah, no, I'm actually working a case, see."

Ah, Griffin mouthed, nodding.

"This is a pretty random question, but... what do you know about the Spit?"

"Spit the *club*?"

Bas raised his eyebrows. "Yeah."

"Not much. It closed down a few years back, before I moved here."

"Oh."

"They call it Axis now."

"Oh?"

"Yeah, Spit was, I think, more new wave? But Axis is grungier. Mazzy Star played there, but so did Primus. Uh, not on the same night."

"So it's still around."

"Right next to Fenway. If you're in the area you'll hear it before you see it. Why, you interested in going?"

Bas blinked. How far down this rabbit hole should he go? A grungy club wasn't really his scene. And what were the chances that this supposed cult was still recruiting from area clubs?

On the other hand, wouldn't it be absurd to leave things here?

"I mean, I go there sometimes on Wednesdays or Thursdays," Griffin said, "since I'm off then."

"Maybe," Bas said. "I don't know, I..."

His fingers closed on his ringless pocket. Lana had disappeared—had died—in the South Station Singularity nearly ten years ago. And just a couple weeks ago, Cynda Bolden had drawn the logo of a cult that might have some remote association to the same event.

"Is it because of Wallace Thaw?" Griffin asked. "Harriet told me about your run-in with him."

Bas nearly flinched on hearing the name. "What does that have to do with Axis?"

"I just thought maybe..." Griffin shrugged. "People I know say

Wallace used to hang out there. So I thought there might be a connection." He put up a hand and backed away.

Bas looked down at the pages of his notebook. How badly was he fooling himself? There might not be any *strong* connections between Cynda and Wallace and I Mine and Axis, but there were enough weak connections that he couldn't dismiss the idea outright. For one thing, he had only seen two people move their arms fast enough to defy observation: the first time was right up in his face, and the second time was on the Cynda tape.

And now, with Wallace Thaw being a regular denizen of this club... well, even a series of weak connections could start to look like a diagram, if you squinted just the right way.

20

TUESDAY, APRIL 23, 1991

DEE STOOD at Gisela's back door with half a cupcake in her hand. Her host had surprised her with the birthday gift before leaving early for work. And that evening, Brenda and Walter would arrive for Dee's birthday dinner. She had no doubt they would want her to leave with them afterward.

But now, as she looked out over the small, overgrown disaster area behind Gisela's apartment, she didn't feel any older. After her parents died, the passage of time had stopped in a way—as if everything that had come after was just part of the vast echo of that singular event.

At least until recently.

Phoebe brushed against Dee's ankle, and meowed when Dee looked down at her. She sniffed the air, eyes fixed on Dee's birthday treat.

No cupcake for you, kitty.

If Phoebe heard her, she made no indication.

Dee popped the last half of her cupcake into her mouth as she descended the steps to the back yard. Gisela had given her permission to tend to the fenced-in area as she saw fit. Though it was unclear there was much of anything left to tend. It appeared that the downspouts had killed off anything but the hardiest of weeds. But upon closer inspection, Dee saw that among the crabgrass and spotted spurge were patches of *Portulaca oleracea*—purslane, with its salty lemon flavor—and chickweed, which Dee had never much cared for.

Dee dropped to her knees and got to work, hand-pulling the spotted spurge down to the taproot. Gisela owned no gardening gloves, but that was okay. The soil—even if it was more like compacted clay here—felt good against Dee's fingers. She would just have to remember to wash off the irritating sap before the rash set in.

Plantae, Tracheobionta, Spermatophyta, Magnoliophyta, Magnoliopsida, Caryophyllidae, Caryophyllales, Portulacaceae, Portulaca.

She might even harvest some of the purslane for dinner. It might convince Gisela to take better care of her yard, modest as it was.

She was soon lost in the ritual of her weeding, piling up the unwanted plants on the stone walk as she crept ever deeper into the overgrowth on dew-darkened knees.

The yard was gone.

Dee adjusted more quickly this time, even as she was pulled away from her body. That was good. If she could get used to this, she could probably get used to anything.

She wasn't in the darkened room this time, but Gisela was there. They were in a media lab of some kind, and Gisela was talking to a man about a video playing on the screen before them.

Dammit, Gisela.

She had lied.

And worse still, she was now getting other people involved.

Where was this place? It was different, so the remote viewing wasn't tied to a specific place. And though Gisela was here, Dee knew it wasn't tied to her, either. This happened only when Gisela watched the tape.

It was the tape that was triggering these episodes.

"Yeah, I think I see what's happening here," the man said. "But it's probably easier to show you." He was a compact man with short gray hair and thick glasses. It looked like he had been staring at screens for decades.

"Yeah, you drive," Gisela said, rolling her chair to the side.

The man punched some buttons and took hold of a puck-like controller. The video rewound on one monitor, while a second monitor held a frozen frame of the alleyway just after the woman on the tape had disappeared from view. When the video on the first monitor had rewound all the way, the man pressed more buttons. The start and end frames were then superimposed onto the second monitor.

"This is the first thing that stands out to me." The man made further adjustments to the composite image, until only the differences between the two frames were visible. "If this had been shot with a fixed CCTV camera, everything but the subject should cancel out. If the camera was posted to a pole or a bridge you might get some variance due to wind or the weight of the traffic. But..."

"The camera was *moving*," Gisela concluded for him.

Dee's stomach dropped as her friend said those words. Gisela might have been describing Dee's own viewpoint just then. She had never been in control of what she was seeing during these remote viewing sessions—she couldn't spin around to look at the other side of the room even if she wanted to. Yet her viewpoint had never remained fixed. It was in constant motion, drifting almost imperceptibly with Gisela's movements. If someone had been recording that woman on the screen, did that mean someone was recording Gisela right now? What was Dee tapping into?

And the woman had disappeared.

The man allowed the video to proceed slowly. "Yes. Which makes me think you're looking at a voyeur, not surveillance footage."

As the woman in the video finished her sketch, the video switched to color. Gisela's colleague stopped it there, then rolled it forward and back over that transition point.

"Another weird thing here: the video quality. The black-and-white footage looks like it's from a different camera, like these two parts have been spliced together. But there's no change in orientation, so..." He shook his head.

The tape rolled forward once more, and the tunnel effect reappeared at the center of the screen.

Gisela pointed. "And *that* wasn't there the first time I played the tape."

The man let the scene play for a moment, then paused to scrutinize the warped image.

"Could it be tape wear?" Gisela asked.

The man ejected the cassette, and the screen went dark. He propped open the top flap of the cartridge with a finger and peered at the tape. "Not worn."

He reinserted the tape into his machine, and the tunnel effect appeared on the monitor once more: the alley, with a whirlpool of repeated alleys disappearing into a dark blur at the very center.

"Whatever this effect is, it's part of the video," the man said. "You can see the artifacting here. The CA is consistent across the frame."

"What's CA?"

"Chromatic aberration. It's one way to tell if something was composited after the fact."

"Well, I'm telling you the video is different now. The first time I watched this scene straight through, and there was never this distortion at all. I made a dupe, and it was fine, too. It was the second time I watched the tape that that thing showed up."

Dee had been watching the tape too, that second time, from far away. She had watched the scene so closely that she had felt drawn into it. And that was when the distortion appeared.

Had that been a coincidence?

Did I cause it?

Dee watched the distortion now, and she felt the familiar compulsion to let her eyes swim in the spectral swirl. Why had she resisted it before? If there was any purpose to this remote viewing, then maybe the distortion on the screen held some clue.

So why not let it happen?

Follow the tunnel to the other side.

Already the effect was mesmerizing, not just for the smooth undulation of kaleidoscopic patterns, but for the feeling of motion. She felt herself being pulled in closer, though her viewpoint remained fixed. And as she peered into the chiaroscuro spiral within the glass tube, as she studied the bloom of detail within the dark mass, she realized... there was something there.

Underneath.

Just below the surface.

Dee strained to make sense of what she was seeing, until the edges of the screen seemed to pull past her field of view. Then her eyes adjusted to the relative darkness, and a second scene came into focus.

Two men.

At first Dee saw only them. Both men were dressed in black robes, and the one on the right had hair as red as flame. She could not see their faces, as they were both looking away, staring into a monitor much like Gisela's.

And on their screen was the room Dee had just left.

These men were the ones who had been watching Gisela.

Now Dee was watching *them*.

Watching the watchers.

Like an echo. But coming from where?

Without control of her perspective, it was impossible to get a better view. And that numbing, disembodied feeling was strong here. Very strong. She imagined losing her connection back to herself completely, becoming lost, like a ghost, with no way to return.

As a wave of claustrophobia settled over her, one of the men spoke.

"There, see that? It's like some kind of interference."

Was he talking about the scene on his screen?

"Caused by what though?" asked the redhead. "Have you seen it before?"

"It's that fucking tape. It's out in the wild now, and this is exactly what she warned us about. Make sure you're getting this."

The redhead pointed at a flashing light, as if in answer. "Where is this? Where are we looking?"

"I don't know. Somewhere close is all I can tell."

"How long till we find her?"

The words sent a chill through Dee that she could feel from miles away.

She fixed her eyes on the image in their monitor, never looking away from it. And the image began to melt, until Gisela's room was little more than an empty smear.

"Whoa, whoa. What's going on?"

Red frantically tapped buttons, but to no avail.

"Get it back!"

"It must be the feed."

"Fine. Whatever. We got enough. Roll the tape back. Let's see."

Red rewound the tape, then hit *play*.

There was the room again. Only now there was no sign of Gisela or her colleague. Just the room, the monitor, and a blur at the center of the frame.

"Can you please go back to the start?"

Red exhaled. "This *is* the start." He rewound again, until some internal component clicked and the screen went dark. When he played the video again, the scene was the same. "See?"

"That doesn't..." The man next to Red was silent for a moment as they both watched the screen. "This isn't what we just recorded. What's with this blur? Is this the live shot again?"

"No, look." Red paused the video, then started it again. "This is what got recorded."

"What the *fuck*? This isn't what we saw two seconds ago! We were *watching* it. How did we not record it?"

"We did," said Red. "Look at the timestamp."

"In other words, our fucking sys—"

Dee was out.

The soil had dried on her hands.

Her legs tingled from squatting for too long, and every nerve buzzed with the flood of pent-up sensation.

And Gisela was in trouble.

People were keying into that tape of hers, using it to trigger their remote viewing, the same way Dee used her head-hopping.

But I never spied on anyone.

Except, wasn't viewing the world through someone else's eyes a kind of spying, even if you were doing nothing at all?

Dee shook the dirt from her hands and got carefully to her feet, waiting for the blood to circulate the tinglies away.

This time it was Gisela's fault she was being spied on. Dee had warned her not to play the tape.

It didn't matter. Gisela was in trouble.

Dee couldn't leave her now.

Brenda and Walter arrived before Gisela.

Dee let them in and hugged them both before they could remove their jackets. She had scrubbed the dirt off her hands, but her fingertips were slightly sore from letting the spurge sap sit on them for so long.

"Someone left the hug machine on," Walter said with a laugh.

But Brenda leaned into Dee's embrace, cupping the back of her head just the way Dee liked. "I couldn't be prouder of you, sweet pea," she said into Dee's ear. "You know that? I wish I'd known your plan before, but... this is the *perfect* time to celebrate your transition to adulthood. You just surprise me at every turn."

You don't know the half of it.

"Gifts are getting heavy," Walter said, feigning fatigue.

Dee let them go and made a move for the bag hanging from Walter's hand.

"Uh-uh, these are for later," he said, pivoting to keep her gifts out of reach.

Dee hadn't meant to be so impulsive, but there was that part of her brain that wanted instant gratification, and it took the wheel at any opportunity.

"Where's Gisela?"

Brenda was asking Phoebe. The cat didn't respond. Brenda handed her jacket to Walter, then picked up Phoebe and headed for the living room.

"You look good," Walter said over his shoulder as he hung their jackets in the front closet. When he turned, the gift bag was nowhere to be seen. Probably in the closet. He gave Dee's shoulder a squeeze. "This is the longest you've been away from home, you know? Four days. That's quite a feat."

Dee provided vocal accompaniment to Walter's praise, which he read as contentment. She allowed herself to enjoy the moment. She would have to face the other things soon enough. She only wished this moment could last.

"I don't think she's here," Brenda said, shuffling back into the foyer, cradling Phoebe in her arms like a baby. "But why are we standing in the hallway? Come on, we can get things started."

―――――

"Hey, everyone!" Gisela said, carrying two carton-filled plastic bags. She tried to extract her keys from the front door as it swung away from her. "Sorry I'm late."

Walter jumped up from the couch and trotted over. "I got it."

Brenda left Dee on the couch as she went to hug her long-time friend. "Ooh, something smells good."

"I hope Mediterranean is okay. I swung by Rami's in Brookline since I was out that way for a work thing."

Dee eyed Gisela from the living room and whispered into her head. *For a work thing?*

Gisela shot her a guilty look. "Hey, Dee." She followed Walter to the kitchen. "Oh good, you have everything laid out. How long ago did you get here?"

"Not long," Walter said, placing the cartons on the counter and opening their top flaps.

"We've been catching up," Brenda said. "Dee, wash hands?"

Gisela's eyes flicked over again as Dee went to the bathroom to wash up, and her face said it all: she knew full well that Dee had watched her play that tape. But she didn't know the half of it. And now Dee would have to sit across from her through dinner without being able to tell her how much trouble she was really in.

"So what happens now?" Gisela asked as Dee regarded her from across the table. "I mean, with school and work?"

"Well she's considered an adult at eighteen," Brenda said. "Which means she's competent to make her own decisions. But since she'll continue living with us, there'll be a lot of consent forms to be notarized, just so everything can be seamless."

These things had been at the forefront of Dee's mind less than a month ago. But now, in light of Gisela's predicament, everything else seemed less important.

Gisela took several pitas from a stack in the center of the table, and helped herself to hummus and tabouleh. "So her day-to-day won't change much."

It will if you keep playing that tape.

Gisela cleared her throat, as if she was worried the others might hear their private exchange. Dee couldn't help herself. The table discussion felt like a distraction.

"Anyway," Walter said, dipping a falafel ball into a container of baba ghanoush, "in Massachusetts Dee's IDEA doesn't run out until she's twenty-two, so she has some runway ahead of her."

Dee tried to distract herself with the hummus, which she could have eaten by the spoonful. It was drizzled with olive oil, and contained flecks of parsley and a dusting of sumac. But she couldn't keep her frustration from coming out. With each breath she let out a sigh.

"It sounds worse than it is," Walter said, patting Dee's arm.

"After graduation she'll be finishing up her transition planning," Brenda said, "which was part of her education program. Kids Kan actually came from that."

"Oh, I didn't know that."

"Yeah, it was a pilot program, so it was really good timing."

"And, you know," Walter added, "she's taken to it so well, with the gardening and all, they said they'd provide references so she can find a more permanent role somewhere."

Gisela raised an eyebrow. "Yeah, somehow I don't think it's going to be so hard for Dee to find her way."

Are you serious? I can't believe you.

Gisela didn't even look at Dee.

"Well, she has something she loves to do," Brenda said, "and she's so good at it. Speaking of good, this food is to die for! We should have Mediterranean more often."

The conversation lapsed as they concentrated on their meals. Dee tuned in to the clanks of silverware and the sounds of their chewing. The ambient din wouldn't have been so prominent if she weren't so concerned. She wished she had her brain muffs.

"Anyway, we're certainly not going anywhere!" Walter said. "It's not like she'll be cast out."

"Oh, of course." Gisela chuckled. "You've done so well together, all of you."

"But Dee will be relying on herself more," Brenda added after wiping her mouth. "I've talked with her about it. As an adult, the details of her continued education, and her medication, those will be her responsibility now. And then, if she gets to the point where she's ready to explore shared living options with her peers, she's in the driver's seat. Like, there's this innovative housing development opening downtown, especially for adults with autism. It's new, which just shows you that people are thinking of these things. And we're not pushing her out the door, like Walter said, but if an arrangement like that would give her, you know, the independence she wanted... but still, a place where she would fit in... I think..." She trailed off and shrugged, face tight.

"These are *good* things," said Walter.

"Oh, of course. It's just, I always encouraged her to be self-sufficient, and now that she is, it's like..."

Brenda was sad—that's what that look was. Recently, Dee had seen it play across her face more and more. Brenda liked to come across as strong—and she was—but the idea of Dee's transition was going to be almost as hard for her as it would be for Dee.

"If anything," Walter said addressing Gisela and Dee, "she's done her job too well."

"Hear hear," Gisela said.

Brenda smiled her sad smile.

Dee listened to the hushed voices of her foster parents from the living room. Gisela spoke in assured tones, but the only words Dee caught were *she'll be fine*. Empty words, but coming from a good place. It wouldn't do to have them as distressed as Dee was. Especially not now.

"They wanted you to go home with them," Gisela said once she had seen them both out. She joined Dee on the couch and let her shoulders slump. Phoebe hopped up and got busy exploring Gisela's lap.

Of course they did. I'm sure you didn't tell them why that's not possible now.

Dee was rocking again, thrusting her back against the cushions.

Gisela rubbed her eyes. "I had to find out, Dee."

What did you find out? Because I can tell you what I found out.

"I'll destroy the tape."

You said that before. They were watching you again, and they used the tape to find you. I saw them. I followed them back to where they are.

"What?"

They were recording you, but I think... I may have messed up their tape. And they were wicked upset about it, but we can't assume you're out of the woods.

"Jesus, Dee." Gisela stared out the front window into the night, as if she might catch a glimpse of something malicious. "I'm sorry."

Don't apologize. Dee's fingers found her favorite pillow, and her rocking abated. *But I have to stay with you now.*

"I told you—"

I trust you. I just have to make sure they don't come back.

Gisela sighed and shook her head. After a moment she stood—sending Phoebe into a brief panic—and went to the kitchen. "Did you want tea?"

No.

The sound of water running issued from the kitchen, along with Phoebe's impassioned meows. It sounded so normal, so domestic. It would be easy for them to let their guard down. And what if Dee missed something? What was she supposed to be looking out for, anyway? Those men might have other abilities beyond remote viewing.

"I just don't even know what this is," Gisela said from the kitchen. "Is it magic? Is that what we're talking about?"

It's like my abilities.

Gisela returned from the kitchen with a steeping mug of tea. "But what *is* it? I've never heard of anything like this, and suddenly it's all around us. All around *me*. You have these abilities, and even you don't know why."

Dee squeezed the pillow. Its yielding resistance was soothing between her fingers.

Try living in my body for a while. Everyone has abilities, you just don't always appreciate them. You tell your body to do things, and it does. You can talk to anyone you want, go wherever you want. Why can you do what you do, and I can't? Does that make sense to you?

Gisela watched the steam rising from her mug.

Sorry, Gisela. I know this is different in some ways. But maybe I'm a little less...

"Mystified," Gisela said. She sipped her tea, and the sound was like a knife against wood. "Sorry."

Dee thought about it. It might not be all good, but it wasn't all bad either, was it?

Whatever's happening, I'm glad I'm here, Gisela. I'm glad I can be here for you this time.

A hint of a smile softened Gisela's face.

"Happy birthday, Dee."

21

WEDNESDAY, APRIL 24, 1991

BAS PULLED his Monza over to the curb and tapped the gas to keep the old girl from stalling. The gurgle from beneath the hood sounded like late-stage pneumonia.

The passenger door groaned as Griffin pulled it open.

"Hey, thanks for picking me up, man."

"No problem," Bas said, sweeping wrappers off the passenger seat into the street. "Sorry about that."

"This is... *something*." Griffin left one leg out as he collapsed into the concavity of the old seat. "Did you maybe want to take a taxi, or...?"

Bas waved off the suggestion. "She'll make it just fine, don't you worry. It's just ten or so minutes away anyway."

Griffin pulled his door shut and settled in as Bas pulled into traffic. The city's sodium-vapor radiance bounced from the low cloud layer, suffusing the streets with a spectral pink-orange glow.

"I'm surprised you fit in here," Griffin said.

Bas eyed his knees, which were possibly too close to the dashboard.

But Griffin was already on to something else. "Yeah, I was telling Harriet I thought it was cool that you wanted to check out Axis."

Bas sniffed. "Because I'm old?"

"You're not *that* old. Anyway, she said anything you did you were doing for work."

Bas shrugged.

"So it's true? Are you looking for that guy, Wallace Thaw?"

"Griffin, I asked you about the club before I knew about Wallace. Anyway, I don't need—"

"I'm just saying, I could help."

Bas shook his head, but managed a smile. "Look, I appreciate it, but what helps me is if you just do your thing. I just want to scope things out."

"Sure, man. That's cool."

Griffin peered out the window, seemingly taken by some of the young women they were passing. Then he turned back, cupped his hand over his mouth, exhaled, and sniffed. Apparently satisfied with his breath, he ran his fingers through his hair and smoothed out his shirt. Bas watched the man's preening from the corner of his eye, glad that his thirties were so far in his rearview mirror.

"Oh, and don't worry about driving me home," Griffin said as they cruised past the hulking black-and-red facade of the Axis. "I like to barhop my way home."

As he stepped inside, Bas was hit by a blast of warm air that smelled of cigarettes, sweat, and, for some reason, paint. He was unfamiliar with the local band on the set list, but whoever they were, they were projecting a wall of metal that sounded like it was all crescendo.

Bas got Griffin's attention, then tapped his own chest and motioned deeper into the club. The younger man nodded and gave him a wave.

Bas moved into the main room, and people parted for him as if he were the head bouncer. The Wednesday crowd wasn't especially dense, but a few enthusiastic participants were demonstrating floor-sweeping lunges that looked sure to spark a brawl at some point. Bas gave them a wide berth as he worked his way along the periphery, scanning the crowd, uncertain what he was looking for. Probably not a recruitment booth with the *I Mine* banner flying over it. Normally he would look for people who were watching other people. That wasn't going to work in a club. Instead he'd have to look for people holding a conversation that seemed too earnest for the venue. Or, more generally, anyone who didn't quite fit in. Someone much like Wallace Thaw.

Or maybe Wallace Thaw himself.

But the incessant din assaulted Bas's eardrums, and he soon found himself seeking refuge as far from the speaker towers as he could get. Less than an hour had passed before he made it all the way to the restroom, where the relative quiet was so profound that it induced a momentary dizziness.

Another kind of crowd had collected in here. Some came to straighten themselves out before heading back into the thick of it, like racers at a pit stop. Others came to conduct business—mostly involving pharmaceutical options or personal services—within makeshift stall offices. An obvious lookout at the sink kept a wary eye on Bas until a free urinal opened up.

Bas listened to snatches of conversation over the ringing in his ears. Most of it was innocuous chatter, meant only to reassure its stakeholders that everyone was legit, or cool. The most surprising discussion, as far as Bas was concerned, involved Johnny Carson's recent retirement announcement.

"He ain't really out till next year," came a voice as rough as a cement truck rolling over a pothole. "But symbolically though, it's heavy because he started when I was born, in 1962, you know?"

There followed a sharp inhalation that reverberated against the tiled walls.

When Bas got to the sink, the lookout's eyes were back on him. As he dried his hands, Bas leaned in toward the man. "I Mine?"

The man's face didn't crack. "No thanks."

Bas chuckled as he scored a three-point shot with his wadded-up paper towel.

Back in the main room, the metal act had exited the stage, and the vacuum had been filled by some anodyne music while a DJ set up his rig on the dais for the next set. Bas imagined it was the closest thing to an intermission the Axis would get, and he made a beeline for the bar. He ordered himself a Sam Adams, fishing out the cash to pay as he scanned up and down the bar. Down near the corner, a man in a fedora stood alone, half watching the floor as he finished something sap-yellow.

The bartender set a sweating bottle before Bas.

"Thanks."

Bas took his drink and moved down the bar, finding a spot next to the man. There he turned to lean against the bar, getting a better look at his neighbor in the process. The man was holding on to his glass of half-melted ice as if it might refill itself. Cigarette hanging from his lip, the brim of his hat pulled low—less for style, more for concealment.

Possibly a good target for recruitment.

"Pretty good for a Wednesday," Bas said.

The man looked over, then up. His eyes remained in shadow. "New in town?"

Bas took a swig of his beer. "What makes you say that?"

The man shrugged.

Bas looked out over the crowd. Some listened to the music, but most of them were milling around waiting for the next thing. Bas's feet were already getting sore.

"Actually, it *can* be hard to find your footing when you're new in town," Bas said.

"You a cop?" The man swirled his glass of ice.

What the hell? "Just making conversation, man. Not a cop." Definitely not a cop. Bas was probably less of a cop now than he had ever been.

"Well, good luck," said the man, his voice barely audible over the music. He took one last pull on his cigarette, then stubbed it out in the ashtray by his elbow. "Sometimes there *is* no place for you."

Hitting pay dirt on his first try wasn't unheard of—Bas had learned to rely on his instincts over the years—but this might go better than expected.

"Hey," he said with a chuckle, "one lone wolf to another." He sipped his beer. "In my experience, you keep your eyes peeled long enough, that's how you find the crowd who gets it."

"Yeah. Not really into crowds." The man raised his glass to his mouth, and the ice clanked as it hit his upper lip.

Weird place for a solitary guy to be hanging out, unless he was looking for something. "Right, right," Bas said. "Or, you know, like a group. That's what I look for."

The man nodded, but his body language said he wanted the conversation to be over.

Bas's bottle had warmed in his hand. He hadn't been a lone wolf before. Not originally. That was something he had cultivated after Lana disappeared, building a buffer wall around him so nothing else could get to that raw place. He hadn't even had to push anyone away —he'd only had to disappear into his self-styled world of hide-and-seek.

What was this guy's excuse?

Bas set his empty bottle on the bar. Fuck it. "Ever hear of a group called I Mine?"

The man stared into his empty glass. "Can't say I have."

Just then the filler music cut off, and for a moment there was only the sound of the crowd. Bas turned as the audience broke into applause, and the club was filled by a rhythm-and-blues strain that sounded like it had been plucked from the mid-sixties. That was unexpected.

A moment later, the music looped back on itself, and an avalanche of drums weaponized the retro sample into something the club goers could fight to.

This is useless.

Bas pushed away from the bar and scanned the reinvigorated crowd for Griffin. The man had said not to wait up for him, but it was only courtesy. The press of bodies had grown denser now, and colored lights painted syncopated patterns over the dancing masses, making it impossible to find a familiar face among them.

He should have dug deeper on the internet. That would have been a better use of his time, instead of clawing his way through some mid-week rave. He peered into the throng one last time before giving up. Maybe he would swing by the Red Bell on his way home.

He had nearly made it out to the front hall when he felt a tap on his shoulder.

"Bas!"

Griffin stood framed against the light show within, his shirt sweat-soaked.

"I was just leaving!" Bas shouted over the rhythmic cacophony.

"Wait!"

Griffin said something Bas didn't catch, but had his hand hooked around Bas's arm. Griffin was trying to get him to follow.

Bas shook his head—it had been a bust.

"... *talk to you!*" was all Bas heard.

Whatever Griffin was saying, he didn't want Bas to leave. Bas put up his hands, then motioned into the club. Lead the way.

Griffin plunged straight into the crowd, crossing the floor like a plow through snow. Bas hurried to keep pace. They were heading toward the door that led backstage. Only there was no backstage area, just an open-air alley between the Axis and the neighboring club.

The cooler air felt good on Bas's cheeks, but now he was even deeper into the club, when where he wanted was to be home.

A decent crowd had gathered in the fenced-in space, half of them smoking.

"Right over here," Griffin said. "Found someone you might want to talk to." He led Bas toward the back fence where a young woman waited in the delicate traceries of her own cigarette smoke.

What was this?

"Hey," Bas said to the woman, meeting her smile. He turned to Griffin. "Actually, sorry, but I was just leaving."

"Just... give her a minute," Griffin said. He waited until Bas acknowledged him.

Bas shook his head. "Yeah. Fine."

Griffin threw a thumb over his shoulder. "I'll be over there."

The woman watched it all play out, then looked Bas up and down as he did the same to her. She wore all black, equal parts lace and strategically torn denim. Spiky black hair framed a face with that flawless quality Bas had come to associate with youth. There was something severe in her eyes though. She was like a walking collage.

"Are you a goth?" he asked, instantly regretting his opener. He was tired.

"I'm just wearing black," she said. "Are you a geezer?"

The corner of his mouth curled. "I just ask stupid questions."

She switched her cigarette to her other hand and held out the free one. "Divya."

"Bas."

She had an accent. British, maybe. This was some setup. What had Griffin gotten him into?

"So I was talking to your grandson there—"

"*Jesus.*" Bas gave her a wounded look, but she was already smirking.

"He tells me you're looking for a Wallace Thaw?"

Bas's hand massaged his empty pocket. No ring there.

Griffin had it in his head that Bas was on some quest to track down Wallace, and had somehow managed to find a friend of his at the club. It was a thoughtful gesture, if misguided. Still, Bas couldn't help his curiosity, now that he was here.

"You know where I can find him?"

She blew out a plume of smoke, and it caught in an eddy, lifting into the night air. "You're probably not the only one who wants to know," she said, "although I'm sure you're the largest."

"Are other people looking for him?"

"Well if you know Wallace, you know he's a bit of a provocateur. Used to turn up here just to row."

Bas mouthed a silent *ah*. "Did he try to pick a fight with you?"

"He tried to pick me *up*."

Bas blinked. "Oh?"

"Not really my type."

Bas looked back toward the door. Griffin was chatting up a woman in sunglasses.

Divya ground the butt of her cigarette under her toe and retrieved another from a pack in her purse.

"So what do you know about Wallace?" Bas asked.

"Not much," she said around the cigarette as she lit it. "I heard he used to bed down at the Shelter on Kingston. Made a name for himself being a grueler. Next thing you know he's cleaned himself up, shaking the tree here, at shelters, anywhere with a grunge factor."

"Shaking the tree?"

"He was always going on about this circle he's a part of. He was trying to score recruits, when he wasn't scoring. Oh!"

She brought her purse back around and snapped it open. After fishing around for a moment, she pulled out a black card, which she held out.

Bas accepted it, and squinted down at it as he tried to find the light.

I, Mine
Fridays

8 PM

On the other side was handwritten contact information.

12 Terminal St.
617-469-6742

"This is your number?" Bas asked, looking up at her.

She scoffed. "Come on, why would I be carrying around my own number? No, this is the card Wallace gave me, see? So that's *his* number... at least I think so. I never called it. You're welcome to try it out. If you reach him, you can tell him Divya still isn't interested."

Bas looked back down at the card. Where had he heard of *Terminal Street* before? It might be the access road outside the Charlestown Navy Yard, which would put it just south of the Mystic. That was still a fairly industrial area. What was a secretive organization doing out there?

He looked back up at Divya. "Why'd you keep the card?"

She laughed, blowing out smoke as she grabbed her purse again and held it open for him to see. "I keep them till they're full. Then I just leave them somewhere, like little time capsules, and I get a new purse."

Bas imagined junk-filled purses left abandoned throughout the city. "Thanks for this," he said, pocketing the card.

She gave him a nod.

Griffin was waiting alone by the door by the time Bas got back to him.

"So? Did I do good?" Griffin asked. But he was already grinning.

"Yeah, man. I think you may have."

PART 2

22

FRIDAY, APRIL 26, 1991

BAS DROVE across a waterfront lot adjacent to the old naval shipyard. It was largely abandoned, holding just a few cars and a cluster of derelict trailers. The sun was just kissing the horizon, throwing long shadows across the tarmac as Bas found a spot close to the other cars.

He twisted the key and waited out the transmission as it muttered on for a while like an old man who's lost the thread of the conversation. As his fingers closed on his empty pocket, Bas felt a bit adrift himself. Then again, if he still had Lana's ring, he wouldn't be here now.

Wherever this was.

He plucked the card Divya had given him from the notch by the air vent. Fridays at eight, it said. A rolling invitation. For a cult, they had their act together. But they might want to reconsider their choice of venue.

Bas waited to see if anyone else would show up, but the lot remained still. Maybe he was the last one to show. He checked his watch. Five till nine. Apparently he was on his own.

He dropped the card into his pocket as he stepped out into a stiff breeze redolent of brine and tar, and headed for a cluster of warehouses. He had come in on Terminal Street, so all he had to do now was find number 12. Some sort of signage or lights would have been helpful, but there were no obvious guideposts. Maybe it was meant as a challenge.

He had almost made it back to the road when two voices drifted over to him in the night air. He peered into the gloom, and two silhouettes came into view a dozen yards away, heading roughly back the way Bas had just come.

"Hello?" Bas called.

The conversation stopped.

"Hey there," one of them called over as they closed the distance between them.

"I might be a little lost," Bas said.

"I can't imagine you're a little anything!" the other man said, then laughed at his own joke. "Sorry, that was bad."

"You must be here for the open house," the first man said.

"Is that what it is?" That didn't sound so mysterious.

"Of course. We can take you there. Are you... alone?"

"Is that okay?"

Bas's eyes had acclimated to the fading light. The two men were clean-cut, but not too clean-cut. The first man looked like he had just gotten off work, his tie loose around his neck. The other man wore a vest jacket and had a tote bag clutched in his hands, like the ones public radio stations awarded patrons for their donations. Was Bas supposed to have brought an offering? Did he need to have a chaperone?

"Oh, no worries at all," the first man said. "Anyway, you're not alone anymore."

They both chuckled.

"I'm Norm, and this is Yahiro."

"Bas."

"Bas, welcome. It's just this way."

"Sorry about the *big* comment," Yahiro said. "You must hear that a lot."

"It's hard to hear anything from up here, the air's so thin."

———

I, Mine's "open house" was being held in an annex structure on the wrong side of the hangar-sized warehouse Bas had parked beside. It was no wonder he hadn't seen it from the lot—the warehouse provided natural concealment from the main road, and the event didn't announce itself with sky beams, loud music, or wind-blown pennants. The sole adornment at the entrance was a placard affixed to the building's sheet-metal hull.

>   Welcome
>   I, Mine
>   Open House

At the entryway to the annex, several greeters—dressed in casual clothing, nothing matching—stood next to a heavy sliding door, the kind that hangs from a track. The open door revealed the entirety of the well-lit gathering within.

Norm handed something to the nearest greeter, and prompted Yahiro to follow suit.

The I, Mine card.

Bas patted his pockets, sure that he had left his card in the car. Would they turn away a visitor without a card? But his finger found the card's edge in his breast pocket, and he pulled it out as he approached one of the greeters, a man with a gray mustache. He had to be around Bas's age.

Norm and Yahiro watched as the greeter accepted Bas's card with a broad smile. "And thank you so much for joining us."

Did he mean that in the casual sense?

J.D. ROBINSON

"Thank you," Bas said automatically when no other words presented themselves.

Following the lead of the other two men, he proceeded inside.

String lights followed the contours of a high-ceilinged space the size of a circus big top. The painted concrete floor was a glossy black, and thick wooden columns stretched upward to steel support beams. Black-painted steel mesh partitioned the interior like lace webbing. From what Bas could see from the entrance, there might be a hundred attendees or more in attendance.

"What a cool hideout," Yahiro said to his friend, his voice almost breaking into a giggle.

"Every time I've been here there's something different." Norm slipped out of his jacket and waved the two of them toward a counter near the front. "Coat check, if you want."

Bas traded his coat for a ticket as he took in the scene. Who were these people? Mostly they had grouped themselves off, clustering among the thick wooden columns, lounging on sectional couches and beanbag chairs, or strolling around the interior sections. Bas drifted toward to the next area, which judging by the nearly impenetrable drove and the smell, had a wide selection of food on offer.

Beyond the doorway the cause of the crowd became clear. Food had been laid out on tables that stretched from front to back on either side—mostly hors d'oeuvres, small sandwiches, and pastries—and almost everyone had a drink in hand.

How much had it cost to run this enterprise? Did they really do this every Friday?

"Bas, is it?" Norm put a hand on Bas's arm. "Hey, I was going to introduce Yahiro here to some colleagues, if you wanted to join us?"

Bas's ears perked on hearing the word *join* again, and he chewed the inside of his cheek. Immediate engagement wasn't the way to go about this. Better to come at it from the outside, to observe until he had some idea what he was observing. He was here because a woman had drawn the I, Mine logo on the ground in some sort of ritual before disappearing. That was all he had to go on. The working theory? Cynda Bolden was a member of this organization. Like a certain ring-snatcher, Wallace Thaw.

"Thanks for the invite, but I think I'm just going to," Bas waved a finger, "you know, mosey."

"Great!" Norm said.

Everything was great.

"Good meeting you," Yahiro said.

The two of them retreated and were swallowed by the crowd. Bas continued through the food hall toward the rear of the annex, which offered some relief from the congestion. Here, people had retreated to chairs and couches with their plates of food. Bas heard snatches of conversation as he strolled, including what he thought might be Japanese and Portuguese.

At the very back a small open alcove had been lit as if for a presentation. A selection of oversized photographs lined the backdrop—world monuments and faces. They looked to Bas like the kind of stock photos found in a travel agent's office.

Bas found a partitioned spot next to the rear alcove and leaned up against the handrail separating the space as he let his eyes drift from face to face. What did these people have in common? They couldn't all be lost souls.

As people circulated through, Bas tried to recall his basic understanding of crowd behavior. Patterns arose from shared intent—how dense a group of people was, what direction they moved—but it was also informed by social affinity. Especially in crowded environments, designated leaders generated spontaneous attraction. People would align around an authority figure, even subconsciously, like shavings around a magnet.

Find who was leading this show. That's what he had to do.

But at the moment, Bas could see no such telltale formations. He glanced at his watch. Quarter to ten. A little late to draw out the dramatic tension.

"Another loner."

Bas cocked his head. A woman had sidled up to him while he was fixated on the migration patterns of his fellow attendees. She was young, with no gray in her long, straight hair. She mirrored him now, forearms resting on the handrail as she watched people pass by.

"Hard to be alone in a place like this," Bas said, amused by her casual disregard for manner.

"Yet here we are." With her voice slightly lowered, she asked, "So what are we looking for?"

Bas sniffed. "Been waiting for a clue as to what this is all about." No reason to hide that from her.

"Ohhh." Then she inhaled sharply. "Hey, what if *this* is what it's about?" Her eyes were wide with mock realization.

"Nah, this is definitely leading up to something." This was the stage. Eventually the act must show, or there would be no point to the production.

She was quiet. Bas made no attempt to break the silence between them, and she made no indication that she was going anywhere.

"This is my first time too," she said eventually. "So your guess is good as mine." She straightened and put a hand on her chest. "Janeen, with two Es."

"Bas."

"I have to ask, even though it's none of my business. Are you a wrestler or something?"

"Not if I can help it." He chuckled. "No, I repair electronics."

"No shit. It's just that it's unusual to see someone so... *big*, just out and about."

"Among the wee folk, you mean?"

She laughed. "Sorry. I'm a beauty therapist, which mainly involves talking a lot. So I say what's on my mind."

Beauty therapist? Whatever that was.

Bas looked over at her. "So, Janeen with two Es. Did you really come alone?"

"In a way," she said, leaning on the railing again. "I mean, my friend got an invite last month, and she came out, but it didn't really click with her. She told me it's run by this couple—like a husband and wife—and they just made their way around the room, talking to people."

Fishing.

Janeen shrugged. "Anyway, I'd pretty much forgotten about it, but then I ended up seeing this guy I met in a little group I belong to —an *anonymous* group—and he just gives me an invite out of the blue. I don't even think I told him about my friend going."

It made sense that they would have scouts trawling the twelve-step groups.

"So this guy didn't come with you?" Bas asked.

She shook her head. "He's not really in the picture anymore. But my friend said I should go ahead and give it a try, so..." She made a *ta-da* gesture with her hands.

As she talked, Bas's attention was drawn to a group of people collecting at the far side of the space. Several of those on the periphery of the cluster were craning to get a better look at something.

"What about you?" Janeen asked. "What brought you here tonight?"

Bas looked at her. A number of dismissive responses popped into his head; some of them he had already told himself. Inertial drift wouldn't sound good. An electronics repairman was probably here for the same reasons as a beauty therapist. It certainly wasn't about a case, because he didn't *have* a case, even if it had started out like one. The prospect of a paycheck had vanished. At this point, he was just hopelessly fixated.

Janeen raised an eyebrow.

"This will sound like a random question," Bas said, "but would you happen to know someone named Cynda Bolden?"

Janeen squinted. "Cynthia...?"

"Cynda."

She pursed her lips. "That *is* pretty random. No, I don't think so. At least not by name."

Bas nodded. "No worries, just a shot in the dark." And a

desperate one at that. Janeen was merely a guest. What he needed to do was ask someone who might have been here long enough to cross paths with the missing woman. Maybe one of the chaperones?

"Thirsty?" Janeen asked, already edging away.

"Oh, no, I'm good."

She gave him a wave as she headed away.

Bas wandered closer to the pack across the room. The general chatter had died down enough that he could pick out snatches of individual conversations. Rising above the rest was the voice of one man whose volume suggested that he was the center of the crowd.

Bas accidentally stepped on someone's foot, and the man's squeal nearly perforated his right eardrum. Heads turned as he caught the man he had stumbled over, preventing him from taking a nasty spill on the concrete floor.

Bas set the younger man back on his feet. "Sorry, man," Bas said hurriedly. "You okay?"

"Yeah, it's cool," the man said, still looking shaken. He had little meat on his bones. No wonder Bas had steamrolled him so easily. "I shouldn't have darted out in front of you."

The crowd had already lost interest and turned back around, but their ranks had broken up enough that Bas was able to see the man at their center, and the woman next to him, who, at that moment, was staring at Bas. Her eyes flicked away as the man beside her resumed speaking, presumably where he had left off.

Was this the couple Janeen had mentioned? They were in their mid-forties, or thereabouts. They were healthy and clean-cut, she with ringlets of hair around a rather stony face, and he with an easy smile.

Power couple.

The phrase made Bas wince. Was I, Mine their thing?

Bas turned back to the skinny young man next to him, who was now looking down at his shoe and wriggling his toes. Bas's eye lingered on the man's rust-red armband, cinched around his left sleeve.

He stuck out his hand. "Bas."

The man looked up as if he had forgotten Bas was there. "Oh, I'm Kit. Kit Lund."

"You on staff?"

Kit's face was a mask of confusion.

Bas tapped his own sleeve.

The man looked down at his arm, then made an *oh* of realization. "Right, I help out at the open houses sometimes. When Fritz and Collette do their meet-and-greet, I usually make sure... Uh, anyway, you should mingle. You know."

"That's them?" Bas said, jabbing a thumb back toward the center of the crowd. "Fritz and Collette? They run things here? Are they members of I, Mine?"

Kit looked distracted, but didn't seem to mind the questions. "Well, I mean, everyone here is I, Mine, as long as we're here. But Fritz and Collette, they really *are* I, Mine. They were right there after the South Station Singularity, counseling family members of the victims. I mean, they've *always* helped people. But it was after that event, really, that I, Mine proper was born." He paused, his cheeks growing flush. "Anyway, I'm just scratching the surface. You should talk to *them* about it. That's the whole idea with the soirée. You know, outreach, connection."

I was the closest thing Bas had gotten to a mission statement. Of course, he was getting it secondhand.

"So you've been here a while?" he asked. "I mean at I, Mine."

"Well, I work there—maintenance stuff, archives, watering the plants—so my situation is different from some of the other members. I met Fritz and Collette a few years back."

Met. Keeping things informal.

"And how many others are there, besides the three of you?"

Kit cocked his head. "Oh, fifty or so regulars, maybe? It varies. You know. People come and go, and a few are long-termers, like me. It's an open-door kind of situation."

"Did you ever run across a Cynda Bolden?" Bas kept his voice even, just slipping the question in as smoothly as he could manage.

Kit's eyes were suddenly nowhere near Bas. "Actually, I should probably... I need to get back to my... helping."

"She was just an acquaintance," Bas said with a shrug. "But if you have any insights into how she did at I, Mine, it would help—"

"Kit." Fritz—the man who had been the center of attention moments before—now stood next to Kit with his arm around his shoulder. He looked over at Bas. "Oh. Don't let me interrupt," he quickly added.

Where had the woman gone? Mingling, probably.

"We were just talking about I, Mine," Kit said.

Would he say anything to Fritz about the topic of Cynda? Bas probably wouldn't have led with that, not with the founders, but if it came up, so be it.

"Oh, well." Fritz gave Bas a warm smile. "You're in the right place. I'm Frederick Frey. Call me Fritz."

"Bas Milius." As Bas shook the man's hand, Fritz appeared to grow several inches. The man's smile was genuine, crinkling the corners of his eyes, but he was definitely standing on his toes. Bas tried not to be obvious about stealing a glance at the man's feet.

Beside them, Kit looked like a man on a roller coaster having second thoughts after the shoulder restraint had engaged. If Fritz noticed, he showed no sign of it.

"I have to say," Bas said, gesturing toward everything around them, "all this has me intrigued."

"Well, this has been a great space for us," Fritz said. "It was completely open when we saw it, so the interior design, from the flooring to the mezzanine on the other side—which I'm not sure if you saw—all the way to the rafters and the skylights, that's all us. We really had the opportunity here to do what we needed to do to present a welcoming environment." His voice grew quiet. "But between you and me, we got a killer deal on the rent."

Sincerity radiated from him like warmth from a space heater, and Bas couldn't help but chuckle. That feeling of directed bonhomie was almost palpable, in a way that Bas had encountered only a handful of times before. The rest of the annex seemed to grow quieter by contrast, as if the only thing that mattered was this conversation, right now.

"It definitely comes across," Bas said.

Kit had a thousand-yard stare, and his smile, long forgotten, was taking some time to fade from his lips.

"Did you come to us alone tonight, Bas?"

"I did." The rogue agent, chasing his ghosts. "Yeah, I came across an I, Mine card. Through an associate."

"Oh, the cards!" Fritz shook his head as if they were artifacts of an early campaign, long-since abandoned. "Those were always meant to be used in context, see. Otherwise they don't tell you much, do they?"

"It's minimal, but it caught my interest."

Fritz nodded. "Maybe you did have some context."

He was digging without making it sound like a question. Bas didn't take the bait. "I wanted to see what you guys were about."

Fritz smiled, but said nothing.

"Does that happen a lot?" Bas asked.

"You mean do people visit us because they happen across one of our cards out in circulation?" He shook his head. "Less often than you might imagine. No, I'd say a good number of people come to us because they feel like something is missing from their lives." He was careful not to lock eyes with Bas, looking away as if they were having a casual conversation.

Maybe they were. Was Bas overthinking this?

"I've heard variations of this same story from so many people. There's this feeling they have of being adrift, even if they're managing to keep it together on the outside. But the key thing is they haven't given up, see. They're searching, even if they don't know it, and it's the search that leads them to places they might not otherwise go. That's the frame of mind they're in when they hear about I, Mine, from a friend or trusted colleague. The next thing you know, our paths are crossing, sometimes only briefly, sometimes longer-term." Now his eyes were definitely shining. "It always fascinates me to hear people's stories, Bas, because even if they're variations on a theme, they are always unique. Does that make sense?"

"It does, sure."

Kit managed to wriggle out from Fritz's arm. "I should probably check the door, before..."

He left it there.

"Right on," Fritz said. "Thank you so much." He turned back to Bas, and rose by several inches again. Was it a nervous habit? Was he trying to lessen the height disparity between them? Even on his toes, the man barely reached Bas's shoulders. "The only reason this engagement runs as smoothly as it does is because of Kit's team."

"Okay," Kit said, perhaps in shock that he had gotten away so easily. "So I'll wait for you after?"

Fritz nodded. "You can drive back with us after we strike the set."

Bas watched as Kit darted away into the crowd. His entire bearing had changed after hearing the name *Cynda Bolden*, and his attitude hadn't improved when Fritz swooped in. Still, he hadn't told Fritz, and that meant something.

"So, you like it?" Fritz's eyes were back on Bas.

Bas nodded. "It's quite a setup."

"Yeah, well, Collette would call it a demonstration of vanity. Frankly, she'd be happy to not be doing these at all. It's kind of my thing."

Bas met his gaze. "But what is *it*?"

Fritz's laugh was loud enough to draw the attention of several people. When he recovered, his cheeks were still pink. "It's easy to lose perspective when you're so close to something. You want to strike a balance, because, you know, you're too up in people's faces and you're a religion, but if you pull back—if you're too secretive—then you're a cult."

Bas couldn't help himself. "So which are you?"

"A little of both," Fritz said without hesitation. He let that hang in the air for a moment. He was enjoying this. "No, Bas, actually, I, Mine is neither. What we do is help people. That's not to disparage religions and cults, but *that's* our focus."

"With the goal being what?"

"Goal?" He sighed and shifted his weight on his feet. "If someone finds value in what we offer, if they leave us better than they came, then we've done what we set out to do."

Bas squinted, biting the inside of his cheek.

"Put it this way," Fritz continued. "Everyone has their own goals in life. Or desires, if you prefer that. *You* certainly do, right? You came for a reason, even if you're not sure what that reason is. Circumstance delivered you here, and now we're talking. We could keep *on* talking. We could decide—formally decide—to keep the conversation going for as long as it benefits us both. Isn't how that most conversations work?"

But surely they were offering more than conversation. If this was a sales pitch, what were they selling? They had been around for at least ten years; they must be doing something right.

"You must have interesting backgrounds, you and Collette."

Down, then back up to his toes. "You're wondering about our bona fides?"

"Just making conversation," Bas said, putting up a hand.

"Well we're not board-certified, but we're not prescribing drugs or issuing advice either. We're not covered by your insurance." He chuckled. "But no, we have our own space—think of a meditation space, or a Zen garden—where we share ideas and promote physical well-being. We work to provide a real sense of camaraderie." He put his hand on Bas's arm. "Like this! More of the same."

Bas nodded as the image of Cynda played in his mind. Frantic, crouched in an alleyway, the whole episode recorded through some unknown means. Had she flunked out of I, Mine?

"So that's how it works?" he asked.

Before Fritz could respond, a woman was whispering something in his ear. It was Collette. "... if you wanted to meet with him while he's in town," was all Bas caught. That, and the faint smell of cigarettes and mint on her breath.

"Thanks," Fritz said, nodding. "Bas, this is Collette Benkopf, my lovely wife." He took her hand in his, but his eyes never left Bas. "To answer your question though, this is how it works, Bas. This is how it *can* work. It can work in a lot of ways, as long as it works for everyone."

People moved around them as if they knew better than to interrupt.

Collette's eyes were on Bas's chest, and he realized then that his hand was there, feeling for Lana's ring. He moved his arm to his side.

"If you don't mind my asking," Fritz said, "do you feel a sense of sadness underneath all this?"

Where had that come from?

"That's not what I thought you were going to ask," Bas said. His hand felt like it was just hanging there. He stuck it in his pocket.

"That's okay, it's what I'm wondering. Am I wrong?"

He looked from Fritz to Collette, then back again. "I'd say I have a lot on my mind. But who doesn't?"

"Let's focus on you for a moment."

Bas blinked. "I wouldn't say I'm *sad*, no."

"Is it a sense that you're facing something that you can't quite put your finger on?"

Collette spoke for the first time. "What are you afraid of?"

Bas's cheeks grew warm, but Fritz smiled before Bas could answer.

"I'm sorry, Bas. I *was* kind of pulling your leg." He gave Bas's shoulder a friendly shake. "Some people get offended."

Collette bumped up against her husband, her shoulder to his. "Good to meet you, Bas," she said.

"Yeah, likewise," Bas managed.

Collette raised Fritz's interlocked hand to her lips and gave it a peck before moving back into the crowd.

"So what do you think?"

Bas's eyes narrowed. "About?"

"Would you like to keep the conversation going? It's up to you."

"I passed the test?" Bas asked. It was a shitty question. It sounded defensive. Too much so.

"With flying colors," Fritz said, already reaching into his pocket. He brought out a card and held it out. How many of those did he have with him? Surely not enough for everyone here.

Bas took the card. In style it was reminiscent of the first card, but the address was different.

I, MINE

82 NORFOLK PLACE

CAMBRIDGE

No time or date.

On the back was the symbol Cynda had scratched into the pavement.

"Several of us are having a gathering on Monday evening, at seven o'clock. More intimate than this. This invite is just for you. Dress casually. No expectations. If you can make it, we would welcome it."

Bas held the card as if he wasn't sure where to put it. "Thanks," he said. "I'll definitely think about it."

"Do that," Fritz said, offering his hand.

Bas put the card in his pocket, then took Fritz's hand and gave it a pump.

Bas wandered aimlessly for the better part of the next hour. The conversation had left him feeling jittery, like he'd had too much coffee and wasn't coming down from it. He saw no sign of Norm or Yahiro, Janeen or Kit. Who were all these people? Did they know why they had come here, or were they just casting about like him?

He hadn't gained any insights into who Cynda was, or why she might have been in that alley that night. The only thing he did have was an invitation—and the weekend ahead to consider whether or not to take it.

Bas pushed through the crowd as if he were swimming upstream. He didn't realize he was headed for the coat check until he was there.

He could attend Monday's intimate gathering of strangers, but where would that leave him? Closer to something, or farther away? Could he even trust his own judgment? He'd regressed since his last conversation with Eshe, he was sure of that much. If he told her how he'd been spending his time, she'd tear him a new one.

Maybe that was just what he needed.

———

"You can't just show up here unannounced at two in the morning," Eshe said, her hand on her apartment door. Inside, the TV was on, playing some schlocky horror film by the sound of it.

"I should have called, sweets. I know."

She sighed heavily.

Bas put his hand on her shoulder. "But I wasn't sure I was coming over, and then I was nearby anyway, so."

"*Don't*, okay? This really isn't cool."

What was that? She actually seemed disappointed, and he hadn't given her reason to be. Not yet. They had left on good terms, and he had given her no reason to believe things were off-track.

"Don't give me that look, Bas. I don't hear from you in almost two weeks, what do you expect?"

"It hasn't been two weeks." His voice echoed down the hallway.

It sounded pitiful to his own ear, that same tone he had overheard often enough through apartment doors.

"Why are you here?"

"Since when did I need a reason?"

Her look was all the answer he needed.

"Just to talk, okay? I've been... you know, working a case."

"So tell me," she said, leaning forward against the jamb so the opening was even tighter around her.

Bas shook his head. "Can't I come in?" He looked over her shoulder. "You got company?"

She pursed her lips. "You should have called."

Unbelievable. They hadn't been exclusive, not strictly. But all of a sudden she was treating him like a stranger, and spending her nights with some other guy?

Eshe turned her head to the side, speaking to someone over her shoulder, her voice softer now. "It's fine. Give me one minute."

"It's *not* fine," Bas said, voice raised as his brow grew hot. She hadn't even had the courtesy to dump him.

Why did this have to happen now? Of all the times she could have lowered the boom, this was the exact worst.

"Calm down," she told him, using her colder voice again. The stranger's voice. Like he was just anyone.

"You're treating me like I've done something wrong, when all I wanted was to have a conversation." His words sounded ridiculous. He had lost any ability to modulate his volume. "So I'm out, is that it?"

"*You're* the one who disappeared! You said you were going to pull yourself together, but I know what it means when you don't say anything, when you disappear off the grid. Now you show up in the middle of the night and everything is supposed to just reset?"

"Not *reset*."

She spoke behind her again. "One *second*, please."

"Eshe, you're the one who set me on this path. Now you turn your back on me like I'm some kind—"

"Oh, *bullshit!*"

Another hand hooked the door and pulled it wide. Standing just behind Eshe was a handsome man, about half Bas's age. He wasn't as big as Bas, but he wasn't small either. And he was anything but intimidated.

"Sir, you need to leave Eshe alone, right now. I know you went through some hard times, but that doesn't mean you can just show up here in the middle of the night. It's inappropriate."

Bas caught sight of Eshe's hanging portraits on the wall behind her and this man. They were more numerous now—a clear sign of someone moving forward with her life.

"Gaétan, *please,* baby," Eshe said, backing up a step so they were all facing each other. The lingering scent of the evening's food wafted into the hall from her apartment. "I do not need you making my arguments for me. And Bas, now is not the time for this."

"This *is* the time for this," Bas said, his heart racing. "You have this narrative of me, that I'm just this lost loser you tell your friends about. But I've been work—"

The other man stepped forward. "Maybe you should get *back* to work, sir."

"Gaétan, *no.*" She put a hand on his shoulder, as if to turn him around. "Just leave him alone. *Both of you,* cool it. I don't have time for this squabbling."

Bas's head was tight. He felt like someone else, someone he didn't like. The pained look on Eshe's face made his stomach drop. She was angry, but just under that was something far worse.

She was scared.

Scared of him.

He forced himself to take a step back, to unclench his hands.

"Okay, you know what? I'm sorry."

Eshe pursed her lips, dubious. Gaétan's face registered something closer to disappointment.

Eshe's face softened. "Bas, just..." She couldn't finish, and turned to her guest. "This is between us. Go get a beer or something. I'll be right there."

Gaétan looked like he was going to say something more, but apparently thought better of it. He nodded once and retreated to the kitchen.

Bas didn't want to be remembered like this. It was humiliating.

"I'll call you, Eshe."

He almost called her *sweets* again, and winced, putting the instant replay out of his head. He turned and headed back toward the stairwell.

"No, uh-uh," Eshe said, her hand on his shoulder. She turned him back around just as her door shut behind her.

"What?" Bas said. "I'm done embarrassing myself."

"That's a start," she said, not unkindly. "What you *need* to do is to figure out your shit."

Her words washed over him, and he didn't fight them this time. It was his new policy. It might even last until the end of the conversation.

"You know, you weren't like this two years ago," she continued. "You never advertised it, but I knew why you went into private investigation. After Lana, after you quit the force, you told me how you felt. Lost. But you found a way to help people, and that helped light the path to your own healing. Does any of this ring a bell?" She took his shoulders in both hands. "Bas, I have to believe that man is in there still, because right now I'm looking at someone who's lost again."

Ten years after Lana, and where was he, really? Getting a pep talk from his latest ex in a hallway? Even the strangers at I, Mine had seen that he was a man adrift.

"I know it was ten years ago, Eshe, but I still feel the weight of it. They never found any bodies at the South Station—never released what they did find. So it never really ended, see? And now I'm supposed to just bury it?"

"Don't *bury* it, but don't wade in it either. I know you still feel her loss, but you don't have to suffer just to prove to yourself how much you loved her."

"Hey, careful." She meant well, but her family was alive and well, even if they were half a world away.

"Do you think Lana would want to see you suffering like this? Or would she want you to be investing in life? *This* life, right now."

Bas looked away and pretended to straighten his jacket. Her kind words said everything about her, but at this point he was afraid they might just bounce off him. Didn't she realize he was too far gone?

"Your photos are looking amazing," he said, hoping she would let him switch gears.

She sighed, crossing her arms. "Thanks." She cocked her head back to her door. "I should get back in there."

"Say, you had a show coming up. An installation. Remind me?"

"An exhibit, not an installation. I told you when. I think you blocked it out."

"Tell me again."

"I'll be doing the final staging on May twelfth at the South Station, lower gallery. That's a Sunday. Curtains come down on Monday."

"I'll try to make it," he said, and meant it. He had avoided the South Station ever since its reopening, but what better occasion to go back? Going there and seeing Eshe's work might help to disperse the dark cloud hanging over the place.

Her hand was on his shoulder again. "Try to take care of yourself, Bas."

She kissed him on the cheek and squeezed his arm before leaving him in the hallway.

Bas stood there for a moment, nodding to himself.

The bars were closed, but he could hit the twenty-four-hour liquor market before heading back to his empty apartment. He would start his Saturday morning on the right foot.

"Yup," he said to himself, and descended the staircase.

23

SATURDAY, APRIL 27, 1991

DEE PULLED THE CURTAINS ASIDE, letting the sun fall across the row of potted succulents she had arrayed before her on the kitchen table. Gisela had surprised her with the birthday gift—one succulent for each year on the planet. Dee had misgivings about plants confined in small pots, but she kept that to herself.

Now, while Gisela ran her Saturday errands, Dee took the opportunity to arrange the plants by name, from *Crassula arborescens* to *Zamioculcas zamiifolia*. The cutest of them were the *Fenestraria rhopalophylla*—known as babies' toes—which were surely superior to their namesakes.

Dee looked over her plants and swayed rhythmically while touching fingers to thumbs, letting her tension channel its way out with each successive touch.

One, two, three, four, three, two, one...

The remote viewers had not reappeared all week, which meant it was time to go home. They had both decided this would be Dee's final weekend with Gisela. Only... Dee couldn't escape the feeling that she hadn't completely returned to herself. She felt like she was still... outside. And she needed to find a way back in.

She had always found sanctuary in her routines. For the past six years, Dee had spent her Saturdays with the Kids Kan group tending to the plant life around designated schools and office parks. But this Saturday found her in Gisela's house, her routine broken. She was eighteen now, and her life was changing. Things would never be the same.

Dee gave the nearest pot a quarter turn so its pattern matched the pattern of the pot next to it. She had managed to keep herself together so far, but the weight of change was bearing down in her. The press of it seemed to have made the air thicker, and if she didn't find a way back in, she might be lost forever.

She stared into the perfect Fibonacci spirals of the *Sempervivum tectorum* until its sun-bathed petals left impressions across her retinas. Here was order and grace more vivid than any remedy she could conjure. Her plant held in its translucent green leaves a labyrinth to get lost in.

In these rarefied moments, time no longer mattered.

Explosions. That's what Dee heard at first. The insistent reports filled the apartment, strong enough that Dee felt each strike through the kitchen table. Phoebe shot like a lightning bolt into the other room.

It was someone at the door.

That was all.

Dee was halfway across the living room before she realized she had gotten up. Not to answer the door, but to be as far from the knocking as she could manage.

From outside there came a scrape, followed by the grumbling of a diesel engine.

A delivery truck.

Just a delivery truck.

Dee paced the room, her heart still trying to break free from her chest. When would Gisela be back? What time was it?

Forward and back, and around the coffee table. It wasn't a large apartment, and it seemed to be even smaller than it had been just moments before.

She might have to go out back just to get fresh air.

On her way to the back door, Dee's eyes fixed on something that stopped her cold. There, by the kitchen table, lingering in the air where she had sat, were eight glistening strands of blue light.

She blinked and moved around the table, being careful not to get too close. The eight streaks were really there, not just tricks of the eye. They hung suspended over the table, weightless, but just as real as the eighteen potted plants.

Dee approached the table with her hands out in front of her, positioned as if she were about to start knitting. As she drew closer, the streaks of light aligned to her fingers.

Eight streaks for eight fingers.

Fingerglow.

That was what this was. Only the streaks were blue, and they lingered far longer than anything Dee had conjured before.

She leaned forward and blew across the wisps as if she were blowing out candles on a cake. Dust swirled, catching first the sun's light, then moving through the electric azure field without resistance.

The marks in the air remained.

What had changed? She had been able to pull light from the air for a decade, but never like this. Was it because she was eighteen? Or maybe the delivery person had startled her in the middle of something, like the needle being pulled across a record.

One, two, three, four, three, two, one two three four...

Claw marks. That's what these were. She had injured the air, had left behind a spectral wound.

Returning to the chair by the table, only inches away from the marks she had left, she reached forward with fingers splayed. As her index finger intersected the first line, the faintest resistance registered, like a warm feather yielding against her skin.

A surge of emotion filled her with equal parts excitement and dread, and her hands wrung themselves before her as she watched, until the itchy feeling passed.

This wasn't bad, was it?

No. Or at least, it didn't have to be. But it did mean there was more to *fingerglow* than she had suspected.

She should have known. Just as the remote viewing was like *head-hop*ping—just boosted beyond her control—surely there must be an energized version of *fingerglow* as well. It was like anything, really. If you pushed it too far, even the innocuous could change into something stranger, more potent.

Dee regarded the accidental bands of light hanging before her. She wondered if she would ever be able to re-create the effect. And she wasn't sure she wanted to. The light ribbons showed no sign of fading. What if they were still there when Gisela got home? What if they *never* faded?

Watching Dee from the hallway, Phoebe issued a small meow.

24

SUNDAY, APRIL 28, 1991

BAS LAY ACROSS HIS COUCH, his right leg tingling under his weight. Blue-gray shadows flickered against the walls of the apartment, cast by the tube in the corner. Bas stared at the talking head on the screen, eyes half-lidded. With the volume at two bars, the reporter's spiel was barely audible over the pained murmur issuing from the fridge.

Which was good. It was the ten-year anniversary of the Singularity, and the thought of listening to ten-year commemorations and saccharine retrospectives was too offensive for Bas to contemplate. Yet somehow he couldn't bring himself to turn off the news altogether.

A graphic behind the newscaster read, *The South Station Singularity: How It Changed Us*. Bas looked for something to throw at the screen, but the remote control was just out of reach.

He braced himself on his elbow, looking for the beers. Empty cans lay scattered on the floor, peeking out from the shadows. Tonight should have been a liquor night. He hadn't even gotten that right.

His eyes fell on Mordell Bolden's *Cynda* tape, and the familiar sinking feeling hit the pit of his stomach. Why was that tape still here, tormenting him? He should have chucked it by now.

He slumped back on the couch. He had bought way too many beef jerky strips—a habit Mo had taught him. She hadn't returned, hadn't left any contact information, because most of the time she didn't know where she was going to be. It would have been nice to have some company to distract him.

He should be sleeping instead of staring, but his head wouldn't stay down. He chanced a look back at the screen. The graphic had changed. It now read, *The South Station Singularity: Breaking News.*

"Dammit."

Bas reached over the side of the couch and patted the floor, snatching up the remote from beneath the coffee table. He ticked up the volume until the reporter's voice filled the room.

"The announcement, coming this afternoon from the office of Attorney General Connor, means we may finally get answers to questions that have lingered for years. We may even learn the cause of the Singularity. But this treasure trove of newly declassified materials, including video footage from that day, also seems certain to raise more questions."

The video cut to a montage of imagery so familiar that no one even saw it anymore. The twisted ruins of the South Station. Chaos in the streets. Emergency response units. People in shock. So many people.

The voice of a different reporter spoke over the footage. *"In a split second, everything was gone. Eyewitnesses near the South Station on the twenty-eighth of April, 1981, described how a day that began like any other ended in a tragedy the likes of which the world had never seen. The reports that followed defied belief: solid structures melted like hot wax, stone and steel fused together as if by some furious force of nature, and a series of subsonic shock waves that were blamed for a myriad of health symptoms ranging from dizziness to memory loss."*

A remote shot showed the field reporter strolling in front of the rebuilt South Station.

"But what of the minutes leading up to the South Station Singularity? In the days following the Singularity, federal authorities called for an unprecedented media blackout in an effort to establish order at the crime scene and preserve evidence. Ever since, the public has been left to speculate what really happened on that fateful spring day."

"Bullshit."

"By September of 1981, the site of the former South Station had been swept clean, and would yield no further insight into the Singularity. But even then, the blackout was not lifted. The files were never opened.

"That is, until today.

"In a stunning decision, the local US District Court has ordered the unsealing of an archive of evidence collected in and around the South Station."

A coarse grayscale image depicted a series of interior shots taken in and around the South Station. Security footage from just before the Singularity.

"Released just today, on the tenth anniversary of the incident, this stockpile of artifacts, including personal items, photos, and video footage taken directly in and around the South Station, gives new insights into the Singularity. Although it will take days if not weeks to sort through it, we've prepared a brief montage highlighting some of the released footage. We would like to caution you that some of these images may be upsetting to viewers."

The audio went silent as the imagery flickered by, each short security video marked with a timestamp.

10:46:11 a.m. A mother pushing a stroller past a soft pretzel vending cart.

10:46:47 a.m. Two children cowering in the nook beneath an escalator.

10:46:54 a.m. A woman rushing toward a man, driving her outstretched arms into his shoulders, shoving him toward a railing and over, then peering over the edge as he falls, disappearing from view.

But a second later, just as the man was likely impacting the floor below, the video jumped. The frames that followed were from the same camera, from the same sequence, but the woman was gone.

A moment later the screen turned white.

Bas scrambled off the couch, nearly falling over the table as he got to his feet.

"What the *fuck*."

The montage continued in rough chronological order, showing a haze of video footage, most of it incoherent.

"Okay, what that fuck was that?" Bas asked the empty apartment.

He had seen video glitches like that one twice before. The first time had been on the *Cynda* tape. The second had been on the security footage from the Gulf mini-market.

And now he was seeing it again, among the video footage from 1981, salvaged from the South Station.

Anyone else watching the video would have seen the glitch as nothing more than an aberration caused by interference—a power surge, maybe an electromagnetic pulse. Bas himself would never have given it a second thought it if he hadn't seen the same glitch a dozen times before in Bolden's video.

He stood, swaying, as the voiceover continued.

"*Now, within that video reel, you no doubt noticed this grisly scene of a woman pushing—*"

"Yes, yes, yes," Bas said, rushing around the table, bashing his shin into its corner. He stumbled, barely feeling it, and stood inches from the television screen. "Show it again."

The footage played back again, this time more slowly.

"*It's yet another tragedy on a day of tragedies—a mystery on a day of mysteries. We suspect it may well prove to be only the first of many new mysteries to be unveiled as we work through this archive in the days and weeks to come.*"

Bas stood rapt, his pulse so heavy that he could see it in the retinal throb of ghostly capillaries. His mind was still in a beer haze, but he forced himself to work the pieces.

Cynda had disappeared immediately after a tape glitch. A woman ten years ago had also disappeared immediately after a tape glitch. An anonymous BBS user had suggested, without prompt, that I, Mine had had some involvement in the South Station Singularity—the event that had stolen Lana from him.

He pulled a hand across the stubble on his cheeks.

"It's all related."

He was sure of it. It tasted true.

He crossed the room, grabbed his jacket from the chair in the entryway, and fished around in its pockets until he found the new card from I, Mine.

He chuckled to himself. This almost looked like a case again.

25

SUNDAY, APRIL 28, 1991

GISELA'S FACE was framed by the neon glow of the Ferris wheel spokes. She was saying something, but her voice was lost to the vibrant bloom, and Dee's brain muffs didn't help.

What?

Gisela reached across the table and pulled the padded cup away from Dee's left ear. The outside sound hit her like a wave—amplified talkers and calliope music, the rumbles and screams from thrill rides, all fusing together into a dissonant cacophony.

"I asked if you're *sure* about this."

Dee knew Gisela meant the sensory sensitivity, and she was right to ask. But it was all about anticipation. Sure, an unexpected encounter with an intense environment felt like an assault—a body-wide electric shock that spawned a thousand ravenous brain beetles. But Dee's lifelong fondness for fairs—or was it a weakness? —had overruled her common sense on more than one occasion, and this evening she had come prepared. In addition to her brain muffs, she wore sunglasses and her most comfortable Aran knit sweater. It was far too warm for the thick sweater, but to Dee it qualified as armor.

She pushed Gisela's hand away from her ear. The wall of noise really was making her jumpy.

Come on, we're here, Gisela. And it's our last evening together.

Her friend looked dubious, even as Dee made her impatience vocal, grabbing the edge of the table as she rocked.

I'll tell you if I get overwhelmed, I promise.

She was on her feet before Gisela could get around the table.

Dee moved on impulse, drawn deeper into the crowd by the chaser lights that followed the contours of the twirling gondola ride. She felt a thousand miles from her own body as the vibrant pendulum cut through the night air in a gentle arc. The humid air clung to the day's heat, filling Dee's nostrils with a mélange of buttered popcorn and hot dogs, and she stopped in the middle of the path, where she had an unobstructed view of the light show.

Gisela caught up to her and stood with her arm brushing against Dee's. "Did you want to ride?" she asked by Dee's ear, speaking loudly enough to be heard through the padding.

I don't ride. I watch.

Gisela nodded, and followed Dee's gaze. "It's pretty."

What?

"*Pretty.* The lights."

A little girl floated by, making Dee jump. She was on her father's shoulders, one arm around her father's head, her free hand holding a cloud of blue cotton candy.

Dee impulsively snatched the girl's treat and shoved a wad of it into her mouth.

The girl shrieked—a single note almost too high for human hearing. It pierced Dee's defensive barrier, forcing her hands against her head. She dropped the confection to the ground.

"She took my *thing!*"

Gisela was already between the father and Dee, her hands out before her. "She didn't mean it."

"What the fuck, man? She's *six*," the man said. The girl clung to his neck, her face crumpled and scarlet, like a *Hibiscus rosa-sinensis*.

Plantae, Angiosperms, Eudicots, Rosids, Malvales, Malvaceae, Hibiscus, Hibiscus rosa-sinensis.

"She has a motor disorder," Gisela said, almost tripping over her words. "It's not intentional, I promise."

"Tell that to my stepdaughter!" The man glared at Dee with an expression like flames behind a door. She had to look away, to find the lights again. "If she can't keep her hands to herself, why's she even here?"

"We'll get you another one," Gisela said quickly.

"I *know* you will. Make *her* pay for it."

As Gisela fished around in her purse, the man was pointing at Dee, his finger just inches from her eye, so close that the heat of it felt like it left a smudge on her cheek.

Dee darted into the crowd, barely feeling the bodies buffeting her from all sides.

"*Dee!*"

Dee watched her feet, letting her arms do the work of parting the way before her. This was the main path. If she followed it to the opposite side, she should find the Samba Balloon Ride. The Revere Spring Carnival was laid out the same way every year, which was a comfort.

"Dee, stop!"

Dee pulled away from Gisela's grasp and walked faster.

"Okay, then I'm going with you. But slow down, okay? We're okay now."

Gisela didn't understand.

If Dee slowed down, a lot of bad things would catch up to her.

There was no time to tell her.

Balloon.

It was all she could manage. She was in go mode, no longer enjoying the lights and motion. "Go mode" was what Brenda always called it when Dee's brain handed control to her feet. Usually she and Walter would stand out of the way, having learned that Dee would eventually wind down, like the Energizer Bunny's inferior competition.

Gisela could only do her best to match Dee's pace.

"Balloon. The balloon ride? Is that what you want?"

Ahead.

The Samba Balloon Ride—the kiddie version of the Octopus—was the only attraction Dee had ever ridden. The spinning, undulating motion of the cars made her think of being rocked in her mother's arms. Dee had never been able to figure out whether that fragment of a memory was real, or just a dream she'd once had.

As she rounded the path to the next section of the park, her spirits lifted. No one was in line at the balloon ride, and the last group was just exiting the far ramp. Dee made her way up the entrance ramp and hastily unhooked the chain barring the loading platform.

Gisela said something Dee didn't hear. Then a hand was on Dee's arm, preventing her from proceeding.

The ticket attendant, a short woman whose hair was too curly, had positioned herself in front of Dee.

She smelled of artificial fruit.

Gum.

"Sorry, miss. Uh-uh, we're shut for maintenance now."

Dee watched the woman's mouth move.

"Dee, we can't go in now," Gisela said. "How long will you be down?" she asked the attendant.

"It's unscheduled," the woman said, her words tumbling from her mouth between chews. "So it depends what they see. Could be a half hour, could be till Tuesday when we're open again."

The nearest balloon was just feet away. It wasn't broken. Dee could sit there while the worker worked. She didn't need the ride to be on.

"Miss, you gotta hold up, you understand?"

Dee hadn't realized she was straining against the attendant's hold until she saw the woman's expression change.

"Is she not quite all there?"

Gisela ignored her. "Dee, this way. Let's find somewhere to cool down."

The prompt caused Dee's body to reconnect with her mind, returning some control. She spun around and retraced her steps down the ramp.

"Sorry about that," she heard Gisela say, before she clomped down the wooden ramp after her. "Dee, *wait wait wait!*"

But this was go mode.

A man came out of nowhere, just appearing in front of Dee. Before she could register what was happening, his shoulder buried itself in her chest, and her legs were no longer under her. She bounced off a pink-and-white support beam, sending a white-hot burst of pain through her ribs.

"*Excuse you,*" said the man.

The man from before.

"Looks like I got a *engine problem*, too."

He must have followed her from the other side of the park.

That was worse than the pain, even though she could still feel the impression of his shoulder in her ribs.

Dee inhaled, filling her lungs again, but it was too late.

The trapped feeling was coming back.

It stiffened her limbs.

Pushed her backward, away from herself.

Her heart beat too quickly.

"Dee!"

Gisela was somewhere close, but Dee couldn't focus.

The words weren't there.

"Just 'cause she's fucked up in the head doesn't mean she gets to do whatever the hell she wants. Maybe next time she thinks about that, eh?"

The man's voice filled Dee with fire, and she shrank farther into herself to be safe.

But still his words came, too loud, until her skin crawled with every syllable.

Then the sounds pulled apart from each other until only the sharpest pieces remained. Shattered glass, glittering in the sun.

No, not the sun.

Stars.

Pulled into streaks by her spinning.

She was spinning.

Spinning.

Her arms caught air, thrashing like the Octopus, with its black lights and rock-and-roll soundtrack.

The man's eyes, Gisela's hands, the pressing crowd.

A howl rang out, so close Dee tasted it.

The sound was coming from inside.

Dee's wail was in her ears, flooding the night air with everything that had been inside.

Meltdown.

She had freed herself.

She was too far away.

Where nothing made sense.

It was too much.

No control.

Light like spiders, crawling over the man's face.

Dee's arms, pulling the night away from itself.

Spectral legs like needles, pressing in, puncturing, illuminating that man like a pink bulb.

Now his shout.

Now his scream.

And Dee's fingers, tracing something new over something old.

The man, consumed in a brilliant mesh that throbbed with the pounding in Dee's temples.

Meltdown.

The park and the shouts, and the body, and Dee.

And it was all flung away.

Until there was nothing left.

26

MONDAY, APRIL 29, 1991

TWILIGHT SETTLED into the low-rise brick buildings of Kendall Square as Bas took a turn down one of its lesser side streets. Fumbling for the switch, he flicked on his headlights and scanned for a parking spot.

This part of town was undergoing an awkward transition, with small factory buildings abutting minimalist biotech labs, and empty lots festooned with proposed construction notices. Bas found ample parking by the razed remains of a building whose rebar-laced beams reached like hands to the sky. Wherever it was that I, Mine called home—an office? a hideout? a fortress?—Bas was pretty sure Fritz and Collette had gotten yet another killer deal on the rent.

82 Norfolk Place, more warehouse than office building, cut right through the residential and industrial zones. From high-set glass block windows, dim light cast a faint glow over the cracked concrete lot. The building's slatted loading dock door was closed and bolted, but a broad wooden door nestled into a recessed entrance bore the I, Mine emblem. The sight of it made Bas's palms cold.

He wiped his hand on his jeans before pressing the doorbell. He heard no chime, at least not over the diesel motor chugging nearby and the hum of the transformers overhead. He cocked his head. Was the buzzer broken? In the pool of light at his feet was a pile of cigarette butts.

A young woman pulled the door open. She was dressed in a simple black outfit, like one of those karate uniforms.

"Hello there," she said with a smile. "Did you try the front door?"

"Oh," Bas said, looking over his shoulder. Was this the back?

"It's okay." She laughed. "You made it, that's what counts. Did you have some kind of...?"

The card. Bas found it in his pocket and handed it to her.

"Fritz invited me. Um, Bas Milius."

"Of course," she said, not offering her name. She pocketed the card after giving it a cursory glance, and pulled the door wider to allow him to enter. "Watch your head."

The inside—all wood, paper screens, and woven flooring—appeared to have been grafted from another building entirely. Indirect lighting gave the interior a warm radiance, and the mat floors showed no sign of use. The faint scent of lumber suggested construction had happened fairly recently.

"You can leave your shoes there."

"Ah, got it," Bas said. Several other pairs were arranged just inside the entryway, men's and women's both. The woman herself wore slippers. "Is bare feet okay?"

"Of course." She clasped one hand in the other, as if to demonstrate she was in no hurry.

Bas braced himself against the wall as he worked his right shoe from his foot. "Am I late?"

Fritz had told him seven. It wasn't yet seven thirty.

"Mm, no." The question seemed to catch her off guard. "Late for what?"

"I'm not sure, to be honest."

She nodded. "Actually, if you could wait just a moment..." She left Bas there.

"Sure," he said to no one.

Standing in the hall, barefoot, he strained to listen. The hall wasn't just quiet, it had that sound-deadening feel he had experienced only once before, in a recording studio. It was almost dizzying.

He flinched when Collette appeared. She was wearing slippers too. They must have muffled her approach.

"Bas Milius, I'm so glad you came." She looked him up and down, then stuck out a hand. She placed her other hand on his as they shook. Around her waist she wore a kind of cloth purse. "How is everything going?"

Everything?

"We didn't really get to talk the other night, but I sensed you had a lot going on."

"No, I'm good. Good." He felt naked, like his feet. Were they just going to stand in the hall? "I just thought I could come by, since—"

"Yes, of course!" She clasped his forearm in her hand and led him deeper into the space. She had a scent about her—lavender, maybe. "You're just in time. I hope you're hungry."

The hall was straight, with no doors along its sides—just a single room at the end. Through the open doorway, Bas could see the people seated around a table before he could hear their voices. The sound dampening really was remarkable.

Collette released Bas's arm as they entered the modest room. Four people were seated at the table, including Fritz at one end. Full place settings had been arranged before them, and what remained of their appetizers was being cleared by two help staff, one of whom was the nameless woman who had let Bas in. One of the plates being cleared was apparently Collette's.

"It's just so perfect," said a young woman to Fritz's right.

Other than Fritz, Bas recognized none of these people from the open house.

"Look who's here," Collette said.

"Excellent!" said Fritz, rising. He came around the table and embraced Bas while the other guests watched. "So glad you're here. Look, we have one extra chair for you right here at the end."

An extra place setting had been laid out, as if they had known to expect him. He should have gotten here earlier.

"We always leave one chair open," Collette explained. "Just in case."

Bas mouthed an *ah*. "So what if someone else shows up?"

"Well then too bad," Fritz said, mocking an imperious tone. "We're full now."

He smiled at their exchange and gave the others a wave, feeling annoyed at himself for being so self-conscious.

Fritz returned to his seat as Bas took his own, next to Collette.

"Okay, intros for Bas," Fritz began. "Bas, I'd like you to meet Darian Rutten, chef, and this is Olivia DeLaria, who is a marketing director, and over here we have Nora Bailey, who is a radio...?"

"Radio presenter," she finished for him, and gave Bas a nod.

"That's right."

"What do you do?" asked Darian the chef.

"Stumble around, mostly." Bas was nervous. But at least it got them laughing. "I'm retired. I was a cop."

"There, see?" Fritz said, giving his wife a meaningful nod. He looked at Bas. "I have a pretty good sense about these things—well, hey hey *hey!*"

The wait staff had just returned wheeling in a cart of food that looked like something from the cover of a *Bon Appétit*.

"Are you okay with lamb?" Collette asked Bas quietly while the other guests gawked at the meal.

"That's... yeah, fine." A draft from the open doorway drifted across his bare feet.

"So how have you been, Bas?" Fritz asked, waving several glazed carrots on the end of his fork. The small talk had petered out. "Last time I saw you it looked like you'd been having a rough time."

Bas's cheeks grew warm as he forced his hand away from his

empty shirt pocket. What if he just came out and asked them about the South Station Singularity? That would make for a good distraction.

"Oh, you know, I can't complain."

"You show great restraint," Collette said, to titters around the table.

"Well I'm glad you're here," Fritz said, "joining us!"

Bas gave him a look, but Collette leaned over and patted his hand. "He means joining us for dinner."

Darian the chef turned to Fritz. "I just love what they did with the demi-glace."

Fritz lit up. "Oh, of course you'll have to meet Quinlan. One chef to another. He came from nowhere, but I'd put him up against the best chefs in the city. He's just twenty-three, would you believe it? Been with us now for almost two years." He sighed. "I'd hate to see *him* go."

"Ugh, so good," said Olivia the marketing director.

Bas agreed. The food was better than anything he had tasted in years. Definitely better than beer and beef jerky. He was out of his league in this place, and the others probably felt it. A retired cop? He might as well have wandered in from the street.

Still, Collette and Fritz were the ones who had opened their doors to him, so what did that make them? Was this all for charity?

Fritz was watching him. "So Bas... what do you think of our setup?"

Bas blinked, and dabbed at his mouth with his napkin.

Fritz continued, "We keep making small improvements, as we can. For comfort or, you know, just to shake things up. Get us out of our own complacency."

Bas nodded. "Right, it's nice."

The wait staff had begun clearing the plates, ducking in and out between the guests.

"So you like what you see?" Fritz said. "The overall presentation?"

What was that look? Was he fishing for something specific? If so, Bas wasn't sure what it was.

"Yeah, I mean, it's a nice spot. I'd never have expected it, seeing it from the outside."

Fritz shrugged. "The outside is for others. This is for us and our guests. What you'll notice is that we think through every detail. That's why I'm so interested in your opinion, you know." He was smiling now. So it wasn't a test, not exactly.

"He's not an *aesthete*," said Collette. "Don't make him sorry he came."

Bas had been more focused on the company than the room, but Fritz did have a point. The place was pristine. Every feature, fixture, and surface was free of wear and dirt, from the light switches to the centerpiece, which was some kind of cut flower and bamboo arrangement. In fact, it was so flawless that it looked staged. Which it probably was.

Something in the corner caught Bas's eye. Only—no, it was just a shadow cast along the framed mirrors set into the wall. Still, his eye lingered, tracing the detail etched into the wood, where blade had cut along the grain, revealing an undulating form that was part nature, part sculpture. The details were so crisp that Bas imagined his vision had improved. Everything in the room, every edge and corner, was uniformly sharp, no matter how close or far. If he didn't know better he might have thought that someone had slipped him an acid tab.

"Nice, right?" Fritz asked again, his gaze holding steady on Bas.

"I see what you mean."

The man nodded to his wife, justified. "There, see?"

Collette ignored him. "No one's going to finish the polenta before they clear it? Bas?"

He put up a hand. What he really wanted was to loosen his belt.

"I'll kill it," Darian said, waving the serving bowl over.

"The decor is mainly Japanese," Fritz was saying. "*Shinden-zukuri*."

"*Ish*," Collette said, returning her attention to her husband.

He sniffed. "Right, *loosely* based. I mean, we used real hinoki, but the chairs are a concession to the Western aesthetic."

"We were inspired by a retreat we attended in Kyushu," Collette added.

"Oh, that sounds amazing," said Nora the radio presenter.

"It's *beautiful*. You should go."

"I should," said Nora, more thoughtfully.

"It's easy to overlook the details," Fritz said, "but I admit it, I obsess. To me, an attention to detail can make or break an experience. In fact, I'd argue that you can't fully appreciate the grand scheme until you have a base understanding of its component parts."

"How do you mean?" Olivia asked.

"I'm saying you could apply it as a base principle to anything."

Olivia wasn't satisfied. "Give us an example."

Fritz clicked his tongue and looked off into space for a moment. "Okay, let's say you go to a therapist. She doesn't begin by declaring what happiness is and prescribing the actions to achieve that state. No, the desired outcome is something that emerges over time, as the manifestation of its underlying details, *sui generis*. You can't get to the truth otherwise, subjective or objective."

"There's a strained analogy," Collette said. "We were talking about the quality of an experience before, now you're talking about... diagnoses."

Bas observed their exchange coolly. It was unusual for one spouse to call out the other in front of guests. But her tone was bemused, without guile.

"It still illustrates my point, I think. There's the utility of a thing, and the presentation of a thing. One is required, the other is desired. I think the result speaks for itself."

"Well, I guess now we'll never know," she said with a wink. Fritz may have been comfortable with his oblique turns, but Collette was on to him.

Fritz only laughed.

Darian put his balled-up napkin on the table and gave a little moan. The wait staff took immediate note, and cleared the final place setting.

Bas was still thinking of Collette's comment. "So which would you say I, Mine's is about: quality or diagnosis?" He didn't mean for it to sound confrontational, but the conversation had floated above the clouds for too long now.

"I can tell you which one *sells*," Olivia said with a laugh.

Collette didn't jump in, instead casting a glance over at her husband with a look of expectation.

Fritz was unfazed. "I, Mine has always been about what its guests bring to it." He leaned back as the server placed a fresh napkin at his place. "Thank you," he said to the nameless woman with a quick smile, before continuing. "And I'm aware that that sounds like a non-answer, so let me try again." His brows furrowed. "Collette and I founded our group to give people space to find their own meaning, but in a structured way. My *personal* belief is that there's an inherent absurdity to this life, but I don't go so far as to say that nothing matters. There's no denying that people find comfort in meaning, though there's never just one way to get to it."

"Well, that's true," Collette said. "But don't give them the impression that it's '*anything goes*' here." She looked at the rest of them "The structure part of it is important to us. Not prescription, but the discipline, the rigor. We provide that."

"Well at least we *encourage* it."

Collette nodded. "And we're here to generally keep things on track."

They were getting warmer, but it still sounded like they were talking around something.

"But are you mostly talking meditation, or martial arts, or what?" Bas asked. Had they trained Wallace, the multi-armed menace? Was that one of the benefits they offered? What about causing a father to disavow any knowledge of his daughter's existence? Or even his own existence? Was that "keeping things on track"?

Fritz waved his hand in a so-so motion. "There is a meditative component here, yes, but it's nothing so internal as, say, *svapnadarshana*. Our practice is rooted in the physical. It relies on group movement."

"Like aerobics?"

Nora laughed. "I didn't bring my leg warmers."

The servers brought out a covered platter, then lifted the dome, revealing fancy cupcakes sprinkled with powdered sugar.

The male server announced, "We have *petits gâteaux*, in chocolate and citron."

"Holy shit," said Nora. Then, quickly, "Sorry."

Fritz seemed not to have heard the exchange. "We can show you, Bas," he continued. "What our practice looks like. If you stay."

Collette put her hand on his again. "If you think of interpretive dance as arbitrary movement, this is more deliberate, like tai chi."

Bas shook his head. They weren't talking about Jazzercise, clearly, but that was the first thing that popped into his head.

When the dessert platter came around to him, he chose the citron, since it seemed lighter. It smelled of lemons. Fancy French lemons, no doubt.

Fritz laughed, seemingly for no reason. "What are we about? I love that question, Bas. It's so unassuming."

Bas shrugged. If he said so.

Whatever the *petits gâteaux* were made of, they melted in the mouth, sweet and tart combining into a flavor that could have lifted Bas out of his chair. His only regret in that moment was how soon it would be over.

"The way I think of it, we're all looking for contentment, I suppose. That's not to say we're always *comfortable*, but finding our way regardless of our circumstances—through analysis or meditation or even medication—that in itself is a kind of reward. I think of Nagel when he suggested approaching our absurd lives with irony."

Maybe. But there was more to life than contentment. Contentment usually meant giving up on something else.

"What Fritz is saying," said Collette, *"that's* why we're here.

Because it's not just about finding a way to muddle through. People want to find their own sense and meaning in things. The specifics are always down to the individual. What do you bring to us, and what are you looking for? Our guests are the players. We can provide a stage."

"But hold on," said Bas. Something about their glibness grated on his ear. Maybe they had always had it easy. "Don't you think contentment is maybe what you see through rose-colored glasses?"

The sounds of silverware seemed suddenly too loud.

"I mean, say you're looking for contentment in the face of tragedy or loss, then you must be ignoring something. Life can be harsh. The truth may be harsh. Sometimes that's just the reality of it."

"Then we can make our own reality," Fritz said, smiling at his wife. He looked positively pleased with himself.

Bas's hand was up at his pocket again. He forced it back into his lap. "What I'm saying is, sometimes you don't have a choice."

Fritz must have heard something in Bas's voice, because, to his credit, his impish grin vanished. "Bas, did you ever hear of the Allegory of the Cave? Plato?"

Bas shook his head.

"The basic premise is that a group of cave-born prisoners are chained up and forced to face the wall. All they know of the world are the shadow projections cast on that wall by the light behind them. The shadows, to them, are the real world. That's their reality.

"Then one day a prisoner escapes, goes into the light, and realizes the shadows weren't reality at all, but rather a poor imitation of the real world. The truth—the light, or the sun—was right behind them."

"Enlightenment," Bas said.

"Right, so we're nothing new in that regard," Collette said. "I, Mine is a means to that end."

"I love that," said Nora.

For a moment, Bas imagined that the other guests were shills. Maybe the whole thing was an act—on a stage, as Collette had suggested—all for his benefit. Then again, that line of thinking might be the path to madness.

Fritz had finished his chocolate delicacy and was finally leaning back in his chair. "You're never supposed to overthink an allegory," he said to the others, "but for me the truth has always been beyond the scope of Plato's little story. Think about the light; about what it is. If you consider that it's inherently impermanent, then in the end, after the heat death of the universe, there will only *be* that last shadow. Looking at it that way, it's the *light* that's the lie. The truth is actually the darkness."

"But darkness and shadows aren't the same thing," Olivia said.

"Well, granted," said Fritz. "But you're making my point. Shadows are the light's own lies."

"Wait, I wasn't keeping score," Nora said. "Who's winning this argument?"

Collette pointed at Fritz, who chuckled.

"I'm just saying," he said, "once we get past whatever illusions stand in our way, the truth we eventually choose to take comfort in may itself be circumstantial and fleeting."

"Maybe that's okay," said Darian, and shrugged. "At least for me. I try to live in the now."

"Sure, you get to decide that," said Collette.

Bas felt like he was treading water, and the dessert had made him sleepy. Time to change the subject.

"So are you three new here?" he asked the guests.

Olivia answered first. "I've been with I, Mine for almost a month."

"We like it if someone more seasoned joins introductory dinner," said Collette. She nodded to Nora. "But Nora here was at the same open house you attended. And Darian is new, as of earlier today."

"I don't want to speak out of turn," Fritz said, his sparkling eyes back on Bas, "but I believe Bas is on a kind of quest."

Bas blinked. *First I'm sad, and now I'm on a quest?*

"Stop me if I'm off base," Fritz said, one hand up.

"No, please." This should be good.

"At the open house I think I got a sense of your inner turmoil, and

I have to say, I was moved. Even before we talked, I mean. I saw it from across the room, in the way you held yourself. And to be frank, I don't know that I, Mine can do a thing for you. I really don't. But I wanted to tell you that, whatever burden you're carrying, it's optional."

Bas opened his mouth, but words failed him. There was no doubt Fritz was being sincere. But he didn't know about Lana. Bas couldn't just leave her memory behind like some old backpack.

That enduring echo of their final fight.

The suitcase in her hand as she walked out the door.

Bas tried not to wince.

Was Fritz expecting a thank-you for his insight? Or maybe Bas should be defending himself. But to what end? Why expend the effort to set the record straight? He had no stake in this.

"He means," Collette said, "that you can honor the things you care about without continuing to internalize your suffering."

Bas looked at her. Fritz might have meant that, or maybe not.

"I'll tell you what I told Nora and Darian," she continued. "What I, Mine can provide for you here is as far from esoteric as you can get: just floor space and a bunk. That's the minimum. But I believe you would get a great deal more out of your time here. Because the fact that you're even here says to me that, whatever else is going on in your life right now, you're not content. Am I close?"

Bas thought about it. "Yeah, that's true." The other truth was that they were finally closing the circle, and not without some skill. Now the conversation had turned to him and his place within their little commune.

"You're braver than a lot of people I've met, Bas," said Fritz. "And I've met a fair number."

The conversation had taken a circuitous route, but it wasn't a bad sales pitch, all told. Still, assuming I, Mine wasn't so much a cult as it was a meditation retreat with a hint of spirituality, what was their connection to the Singularity ten years ago?

"Would I have to sign anything?"

Had the white rabbit made Alice sign anything?

"No signatures," Olivia said.

"I like that," said Nora.

"No signatures, and no payments," added Fritz.

"We can talk about the terms later," said Collette. "but I promise we'll never ask for a dime, and the front door is always open."

Fritz cleared his throat. "We do lock the back door sometimes though, because we had warehouse workers from next door using our restrooms."

Collette rolled her eyes and Darian laughed.

Was that it then? Were all three of them being invited to join? Or had the others already passed the test?

Bas thought about the offer. Going along with it would be his best chance of talking to Kit Lund again, who definitely knew something about Cynda. And if Bas managed to find their connection to the South Station Singularity, all the better.

"What have you got to lose?" Fritz asked him, then turned to the other guests. "Really, any of you."

Olivia was silent, but her smile said she hoped they would join.

"Don't get the wrong idea," Collette said. "This isn't a hotel. We believe in deliberate work, hard work."

Work? Maybe they would pay him for it.

"We've been waking up at six," Olivia said.

"And there will be motion practice," Fritz added.

"Actually," Bas said, "can I ask something?"

They all looked at him.

"What about the name? 'I, Mine'?" He had to know.

"Oh!" Fritz laughed. "Well it has *two* meanings, really."

Collette nodded. "At least two."

"First, what we first do for ourselves, we can then do for our loved ones. Our, ours."

"Oh, so *I*... and *mine*," Darian said. "That makes sense."

"Exactly. But we also say that we're *mining*. All of us, mining toward something deeper."

27

MONDAY, APRIL 29, 1991

THE SUN FALLING across Dee's lap was like a warm blanket made of light, but there was little comfort to be found in it. She looked to the driver's side, where Brenda had a hand on the wheel and her arm on the window ledge. Cathy, Dee's personal aide, was standing outside the window, and she and Brenda were talking about Dee's bad day at school.

"Well this week we're back to the routine," Brenda said. "So that should definitely help."

Cathy smiled. "Yeah, she was just a little checked out today, that's all. It really wasn't a big deal."

Dee's concentration had been shot all day, and as a consequence she'd heard nothing Mrs. Siméon had said up at the blackboard. Her distracted state was only partly due to the doozy of a meltdown she'd had last night at the carnival. Mostly she was concerned with what Gisela had told her after she'd managed to come back to herself.

"Thanks so much for hanging in there, as usual."

"Oh, no, we're buds." Cathy leaned down and peered into the car. "Isn't that right, Dee? We're buds."

Buds with the autistic girl who'd flayed a man to death with a web of light?

Only no, that hadn't happened at all. Not according to Gisela.

"Well, we'll see you Wednesday, Cathy."

"Bye-bye, Mrs. Luckie. Bye, Dee!"

Brenda rolled up her window and pulled away from the Higashi School's pick-up lane. As she got back to the main road, she reached over and gave Dee's shoulder a squeeze.

"You doing okay there, toots?"

How much had Gisela told her? Brenda knew about the fair, and the meltdown, of course. But Gisela wouldn't have spoken of Dee's delusions.

And what had all that been anyway? It was one thing to have sensory-based visions, especially when she was over-stimulated. Flashes of color, and foul smells, weren't uncommon. But to see such a detailed scenario play out before her eyes? And then to find out it hadn't happened at all?

That kind of full-blown hallucination was something entirely new.

"I think you've just been through a lot, and, you know, your body just has to process that in its own way."

Dee's memory of last night couldn't have been clearer, even through the sensory haze of her meltdown. She had lost control, had summoned ribbons of electricity—had torn them from the air—and the gathered crowd had responded in horror as events unfolded from there.

Only...

It never happened.

None of it.

According to Gisela, the man had never even returned after their first encounter. He had never knocked Dee off her feet as she exited the Samba Balloon Ride.

And those memories were from *before* her meltdown had set in.

"You just have to be careful not to push yourself," Brenda continued. "You know what I mean?"

Maybe there was something to that. Dee didn't doubt Gisela—after all, there had been no police, no news reports. But her recollection was so vivid, so specific. *Was* it a hallucination? Some kind of mental interference caused by her abilities? Was Dee her own kryptonite? She hadn't intended to push herself, it was just that circumstances had led her to the breaking point. The same thing had happened, on a much smaller scale, when the delivery person had startled her at Gisela's, resulting in that long-lasting, unintentional *fingerglow*.

Were her abilities becoming more erratic over time? And, if so, how long would it be until they became too strong for her to control at all?

As Brenda pulled onto the highway, she glanced over at Dee. "I know it's hard, Dee. I know you can't always predict what will happen when you're out and about. And I know how much you love the fair. You always have. But you know it's a risk, too."

Being alive was a risk.

Dee didn't have a choice. She couldn't just avoid using her abilities altogether. That would be like cutting herself off from her own senses. Her abilities were a part of her. The way forward was not to shrink from them.

She had to practice, until she gained true mastery over her abilities.

What happened at the fair—whether or not it had actually happened—must never happen again.

"Welcome back home, you," Junmo said.

Dee looked up from the eighteen plants she had arranged on her dresser.

Hi, Junmo.

She braced for his hug as he came into her room. He was big on hugs, though he didn't like to be hugged back. As a result, he usually pinned her arms under his. It wasn't so bad.

It's so good to see you.

He cast a glance behind him, then whispered to her. "You went on a real adventure, I have to be honest. You left on April nineteenth, and now it's April *twenty-ninth*. That's ten days, total. I didn't say anything about your mind-talking secret, Dee, rest assured. Also, I really like your plants, but I won't touch them."

He sat down on her bed. He had missed her, even if he wasn't likely to articulate it. She had missed him, too.

Thank you, Junmo, for everything. I appreciate it.

Brenda called from the base of the staircase. "*Junmo, you give her some space.*"

He hopped back on his feet. "Yes, I'm giving her space!" he called back. Then, to Dee, he added, "But it's good that you're situated. So, I'm going to leave you to it. You know where to find me."

I know where you live.

"Ha!" he barked without looking back.

In her mind, Dee saw the man from last night, his finger an inch from her face.

That had happened.

Dee sat on the edge of her bed and attempted to still herself. Her body was behaving fairly well, neither carrying her to other rooms nor locking up entirely. She had only to contend with the usual stims—the finger-touching and some gentle rocking.

She couldn't help but feel the call of her old routine beckoning her. Normally at this time she would be out back, tending to her garden. And after more than a week of neglect, it could probably use the attention. But routine was not her friend, not right now. She had to work on her *fingerglow*.

She glanced at the door, making sure she'd shut it, then held her hands out before her and ran through one of her go-to sequences, hoping she could find the trigger for the effect within the pattern.

One, two, three, four, one, three, two, four...

She hadn't even finished the full sequence before the glowing filaments—still blue, but less blue than they'd been in Gisela's kitchen—streamed from her fingertips, carried on the stirred air like luminescent smoke.

This, too, was new. She had never been able to conjure the effect so quickly before. It was almost as though she had simply picked up where she'd left off the last time. The digital phone downstairs came to mind, with its speed dial that could summon a full phone number with the press of a single button.

Speed-dialing fingerglow.

Dee didn't stop at the sight of the spectral threads. She pushed on with her finger sequence, touching fingers to thumbs as quickly and as precisely as she was able. The thrill of it was like the sensation she felt during the momentary drop of the balloon ride at the fair: a predictable but surprising loss of control that shot from chest to spine but was over before true panic set in.

Her heart raced as the filaments hanging before her formed a kind of light brocade, a beautiful silvery sculpture with delicate arcs sprouting from a central seam. Very quickly the shape before her was more substantial than anything she had ever summoned.

After a minute her wrists began to cramp, and she stopped her stimming, half expecting the entire form to vanish. But it persisted, hanging weightless before her, bright enough to cast shadows against her walls.

Dee stared at her creation until she could see it even with eyes shut. It wasn't holding still, like a photograph. Every whorl and knot of it *crawled*, like electric sinew, retracing and renewing itself as it pulsed.

What was it? Had she summoned something that had always existed, or had she built this pattern in the air from nothing?

She heard feet on the steps. That had to be Walter. Adrenaline flooded her system. She reached forward to wave the shapes away—

but they refused to be waved away. Instead, she watched with wide eyes as her fingers flickered in and out of existence.

She yanked her hands back as Walter passed by her room without stopping.

She was safe, at least for the moment. But what had she just seen?

Dee drew her hands up to her eyes, examining each finger in the glow of the strange creation hanging before her. No damage as far as she could tell, and the static tickling sensation had vanished almost immediately.

She leaned toward the light streams. Still no sign of fading.

She intended to touch only the edges of the form, carefully. But her body was finished cooperating, and she thrust both hands directly into the glowing mass.

Both hands vanished.

She could still feel each finger, and she was able to ball her hands into fists. But wherever her hands were, they were no longer in her room. It felt as if she were reaching into a warm pocket.

Her impulsive episode over, Dee withdrew her forearms—relieved that her body had decided to obey—and watched her hands reassemble as they returned from across the threshold.

Light pockets.

That was a new twist.

Was this what mastery looked like? Was she on the right track? Or was she getting herself into deeper trouble—and maybe flooding the entire household with radiation in the process?

She had to pull herself together. She had never hurt herself, or anyone else, with her abilities. She wasn't counting the man at the carnival. That hadn't happened.

Right now there was only one thing Dee needed to do. She had to figure out how to turn this shimmering hand teleporter off.

Preferably before dinner.

28

TUESDAY, APRIL 30, 1991

BAS RETURNED to his room and slid the pocket door shut behind him as he towel-dried his hair. The raw silk of his black uniform was soft against his skin, but textured like cotton. The woman who had answered the door last night had been wearing the same outfit, and Bas hadn't been surprised to find one draped across his cot when he was finally escorted in last night.

His modest room continued the building's Eastern motif, with tatami flooring, minimal slab surfaces made from some pale wood, and parchment screens. A single shelf by his cot held his rucksack, which he had packed with several days of clothes during a late round-trip to his apartment and back. His hosts had made no mention of the terms of his stay yet, which was fine by him. Better to leave things open-ended and play it by ear.

He gave his towel a final snap and hung it on a peg, then frowned at himself in the mirror over the sink. He needed a haircut, and that was really the least of it. He had let himself go by almost every measure, and the old man staring back at him bore only a passing resemblance to the sharper, more refined Bas of his mind's eye.

He walked to the room's single window. The flared eaves overhead blocked his view of the sky, but streaks of rain caught the sun and darkened the grass of a courtyard outside. That meager patch of nature was the only thing separating his room from another one opposite. He could make out no tenant though its darkened window.

Bas mused on Fritz and Collette, he the more philosophical and she the more pragmatic—or so it had seemed to Bas. Though they were quite different, they shared an earnestness that bordered on the aggressive—there wasn't a note of disingenuousness between them. They were charmers, both; that was the truth of the matter.

Maybe Bas was being too easy on them because they had professed to see something in him. And apparently—judging by the free meals and comfortable, if compact, room—they thought he was someone worth investing in. But to what end? What were they after? Even if they were completely above board, nothing came for free.

And what was Bas after? He certainly wasn't here for the meditation. No—he was here for a genuine mystery. Could he help it if he was leaning toward obsession? The things he had seen over the past weeks—that mind-altering fight with Wallace, Cynda's disappearance, Bolden's change of identity, the tape glitches—might each have been explained away in isolation. But taken together?

"Or maybe I've lost my fool mind," he said, voice still morning-gruff.

His shot a glance at his door, suddenly self-conscious. There was no telling how thin the walls were in this place. He had to be careful as long as he was here.

As if responding to his thought, a quick rap sounded at his door. Bas looked over his room to make sure it was presentable, then slid the door aside.

Fritz and Collette stood outside, talking to each other about something. Bas heard only the word *cycle*.

"Good morning!" Fritz's face was mostly grin. Bas noted that he was already up on his toes. Maybe that was a good sign.

"Morning." Bas gave them both a smile.

"Oh good, it fits," Collette said, looking him up and down.

"Oh." Bas plucked at his shirt. If the uniform weren't loose by design, it would probably have been comically small on him. As it was, it only pulled if he fully extended his arms.

"Did you sleep well?" she asked. "Find everything you need?" She peered around her husband as if looking for signs of disarray in the room.

"Everything was great. I slept straight through, probably because it's so quiet."

"It is *profoundly* quiet, yes sir," Fritz said, almost conspiratorially. "So are you ready to join morning practice?"

"I *think* so?" Whatever that was, it didn't sound too challenging. Then again, were there any other sixty-year-olds in their ranks?

"You'll do fine," Collette said.

"I don't need anything?"

Fritz gave him a gentle poke in the chest. "You've got all you need."

Collette hooked her hand on Bas's forearm, coaxing him from his room. He heard Fritz slide his door shut behind him—no locks—and they made their way to the end of the dormitory wing.

"We thought it'd be nice to walk you to the courtyard," Collette said.

Something was brushing against Bas's thigh—her hip? But a quick glance revealed that it was a cloth pouch tied around her waist, the same one he had seen at the opening last week.

"Does everyone get this kind of personal attention?" he asked.

"We're not a factory, Bas," Fritz said, a smile in his voice. "This is our home."

"How many guests are there?"

"We have, let's see... fifty-two people staying here—"

"Fifty-three now," Collette interjected. "And most stay for a good amount of time."

"So you're not keeping us from pressing appointments," Fritz said.

The dorm wing fed into an open area, at the center of which sat a spherical boulder as tall as Bas. Pockmarks on its surface gave it a moonlike appearance, and water flowing from a concealed fountain at the top created a transfixing shimmer over its bulk.

"We excavated it when we were digging the foundation for the expansion," Fritz said. "We brought it up and had it retrofitted."

"The basin and the pebbles of the bed, they're all from here too," Collette added.

"Good morning, Shane." Fritz gave a nod to another man passing through. "I'll see you all in a bit."

Shane wore the same all-black garb as Bas. He smiled and nodded back.

They took a sharp turn, practically turning around to enter a wide corridor that ran at an acute angle to the dorm hallway. Bas's eye was drawn to the high transom windows, expecting to see part of the dorm from here, yet only pale morning light flooded in, unobstructed. Something about the layout definitely seemed disjointed. Then again, sleeping in an unfamiliar bed had always left Bas feeling somewhat adrift. He was probably thinking too hard about it.

"Oh, here's something you might like," Collette said.

Ahead, the wooden support beams along the ceiling gave way to open slats, allowing strips of sunlight to fall across a tree-lined pergola. At the center of this wider area sat a squat display case, like some abandoned museum furnishing.

They must be taking him the long way around, showing off their space. Their pride in the hidden industrial park retreat was oddly endearing.

Bas approached the self-lit display case, its glass shelf teeming with oddments. The collection wasn't made up of prized rarities, but of commonplace personal effects. It was as if someone had upended a dozen purses. Matchbooks, watches, money clips, lipstick cases, glasses—all were laid out as if they were precious stones. Some of the items weren't even in good condition. There was a pill bottle with half its label missing, a warped emery board, a torn two-dollar bill.

"What are these?"

Fritz sidled up behind him. "I, Mine operates at no expense to its guests. But one thing we do ask for is a token gift of some kind, as a gesture to symbolize a person's commitment—to us and to themselves—during their stay here."

"Those are the terms I spoke of before," Collette said.

Bas scanned the collection as if he were looking at the emptied-out contents of an evidence box. What picture did this paint? And why display everything like this? Who was it meant for?

Then an artifact at the very back of the display caught his eye. At first he wasn't sure what he was looking at, but that was only because it was two items merged into one. The polished wooden barrel of a fountain pen had been crudely intersected by a brushed chrome flip lighter. The two were fused in such a way as to render either article unusable. They hadn't been melted together—their individual geometries were warped only slightly—but rather they were joined, one through the other, as in one of Eshe's double-exposed photographs.

Bas caught his hand fumbling around where his pocket would have been. The composite object recalled Lana's ring, its delicate form warped by the forces of the South Station Singularity.

"Ah, yes," Collette said, following Bas's gaze. "Our hapless little amalgam."

"I always liked that one," said Fritz.

His wife chuckled. "Yes, well, there's no accounting for taste."

The air grew sharp as they approached the courtyard garden with its open roof and moss-covered stone floor. Bas couldn't help but stare as a crowd of twenty people, each dressed in the same black garb, went about a series of movements in perfect synchrony, like a kind of structured performance.

"Holy shit," he said under his breath.

It wasn't quite dance, but it wasn't exercise, either. What then?

Some home-grown, post-aerobics workout geared to stimulate mental focus? Motion practice, Fritz had called it. That was as apt a description as any.

"This is the assembly," Fritz said, looking on the group with something like admiration. "Sixteen or twenty-four of our residents are out here every day, rain or shine."

As Bas watched, it became apparent that their movements were more complex than he had at first realized. Most of the participants did move together, but within their number was a smaller group whose tai chi–like progression was out of step with the rest. There had to be a pattern to it—they were moving together, after all—but Bas was unable to anticipate how they would move from one step to the next, even after watching quietly for a minute.

As they reached some unseen inflection point, about half the practitioners broke off from the others, lined up at the far side of the garden, and deposited something into a basket, one after the other. A lone scribe stationed by the basket marked something on his pad with each deposit, then immediately scratched it out. Each person in the queue then picked something up from a second basket, which they clutched in their hands as they resumed their motion practice.

Bas looked around at the rest of the group. Every one of them had something clutched in one hand or the other.

"What is this about?"

"I'm going to make the rounds," Collette cut in, as if taking that as her cue. She gave her husband a peck on the cheek. "Bas, I'll see you later on today, probably."

Bas nodded without taking his eyes off the assembly. Another subset of the group made their way to the edge of the courtyard and lined up by the first basket.

"Stones," Fritz said, letting the explanation hang in the air. He turned to Bas. "The stones are just for focus. It's not something you need to concern yourself with now."

It sounded like a partial answer. If the stones were just for focus, why the steady supply of new ones? Maybe they were being sold as monk rocks. Maybe that was how I, Mine continued to operate tuition-free.

"Join in whenever you feel comfortable," Fritz said, his eyes on Bas. He grew several inches as he stood on his toes.

Bas's nervous laugh came out like a bark. "*How?* I don't know how to do *that*."

The group sidestepped across the mossy stones, left arms out, right arms down at their sides. At the far edge they paused, bent slightly at the knee, and moved their arms in slow opposing arcs. Then turned their backs on Bas and Fritz and moved simultaneously backward.

"None of them knew the movements when they started," Fritz said. "That's the magic of it. You just... fall into it."

The man had to be joking.

"I've never seen anything like this is my life, man. I can't see myself just '*falling into* it.'"

But as foreign as it was, something about it did seem familiar. It took Bas a moment to figure out why.

Cynda.

That little ritual she had gone through after drawing the I, Mine symbol on the pavement. It wasn't *exactly* what Bas was seeing now, but it wasn't too far off. She must have picked that up here. But why reenact it in an alley at night? Had she bought into Fritz's assertion that there was some kind of magic to it?

Fritz was squinting up at him, as if attempting to read his thoughts. "I think you're thinking there's a wrong way, and you feel intimidated."

Bas gestured toward the group. "Look at them!" It came out louder than he'd intended, and he glanced at the assembly to see if he had disrupted anything. They went about their routine as if Bas weren't there. "What I mean is, they're all doing that in unison, so obviously there's a right way."

Fritz nodded, and whispered. "I'm going to let you in on a little secret. What you're seeing here, now, we didn't come up with it. How could we have? This happened over many years. Is there a sense to it? A rhythm? Well, sure. But just because you see people swimming laps at the pool, does that mean you're not getting in?"

Bas looked at his host. "You're sure about that?"

"Everyone here started out like you, Bas. They have no formal training. And there's no need for training anyway. So I encourage you to get in there and do what moves you. Start with what you see if you want. Or don't. Just get your blood pumping. At the very least it's a workout."

Bas's palms were wet. Was he really considering this? It might give him some clearer insight into Cynda's state of mind. Or maybe he was just fooling himself, and was joining a cult to cover up the fact that his life had gone off the rails.

"For how long?" he heard himself ask.

"When you're ready to stop, you stop."

Bas looked at Fritz, who was still up on his toes. "You're not joining me?"

"No." He smiled.

The moss under Bas's slippers made it feel like he was walking on clouds. Fritz had already left, probably to spare him the added humiliation, which he appreciated.

Bas kept as far away from the assembly as possible, standing in the shadow of the eaves as he did some warm-up stretches. He had never been a dancer, but in his boxing prime his workouts would routinely have him sweating for hours every other day. Now his joints sounded like someone stepping on a Cracker Jack box, and the threat of pulling something seemed all too likely.

Soon his warm-up was only making him feel even more conspicuous. So Bas planted his feet on two of the flat, round stones, and moved his arms in a slow arc, as if he were doing slow-motion jumping jacks. The movement bore some passing resemblance to the patterns of the others, at least in spirit. If anyone asked, he could say he had given it a shot.

He would stick with it for a few minutes, then take a tour of the rest of the facility. If he ran into Fritz or Collette—or one of the other residents—then he could try to get some answers about Cynda, and see where things led from there.

Thinking of Cynda, Bas closed his eyes and played the tape back in his head. She had been squatting during her performance, but most of her movement had been in her arms and hands. She had begun with broad symmetrical gestures, and then one hand would freeze—palm facing in—while her other arm went through ever smaller versions of the initial movement, until her two palms were facing each other, an inch apart. Then she would do a variation on the same thing, only favoring the opposite arm.

Bas aped what he had seen her do, not attempting to match the motions of the assembly in any way. Fritz had said it didn't matter, and he was right. This was just a means to an end.

After a few minutes the stiffness in his joints began to fade, and as his heart rate rose, Bas was grateful for the morning's lingering chill. At first he kept an eye on the rest of the assembly—if only to avoid tripping over them, though he never strayed from his corner of the courtyard. But he decided it was easier to run through his improvised routine with his eyes shut.

Once he gave himself permission to look like a fool, the initial sense of awkwardness vanished, and he became engrossed by the repetition of his movements. His pulse throbbed behind his ears, but unlike his basement match with Wallace, this time it wasn't accompanied by an onset of seasickness or impending doom. The truth was, he hadn't felt this invigorated in years.

Runner's high, that's what they called it. That, and something more. It was almost as if his movements were forming a picture in his mind's eye. He imagined strings trailing from the tips of his fingers, each motion tying off another row of color before moving to the next, his hands working an invisible loom. Eyes still shut, he fell into a tempo that vaguely matched that of the group, while maintaining his unique interpretation of Cynda's ritual.

Suddenly he thought of Lana—and he saw her more clearly than he had in years.

The chicken pox scar on her forehead that crinkled when she smiled.

The way her laugh went hoarse when she gave herself over to something joyful.

Her steady gaze on him, which never failed to stir a feeling of intoxication and unworthiness.

He hadn't felt that way in more than a decade, and though he now braced himself for the inevitable stab of loss, he felt only a gentle reassurance, and even nostalgia.

What bullshit.

Bas let his hands fall to his sides and opened his eyes. The sun was directly overhead now, creating a perfect square of light on the moss. His mouth had gone dry.

Heart racing, he overcame a moment of disorientation and made his way over to the far side of the garden, where a spout dribbled fresh water into a stone basin. He grabbed one of the paper cups stacked to the side and filled it several times before he was sated.

How long had he been out here? It must have been hours, judging by the sun. But it had seemed like minutes.

He wandered over to the scribe—it was a woman now—still careful to avoid the assembly. As he approached, she looked at his hand, then met his eye with a curious look.

The stones.

"Uh, sorry. I didn't get one."

"Pardon me."

Bas jumped and nearly spilled his water as someone tapped his shoulder. A line of motion workers had queued up behind him.

He moved to the other side of the scribe as she read the stone of each person in line. Her pad was full of half-erased gibberish—a series of freeform doodles, one after the other, each one followed by the I, Mine logo. None of the squiggles took more than a few seconds for her to draw, and she crossed them out—and the logo—as soon as they were complete, just in time to examine the stone of the next person in line. Pulse still quick in his chest, Bas remembered a documentary about Tibetan monks painstakingly creating their sand mandalas, only to destroy them immediately upon completion.

As he looked out over the assembly, a flood of adrenaline made his heart skip a beat. Had he fallen for it? Was that feeling of euphoria nothing more than the power of suggestion? Fritz and Collette had intimated that their rituals might invite the mystical. And now he'd ridden an endorphin high through several hours of arm-waving.

But it wasn't mystical. And it wasn't just the endorphins, either. It was Lana. Over time, Bas had discovered that boxing up his grief allowed him to approach her memories without succumbing to the despair. More than once, Lana herself had remarked—more with curiosity than appreciation—on Bas's tendency to compartmentalize. Another memory. The Singularity had taken everything else. So what choice did he have? If there was a better way to push through the bad days, Bas had never discovered it. But today he had experienced a more intimate kind of recollection. Not just a memory, but a vision. Something electric, vital. Something dislodged only after he had forgotten himself.

Or maybe it was all just a coincidence.

―――

Fritz was waving to him from the edge of the main passage. Bas gave him a nod, then circled the perimeter of the garden. How long would the assembly be out here? If new members had tagged in since the morning, Bas hadn't seen it.

"Hey there, Bas," Fritz said. He had changed since the morning, and now wore a suit and tie. "I was wondering if you wanted to get some food. I imagine you must be hungry."

"I could definitely eat," Bas said with a chuckle, joining his host down an adjoining corridor.

He was still up after his experience in the courtyard. Fritz read it on his face.

"I hope you don't mind my saying, but you look like a new man."

"Yeah." Bas shook his head. "I admit, I didn't know what to expect, but that was really something. I don't know if I did it right or wrong, but..."

"It's hard to describe, isn't it?"

The corridor ended in a T, and they took the left leg, heading up a shallow ramp to the second level. At the top, a cloistered hall was open to a broad court on one side and more of the paper panels on the other. With the natural light setting the area aglow, there was no need for extra interior lighting. More I, Mine residents were in evidence here, some walking in pairs, others sitting in small classrooms.

Bas looked at Fritz. "Do you and Collette participate?"

"In the assembly, you mean? Or...?"

"Yeah."

His lips tightened. "You know, *I* do on occasion. But Collette..." He cocked his head, then motioned down another hall, this one lined with thin-leafed trees. "Well, that's actually a larger question. To be honest, my wife and I sometimes have very different ideas about how to proceed with this endeavor of ours."

Fritz managed to avoid making it sound like he was gossiping. But why such candor, and with someone he barely knew? It might just be who he was, or maybe it was something else he could show off.

"How do you mean?" Bas asked.

"Well, I'm sure you've noticed, but I tend to be more spiritual. Touchy-feely, she'd call it, and she's not wrong. She's always been more pragmatic. I'm not saying we don't see eye to eye in the broadest sense." He shrugged. "I'd say her path is parallel to mine, just maybe one track over."

Bas thought of Lana's painting, which she would often disappear into when she got home from the animal shelter. It had been an inherently solitary practice, and had often meant evenings spent in separate rooms.

"Do you miss it?" Fritz's eyes were on Bas's hand, which was up by his chest again.

No pocket, no ring.

"What's that?" Bas asked, trying to play it off as a nervous habit. Which it surely was.

"You probably don't even know you were checking it—your pocket, I mean—but I saw you doing it at dinner the other night, too. Something's... missing?"

Fritz didn't acknowledge a guest as she passed them going the other way. The man's full attention was on Bas.

Bas drew a breath. "My wife's ring."

"Oh?"

"She died in the Singularity," Bas said.

Fritz stopped and put a hand on Bas's shoulder. "I'm so sorry, Bas. Of *course* it's been on your mind."

Bas nodded. "They sent me her ring after they were done sifting through everything. I carried it with me every day. At least till recently, when I... lost it."

"Oh, no. I absolutely see it," Fritz said, standing up on his toes. "Believe me, I do."

Bas believed him.

Before their quiet moment became awkward, Fritz gave Bas a pat on the shoulder. "Come on, the cafeteria is just this way."

The smell of food wafted into the hall from up ahead.

"You know, I felt close with her again today. With Lana."

Fritz glanced over. "Close? During your practice, you mean?"

"Almost like she was... not *with* me, but yeah, close by somehow."

Fritz didn't say anything, as if he was going over what Bas had just told him.

"That sounds weird, I know," Bas said.

"No, no, I was just thinking about how impressed I am."

Impressed?

Fritz stopped again and looked up at him. "Have you done that kind of work before?"

It wasn't the question Bas had expected after such an admission.

"No," he said. "Like I said before, I've never seen anything like that, with the assembly."

Fritz's eyes narrowed. Was he not convinced?

But he finally grinned his odd grin, and gestured to the end of the hall.

"Come on, let's eat."

29

WEDNESDAY, MAY 1, 1991

MUCH TO BRENDA'S PUZZLEMENT, Dee had spent the afternoon in her room for the third day in a row. Dee could have whispered to her and Walter that she had something else to focus on now—that she hadn't lost interest in gardening—but she wasn't ready to reveal her whisper ability to them yet. She'd only whispered to Gisela and Junmo because she'd been forced to. And until she figured out where all this led, she would leave it at that.

Anyway, how could she have explained what she was doing in her room? *Don't mind me, I'm only conjuring holes in the air by stimming the special combination?*

Instead, Dee had given Brenda a rare and reassuring hug—one that told Brenda everything Dee needed her to know: *I'm fine, I'm happy. And I'll see you at dinner.*

Dee closed her bedroom door behind her and settled in for another session. Yesterday she had used her *fingerglow* to summon the light pockets again, just to prove the first time hadn't been a fluke. It wasn't. Now that she knew the sequence, she could call them up in seconds, even if their size and location were still somewhat unpredictable.

But conjuring them meant she had to be better at making them go away. Not just better—perfect. She had begun small, calling up the smallest formation she could manage, then unraveling it as if she were tugging the thread of an old sweater. It wasn't easy, especially not at first. She couldn't partially erase a pattern. It was either all there or it was all gone. But the manual work alone had been infuriating—forcing her fingers to run through calculated patterns was far more difficult than the instinctual kinds. It was easier to knock the planter over than it was to clean up the dirt.

Taking her place on the edge of the bed, Dee conjured one of the light structures with a few coordinated finger moves. Today the blueish hue was nearly gone, as if the electrical fields had matured to a more stable silver-yellow, like some common fruit. The complex form hanging before her was made up of smaller pulsing fibers. Together, the delicate construct was about as wide as Dee's forearm, and resembled a flower petal under a microscope, or maybe a butterfly's wing. Whatever it was, it didn't look so much constructed as *grown*, similar to the old *fingerglow* streamers, only more complex. These specimens, Dee had decided, were not sculpture; she hadn't drawn them the way an artist produces a portrait. She had only figured out how to summon them, piece by piece. But from where?

That was what she meant to find out. After all, if a light pocket led from here to somewhere else, she was already halfway to an answer.

She stood, moving carefully around the light pattern, and went to her dresser. Yesterday she had established that she could reliably summon the pocket, and that she could still put her hand through.

Now it was time to push a little farther.

Dee looked over her collection of succulents. For her purposes any of them would do, but she thought it best to start with something compact, something she could easily clutch in one hand. Her eye settled on the lithops. More commonly known as the pebble plant, its signature characteristic was two plump dome-like leaves, each with an intricate pattern over its translucent top. On first seeing the plant,

Junmo had dubbed it a *butt brain*. But its scientific classification was more interesting.

Plantae, Angiosperms, Eudicots, Caryophyllales, Aizoaceae, Ruschioideae, Ruschiae, Lithops.

From *lithos* for stone, and *ops* for face. Stone-face.

Dee removed the small ceramic pot from its neighbors, then took it with her to the bed, positioning herself before the golden filaments.

Ready to go on a little trip, little stone-face?

She held the plant before her, an inch from the opening, then moved it forward, watching as the light glimmered around her right hand, then the pot, then her wrist. She held her arm steady, studying every detail.

Beyond the light pocket, no part of her hand was visible, though her hand was still at the end of her arm, and her fingers still encircled the small pot.

Reaching her left hand around the side of the structure, she waved it through the space where her right hand should have been, and encountered no resistance. Her hand wasn't just invisible, it had punched through to somewhere else entirely. Or maybe into no place at all.

Slowly, she brought her right hand back out, shivering at the tickle along her delicate hairs. On close examination of the lithops she detected no change at all. It was intact, as was her hand.

She dismissed the light pocket, then just as quickly summoned it again. Easy. Both actions now took barely more than a flick of the wrist. She was getting better at this, no doubt about that, even if her secret feat served no discernible purpose.

But this was just the start. She had found the light pocket by accident, after having played with *fingerglow* for years. What could she call forth if she really applied herself?

Delight welled up in her, and she rocked on the edge of her bed until the strain of the mattress springs threatened to draw attention. Time to put everything away, until tomorrow's session.

She got up to return the lithops—or at least that's what she told her body to do. But in her excitement, some circuit in her head must have gone offline, and instead she shoved her arm back through the light pocket and opened her hand. The edge of the pot brushed by her little finger as the plant fell, and then was lost.

Dammit, Dee!

She pulled her hand back, empty. Where had her stone-face gone?

Carefully, she moved her arm forward again. Of course she was back in control, now that it was too late. Reaching into the pocket, she angled herself forward until her arm was inside almost to the shoulder. Fingers splayed, she waved her hand up and down, and from side to side, but felt nothing at all. No surface, no resistance, no heat or cold. As far as she could tell, there was only emptiness, stretching out to infinity.

A question occurred to her: What if she kept pushing forward, and entered the light pocket? What might she find inside?

And would she be nowhere then, too?

30

WEDNESDAY, MAY 1, 1991

BAS RECEIVED no escort on the second morning.

His first day had been so regimented—from the assembly work, to the meals, to the evening classes about sleep yoga and emergent behavior patterns—that the sudden freedom felt a little intoxicating.

Wandering the facility, he spent some minutes debating whether the lack of scrutiny represented trust, or a test. But, he reminded himself, he wasn't here to get invested.

Instead he treated himself to a real breakfast—the better to track down some familiar faces. The buffet offered a wide selection of breakfast fare, with nary a cash register in sight.

Unfortunately, the I, Mine residents must have been observing a different schedule, and the cafeteria was nearly empty at eight in the morning. Bas joined a couple who, before he had even sat down, had already given him their excuses for sitting out today's assembly. The woman had injured her foot during motion practice last night, and the man wasn't feeling well.

Bas settled in for a discussion of I, Mine from the perspective of its residents, but scarcely got a word in. The couple spent the entirety of their meal talking about the end of the Gulf War, the Rodney King fiasco, and an impromptu review of *The Silence of the Lambs*. Bas stayed long enough to be polite, then excused himself.

He set off in search of the immense fountain boulder, which, on reflection, bore some resemblance to the tiny stones used by the assembly. As he padded down the soft mat floors, he couldn't help but wonder whether he was making progress, or just filling time with activity. How close was he to finding a unified explanation of recent events? Or was a regimen of strangely intensive interpretive dance routines and pseudo-philosophical lectures a laughable distraction?

Turning a corner, Bas stopped in his tracks. He hadn't managed to find the ramp down to the ground level, yet here the boulder was. Or maybe this was a second boulder of the same proportions. It was so unexpected that Bas didn't at first notice Kit seated on a bench—until the man hastily rose to depart, and the tool belt around his waist made such a racket that Bas could have located him in the dark.

"Kit, wasn't it?" Bas was across the room in a few strides. "We met at the opening last week?"

Kit stopped in his tracks and turned, his furrowed brow undermining his smile.

"Oh, right. Sorry, remind me...?"

"Bas. Good to see a familiar face."

"Yeah, glad you made it. So how... you know, are you enjoying yourself?"

Bas licked his lower lip. Their conversation had been cut short the first time, right after Kit had gone pale at the mention of Cynda Bolden. Now it was time to tease that thread.

The wood of the bench creaked as Bas took a seat. "How could I not? I mean, hearing about I, Mine is one thing, but seeing the operation with my own eyes is something else."

"The operation?" But Kit had taken the hint. He sat at the other side of the bench and stared straight ahead at the boulder.

"I'm talking about the spread, and the daily routines. Everything Fritz and Collette have built here. Not to mention the perks, like the food. And all of it *free*? I mean really, you wonder why someone would want to leave."

"Yeah, well, you know. So here we are." He sat up and gave his tool belt a little twist, but didn't meet Bas's eye.

No reason to drag this out any further. "So we were talking, before, about my friend."

"Right."

"Cynda Bolden."

"Right, yeah. I don't—"

"And it sounded like you knew her."

"I don't like to speak out of school. You know."

Out of school?

"No, man, we're all friends here." Bas slid an inch closer to him. "I'm not asking you to gossip. We're just discussing a mutual friend. I assume you two were friendly?"

Kit wanted to be gone, that much was clear. He was less willing to make it official.

"You did know her, right? Maybe you were friends, you spent time together...?"

"It was never like that." Kit was looking at Bas now. "Why, were you two—"

"Father and daughter?" Bas put up a hand. "No, as I told you at the open house, we were acquaintances. And I wasn't implying anything about you."

Kit's shoulders fell a bit. "She was just a good person, that's the truth. And she was good here. She made so much progress, and really contributed to I, Mine."

"How's that?"

"Well for one thing, the regimen completely changed. With the assembly, I mean."

"Changed how?"

His eyes were back on the burbling stone. "I don't know how much sense it'd make to you, since you're new. But her approach to the patterns came from pure instinct. What she brought to it was her own thing, you know. Unique. You saw the assembly?"

"Bright and early yesterday morning."

"Okay, you know then. But a big part of the work they're doing now came straight from Cynda."

He made it sound like they were building something.

"I thought the goal of the motion practice was just a Zen thing. Relaxation, physical therapy. It's not?"

The longer they talked, the tighter Kit's face got. He really didn't like the questions.

"The goal... is all about what you bring to it, really."

Now he was just toeing the line.

"What does Fritz bring to it?"

Kit sat up straight and rubbed his palms on his silk uniform. "Hey, look, it's really not for me to... you know. If you want to know about Cynda, that's one thing."

"Fine, let's stick with Cynda. She comes here, wows everyone with her natural gifts, and then what? She hightails it out of here? Why would she do that?"

"I have no idea."

That, at least, sounded like honest puzzlement.

"You miss her?"

"Sure." He glanced at Bas. "How did you guys...?"

"Friends with her father."

Kit nodded. He didn't need to express much; the pathetic look on his face said everything. He was keen on her, even if he didn't acknowledge it to himself.

"She was the restless type, and a total skeptic. But that kind of fell away, a lot of it, during her time here. I was here when she showed up, January of last year."

"And she left?"

"Few weeks ago. April seventh. That morning she didn't come to assembly, and by the time we thought to check her room she was already gone. She hadn't even taken her stuff with her." Kit unsnapped one of the compartments on his utility belt, then snapped it again. "We sometimes keep tabs on our residents on the outside."

Bas remained still. Was this a confession?

"It's just for their safety. You know. I help out in the video lab, so... I know it sounds weird to say we check in on former guests, but it's really more like a guardian angel thing. Anyway, it didn't matter with Cynda, because she..." He looked at Bas. "She still managed to fall off our radar. We don't know where she is."

"So what did you do then?"

"Tried to let it go. Except I couldn't. Then I wanted to tell her family, but I couldn't do that either. So I... I have access... I went into her records, here, and copied the latest video we have of her. And then, at the next open house, I—"

"You smuggled a tape out?" It was the Cynda tape. It had to be.

"I know, it wasn't the explanation her family would have wanted. And maybe I'm a coward, and I—"

"A cryptic surveillance tape? *That's* what you send them?"

"I couldn't do the right thing, man, okay? But I could do *something*. So that's what I did. It's more than anyone else did. If it were up to them..."

Bas put his hands up on hearing the desperation in the man's voice. The prospect of passing along even a partial explanation to the outside petrified him. But had Kit really thought a tape with zero context would be better than nothing at all? Bas thought back to his brief encounter with Bolden that night in his office, and worked his lip as the guilt flared up.

"Can you at least tell me how it works?" Bas asked. "I mean, if you're all in here, how are you tracking your members on the outside? What are you watching in this video lab?"

Kit shook his head as he stood. "I shouldn't have—"

Bas got to his feet. "Kit, I'd love to tour the lab. Do you think you could set that up?"

Collette breezed into the fountain area. "Kit, I thought you were going to see to the lighting situation."

No hesitation, as if she had known she would find him here.

While she was focused on her handyman, Bas took the opportunity to scan for cameras. If this operation was so adept at tracking people on the outside, they must surely have the inside covered. But if they had mounted cameras, Bas couldn't spot any. Which only made him more suspicious.

"Right, I didn't have my multimeter, so I got it from the exec storage on the fifth, uh, circuit. You know."

Had he just said fifth circuit? Why did it sometimes sound like they were using English to speak a different language?

Whatever he had meant, Collette was glaring at him as if he had just insulted her mother at her funeral.

"And then I met up with..." He indicated Bas. "So we were just chatting. But okay, so I'll just..." He edged toward the hallway.

"Thank you, Kit," Collette said, lips drawn into a smile.

Bas pushed away the notion that he was in trouble for... how had Kit put it? For speaking out of school. Still, Collette did have an air of authority about her.

"Good morning, Collette."

Her eyes were still on the hall, as if to ensure Kit was doing what he said he would do.

"I'm sorry about him," she said.

Over the faint smell of fountain chlorine, Bas thought he detected cigarettes on her breath.

"Nothing to be sorry about. Just shooting the breeze with a familiar face."

"That man will shoot more than the breeze if you get him going. Oh, he means well, but he's... a bit of a '*true believer.*'"

Her air quotes elicited a surprised laugh from Bas. She had to be aware of the shock value of such sudden candor. In that way Collette and her husband were very similar.

"Anyway, I'm surprised not to find you up with assembly today."

Up?

Probably just a figure of speech.

"Right, well I thought I'd see what else you had going here. Shake things up a little."

She raised her eyebrows. Was that surprise or disapproval?

"Did you find anything interesting?"

Besides the disorienting floor plan, the all-day dance rituals, and skittish staff members smuggling out secretly taped sightings of former members?

"I may need to recalibrate, because I'm finding it *all* very interesting."

"A good problem to have, I should think." She put an arm out. "Walk with me?"

Bas obliged, following her lead into the corridor opposite the one Kit had just stumbled down. They passed a series of classrooms on their left, currently empty, while the wall to the right opened up to a multi-level interior garden. A shallow pool set into the floor reflected the frond-filtered sun, creating a dance of light along the walls and ceiling. Only the murmur of water filters broke the silence.

Kendall Square had never been so tranquil as this. The cacophony of industry and construction should have been coursing through the open roof, but Fritz's and Collette's business district tribute to their Kyushu retreat seemed to have transported them away from Boston's biotech gulch.

"Hard to get over how quiet it is here," Bas said. "And at midday, mid-week."

"That was the idea." She paused, as if to prepare an explanation. "Fritz told me about your experience yesterday."

"Oh."

She hadn't just happened on Kit and him. It was Bas she had been looking for, and he now understood why she looked so preoccupied.

"Yeah, that was something." Bas thought about it. "Or maybe it was nothing."

"Don't be so quick to discount it. You're not the first to respond that way, though the experience tends to be different for everyone."

Bas nodded, but kept his silence.

"Then again," Collette added, squeezing his arm in hers, "the same could probably be said for an endorphin high."

Bas laughed. There was that commonsense note slipping out again.

"You don't go for the spiritual thing?" he asked.

"Oh, you know, people see things as they understand them. Personally, it's never been my interest to achieve a higher level of consciousness, or whatever you want to call it. I'm fine where I am, thank you. But what I, Mine *is* is about the people. That's what it comes down to for me. If you want to call that spiritual, be my guest, but I never have."

It was the other side of Fritz's conversation yesterday. Was that purely by chance, or were they employing their spin on the old joint questioning routine?

"But our assembly really seems to be getting a lot out of the motion work, and that keeps us going as much as them."

They had somehow made it back to the mouth of the residential wing, with the immense stone on their right. So there were two of these stones—perhaps more. But Bas hadn't recognized their approach. The I, Mine facility was a labyrinth without appearing the least bit labyrinthine.

The thought reminded him of Kit's words. The fifth circuit. What had he meant by that? Circuit. Assuming it wasn't just a nervous slip-up, what could that be?

Collette unhooked her arm from Bas's and gave him a look that made him feel like there was something on his face.

"Uh, so what did you do before I, Mine?" he asked.

"Programmer," she said, without changing her expression. "It ended up being a lot of database work, but editing code was always where I was happiest."

A woman emerged from the residential hall and gave Collette a nod as the two of them parted to let her pass.

Bas was getting preferential treatment, that much was clear. But why? Why did Collette and Fritz think he was here? They had surely compared notes on him—and why wouldn't they?

As he looked at her, Collette raised her eyebrows and cocked her head, as if to say, *Anything else?* In that moment he felt like an interloper who had infiltrated their compound for ulterior motives. Maybe that was a choice.

Bas tried to get his thoughts straight.

The idea of inquiring about Cynda Bolden outright might have seemed careless before his little powwow with Kit. Bas's knowledge of her had been the ace up his sleeve. But that had changed, hadn't it? He knew more about the missing woman now—namely, that Kit had known her. Collette and Fritz had to have known her too, which provided Bas with a more playable ace.

"I didn't mention it before, but I knew someone who used to be here. Do you remember a former I, Mine guest named Cynda Bolden?"

Now he would see if Collette was a guileless as she came across.

Her expression changed like the sheerest cloud passing between Bas and the sun. She looked off, squinting as if reassessing something.

"I do remember Cynda. How could I not?" Her eyes returned to Bas. "Were you together?"

"Friends."

"She was a real handful, that one. At least at first. Which always struck Fritz and me as strange, since she had come to us. But everything we did or said, she would challenge. It took us some time to realize she wasn't just being difficult, she was trying to figure out how it all worked." Collette sighed. "I guess I shouldn't have been so surprised at the suddenness of her departure. For all I know she's running another I, Mine somewhere out there."

"So you don't know where she ended up?"

"She didn't leave us a note." Her eyes lingered on Bas. "Not for you either?"

Bas shrugged.

"Did you just make a confession to me, Bas?"

He wasn't sure how to answer that one.

She gave his arm a friendly shake. "Don't get me wrong. I'm glad we can talk like this. And I wish I had more information about your friend."

Didn't she? Had she just confessed something of her own? Kit had mentioned records, not to mention the video.

"It was worth asking," Bas said. He needed time to chew this over.

"It's always worth asking. Nothing is as important as the connections we forge with others. Even with those who are no longer with us."

Bas checked his hand, to make sure it was nowhere near Lana's phantom ring. Collette knew—he saw it in her eye. She didn't miss much, but there was more to her—more to both of them—than she let on.

"I hope you'll consider attending one of our evening classes." Collette's hand had gone to the pouch around her waist. "You'll have seen the schedules posted everywhere. We have everything from mindfulness meditation to sand sculpture. I sometimes lead a class I call 'Statistics All Around Us,' though not this evening. But it would be great to see you there. Shake things up a little, as you said."

"I may take you up on that."

Bas's mid-afternoon nap had lasted far too long, and he awoke just before nine p.m. clumsy with fatigue. Maybe it was the I, Mine uniform—the loose-fitting silk fabric was just too comfortable.

In an attempt to make up for lost time, he hastily made his way out to the common area, his hair still a mess. Maybe he would sit in on a class, or just go for a spirited walk.

But most of the meeting rooms were empty. He had missed the evening classes, save for one called *'Making Peace with Your Neurobiology,'* whose instructor was delivering a sermon-like address. It was a popular topic judging by the crowd in the room. Bas lingered by the entrance for a minute, standing in the relative dimness of the corridor, but the subject left him cold. A walk it was then.

He retreated back into the main hall, strolled past the trophy case, and continued around to the second boulder. Maybe I, Mine wasn't as labyrinthine as he had assumed—another day or so and he would have the layout down.

As he walked, he considered his next steps. Tomorrow he would start over, maybe find Kit, and ask around about Wallace. He might even put in some time with the assembly if he was feeling up to it.

By the time he had completed a lap around the perimeter corridor, his stomach was complaining. He had skipped dinner, and he had no provisions in his room. A vending machine would have come in handy, but Fritz would never have allowed such a thing to blight the premises.

A quick visit to the cafeteria then.

Bas passed by the classrooms area once more, but now found them all empty and the lights out. Had everyone made peace with their neurobiology so quickly?

He passed by the display case a second time, then paused at the ramp to the second floor. His stomach was still making rude sounds, but something Kit had said had been replaying in his head, and now it stopped him in his tracks.

On the fifth circuit.

The way Kit had said that made it sound less like a thing, and more like a *location*, as if he had left his tool there. Maybe "The Fifth Circuit" was a place. Bas had certainly lost the time of day in pubs with more entertaining names.

But something about that particular turn of phrase was proving hard to dismiss, especially given I, Mine's unreliable layout. The stone fountain hadn't always seemed to be in the same place, and earlier that day Collette had wondered why he hadn't been "up with assembly," even though the courtyard garden was on the same floor.

Either people were rearranging things when he wasn't looking, or... what?

Bas shook his head. Maybe his session with the assembly had scrambled his perspective. He chuckled at the idea, picturing himself lost in a simple loop.

And yet a thought remained with him for far too long as he stood in the empty corridor. Holding such a thought might leave an impression, like staring too long at a photograph.

What if the perimeter walk wasn't as linear as it appeared?

Even the slightest incline might induce disorientation. But then a circuit really could mean something.

It was nonsense.

But...

Bas eyed the ramp. One last chance to forget this nonsense and grab something to eat. Food was another way to alter his mental state —and give him all the perspective he needed. With none of the woo-woo.

Well. The two options weren't mutually exclusive. Three and a half more laps and he could stop by the cafeteria, a little hungrier and only slightly humiliated.

On his third time around, the *Making Peace with Your Neurobiology* class was back in full swing as if there had never been an intermission. The logical explanation was that the participants had all gone on a late-night field trip, then returned in the time it took Bas to complete a lap.

But seeing that room full of people quickened Bas's heart. If he had only paid more attention the first time around he could be more confident that everything in that room had been restored to its prior state—not just the people at their desks, but the instructor's place in his lecture, the postures of the participants, and even the positions of their pens on their notepads. Yet he suspected everything wasn't *quite* the same. Even without a photographic memory, the scene before him felt like the continuation of a film reel with one frame missing.

As he walked, he only grew more certain that he owed it to himself not to dismiss his intuition. He had sensed something off since he had first stepped foot in the I, Mine complex—the disorientation, the odd details, the inconsistencies. Brushing those things aside had seemed like the sensible thing to do at the time. But now...

Assuming he *wasn't* losing his mind, what other explanation could there be?

He did a double-take when he next reached the display case.

The shelf within was empty.

Palms sweating, he went over for a closer inspection. Same case, same place, but the junk inside had been cleared out.

Or it was still there and he wasn't seeing it.

Why would he even think that?

He leaned close to the case, peering at the glass shelf within. No trace remained of the artifacts he had seen previously, nor even dust silhouettes or handprints. The display case was as empty as the classroom had been on the second circuit.

Same case.

Now empty.

And it wasn't because someone had emptied it out.

Bas moved away from the case and surveyed the pergola, the trees, and the corridor. Had he been following a cleverly camouflaged spiral the whole time? And if so, to what end? This was no mystery house. No—he definitely would have detected even the subtlest grade as he made his way around the outer loop.

He eyed the hall ahead. It was clearly the same hall.

Maybe this was a lucid dream. If it was, he could do anything he wanted. But anything might happen, too. He remembered reading that the trick to extending a lucid dream was to spin. Did walking in slow circuits count?

Rubbing his moist palms together, he continued.

The fourth time around, the classrooms were empty again, and dark. In fact, most of the indirect lighting along the corridor had been dimmed or turned off completely. Though that wasn't unusual in itself—it was fast approaching midnight. He noted the empty trophy case once more as he passed—no change there.

But then, another surprise. On the next leg of the corridor, where there should have been a ramp to the upper floor... it wasn't there. The outer wall was solid, as if there had never been a ramp.

Bas pressed on unabated, letting the questions flit around his mind like moths. Was this real? If it was, then where was he? And what if the way out wasn't the same as the way in?

As he rounded the last half of the fourth circuit, he encountered no boulder. The open area was large enough to accommodate one, but it simply wasn't there, and never had been by the look of it.

Heading down the final leg of the walk, Bas stepped carefully. The residential wing was still there, albeit in complete darkness. But the classrooms along the next leg were missing entirely.

He was in unmapped territory. Or maybe "unmappable" was more accurate.

In place of the classrooms were several paper-lined sliding doors. Bas read the inscribed plates over the first few.

Maint. Supply
Elect. Control
AV Lab

That last one caught Bas's eye, not just because Kit had mentioned the video lab, but because the framed paper panels were illuminated from within, casting a faint blue glow into the hall.

"Tomorrow, most likely."

A man's voice, coming from the video lab. Judging by the silence after, he was speaking to someone over the phone.

Bas crept closer to the door.

"Yeah, already did, but I can leave it out if that's..." Pause. "Okay, yup yup."

Adrenaline coursed through Bas's system. Someone's conversation had just ended, and if they emerged from that room now it would be bad news. There was nowhere to hide. Damn the minimalist interior design.

Bas slipped farther down the hallway, hoping the relative darkness there might be enough to avoid drawing attention to himself.

The video lab door slid to the side.

Bas pressed himself to the wall, feeling about as invisible as one of the boulder fountains.

But the man who came out was preoccupied with something in his hand. He slid the door shut behind him and headed back the way Bas had come, all the while rolling something around in his palm.

Bas's muscles remained taut until the padding of the man's feet faded. He might come back, or they might be in the middle of a shift change. In any case, it was a bad idea to linger.

Bas went to the door of the AV lab and gave it a quick once-over before trying it. There were no locks or scanners that he could see. And why should there be? This room didn't usually exist. Which was by far the best security scheme he had yet come across.

Sliding the door aside, Bas found himself face to face with a wall of screens framed by packed shelves on either side. Most of the screens showed a close-up of one or another of the sleeping residents of I, Mine. And as he watched, the faces swapped out with new faces, one after the other.

Everyone here was being actively monitored.

"No shit."

Bas entered the lab and slid the door shut behind him. Two office chairs were positioned before a control console in front of the monitor bank. Balanced on the edge of the console was a log book with "05/1991" on the cover, next to a secure telephone. This was a small security operation, largely automated by the look of it. The equipment was top of the line, with color monitors, an integrated frame buffer, and a video printer off to the side. Collette and Fritz had spared no expense.

As the marching array of residents flashed up on the screens like the subjects of some intricate lab experiment, Bas found his analytical side kicking in. His eyes flicked from tube to tube before he spotted the single constant. The framing of each face was as precise as a mugshot, tight and centered, whether the person slept on their side or on their back.

Then one of the young women switched from sleeping on her left side to her right. And as she turned over, her camera rotated with her, as if it were mounted to a jib, remaining locked to her face the whole time.

How?

"This is how they taped Cynda."

Bas tried to picture it. Maybe I, Mine had figured out how to mount tiny cameras to silent miniature helicopters. But that wouldn't explain the insomniac on the next screen, head on his pillow, eyes wide open, staring straight ahead through the space where the camera would have been.

If there was a camera there—much less a miniature helicopter—he clearly didn't see it.

The few screens that weren't trained on the residents were focused exclusively on the exterior of the warehouse—mostly doors and windows—plus one wide shot of the courtyard garden and its few assembly participants, going about their ritual late into the night.

Bas turned away from the wall of surveillance and studied the shelves. Spines of tapes faced him in rows, sorted chronologically, twenty-four hours a day, going back... years, according to their labels. Something had to be driving that kind of dedication. Why monitor every moment of every resident's movements? And why keep those recordings even beyond their stay here?

Bas could only assume he was somewhere in their archive now, too.

At one end of the console was a single VHS tape sitting inside its case. The plain label on its spine—1981—made Bas's stomach drop. A Post-it note was affixed to the top.

Fritz, tape #1

So. I, Mine had been making these recordings for at least a decade.

Bas had popped the case open before he thought to hesitate. He had no reason to play it—not even curiosity—except he would probably never get another chance.

He would give it a look, and then leave. He would try to get some rest in his monitored room, and he would check out first thing the next morning. Then he would call Mitch and beg for a regular post, anywhere. Something reliable.

Something boring.

He pushed the tape into the closest player and sat in one of the chairs. The leftmost monitor on the bottom row went dark for a moment as the spooling mechanism clicked into place.

The face that appeared on screen was absolutely the last face he expected to see.

Lana.

There she was, in the South Station, center frame, in full color. On her face, crisp and clear, was an expression so neutral that it resembled a mask. She was far less emotional here than she had been an hour before this footage was captured.

"A dream. I'm dreaming..."

Lana strode forward with purpose—hands free of luggage or personal effects—and pushed a man backward, over the railing of a second-floor balcony. The man struggled to remain upright, but his center of gravity was too high, and he grabbed for her arms in an attempt to pull himself forward. As stunned travelers and commuters rushed to provide assistance, Lana continued her shove, sending the man right over the edge.

Her arms dropped to her sides, and as the first responders grabbed her, or the railing, the video glitched and went white.

Bas stared at the white screen until it was burned into his retinas.

His hand went to the jog wheel and he rolled the video back, playing it once more at the slowest speed.

Lana.

Eyes fixed on the man passing by.

Reaching forward with both hands.

No hesitation.

Pushing him back.

Bas tapped pause, freezing the moment. The skylights glinted off Lana's wedding ring. A few months later Bas would pick up that same ring from a utilitarian trailer set up to distribute personal belongings recovered from the site.

Evidence deemed irrelevant.

Bas had seen this same footage only days before, along with everyone else watching the news. Except that the television broadcast provided only an indistinct black-and-white blur. This footage was in full color, as crisp as the video on the *Cynda* tape.

No surveillance camera from 1981 could have captured such a high quality picture.

Only I, Mine had the means to pull that off.

Bas heard a sound from the hallway, and his finger stabbed at the eject button. He tore the cassette from the mouth of the machine and tucked it into his tunic. As he crossed the lab the tape settled by his waist, just above his cinched belt, cold on his skin.

His shoulder to the wall beside the door, Bas strained to listen. For all he knew, he was being recorded even now, his personal camera flitting around his head like a mosquito. He hadn't seen his own face on any of the monitors, but he didn't doubt he was being watched.

His pulse throbbed at his temples as he waited for the door to slide open, though he had no idea what he would do when it did. Instead it was a neighboring door that slid open. Only when it slid shut did he move. He opened the lab door only wide enough to slip through, then slid it silently back into place.

What now?

Back the way he came.

Five times around.

Back to the first circuit.

———

The clock in Bas's room read 1:03 a.m. He hadn't encountered anyone on the way back, but he hadn't relaxed, even a little bit, until the final circuit.

Now, standing just inside his door, he felt unable to move. Was he dreaming or awake? Was he staying or leaving? Did he know his own wife, or had Lana lived some parallel life? Could she really have shoved a man to his death? And what did I, Mine have to do with any of it?

"*Fuck*. What the *fuck*, Lana."

Bas's gaze crawled along the contours of his dark room, searching for any sign of a camera. It was hard to imagine a camera being hidden in such a spartan environment, but he had seen with his own eyes the evidence that it was there. He moved to the center of the room and waved his arms as if snapping spider webs—or batting away miniature helicopters.

Only when he was satisfied that the air was clear did he realize his door was still open. He moved to close it.

A shadow moved forward to meet him, and the next thing he knew the tatami mat was pressed into his cheekbone. He was jerked from the floor—not by hands, but as if the room itself had been upturned—sending bolt of pain up his side. He was forced upward so hard that a flash of light went off behind his eyes. He thought of Lana shoving the man over the railing.

The dark figure slid forward like a jaguar through underbrush. His black tunic and hood provided ample concealment, but there was something more at work. Every shadow in the room appeared to be drawn to his form, as if unable to escape his gravitational pull, creating a kind of ghostly silhouette.

"What do you want?" Bas croaked as he struggled to get back to his feet.

No answer came, save for the hiss of air as the figure exploded forward, unraveling all at once like a ball of elastic. At the same time the floor seemed to bank sharply forward, sending Bas directly into the whirlwind. The rain of blows to his solar plexus forced his lungs to empty all at once.

Whatever was happening, his opponent's skills far surpassed Wallace's, and this time there was no ring to be won.

As he drew his arms in to shield himself from the worst of the attack, great dark blotches danced at the periphery of his vision. And if he blacked out now, he might not wake up. His only chance was to make it to the door.

Bas ducked to the side, catching the shelf by his sink to steady himself. The metal slab came off in his hands, sending his toiletries skittering across the floor, and without thinking he swung it around in a great arc, forcing his adversary to dodge. Bas was at a vast speed disadvantage, but one solid blow might be enough to take his opponent out. At least, that's what he needed the shadow man to think.

Feinting with his slab, he edged around until his back was to the door, then did the counterintuitive thing: he rushed toward the shadow, bellowing like a mad bear.

Just as he'd hoped, the floor lurched backward, sending Bas tumbling away from his assailant. As he caught the edge of the door jamb across his left shoulder, he had just enough balance to hurl the shelf square at his intruder's head. That bought him only a second, but it was enough for him to leap into the hall and sweep his arm around to slide the door shut.

He loped down the residential wing, sliding his hand along the wall for balance. Whatever he had just faced, he felt like he had finally broken its spell. That sense of heaviness had lifted, and now that he was free of the cloying darkness of his room, gravity seemed to have returned to normal.

His head was another matter.

After testing his apartment door to make sure it was locked, Bas used his spare house keys to get in. It had been three days since he had dropped by to pack provisions for his stay at I, Mine, but it felt more like a month. Now, with only his keys, his black cult uniform, and the tape he had stolen, he entered his apartment like the rogue deserter he was.

He flicked on the lights and dropped the keys on the side table.

"Hey, Mo? You—"

Half his living room was gone—or... transformed. Everything that had been beyond the sectional couch was now missing: the ailing palm tree in the corner, his entire home theater setup, several guest chairs, and every one of the photos Eshe had hung on the far wall to liven up the place. And that half of the room—the floor, the walls—was itself different. A distinct line separated the two halves of his living room—one side sooty and weathered, the other as fresh as the day it was painted—as if two different living rooms had been grafted together.

"What the hell? *Mo!*"

If I, Mine was behind this—and who else could it be?—he couldn't let Mo get caught up in it.

Bas kept one eye on the empty portion of the living room as he crossed over to his bedroom. No sign of Mo there, nor in the study where she had been known to lay her head, nor in the bathroom. And all the other rooms looked normal. The apartment was empty, and to his relief, Mo had cleared out her toiletries. She must be staying at one of her other ports of call.

Bas exhaled and returned to the living room. Whatever had happened here, it looked intentional, surgical. It was as if someone had selected a computer file and hit the delete key. Half his living room had been magicked into oblivion. But to what end?

Bas eyed the bare corner at the opposite side of the room. There was his answer. The Cynda tape had been there—along with anything he could have used to view it. It was all gone now. That had to be it. That was what they were after.

At least Mo was safe. But what about Zelda?

Stomach tightening, he went to the phone and dialed. He squeezed his eyes shut as the dial tone purred in his ear.

He saw Lana, eyes blank, marching forward, hands planting into the chest of some hapless commuter.

"Come on, pick up."

The line clicked, followed by a series of muffled thumps.

"You best have a good reason for calling me at two in the a.m."

"Zee, it's me."

"Bas?" More clicks as she adjusted the phone. "Are you okay? I'm mostly asleep right about now."

"I'm fine. I just got home and..." Lana is a murderer. "I just wanted to call, make sure you were good."

That gave her a chuckle at least. "Bas, baby, I don't even want to know. As far as I'm concerned, everything is in its right place."

"Good, okay. And hey, I'm sorry to call so late. This case..."

He cursed himself. He was babbling, and had said too much. She didn't need to hear this, not now.

"What was it you said the other day about quitting all that?"

"I know. I tried." Bas shook his head. "Things got complicated after my client disappeared and... now it's kind of personal. Anyway, you don't need to—"

"Well that's not a case, baby. What you have there is a crusade."

"No, Zee, it's not a crusade."

She laughed again. "If you're ever in doubt about which one it is, best clue is only one of them pays."

Zelda was fine.

After wishing her good night, Bas hung up and reconsidered his modified apartment. The Cynda tape was gone, which meant they had effectively covered their tracks. But what about the Lana tape? Bas fished inside his tunic and brought it out. The case had cracked in several locations, but the internal mechanism appeared to be intact. How long would it be before Fritz and Collette realized *the Lana tape* had gone missing from their collection? Would they send another shadowy emissary to retrieve it? Nothing was stopping them. As he imagined how a call to the authorities would go, he winced. Even if he left out anything to do with their mind-altering tactics, he couldn't risk being questioned about the stolen tape.

He had to watch it again. And it would probably be smart to make a dupe before the vintage 1981 tape wore out. But not on his equipment at Hawley Hill. He couldn't risk being seen by one of I, Mine's invisible eyes. He needed to go somewhere less obvious.

What about Gisela Andie?

She would help him dupe the Lana tape—and she would definitely take an interest when she saw who the star of the show was. Besides, Bas couldn't help but think that, after everything he'd just been through, he could use another pair of eyeballs on this.

Reckless. Selfish and reckless.

Edging carefully around the erased part of the room, Bas went to his bedroom—tape firmly in hand—to grab some normal clothes. He couldn't stay here. I, Mine had gotten what they wanted, but who was to say they hadn't left some invisible cameras behind?

Before leaving, he left a terse note for Mo on his door. Then he headed back down to the Monza.

"Jesus, I'm not having this again."

Eshe tried shutting her apartment door on Bas, but he shot his hand out, blocking it. A jolt of pain ran up his arm. He had twisted his arm during the assault, or maybe he'd had it twisted for him.

"It's not what it looks like!" he said.

She glared at his hand, and he pulled it back.

"Eshe, I promise. I know I'm a mess, but... I was ambushed."

Her eyes surveyed his face, but she opened her door no further. "Listen to yourself. Who gets ambushed?"

"It sounds bad, I know. But I was attacked in the dark, and... someone got into my apartment. They're gone now, but I didn't want to stick around there until I've had time to investigate. It's just... it's late, and—"

"They didn't follow you?"

Bas chuckled, mostly out of surprise. "They're long gone. I would never endanger you, you know that."

Eshe nodded and pulled the door open, then turned and shuffled toward the bathroom without a word. Bas entered and shut the door behind him.

The familiarity of her apartment made him drowsy, but he didn't dare to relax, not yet. Eshe might change her mind any second, and who could blame her?

A few hours of peace, that was all he needed. Just enough time to regain his equilibrium and sort through the mess in his head.

When she returned, she had her little med kit in hand.

"Sit." She stabbed a finger toward the couch.

Bas shrugged out of his jacket, doing his best to mask the ache that had set in as the last of his adrenaline had burned off. He didn't need sympathy.

"Tell me," she said, turning on a gooseneck lamp and angling it at his face like it was an interrogation lamp.

There was nothing he could tell her; no way he could back up far enough to make it make sense to her.

Crusade.

He winced as she touched something cold to his cheek.

"You're not going to tell me." Not a question. "Then at least tell me you're not in trouble."

"I'll be fine, Eshe. I was caught off guard, that's all."

As she dabbed at his forehead, his eyes went to the photos around her living room. Most of them had been taken down. Packed away, he assumed. He had written down when her show was. What day was that?

Her hands dropped into her lap as she examined him. "Well you're no longer bleeding, at least, so I think we can just let the wounds breathe."

"I really appreciate it." He caressed her shoulder, then thought better about letting his hand linger there.

It was too quiet. Was she waiting for him to say something?

"Where's your friend?" he asked.

Eshe snapped the med kit closed and got up. "Gaétan isn't here tonight," she said over her shoulder, heading back to the bathroom. When she emerged again, she was rubbing her temples. "It's late, old man."

"Seriously, thank you."

"Yeah, you said that. But the couch is as far as you come. You and me, that's not something that's still happening."

"I know. That's not why I..."

She nodded. "You know where the pillows and blankets are."

"That's fine. That's perfect."

Her gaze lingered on him. He felt like a kid who had gotten into a scrap at school.

Bas thought of I, Mine, the magic cult located just a couple of miles from MIT. The last three days felt like some kind of dream he had allowed himself to get pulled into.

This was real. Eshe, her apartment, her photos, her spices in the air. Bas only needed someone to remind him of that.

Eshe turned toward her room. "Something needs to change, Bas."

31

THURSDAY, MAY 2, 1991

HER GARDENING GLOVES squeezed tight in her left hand, Dee caressed the deep coral petals of the peonies Brenda and Walter had bought for her. It had been a sweet gesture on their part, and the perfect opportunity for Dee to start over, after she had trampled the previous assortment.

Plantae, Tracheobionta, Spermatophyta, Magnoliophyta, Magnoliopsida, Dilleniidae, Dilleniales, Paeoniaceae, Paeonia.

The words tumbled forth in her head, inert, failing to kindle that old excitement.

Her foster parents had seen the change in her. How could they not? Ever since she had returned from Gisela's, all she could think about was honing her abilities.

Now Brenda and Walter were out on the deck, and Dee felt their eyes on her back.

"You worry too much, you know that?" Walter's voice was quiet, but they weren't quite out of earshot.

"Something changed," Brenda said, matching his volume. "She's withdrawing, and it feels like regression. She's eighteen. I just think it's time... She can't live in her room."

She can hear you right now.

Dee was up and on her feet without thinking about it, gloves still clenched in her hand. Her abrupt abandonment of the garden was as automatic as any reflex, but she didn't bother fighting it. She had left her brain muffs in her room, apparently to spare them from the awkwardness of overhearing such conversations.

"Dee, wait," Brenda said, hands up. "There's an hour of sunlight left if you want to work out here. I'll help you."

Walter—always the less insistent of the two—stood behind his wife with a leery expression.

If Dee knew of a way to tell them she was fine without complicating things, she would. Instead, still on autopilot, she handed her gardening gloves to Brenda, who accepted them without a word. But her frown said enough.

"Let her go," Dee heard Walter say quietly as she headed inside.

―――

Dee stood in the middle of her bedroom, bathed in the golden light of the sinuous form suspended in the air before her. How easy it was to call up the macramé-like construct now. Maybe too easy. If it became automatic—if her hands ever took it upon themselves to conjure a light pocket on impulse—the consequences would be far worse than her whispering being discovered. But—so far at least—her ever more ornate *fingerglow* creations had been strictly intentional.

Still, seeing the writhing shape before her was unsettling, like watching a fish pulled up onto the dock, flipping to and fro as it suffocated. Were they alive, these twisty light specimens she had been summoning forth? Was she witnessing suffering? Did this glowing formation not want to be here?

But these questions were fleeting. She didn't need answers. At least, not yet. Because behind it all she had a certainty—frail as the first light strands Dee had pulled from nothing—that none of this was by accident.

Besides, she couldn't stop now.

Dee checked the Polaroid OneStep 600 in her hand to make sure her finger was on the shutter button. The camera had been a birthday gift from Brenda and Walter on her fourteenth birthday, and Dee's first response on unwrapping it had been dismay. She didn't have the dexterity to operate most mechanical things. But Walter had shown her how her camera—with its rainbow stripe down the front—was different. It had only one button. All Dee needed to do was flip up the plastic flap, wait for the LED to illuminate, and then click.

Dee had retrieved the camera, now covered in dust, from her bookshelf. The battery still worked, and the film pack showed eight exposures remaining.

Now, with her hand poised before her, Dee's pulse thrummed in her ears. She took a step forward, toward the light pocket, and her arm disappeared—camera first—to the middle of her forearm.

And... something new happened.

Dee felt herself being pulled from her body—but with only the slightest feeling of displacement. She wasn't transported to some darkened office this time, but to a point just over her own right shoulder.

She was looking down at herself.

Two thoughts immediately flooded her mind, each vying for attention.

The first was that whoever's eyes these were, they weren't seeing the world quite the way Dee did. Her outstretched arm still intersected the glowing formation before her, but now her hand emerged on the other side of the light pocket as normal, the camera—still quite visible—in her grasp.

But the second thought, far more urgent, overwhelmed the first. Someone was here, right now, *in her room.*

She had pushed her experimenting too far.

Dee tried to pull herself back into her own body, but she might as well have been trying to move a third arm. Whatever had snatched her from herself now held her fast, and she was forced to watch her immobile body with the full realization that someone might, at this very moment, be locating her.

Don't squeeze.

The oft-repeated prompt struck just as fear edged into panic.

Don't squeeze, Dee. Release.

How many times had her instructors uttered that phrase? Dee's executive function exercises had been geared to stem her impulsive tendencies, to encourage her to form a plan in her mind, then take action on it. The training provided no guarantee of success—impulse was impulse, after all—but it had definitely improved her ability to remain aware of her body as it moved about in the world.

Now she just had to do the opposite—to turn her body off completely. The key to that was head-hopping, which had the pleasant side effect of relaxing every muscle in her body. If she could call on that ability now, she might be able to sever this connection before she put her foster family in jeopardy.

You're in control.

Whoever's perspective this was, they probably didn't know she was now seeing what they saw. They wouldn't know she was aware of them.

It was small consolation.

Dee fixed her attention on the back of her own head and pushed, urging herself to bridge the space between them.

Nothing happened.

She was still too wired.

Relax.

Refocusing, Dee took in the scene. The room. The girl standing in the center of it.

Herself.

She focused on her dark hair, the pulse in her neck, the rise and fall of her chest, the hairs on her outstretched arm.

And she pushed.

Dee drove her mind forward with all her might, picturing it as electricity across a conduit.

Straining...

Straining...

Straining until her consciousness wavered like a mirage.

The edges of her vision darkened, and her bedroom started peeling away like an old poster. Behind the picture of the girl in her room was something hollow. She felt its hunger. It was ravenous, all too ready to devour the last sense she had left.

Stop.

Stop.

Dee let go, and the void receded.

Panic surged through her from some unknown place, but had nowhere to go. It was trapped in her body, maybe, or buzzing in circles somewhere behind her eyes. Had her spies sensed the lure of that great emptiness behind everything? Or was she alone in that, too? Could there be something worse than her remote viewers, lying in wait still?

The questions were a welcome distraction, but she had to keep her focus. She had pushed too hard, that was all. She had overstrained, and had almost blacked out as a result.

Stupid.

She could have avoided this if she'd had the presence of mind to think her circumstances through. They were too far away. That was the problem. Her point of view might be only feet from her body, but the *source* of this point of view, the unseen observer, wasn't in her room at all. They might as well have been looking at her through a telescope. And she was now in that distant observer's head—too far away for her to be able to head-hop back into her own body.

She was out of range.

Dammit. Stuck.

She took a deep breath—mentally—and observed herself once more. In her absence from her own body, her grip on the camera had loosened. At first, the sight of it sent a chill through her heart. Only... wait. Her faulty grip might be exactly what she wanted. The remote viewers had latched onto her as soon as she had passed the camera through the light pocket. It might have been a coincidence; whoever this was may have already been trying to find her ever since she had first meddled with their recordings. But every instinct in her screamed that she had set off some sort of remote alarm. *She* had let them in, unintentionally, the same way Gisela had with her tape.

Dee couldn't imagine how this all worked, but if there was something in the arm-to-hand-to-camera-through-pocket chain that was forming this connection, a break in that chain might be exactly what she needed.

She watched through unfamiliar eyes as the device slipped from her fingers. After several slow seconds, the camera dropped.

And Dee fell to her knees, returned to her body.

She had severed the connection.

Her vocalization, lowing and steady, like an ache in her throat, encapsulated her experience over the past five minutes. Her shoulder burned, and she felt a tingling in her feet like biting ants. Around her temples, a sheen of perspiration cooled as the air from the hallway drifted in.

Her fall must have sounded pretty bad, because Junmo was at her door moments later, and rushed to her side.

"For crying out loud, Dee. Just look at you." His hand was on her shoulder.

I'm okay.

"Well I know I'm not supposed to come barging in, but you made quite a racket, so you didn't leave me much choice. Here, let's get you up."

Junmo moved his hand under her armpit, which made Dee flinch. It was also enough to get her unstuck. She got to her feet and let him escort her to her chair, where he stood over her, hands on his hips.

"I hope you didn't just have an atonic seizure, like I used to. And still do sometimes."

It wasn't a seizure. I appreciate your concern, but I promise you, I'm fine now.

Junmo threw a look over his shoulder, then shut her door. "Did something happen related to your special powers?"

What could she tell him? That she had potentially put a target on the backs of everyone in the house? As long as she was here, everyone was in danger. Even if she stopped playing with her *fingerglow* creations, it might already be too late. She had pushed too far, and had led someone straight to her.

I got carried away.

Would he understand? For all Dee knew, whispering might be risky too. How stupid she had been.

I have to be more careful.

"What does that mean?"

She considered her options.

Can you do me a favor, Junmo? Would you call Gisela for me?

His answer came quickly. "Well you know I really don't like talking on the phone. That's something I leave for other people."

Dee would have whispered directly to Gisela if she could figure out the long-distance issue.

I know it's hard for you, but it's even harder for me. I wouldn't ask if I didn't need your help. You'd be doing me a huge favor.

It looked like he was counting something on his fingers, but he remained silent.

I'll be right there with you the whole time. Will you help me?

Finally he took a deep breath. "Okay, sure, Dee," he said, his face as inscrutable as ever. "I guess, what's the worst thing that could happen, right?"

32

THURSDAY, MAY 2, 1991

"YOU'RE SHITTING ME—BAS fucking Milius."

Bas approached the front desk. It took a second for the smiling face to register. "Reggie Turner?"

Reggie had started with the BPD in 1978, several years before Bas's departure. He had been young then, and bright-eyed, and Bas barely remembered seeing him outside of morning roll call and compulsory department functions. He was still young now.

Bas had found the Metro Discovery office on the bottom floor of a nondescript brick building in Boston's central business district. Inside, the smell of adhesives and paint still hung in the air like a pall, and shrink-wrapped boxes of furniture parts were stacked on either side of the front office.

"Man, it's been forever and a day," Reggie said. "What you been up to? Look like you got into an argument with a bus." His eyes were on Bas's face. The wounds were better, thanks to Eshe's attentions, but there was no way he would be mistaken for a man with a desk job.

"Oh, you know what it's like out there." That sounded cagey. "I'm actually working a case now."

Close enough to the truth.

"Gumshoe, huh? I love it, man. Guess it can get pretty rough, by the looks of it. Someone your size, it's not like you're gonna be sneaking up on anyone. I swear you've grown since I saw you."

"Grown sideways," Bas said, patting his stomach.

"You and me both, brother. So what brings you out this way?"

Bas leaned on the front desk. "A little birdie tells me Gisela Andie is here now." He had made it a point to keep up on his former colleague's whereabouts. The way he saw it, that was no different than maintaining common situational awareness.

"She sure is. A bunch of us are. I think we all eventually got fed up babysitting the blue flamers and running code." Reggie leaned closer. "I still hear sirens in my sleep, know what I'm saying?"

Bas sniffed. "Memories."

"*Man.* Going private is where it's at, and the pay ain't bad either, if you know what I'm saying. Anyway, Gisela should be in her office." Reggie slid his clipboard in front of Bas. "Just sign in and you're good to go."

———

Gisela's name was handwritten on a strip of drafting tape stuck to her open office door. Bas was about to knock when he saw she was on the phone.

"Okay, I understand."

When she saw Bas in her doorway, her jaw dropped a little. He hadn't seen her in nearly a decade—not since he had quit the force. She still looked like herself, only more mature somehow. Maybe it was just the way she was looking at him.

Bas pointed down the hall. *Should I go?*

"No," she said into the phone, then switched the handset to her other ear. She looked distracted, but gestured Bas toward a chair, mouthing *Sit*. "She's okay though? Good. Tell her I'll talk to your mom after work, okay? It's just such short notice, so I'm not sure. Did you tell her? Yes, I will." She flashed Bas a smile, but her eyes drifted away before he smiled back. "Okay, I'll explain it to her. Of course not, I know. I will. Okay. Bye, Junmo."

Gisela hung up and took a deep breath before turning to face Bas. For a second he thought she might stand up. But if so, she thought better of it.

"Sebastos," she said, regarding him over her desk. The formality had been in in-joke between them, based on the fact that he hated his full name.

Bas had always been good at reading faces, but never hers. She had a way of presenting several expressions at once, making him feel illiterate. The look on her face now was something between surprise and disappointment. How did she even do that?

"You look good, Gisela Andie."

"You *lie* good. What's it been?"

"Ten years."

She nodded. "Yeah, since…"

"Since." No need to get back into it. Bas studied her office. "New digs, huh?"

She sat back in her chair. "We've only been here a couple weeks, as you can probably tell. But business is good. Everyone wants to make sure applicants are on the up and up."

"Sure they do."

"Is that why you're here?"

"Is what?"

"Do you need someone checked out? Maybe whoever did that to your face?"

Bas touched his cheek. "Nah."

"Because I can't help you there."

The glimmer in her eye said she was being playful. Maybe she was actually glad to see him. Maybe time really did heal all wounds.

Well, not all.

"I actually wanted to thank you."

Her eyes narrowed, then she nodded. "For Mr. Bolden? No problem. You were doing me a favor, since locates aren't really in my wheelhouse these days."

"So you do know a Mordell Bolden?"

"Was that... not what you meant?"

"No, I mean, you've heard the name? Mordell Bolden?"

"You've lost me. I thought that's who we're talking about."

So Gisela still recalled the name, just as well as Bas did. That was good to know. At least in their minds, the man existed—not Alton Griggs, but Mordell Bolden. Even though his own garage denied ever knowing him.

That was something Bas could have cleared up earlier if he had merely contacted Gisela. But reconnecting would have felt like picking at the edges of an old scar. Now it was Lana's tape—and the irony was hardly lost on him—that had convinced Bas he had to seek her out.

As for Bolden, had he been lying after all? That he'd had prop mail made, had hired actors, all just to sell a lie? Had the whole thing been a carefully choreographed production, just to lead Bas through I, Mine's doors?

He shivered.

"Are you having an off day or something?"

Bas looked up at her. "Sorry, I was just... Was there a specific reason you sent him to me?"

"Well, like I said."

She was nervous. Bas hadn't seen it until now. As soon as he'd mentioned Bolden's name, something had changed. Which meant something was there.

"How well did you know Mr. Bolden?" he asked.

"Well I never ran an EBI on him or anything."

"He wasn't a friend of yours?"

She shook her head. "Friend of a friend. I met him at a party." Gisela sat back. "A small group of us got to talking, and he ended up telling us about his daughter, who had skipped."

"Some party."

"Well, he was worked up about it because he had just received a security tape with his daughter's name on it. He explained?"

Bas nodded.

"So I pulled him aside when things were winding down, and told him I could help him with the tape if he just needed it converted, since we have a pretty nice setup here. And that was the last I expected to hear about it."

"I assume you watched it?"

She studied her fingers. "Hard to convert it without seeing it."

"Any chance he left the original with you?"

"He has the original, but I duped a copy for reference. He never called me back, so I archived it. Hey, you know it's good to see you, but... what's up with the twenty questions?"

A new note in her voice made Bas's heart race. She was talking around something.

And why should she trust him after all this time? He had given her no reason to, yet here he was, from out of the blue, with a head of gray hair and a messed-up face.

If he was going to make any headway, he was going to have to make the first move. What did he have to lose that he hadn't lost already?

"The first time I met with Mr. Bolden, I turned down the case."

Gisela listened.

Bas took a breath and smoothed his hair back. "The second time I met up with him, I went to his apartment to tell him I'd take his case after all. Only he was no longer answering to the name Mordell Bolden."

"I don't follow."

"He claimed his name was Alton Griggs. And he had the address labels to prove it."

She frowned. "You're losing me."

"That's exactly how I felt. Why would he stand in front of me and lie to my face? He didn't know who I was, he said, and he definitely didn't have a daughter named Cynda."

Gisela shook her head. "Well I can't vouch for the guy. Maybe he just had a change of heart."

"There's more. Before I went to see him, I called the garage where he worked. Got the phone number from the business card he gave me—with the name Mordell Bolden on it, of course. They gave me his address. After I went to his apartment, I called them again. They claimed never to have heard of a Mordell Bolden."

Gisela raised her eyebrows. "Okay that's starting to sound like a lot of theatrics. Did he seem nervous? You could check to see if he'd been paid off, or threatened, but... who would have a bigger stake in his daughter's whereabouts than him?"

"Maybe I, Mine," Bas said.

"Your what?"

"Yeah, I hadn't heard of them either. They call themselves 'I, Mine.' They're a secretive collective—based in Kendall Square, if you can believe that. Long story short, that's where the *Cynda* tape led me." The look on his old friend's face wasn't reassuring. "Cynda was involved with the group. They offer a kind of... like, therapy retreat, for people with nowhere else to go. But there's definitely an exploitation angle to it." He shook his head. "I think. Anyway, the reason I *know* all this is because I actually stayed there for three days, as a guest."

"Hold on. You infiltrated this self-help group even after Mordell Bolden brushed you off? Why?"

"If you'd asked me then, I'm not sure I could have articulated why. Just, there was something about it I couldn't let go of." Bas patted his jacket. "But now I know why. Call it instinct or whatever, but I was *right*." He produced his stolen tape and set it on Gisela's desk. "It was at I, Mine that I found this."

"'Found,' huh?" She turned the tape around to see the label. "1981. Okay, what is it?"

Bas's heart beat in his chest like it was trying to escape. "They have a collection of hundreds of these. Maybe thousands."

"You're telling me this tape came from the same place as Bolden's?"

"I'm sure of it. But there's more to it than that." Bas wiped his hands on his pant legs. "Gisela, Lana is on this tape."

"*Lana?*" There was a name she probably hadn't expected to hear today, or maybe ever again. "Jesus Christ. How?"

Bas reached across and pointed at the label. "1981. It was recorded at the South Station. April twenty-eighth. The day of."

"Holy shit, Bas. They caught Lana on tape before the Singularity?"

"Yeah. And it's not a security feed. It's like the Cynda tape—they were focused right in on Lana. And the footage shows her... Gisela, it's fucked up, what she did."

Gisela pursed her lips and put the tape back down. If she had any more questions, she wasn't asking them. In fact, she had gone pale.

"I can show you," Bas said.

"No, I believe you."

And she did, judging by her face.

"I need to see it again anyway. I'd really like it if you're with me when I do."

"Let it go, Bas." Her teeth were practically clenched.

"*What?* After everything I just told you?" Bas waited for a response, but she only crossed her arms. She was pulling back. "Gisela... I can see there's something you're not saying. As soon as I brought up—"

"I think it's dangerous."

The tape was still in front of her, but she had backed away from it like it was radioactive. Bas reached across and took it back. "Tell me what that means."

"It wouldn't make sense."

"That just about describes the past three weeks." Bas leaned forward. "I didn't just wander in here for old time's sake. Something's been going on, maybe ever since the Singularity, and this group is behind it."

255

"Which is exactly *why* I think it's dangerous."

"What, you think I had a tail? No one knows I'm here."

"Mm."

"Gisela, you know I can't let this go. Not after seeing Lana."

She peered into his eyes like it was the last thing she wanted to be doing. "It's complicated, Bas. Don't you think there's a reason I'd rather not talk about this?"

She was throwing it back at him just to see if it stuck. But leaving was no longer an option.

"Tell me how it's complicated."

She bit the inside of her lip, giving him a look like she was sizing him up. "I can't make this make sense," she said. Before Bas could protest, she added, "But I know someone who can."

What was she talking about? Who else could know about any of this?

She wrote something down on a sticky note. "Did you drive here today?"

"Yeah, I'm in the side lot. Why?"

"Okay, this is my address." She pressed the slip of paper into his hand. "Meet me at my house in about an hour. There's someone I need to pick up."

33

THURSDAY, MAY 2, 1991

BAS PARKED across the street from the address Gisela had written down, and listened as his Monza knocked and burbled itself to sleep. The house was compact but well-maintained, with a small white picket fence that wrapped around the front to a driveway on the side. It was almost cute. Gisela definitely hadn't owned a home back when they worked together. She'd been making changes. For the better.

Meanwhile Bas was still living in the same apartment he'd been in since quitting the force.

Ten minutes later Gisela pulled into her driveway. She circled her car and opened the passenger door, and a teenage girl got out. Something about the girl felt off. Her arms were stiff, and she was up to the front porch without even once looking at Gisela.

"This should be interesting," Bas muttered to himself.

He got out and pulled his jacket more tightly around him as he crossed the street. He pressed her doorbell, then gazed down at her *I Hope You Like Dogs* doormat while he waited.

Gisela pulled the door open. "Perfect timing." She had an empty mug in one hand. "Come in, I was making us tea. Or hot chocolate."

Bas ducked as he entered. Her place smelled foreign, but not unfriendly. "Where are the dogs?"

"Dead."

Bas took off his jacket. "Shoes off?"

"Either way." She headed into the kitchen while Bas looked for a place to put his jacket. He hung it in the open hall closet, wedging it between two of Gisela's jackets.

She stopped him in the dining room before he made it to the kitchen. "We're in the living room," she said, three mugs in her hands this time. "This way."

Gisela's guest was waiting on the sofa. Up close she looked older. And... was she talking to herself?

"Hey," Bas said, giving the young woman a wave. She didn't respond.

"Just a sec," Gisela muttered, as though talking to herself. She put the mugs on the coffee table. "Bas Milius, this is Dee Khalaji. I told her a bit about you on the way over. Dee is... a good friend. She lives with my friend Brenda Luckie and her husband Walter."

"Lucky?" Bas asked, taking a seat at the other side of the sofa.

"L-U-C-K-I-E. They run Luckie Landing, a foster home. They've been parents for Dee and her brother for a long time now."

"Orphans?" Bas asked.

"Just a *sec*," Gisela muttered again. She placed the mugs on coasters and slid one in front of Dee and another in front of Bas. "Dee has been helping me out recently," she said. "And it's related to that Cynda Bolden tape."

Bas looked back at the girl. Her eyes were on him, then not. There was definitely something wrong with her. Was she even paying attention? The girl didn't seem to be in a condition to help anyone. From the look of it, she could barely hold still.

As if to underscore Bas's suspicion, she started moaning just then. No words, just meaningless noise.

"Helping you," Bas repeated, talking over the girl's sounds. "How's that?"

"You watched the tape."

"More than once."

Gisela put her mug to her lips and slurped. "Did it look like a security video to you?"

"More or less." What it really looked like was his *Lana* tape.

Gisela set her mug down. "Less, I think. What it *really* looked like was a POV shot from a voyeur."

Of course she would have picked up on that too. But she didn't know about I, Mine. She hadn't seen their video lab.

"I wasn't sure what it looked like," Bas said. The less he said the better, at least until he knew where this was going.

"Oh, don't play coy. You know exactly what I mean. And so does Dee, because she's caught them in the act."

"Caught them? She's caught them how?"

"Okay... now stay with me, Bas," Gisela said, moving to the edge of the couch, leaning closer to him. "Dee here can do some remarkable things. She has certain talents that seem... like magic. At least at first."

She paused, as if she wanted those words to sink in.

"You mean like Rain Man?" Bas asked.

"No. That's—" Gisela held up her hand to Dee as if she were directing traffic.

Bas looked from one to the other. There was only the silence hanging in the air, growing heavier by the moment.

After a moment, Gisela directed her attention back to Bas and composed herself. "It's not like that. What Dee can do is... she can throw her words."

"Like a ventriloquist."

"Sort of. Only she can make it so you can hear her in your head. She can do it without using her voice at all."

Bas ran the words through his head. A week ago Gisela's assertion would have sounded crazy. It still did. Only now it sounded like something he could have experienced in that warehouse in Cambridge.

"Why is this all happening now?" he asked, his voice quieter than he intended.

"Hey," Gisela said, waving her hand. "No questions about what I just told you?"

She sounded surprised, which made sense. Bas should have challenged her. But he ignored the question.

"What you said about the tape..." He sighed. "There's something to that. I couldn't figure out how it was recorded either, and the tape from 1981 is the same. And..." He wouldn't tell her about the video lab. Not yet. "If you're telling me this girl can do magic..." He looked from Dee back to Gisela. "Show me."

Gisela looked relieved. The girl's expression, on the other hand, hadn't changed at all. To all outward appearances, she was completely checked out. Had she even followed their conversation?

"You're sure?" Gisela said.

"Why am I here?"

Gisela nodded, then looked over at Dee. "Okay, it's all you."

Bas watched Dee's face, but saw no sign of acknowledgement or understanding. She looked agitated, with her arms and fingers in continual motion.

Hi.

The word came from somewhere close, but Bas wasn't sure where. He hadn't been ready for it. It was distinctly feminine, but nondescript. And it wasn't Gisela's voice, which was of a slightly lower register.

Bas looked at Gisela. "Did you...?"

"It wasn't me." She pointed at Dee.

I'm speaking to you.

The voice sounded like it was coming from somewhere in the room. Only no one's mouth had moved.

"What is this?" Bas asked.

I'm speaking directly to you. No one else can hear.

Bas studied the rocking mute girl more closely.

It couldn't be her.

"You hear her?" Gisela asked.

"I hear *someone*."

"I know, it's weird. There's no escaping that."

"But I mean... Isn't she..."

"Dee's autism locks her into herself a lot of the time. Maybe this ability of hers—call it telepathy, or a magic trick, or whatever it is—is a kind of compensation."

Bas turned back to Dee, squaring himself up on the couch so he could really see her. "So right now, you can understand me?"

I know it doesn't look like it, because my inside doesn't connect well to my outside. But I'm always paying attention.

Bas had heard of autism, but he'd never seen anyone like Dee. If she was truly trapped in a body that looked oblivious to what was going on around her, it must be hell. If it weren't for this special ability, no one might ever know she was even *capable* of paying attention.

"And you can do this with anyone—talk into their head?"

I think so.

"But right now Gisela can't hear you."

If I'm talking to you, it's just to you. If I talk to her, only she hears.

"How long have you had this...?"

I'm not sure. At least since my parents died, when I was eight.

For a moment, Bas didn't know what else to say. Who was this girl?

He turned to Gisela. "Is she the only one who can do this?"

"No idea. This is all new to me, too. I can't imagine it's common."

When Dee looked at him, she did see him—now that he knew what to look for, it was obvious. The vocalizations and movements were only a distraction.

"It's hard to wrap my mind around it."

"Tell him about the tape, Dee. That's why we're all here."

The tape wasn't recorded with a camera like you're thinking of it. I don't know how they do it, but I'm pretty sure it's not mechanical at all. I think it's a special ability, like mine.

Only I, Mine weren't just watching. They were recording—and had been for more than a decade.

There's something else I noticed about the tape. It's like a beacon to those people. As soon as Gisela watched the tape, they started watching her. So if you watch your tape—

"Then they'll be able to find me?"

They'll be able to see you. If they want to spy on you, that's the key they need to start. That's how they found out Gisela had the tape.

Bas looked at his old friend. At least he hadn't brought I, Mine into her life; they were *already* on to her.

"Well I'm sorry," Bas said as he brought the 1981 tape out of his jacket pocket "I didn't know all that, obviously." Gisela would only have heard half the conversation between him and Dee, but she would understand why he sounded apologetic about it.

Dee made a sound.

"Yeah," Gisela said, "that's the one." She turned to Bas. "It should be fine as long as you don't play it."

"That's one thing I don't get." Bas looked at Dee. "You said you *noticed* them watching. How?"

I can see what they see.

Bas massaged his temple. Was that any less believable than this head-talking trick? "So you throw words, and your eyes, too."

Basically.

"Okay, so if you saw them, you could identify them?"

I caught a peek of several men watching a monitor once, but not long enough to see who they were. All I know for sure it that they've been alerted every single time Gisela has watched that tape.

Bas sat back on the couch, sinking into the cushions' embrace. Kit had leaked the tape to Bolden, and Gisela had gotten caught up in it. She would be tangled up even worse had Dee not alerted her to the fact she was being watched. No doubt by I, Mine.

Bas took a sip of his cocoa and looked around the room. It was cozy, spare on the memorabilia and decoration. Gisela did have some photos perched on the mantel, but they looked like family excursions. Had she been seeing anyone?

As he rolled his mug between his fingers, he told Gisela and Dee about his experience at I, Mine. He told them about Collette and Fritz, about their disorienting headquarters with rooms that existed only sometimes, about the assembly, and about their archive of tapes. He told her about the tape labeled *1981*, and the horrific footage it revealed. Through it all Gisela listened intently, taking it all in as if Bas were recounting the details of his latest vacation. Dee looked like she was in her own world, but apparently that was just her autism lending her a kind of social camouflage.

Bas left out no detail, taking them up to the point of the masked assailant and his own subsequent escape. When he was finished, he raised his mug to his lips and emptied it.

"So what are they after?" Gisela asked. "If they can do the things you say, where does that lead?"

When I saw them watching Gisela, they talked about wanting to find her.

"Dee says you got them interested in finding you."

Gisela crossed her arms over her chest.

"I think she's right," Bas continued. "I think they must be collecting anything that can conjure this magic."

"Well I'd disappoint them then. But Dee?"

Bas wondered. It was clear why Gisela had gotten the attention of I, Mine: she had something of theirs that they didn't want in circulation. But Dee was another matter. Bas hadn't seen any evidence to indicate the I, Mine residents were endowed with natural gifts like Dee's. If they knew about her... If they thought they could exploit her abilities...

Frowning, Gisela got up and left the room.

I don't think 'collecting' is the right word.

Bas looked at Dee.

The group you found aren't just gathering things. They're studying them. They watch.

Bas mulled this over. I, Mine had dedicated a fair amount of their operation to surveillance, and they were definitely playing the long game. The Cynda case had made clear that when something got out—incriminating evidence, or someone who knew too much—they had ways of covering their tracks. That kind of commitment proved how serious they were.

"I, Mine are building toward something. I mean, they *believe* they are. I saw it myself, in the rituals they do all day and all night. They're methodical about it—everything is centered around it, like it's leading them somewhere."

I just don't want it leading them here.

"Yeah, well."

Gisela's voice issued quietly from the other room. Was she talking on the phone?

The girl swayed gently and plucked at the fringe of one of the three hundred pillows Gisela had festooned across the couch.

"Bad news," Gisela said, returning.

"What's up?"

She took her place between them on the couch. "That thing you said about Bolden earlier, about him becoming someone else, it got me thinking."

"Gisela, I'm telling you—"

"No, hear me out. I think you may be right."

Bas fell silent and put a hand out for her to continue.

"I just got off the phone with my friend Jenny, the one who introduced me to Mordell Bolden at the party. People knew him there—some of them, anyway. I mean, he was Jenny's mechanic, and their daughters had been in the same class. Right? Well, I just called her—and she had no idea who I was talking about."

Bas raised an eyebrow. "And you're thinking maybe someone got to her too. Paid her off."

"Don't I wish." She shook her head. "No, I'm wondering if this I, Mine could have done something to him."

A chill took root in Bas's chest as the thought ran through his mind. He saw Lana shoving that man from the balcony, and winced. None of it made sense.

"What are you thinking I, Mine did to him?" Bas asked.

Gisela just shrugged.

Dee barked, as if in response. Bas shot her a glance. What did she make of all this?

"What I'm asking, Gisela, is how they could make everyone forget that a man ever existed. Because *that's* what they'd have to do."

"Not everyone. Not us. We're immune somehow."

That much seemed true. Here they all were discussing the matter, after all. But maybe that was their silver lining.

"Let's take advantage of that," he said, pointing the 1981 tape at her. "This is the only link I have to Lana. So let's review it. I have to know what happened, even more so if Dee is right about how these tapes are created. If I, Mine was alerted to Gisela because of a tape, then something might have alerted them to Lana on the day of the Singularity. There has to be a reason she's being tracked on this tape, even if it's only for ten seconds."

Dee stood up and walked out of the room. A moment later, a door opened and closed, announcing her exit.

"She goes out back when she's stressed out," Gisela explained.

Bas put his cold mug on the table. "Sorry for raising my voice. But this is Lana we're taking about."

"Is it?"

What did that mean?

"Let me show you the tape."

"After what we've just told you about the Cynda tape? After what you've seen yourself?"

"We're *immune*, right?" He tucked the tape back into his jacket. "What, so I'm supposed to drop it?"

She moved closer to him on the couch. "However you want to look at it, it's a cold case, Bas. Poring over ten-year-old footage isn't going to bring her back."

"No, but knowing what happened may help me let her go."

Gisela gave him a dubious look. "You're a terrible liar."

Maybe so, but Gisela hadn't lost anyone. She couldn't know what it was like to experience the loss of a partner, to haul around the all-consuming pit formed by all the unanswered questions.

Bas *had* to watch the tape again. He had to understand what happened, even if the truth was worse than not knowing.

"Maybe it was the man the tape was following," Gisela said. "Maybe Lana wasn't the focus at all."

"It doesn't *matter* what started the recording. I need to make sense of what I saw!" Bas took a deep breath and put up his hands. He was getting worked up again.

Gisela put a hand on his knee. "Bas, if you're looking for some kind of peace of mind, I don't think this is the way to get there. These things are happening all around us whether we like it or not, and from the look of it they have been for a long time."

"So we just go on with our lives? We just let it all go?"

"Maybe what's done is done. We may *never* understand it, but why press our luck? Why risk what we have now?" Fear—that was what she had been hiding. It was there, in her voice. "Okay, think of it this way then. If this I, Mine group wants those tapes so much they're coming up with magical spying schemes to track them, is that really something you need to be tangled up in? Because I don't see it. To me, if that's not an excuse to back off... then what is?"

34

THURSDAY, MAY 2, 1991

THE PORCH LIGHT had burned out, and the glow from Gisela's kitchen was too weak to do Dee much good. But sitting among the plants was good enough. She didn't need to see them.

Gisela's giant friend was one of those loud people whose movements shook the floor. As the evening had drawn on, being around him had filled Dee's head with little exclamation marks, like springs pressing into her brain. But Bas had left, finally, and now the sound of ceramic on metal issued from the kitchen as Gisela put their empty mugs in the sink.

She emerged onto the back porch a moment later. "Dee?" Her voice was quiet again, now that she didn't have to match Bas's level.

Your friend is weird.

Gisela let the screen door shut. "He's fine, he just hasn't been the same since his wife died."

He doesn't know what he's messing with.

Gisela sighed as she squatted next to Dee, putting a warm hand on her back. "I think he does know, now. You just have to give him some time to let it sink in." She rubbed Dee's back. "Thank you for helping me. I know that wasn't easy."

The breeze kicked up, rustling leaves still wet from earlier rain. The chill found the gaps in Dee's clothes and raised goose bumps across her skin.

So what you told me in the car, about working with him... You were friends then, before his wife died?

For a moment no answer came.

"Yeah."

Just friends?

Gisela's warm hand disappeared. Now she was rubbing her own arms. "We got close, briefly. But... Lana found out, then it was over."

Which part?

Gisela stood. "I don't know. All of it."

35

FRIDAY, MAY 3, 1991

BAS WATCHED Gisela enter the Metro Discovery office, and waited a few minutes. By then, he guessed, she should be in her office, which would provide him an easy excuse to head back there himself.

But as he walked inside, the man who looked up from the front desk was not Reggie Turner.

"Good morning," he said, a bit too cheerfully. By the look of him, he might have just started shaving that year.

"Morning," Bas said, doing his best not to tower over the kid. The name on his badge read *Tobias*. "Say, Tobias, I'm wondering if you can help me."

"I'll try!"

"My name is Bas Milius, and I was here yesterday to visit an old colleague of mine, Gisela Andie."

"How cool is that?"

"Yeah, she was actually on the force with Reggie and me, a couple hundred years ago."

"Oh, Reggie too! Like a little reunion."

"Exactly. Only, thing is, I forgot and left some old photos in her office by accident. You know, when you reach a certain age..."

The kid chuckled. "Well she stepped out of her office a minute ago—I mean I literally just saw her. But if you wanted to wait here...?"

Dammit. Reggie would have let him go back anyway.

"Well, actually," Bas made a show of checking his watch, "I have somewhere I have to be, so if I could just pop back there and grab my photos... gee, Tobias, you'd really be helping me out."

The kid sucked air in through his teeth as if Bas had just shown him a fresh wound.

"Just in and out," Bas assured him. "Won't take but a second. Here—" He scanned down the sign-in sheet and pointed out his name from yesterday. "That's me."

"Maybe, if you—"

"Thank you, Tobias." Bas started toward the back offices before the kid had a chance to change his mind. "You're a life saver."

———

Bas passed by Gisela's empty office and tried to look inconspicuous as he kept an eye out for a video library or editing room. The floor wasn't so large that he had to worry about missing it or getting lost. He took an adjoining hallway past a kitchenette that smelled of coffee and burnt toast, and kept his head down as he walked past several of Gisela's colleagues.

At the end of the hall he spotted a door with "208 - *Media Lab*" etched into a tile above it.

The room, lit only by LEDs, was awash in the sound of humming internal fans. Bas flicked on the overhead lights and was greeted by a setup even more extensive than I, Mine's, though without the video collection. On one side of the room, an all-black NeXT computer sat beside an older PC, with a myriad of peripherals and software boxes littering the table between them. Opposite the digital equipment was a compact but modern analog video rig, complete with a fancy Sony thermal video printer.

Once Gisela saw Lana in her final moments, she could explain it to Dee in a way the girl could understand. Not that he needed their blessing to pursue the case, but it would be nice to have some allies who understood that they were up against an organization that defied rational explanation.

Bas removed the Lana tape from his jacket pocket. He had to watch it again, and he no longer had a TV or VCR of his own. Besides, if Dee was right about the video triggering I, Mine's magic surveillance, this was the safest place he knew of to watch it. At least it wouldn't lead them to anyone's home.

He powered up the VCR, loaded his tape into the deck, and rewound back to the start. As the machine whirred, he flicked on the printer, which flashed OK on the LED readout just as his tape reached the beginning and clicked into standby.

Bas turned on the monitor, steadied his hand, and punched play.

The monitor flickered to life.

A sea of morning commuters packed the South Station concourse. Bas saw no sign of Lana, but the camera—if it was a camera by any traditional measure—was tracking an elderly man as he made his way steadily through the throng, like a tortoise fording a stream. As Bas watched, the camera pulled ever tighter on the old man, following from above and slightly behind.

There had to be a reason he had earned the attention of his gravity-defying observers. But who was he? From this vantage point it was impossible to get a look at the man's face.

The man walked over to a lone woman who was leaning against a column with one hand, as if for support. He approached her with no hesitation, and tapped her on the shoulder. Only when she looked up at the man did Bas realize it was Lana.

The bottom dropped out of his stomach.

Then the video glitched, and the image yielded to a white blur.

Bas rewound the sequence and watched it again.

The man wasn't just meandering through the South Station. He was making a beeline for Lana. Had they known each other? Or maybe the man had seen something in Lana that had drawn his interest.

Bas forwarded through the white blur, to the next sequence.

The camera had found a new target in Lana, without a doubt, as if the operator had lost interest in the old man. Now Bas watched with sick resignation as the camera tracked her to the escalator to the second floor. He wanted nothing more than to tell her not to go there. Did she know what she was about to do? Had it been premeditated? What had that old man said to her?

When she reached the top, she just stood there for a moment, as if she had forgotten something. The people behind her squeezed past, pushing her forward, and Lana didn't even react.

She walked purposefully to the center of the space, stopped, and did an about-face, turning toward the railing beside the escalator—and toward the camera.

Bas recognized this part of the video. He had watched it at I, Mine. He didn't want to see it again, but he watched anyway, hoping, somewhere at the back of his mind, that this time things could be different.

Lana marched forward and plunged her hands into a young man's shoulders, sending him to his death.

The image went dark, and Bas sped through the rest of the tape to the end.

Blank.

His mouth was dry, and his palms had gone clammy. He tapped rewind, stopped the tape at the moment Lana spun around to locate her target, and pressed pause.

Lana's face, neutral as a mask here, stirred something in Bas that had long since gone dormant. For years after the Singularity, memories of her had cropped up like shards of glass in sand, every lance and pinch reopening the wound. With time those memories had diminished, leaving behind only inert impressions of her, and the dull guilt over the things he had done to push her away.

But now, as Bas stared into her blank eyes, the sting pushed inward once more, pressing into that old wound. The contours of her face were as familiar to him as his own. But who was she? How was it possible not to recognize something so familiar?

Bas felt watched, and he thought of the words the autistic girl had whispered to him. *If you watch the tape, they can watch you*—or words to that effect. At the moment, he was starting to feel she was right: his skin prickled as if he had walked through an electrical field.

He pressed print on the thermal printer. The machine whirred and clicked to life, then began committing every glowing raster of Lana's final moments to paper.

"*Asshole.*"

Bas spun around to see Gisela with her hand still on the door.

"How did I know you'd be in here, even after everything Dee told you?"

"Sorry, but I have to show you this. Someone put Lana up to it, Gisela. It's all right here. Someone talked to her before she went up—"

"*What are you doing, Bas?*" She was petrified, hands balled into fists, pupils so dilated he could see them from across the room. "I know you want answers, but this isn't the way!"

"It'll just take a second," Bas said, turning back to the deck. He pressed play before she had the chance to object, but Gisela covered the distance between them, shoved him out of the way with surprising strength, and traced her finger along the component rack in search of the active machine.

On the screen, Lana was driving her hands slowly into the man's shoulders, shoving him back.

"What the hell?"

Now, finally, she understood why he had been so adamant.

Only Gisela wasn't watching the playback.

Bas noticed the reflection in the screen's glass a moment after she did, just as she was looking back toward the door. Bas turned—and shielded his eyes from the rippling ball of cold light hovering in midair just five feet away.

His ears popped, and all sound was pulled from the air, save for a kind of muffled rupture.

Gisela backed against the console. "What did you do?"

She sounded like she was underwater.

The floor seemed to pitch, and Bas grabbed the edge of the console.

The sphere grew to fill the room, writhing like a tightly coiled snake. Bas pulled himself closer to Gisela, trying to remain between her and that strobing thing.

It was no use.

The flash swept the room away.

And Bas fell.

When he regained his senses, he was on the floor of the media lab, chest heaving. He didn't think he had lost consciousness—not exactly. But for a moment he had felt... somewhere else.

No sign remained of the miniature sun, save for a scattering of loose papers on the floor.

Bas's ears popped again as he looked over at Gisela, who was already pushing herself up. He shot a glance at the dark monitor. The recording had run out, leaving nothing but empty tape, dispelling whatever it had summoned.

"You okay?" Bas asked. His ears still felt clogged.

Whether Gisela heard or not, she didn't answer, just headed for the door.

"Wait, hold up." He went to follow her, then remembered the tape and his printout. He went back and stabbed at the eject button, then took the printed still image from the printer and the tape from the VCR.

Gisela was practically at the lobby by the time Bas caught up with her.

"Hey, *hey*. Are you all right?" He put a hand on her arm, but the look she gave him stopped him where he stood.

"Excuse me, did she sign in?"

It was Tobias, peering over at them from the front desk. He didn't seem to recognize Gisela.

"I'm leaving," she said, paying the security officer no heed. She pushed through the doors into the lot.

"Uh, she's with me," Bas said, then headed outside, where Tobias's protests were lost in the sound of traffic.

Gisela was already halfway across the parking lot, with no briefcase, purse, or coat. Bas hurried to catch up with her.

"Hey, hold up," he said, matching her pace. "Tell me you're okay at least."

"Leave me alone, please."

She sounded rattled. Maybe she was in shock. But when she stopped and turned to face Bas, he took an involuntary step back.

There was no recognition in her eyes. She sincerely had no idea who he was.

"You just gonna keep following me?" she snapped.

It was subtle, but her voice was different. Something about the intonation, or cadence. She sounded like a stranger doing a Gisela impression.

Whether she recognized him or not, Bas wasn't going to just let her wander downtown Boston. Certainly not in her current state.

"Let me drive you," he said. Not the kind of offer someone would accept from a stranger, but he didn't have time to think it through. "I can drop you off at home."

"Can you just leave me alone?"

"But if you're headed to Somerville anyway, I can drive."

"I'm not going to Somerville."

As she turned to go, Bas's heart raced. The ball of light had taken something with it. Something of Gisela. He couldn't let her go now. If he did, he might never find her again.

Bas followed her at a safe distance as he racked his brain for ideas. She definitely had a destination in mind, judging by her purposeful gait. The bus stop was just ahead—the red line, which meant Somerville was out.

Bas fished his notebook from his pocket and rushed ahead. "Uh, sorry, ma'am, one last thing."

"I thought I told you—"

"I know, sorry about the confusion, I had my notes wrong." Bas waved his notebook around like he had just caught a wayward bird. It was enough to get her to slow down at least. When he was sure she wouldn't leave, he took out his last business card. "Now, I'm going to leave this with you."

"I'm not interested, man."

"Don't misunderstand," Bas said, holding the card out. "I'm a detective and we're working a case at Metro Discovery, where you just left."

She looked back at the office, shaking her head. "I had no reason to be there. It was a mistake."

"Regardless, we're going to have to reach out to everyone who was in the area, just as a matter of procedure."

She pursed her lips and took his card, glancing at both sides of it. "I don't know anything."

Bas opened his notebook and slid the pen from the spiral binding. "I need to take your number, just for the record."

With a sigh, Gisela snatched the notebook and the pen, wrote something down, handed them back, and resumed her hasty stride.

Bas looked down at what she had written. The phone number put her somewhere in the greater Boston area, at least. Just as Bolden had had his mailing labels, she had her phone number. And probably a new house, possibly a family, and a full back story to go with it. He had no doubt of it. And it had all happened in the space of a second, with no coordination required. How was this possible?

Beneath the phone number Gisela had written *Isabel*.

"Jesus."

When Bas looked up, she was already at the bus stop, presumably ready to pick up her life where she thought she had left it.

So what had happened to her *old* life?

Bas thought of Dee.

"Dee," he muttered, "I don't know if you can hear me right now, but things just got more complicated."

36

FRIDAY, MAY 3, 1991

DEE MANAGED to find her backpack in an upstairs den, which Gisela's house hadn't had before. But this wasn't Gisela's house, because Gisela didn't exist anymore. Bas had seen to that. Now Dee had to get packed before whoever lived here now came home.

She had been practicing her *fingerglow*—to Phoebe's amusement—before Bas's tape had gotten the attention of his cult. Dee had been torn from her body as soon as their remote viewing was triggered, and had been forced to watch as they set off some kind of slow explosion.

Dee continued to watch as Bas chased after the Gisela-looking stranger. But whoever was watching lost interest then, and Dee returned to her body in this house with no garden, no smell of tea, and no Phoebe. The glowing wisps of Dee's interrupted *fingerglow* had remained, but she dismissed them with a wave of her hand.

Now her body wasn't cooperating. Her agitation was like gravel in her shoe, and though her backpack was in sight, she could only pace the room and flap her hands. How would she get home? Reversing the route she had used to get to Gisela's house would only get her as far as the Haymarket subway station. She could use maps to get to a closer stop, and she could head-hop to maintain her composure, but there were just so many variables to contend with.

Downstairs, a clock chimed the hour.

The interruption helped Dee regain some control. She rushed to her backpack and shoved her things into it—clothes, toothbrush, seed packets, brain muffs, and Walkman. The sound of a car door slamming outside sent an adrenaline wave through her body, and she dropped everything to dash to the window, fearing the worst. If some random person caught her in their house, her evening was about to get a lot more complicated.

But it was Bas, speed-walking up to the front porch.

Dee made a low groan in her throat. A stranger might have been preferable.

And he didn't have Gisela with him. That confirmed all her misgivings about him. Not only had he caused Gisela to forget who she was, he had also let her go.

A series of rapid knocks sounded on the front door, and the doorbell's insistent chime added to the commotion.

Dee grabbed her backpack, squeezed it to her chest, and tried to let the noise slip by her. She had to think about Gisela.

"Dee, we have to talk."

The knocking had stopped just as suddenly as it had begun.

Dee exhaled as the world grew softer again. From the top of the stairs, she watched Bas's shadow through the frosted glass of the front door.

"Come on, Dee. I know you're in there."

He wasn't going away. And maybe he had a point. Bas was the last one to have seen Gisela, and despite being aggressively clueless, he might have ideas about how to find her again.

She was going to have to deal with the man, like it or not. At least until they got Gisela back.

"Were you leaving?"

The big man stood at the open door, filling its frame. His eyes were on her backpack.

I don't have much of a choice, do I? This is someone else's house now. Even the cat is gone.

He stood there, silent, blocking her way.

I need to get home, okay? I hope you're happy.

"Hey, I'm so sorry that whatever happened happened. But how could I know it would turn out like that?"

Dee's fingers tightened on the strap of her backpack. *You are seriously the biggest idiot I know. Not only did you cause Gisela to be... brain-zapped, but then you just let her go!*

"What am I supposed to do, stalk her?"

She whined at him, and he winced, unable to cope with her autism. At least he didn't try to hide it. But he definitely understood what her vocalizations meant.

"Dee, finding Gisela won't be an issue. That's what I do."

Only there is no Gisela, which basically means you killed her.

"Oh, come on, I was *just* speaking with her. I got her phone number."

Did you try calling it?

That made his cheeks flush. "Okay, yes, it's a fake. No surprise. Doesn't matter, because there are other ways—"

The point is she thinks she's somebody else now. She is somebody else. She doesn't live here *anymore. Ugh, why couldn't it have been you instead of her? We would have been so much better off!*

The man fumbled around in his jacket pockets, looking flustered. When he pulled out his tape, Dee wanted to launch her backpack at his head.

"We still have something they want."

You're still waving that thing around. Have you learned nothing?

"I'm saying—hey, *listen*. Look, whatever I, Mine is doing to people, they're the only ones we know who might be able to reverse it."

Dee dropped her things, snatched the tape from him, and retreated into the living room.

"God *dammit*, Dee!" he shouted, taking several steps forward. "Hey, now come on."

She triggered the light pocket without even thinking of the finger sequence.

"What the fuck?" He stayed where he was. "Is that you, or I, Mine again?"

Oh, so now you're worried about I, Mine. Well now we agree on something, so I'm going to make sure you don't get their attention—

But he had been waiting for an opportunity, and swiped the cassette from Dee's fingers before she finished whispering. He moved away from her, retreating toward the front door. "You can do your magic all you want, but we need this tape. It's the only proof I have of the connection between I, Mine and Lana."

It's too dangerous. It might as well be a weapon. After I get rid of it, we can focus on getting Gisela back.

"Get rid of it? Uh-uh, fuck that. Not when I'm finally getting close to something."

That cult just erased Gisela, Bas. How is a tape supposed to convince them to tell you anything about Lana? All it's going to do is make them madder than they already are. And I'm done trying to hold them off for everyone.

"If they erased her, they can bring her back. *Think* about it."

You're making that up! You're not even thinking about Gisela. You're thinking about your wife. That's what got us here. Are we all expendable to you?

"I told you, Dee, I didn't know that would happen!"

Dee rocked back and forth, stealing glances at the tape in his hand. If he noticed her looking, he would put the tape back in his pocket, but Dee's constant movement did a pretty good job of masking her intentions.

You expected *something to happen.*

"Sorry, Dee, but unless you have a better idea..."

We should forget about I, Mine and your dead wife, and find Gisela. If I can just talk to her—

"I can't believe I'm wasting my time debating this."

As he turned to leave the house, Dee's body took over, and she accidentally initiated a light pocket at the same moment that she head-hopped to Bas. To her surprise, the light formation streaked across the room with her awareness, like taffy pulled from its origin. It now stretched from her body to a point just in front of Bas. She had never done anything like that before—would never have *thought* to do it. But if this construct she had summoned still behaved like a light pocket, then maybe...

Dee instantly returned to herself. The mutant light pocket stayed where it was, a tube hanging between the two of them. She shoved her hand into the tube at her end—and it emerged feet away, beside Bas, who had turned and now stood in open-mouthed stupor.

She grabbed the tape from his fingers before he realized what was happening.

Bas lunged for her. But Dee had anticipated that move, and she released the tape before she pulled her hand from the pocket nearest her.

Only her empty hand emerged.

Bas stopped dead, lit from both sides by hanging light patterns, his own hands conspicuously empty.

"Dee, what the hell! Where's my tape?"

No idea.

"Seriously, get it back. Right *now.*"

Dee flicked her fingers to dismiss the light pocket before he got any ideas. It was done.

Dropping things in light pockets is kind of a one-way thing. I couldn't get your tape back even I wanted to.

He shook his head at her, his jaw working for a few moments before he could speak again. "You have *got* to be shitting me."

Dee picked up her backpack from the floor. *I didn't do that to piss you off. But what happened to Gisela is your fault, and you know it. You and I may be immune to whatever happened, but that doesn't—*

"Oh, spare me your rationalizations. You have no idea what you're talking about. You're just a kid with zero life experience." He was patting his jacket as if feeling for a wound. What was he up to?

He turned to leave.

Wait!

Bas was already out the door, but he stopped on the porch. "What?" he asked over his shoulder.

I need help getting home.

"Jesus Christ, kid," he said, turning around. "You have some balls, you know that?"

You got Gisela zapped, and now you're just going to let me fend for myself out there? Who does something like that?

He looked her up and down, still pissed off, but maybe a little guilty, too.

"Unreal," he said to himself. But he held the door open for her. "Come on then."

PART 3

37

FRIDAY, MAY 3, 1991

DEE HAD Bas drop her off at the bus stop so she could walk home as if she had spent Friday at school. It felt wrong, like grafting a blooming peony onto a poison ivy plant.

Toxicodendron radicans.

That's how the day had turned out.

Gisela was gone, and no matter what that idiot Bas said, she might be gone for good. Dee wiped her cheek as she walked the last block home.

She wouldn't give up on me.

Dee didn't have the right to just give up. If Bas really could find out where Gisela was living, Dee could whisper to her, remind her who she really was. And if it didn't work, she would keep trying until it did.

Gisela had been there for Dee when she had needed it most. Now it was time to return the favor.

"Dee, calm thoughts!" Brenda said from the front porch.

What was she talking about?

Brenda caught Dee's backpack, which she had been swinging

around her like a scythe. She had let her body get away from her again, but it was only mirroring what she was feeling inside.

"Calm thoughts, Dee." Brenda hugged Dee close to her and cooed the phrase, as if Dee were a baby. "Did something happen at school?"

A rhetorical question, of course. But what was her foster mother supposed to think? Brenda had no recollection of Dee staying with Gisela. Brenda no longer knew a Gisela at all.

Unable to stop her flailing, Dee head-hopped to Brenda, and saw her own arms fall to her sides as Brenda pressed her cheek to the back of Dee's head.

"It's okay, honey. Maybe you're just having a bad day." Sensing the change in Dee's demeanor, she pulled away and rubbed the girl's shoulders. Dee felt a moment of dizziness as she looked into her own eyes. Distant eyes.

Her cheeks were still damp.

"Come on, I got you some Inka from the Euromart."

Dee jumped back into her own head and looked Brenda in the eye. The time had come to tell her about the whispering. Dee would need all the support she could get. She would just have to outgrow her fears about reaching out to people—especially the people she loved. What Roddy had done to her when she was nine had been a fluke. She had thought whispering to him might calm him down, but instead it had made him crazy. No, that wasn't right. He had always been crazy.

Brenda wasn't like that. Dee could trust her not to change when she found out what Dee could do.

Dee sniffed and wiped her cheeks again as Brenda led her inside the house. But in the foyer, Dee started for the stairs without letting go of Brenda's hand. Brenda was obviously confused, but she let herself be drawn up to Dee's room.

What's happening?" she asked as Dee ushered her to her chair and closed the door behind them.

Dee's nerves felt like they had been severed then incorrectly reconnected. Pacing might help, at least a little bit.

Brenda watched with concern as Dee moved back and forth. "Hey, you're okay, Dee." But she sounded uncertain, as if she was trying to convince herself more than Dee.

Dee managed to stop pacing long enough to look Brenda in the eye.

Brenda, it's Dee.

Her foster mother inhaled as if she had just cut herself. In an instant she was on her feet, her hand on Dee's cheek. "Did you just say that, honey? Did you talk?"

You can hear me, right?

Brenda yanked her hand away, and her look of elation vanished as she took several steps back. The problem was that she hadn't seen Dee's lips move, which changed everything.

She looked around the room as if she might spot a hidden speaker, then returned her wary gaze to Dee.

Her voice was only a whisper. "What is this?"

Dee was losing her.

Brenda, there's nothing I can say that will make this make sense. I can only try to reassure you that you're not imagining this. It's really me. I don't know how this works, but—

Brenda's eyes searched Dee's face. "Are these *your* words, Dee?"

Yes. I promise, these are my words.

Brenda looked more conflicted than reassured as she moved her hands to her temples. "What do I do?" It sounded like she was talking to herself. "I need to... think."

As Brenda turned to leave, Dee fought every instinct to whisper something to her. Dee wanted to tell her that everything would be okay, but the truth was, things were measurably less okay than they had ever been. And of course she couldn't say anything about Gisela. So she allowed herself to rock in silence, and hoped Brenda could find it in herself to stay.

"Tell me it's you."

Brenda hadn't made it halfway to the door before she stopped and turned. Now she stood only feet away from Dee. "I think... I need to hear that again."

Okay. This is me. I'm right here.

"And this... is something you can do?"

Yes.

"You've always been able to do it?"

For a long time.

Brenda stared, a mix of emotions playing over her face. But at least she hadn't bolted from the room. "I want to believe it. The more I think about it, the less sense it makes. When I look at you..."

I know what it looks like, but my body doesn't reflect what I'm thinking. I've been able to communicate this way for a long time, but I've always been scared to let people know.

Brenda shook her head. "Why?"

Because most people wouldn't understand.

The disbelief on Brenda's face ceded to something that looked more like concern. "Has something changed?"

Dee had thought of several ways she could talk to Brenda about recent events in a way she would understand. But nothing seemed right. Despite having opened herself to Gisela, Junmo, Bas, and now Brenda, Dee felt more alone than ever. And telling Brenda everything would be worse than selfish; it might be dangerous.

"Dee? Is something wrong?"

She had taken Dee's hands in hers and was gently massaging her palms. Over the years Dee had managed to impart, without words, how comforting she found the gesture.

I have a friend. Gisela.

Maybe that was the answer. She could tell her the relevant details without revealing everything.

"From school?"

From work.

"At Kids Kan? Is she okay?"

I don't know, but... she's been going through a lot of changes lately, and... I just wish she knew that I was there for her. I want to reach her, even if it means whispering. So I thought maybe...

"That you would try it out on me first?"

Brenda was smiling, and her eyes might even have been watering. That had come out better than expected.

I can trust you. This way of communicating—my whispering—is something I want to keep private. But maybe the people I'm closest with can know. Some of them.

Brenda took a step closer. "I'm sorry I reacted the way I did. I just... I'm not even sure how this is real. I understand you took a risk reaching out like this. But if it's all because you're worried about a friend, that says everything about who you are as a person, Dee."

Dee slumped on her bed, suddenly overtaken by emotion. Brenda was by her side a moment later, wiping Dee's cheeks.

I didn't want to scare you off.

Brenda put her arm around Dee and held her. "You could never scare me off, Dee. I'm feeling... relieved, but also... disappointed in myself. I've always felt like I knew you, that we had a connection, but with your autism, because you're nonverbal, I could never be sure you were really in there and engaged. And I should have known. If anyone *could* know, it should have been me. I could have been more there for you."

There's no way you could have known. And this whispering... this is me as much as my autism is me.

Brenda gave her a squeeze and looked into her eyes. "I want to get to know you, and this new part of you. Walter, too. Can we figure out a way to tell him?"

Dee thought about Gisela again. She might be living another life now, or in some kind of existential limbo. But telling Brenda her secret had made Dee feel hopeful, even if it was irrational. Even though she had no plan.

Brenda would be discreet about the whispering, but she shouldn't have to keep such a secret from her own husband.

Let's sit down with Walter when he gets home. And Junmo, too.

38

SUNDAY, MAY 5, 1991

A HUSBAND, a wife, and their two daughters had taken residence in Gisela's house. Bas watched from his Monza as the two girls chased their dog in the front yard while their parents brought groceries in from the car. One of the girls took a tumble on the lawn and came to a rolling stop on her side. The dog immediately ran to her and licked her face until she was breathless with laughter.

Of course this wasn't Gisela's house anymore, because Gisela was now going by Isabel, and Isabel lived somewhere else. Bolden was luckier: when he changed identities, he got to keep his same apartment.

Bas couldn't help but wonder if the same thing had happened to Lana. If instead of dying, she had been turned into someone else. He pictured her living out her life in some nameless suburb, ten years older than when he'd last seen her, now answering to a different name. The thought was accompanied by a different kind of sadness, less like mourning, more bittersweet. If she was out there, he had to find her, even if she didn't recognize him. It would be worth it just to know she was alive.

But there was someone else whose needs were more immediate. Gisela.

Bas started the car and drove south to the I, Mine compound.

———

The Monza complained mightily as Bas cut the power.

"I know the feeling," Bas said, patting the dashboard as he peered through the grimy window.

From across the street he had a good line of sight down the rear alley where he had entered for his introductory dinner almost a week ago. The Sunday crowd was sparse in the industrial quarter, but it was still hard not to feel conspicuous. Especially because he had no plan, let alone a cover story.

He sat up as Collette exited the rear door, alone. She lit a cigarette, leaned back against the peeling gray paint of the masonry wall, and squinted up at the sky. Bas was half-tempted to get out and confront her right there.

"Stupid," he muttered.

Dee had been right about one thing: he had no leverage with I, Mine. Which meant storming the castle was the most reckless thing he could do. Between I, Mine's invisible surveillance and directed amnesia, Collette and Fritz had him at a serious disadvantage. And he wouldn't do Gisela any good if they zapped his brain, as Dee had put it.

So what then?

Bas's fingers tightened on the steering wheel as a new idea asserted itself. A bad idea, to be sure—but preferable to doing nothing at all.

"Fuck it," he said, and sucked his teeth as he shook his head. "Fight fire with fire."

He turned the key in the ignition, and the Monza coughed to life. As he pulled away from the curb, he glanced over at the alleyway one last time, and saw Collette staring in his direction.

39

SUNDAY, MAY 5, 1991

"DEE, you might want to turn around, because there's an actual giant on our back porch, and I'm not even joking you."

Dee knew who Junmo was talking about without even looking. Setting down her garden shears, she shifted on the edge of the planter box and turned toward the house. Sure enough, Bas Milius was standing there next to Walter, giving her a look that made her uncomfortable. It wasn't like anger, more like intense interest. What did he want? An apology?

"Hey, Dee?" Walter called from the deck. "Looks like you have a visitor."

Dee turned back to her gardening and picked up the shears. It was her own fault that Bas was here. And now that her whole family knew about her whispering, they didn't think it odd that she would have a guest.

"Why are you so big, anyway?" Junmo asked.

"I guess no one told me when to stop," came Bas's voice.

"Hey, Junmo, let's give your sister some time with her friend."

Dee wished her brother would stay, but she resisted the impulse to whisper to him. It would be unfair to him.

Junmo looked at her with admiration. "Friend!" And then he was up and away.

To stretch out her peony season, Dee had alternated rows between early and late spring bloomers. The early spring bloomers had flowered weeks ago, and she had neglected to deadhead the wilted flowers, just as she had neglected just about everything else not related to watching out for Gisela.

Plantae, Tracheobionta, Spermatophyta—

"Hey, Dee."

Magnoliophyta, Magnoliopsida—

"I thought your family would be more surprised when I showed up, but I guess you told them about your telepathic, uh..."

Dilleniidae.

Dilleniales.

Paeoniaceae.

Paeonia.

"Hey, look, can we talk?"

Dee froze, her shears in one hand, a clump of glossy green peony leaves in the other. She heard Bas take a seat at the picnic table next to her, and whispered to the man without turning.

I didn't expect to see you again so soon. What did you tell them?

"I told them I was the father of one of your friends, but before I could get into much detail Walter asked if I was talking about Gisela. I just went with it. That's good, Dee."

I only said she was a friend in trouble, which is the truth. They'll still wonder why you're here.

"So tell them something plausible," he said. "This isn't just a casual visit."

Of course it wasn't. He wanted something, just as she had suspected. Dee stuck the shears into the soil, blades first, before she did something impulsive with her plants.

She turned to him.

Before you say anything, get one thing straight. If you put my family at risk—

"You don't have to worry about that." He seemed smaller than usual on that bench, looking at his feet. "I fucked up, I know that. Sorry about saying fuck. But I didn't think things would go down like that, even after talking to you and Gisela, and seeing what I saw at I, Mine. But I mean, how could I know it would go down like that, when none of it makes any logical sense?"

There is a sense to it though, which is exactly what we tried to warn you about. You didn't try to understand it because you didn't respect it.

Bas squinted at her. "I know that now."

Dee dusted off her gardening gloves and peeled them off as she moved to the bench. She sat at the opposite end, putting her gloves on the table.

So you must not be giving up on Gisela.

"That's exactly why I'm here. And before you say anything: yes, I do think this may be related to what happened to Lana. But I guarantee you that my focus is on getting Gisela back first."

I'm sorry about what I said about your wife.

"Don't," he said, waving it away.

But I was scared. Am scared. It's hard not to feel hopeless. Or worse, doomed.

"I get it. But we can't just sit around feeling doomed. So we both get Gisela back. You and me." He leaned forward. "I'm saying I can't do this without you."

That's why you're here.

Bas moved close enough that the sheen of sweat on his forehead glistened in the early evening sun. "I know you have your own difficulties, Dee. And the last thing I want is to put someone else at risk. But as far as I can tell, you're the only one who can protect us from I, Mine."

Or we can get Gisela back without them.

"They're *already* involved. We wouldn't be here if not for them, and Gisela wouldn't be playing Isabel, taking the Red Line out to BFE—"

What's BFE?

"Uh... the boonies. Look, you had it right before. We don't have any leverage with I, Mine. But there may still be a way to force them to reverse what they did to Gisela."

Dee rocked on the bench, suddenly nervous about what he was proposing. He had said he would be more careful, yet here he was talking about forcing people to do things? And not just any people—people with abilities far greater than Dee's.

"I was thinking about what you did with the tape."

Dee stared down at her gardening gloves. The days of losing herself in seeds and soil seemed long gone.

"I want to try something, with you."

It's too much.

"I know you're scared."

If this weren't about Gisela, we wouldn't be talking right now.

Bas apparently took this as his cue. "So we confront them, only this time we're ready for them. If we do this the way I have in mind, we can get them to undo whatever they did to Gisela, *plus* demonstrate why it would be in their best interest to leave us alone."

Dee flapped her hands and used every ounce of her willpower to stay seated. Bas looked unsettled by her stimming, and for once she was glad. He should know exactly how she felt about his scheme.

I don't think I'm ready to confront anyone.

"You don't have to do anything you haven't already done. In fact, you may not have to leave your seat."

He had a strange definition of confrontation. What exactly was he proposing?

When would this happen?

"Day after tomorrow. We'll need space to do this, but I think I have that covered. I just need to call in a favor from an old buddy of mine."

I don't know about any of this. It doesn't sound risky to you?

"Worst-case scenario is we get no closer to Gisela. Honestly, I fear we face more risk by doing nothing at all." Bas drew a long breath and looked in through the back window of the house. "Dee, by now you may be a lightning rod, and I'd hate to think that's putting your foster family at risk. I, Mine isn't going to back off unless we show them why they should."

Dee rocked, but remained quiet. He was trying to get to her through her family. But he wasn't wrong.

I can't decide on anything until I know what it is we're talking about.

"I'll run you through the whole thing," he said. "It's nothing you can't handle."

So you say.

Dee stood up so her nervous energy would have somewhere to go.

Tell me the plan.

40

MONDAY, MAY 6, 1991

BAS PARKED ILLEGALLY next to a construction dumpster, taking the chance that Parking Control officers would be lying low until after the Monday morning rush hour had died down. Besides, he was only going to be in and out.

Jake Haas was already across the street at the newsstand. The man was nothing if not punctual. Bas crossed, and tilted the magazine Jake had his nose in so he could see the cover. *Time* was running an exposé on Scientology.

"*The cult of greed,*" Bas read aloud. The cover image was of a volcano with octopus tentacles. It seemed rather tame compared to what he was up against.

"There he is," Jake said, dropping the magazine back into the rack. "Yeah, if you ever feel like you've got a handle on what people are about, read that story."

"Oh, I don't have a clue what people are about."

"Well, I didn't want to say anything." Jake cracked a smirk.

"Hey, man, thanks for doing this."

"Don't thank me," Jake said, the smile gone from his voice as he dug around in his pocket. "After this, we're even. That's the only reason I'm helping you out, because this little favor definitely constitutes unethical conduct." He passed Bas a set of keys on a silver ring. "This is my ass, is what I'm saying."

"It won't be anyone's ass." Bas looked over his old colleague's shoulder out of habit. But their interaction wouldn't have looked suspicious to any onlookers. It was just one man handing keys to another. But now that he'd passed them on, Jake seemed less stiff.

"It's funny, but this was literally the only week you could have called me, the way things are moving out at the seaport. You have some luck, man."

Bas chuckled. "Trust me, if I had luck, I wouldn't need these."

A woman elbowed her way past Jake to grab a copy of the *Globe*. Bas motioned for his old friend to follow him down the sidewalk.

"You're not going to tell me, are you? What you need those for? And please don't give me the line about plausible deniability."

"I just need the space for a few days."

Jake waited to see if his old colleague would say anything more, but Bas held his tongue. "Fine, I get it. I'm not pushing." He sighed. "Anyway, the silver one's the outer fence, gold is the warehouse. If security asks, just tell them my name and I'll vouch for you. I'm on the list. But I need these back before the end of the week, or, seriously—"

"I know, your ass."

41

TUESDAY, MAY 7, 1991

AS THEY APPROACHED the South Boston Waterfront, sagging, soot-covered houses gave way, block by block, to patches of rubble and rebar. Bas glanced over at Dee, who had her hand pressed to the passenger-side window, seemingly unable to take her eyes off the desolation. That made sense, given what he assumed had been a sheltered existence. Her disability surely meant she didn't get out as often as other kids her age.

Where are we going?

The voice in Bas's head had a note of apprehensiveness, whether or not Dee had intended it.

"This whole area by the Boston Harbor is about to become a construction zone. So it doesn't look like much right now, but just wait a few years. People like us won't be allowed in."

Oh. Okay.

Bas drove on, entering a lower-density industrial section that was about to become the city's primary target for redevelopment. They passed derelict warehouses and gutted brick facades left over from a more industrial age. The only signs of life were the portable office trailers clinging to the edges of waterfront lots like gray barnacles.

Bas pulled up to a tarp-covered warehouse at Fort Point, parked, and got out before the engine stopped sputtering. Dee remained in her seat. Brenda and Walter had told him that the girl could get stuck sometimes. Bas imagined it was like temporary paralysis, but he also wondered if Dee didn't sometimes use it as an excuse to get out of doing things she wasn't into.

He leaned down, looking through the window. "Dee?"

This place is scary.

He looked around. It did look a bit like a ghost town. "Well, this part is, because that's what we need. But believe it or not, there are some interesting spots near the channel. Art communes, a few museums, even an old ice cream stand shaped like a giant milk bottle."

How did you find this place?

"Because the local news can't shut up about it. The Seaport Association is going to tear it all up, but things are tied up for the next few weeks, and for us, that works out just fine. You'll see for yourself... when you get out of the car."

Bas left the door of the warehouse open to let the light in. When he had come out to inspect the site yesterday, he had found that its few windows had been painted over, and the only other sources of light were a couple of mast-mounted work lights huddled in the corners like scarecrows.

A single chair, a ratty recliner showing too much stuffing, sat in the low shaft of sunlight coming through the door.

If my parents saw this place, they would never have agreed to let me visit your daughter, Gisela... or whatever story you told them.

"I know how it looks," Bas said, standing in the sun's warmth. "But look, we want it to seem imposing, right?" He pointed to a beat-up couch in the corner. Under normal circumstances he would never have asked anyone to stay here, let alone a kid. "You'll be over there, out of sight. I even got you some snacks and a space heater, so you'll be comfortable."

Oh, I'm not going to miss my bed at all.

Bas grimaced. "She has a sense of humor. Well good, you're going to need it."

Don't say things like that, please. I was just starting to forget what we're about to do.

Bas sighed. "We just have to keep it together for a few more hours, then hopefully we can get Gisela back. Stay focused on her, and you'll be fine."

Dee's compulsive moaning echoed off the metal warehouse walls, lending the space an unnerving soundtrack.

What about you?

"I'll do what I need to do," Bas said, hoping that didn't sound like false bravado. He didn't want her thinking about his role in this. She had to keep her focus on her own job. "So you're all set, right?"

I guess so.

"Good. And you're okay working in the dark?"

I like the dark. It's calming.

"Right, right. And if you get nervous and start to do something impulsive?"

I have more to keep me focused now than I used to.

Dee put her hands in front of her, then twisted her left wrist around as she did some complex finger movements with her right. In the space between them, a schematic made of light sprang into existence from nothing. At least it looked like a schematic, if it resembled anything at all. Bas had seen something similar when she had grabbed his tape from him, and again, on a larger scale, when she had demonstrated her ability for him this morning. Bas had no doubt she would be able to pull her weight in this endeavor, as long as her autism didn't throw a wrench in the works.

"I honestly don't think I'll ever get used to seeing that shit. Uh, sorry."

With another twist of Dee's wrist, the entire manifestation vanished, leaving behind nothing but a slight ozone smell.

I wish you could just take me with you.

"We went over that. It wouldn't make sense."

What if they don't use any magic? If I'm remote, and they don't give me anything to connect with, then I'm just here alone sitting in a warehouse on the other side of town.

Bas grumbled.

Or what if I don't pick up on their remote viewing because you're not Gisela? Then you'll just be abducted, or worse.

She had worked herself up again, and started pacing around the dank warehouse while flapping her hands like a wounded bird. This was exactly what Bas feared would happen—that she would become so wrapped up in the risks that she became one herself.

"Dee, listen. From what I saw, everything these people do involves some kind of magic trickery. But the other thing is, you really need to give yourself more credit. You saw me at the Metro Discovery office before Gisela even showed up. Isn't that right?"

She stopped her pacing, but her hands were still going.

Okay, fine, yes. But... I don't like variables. There's no guarantee we can pull off something this complex.

Bas moved closer, but stopped short of comforting her. They were partners by circumstance, but Dee was a stranger. Was it possible to really know someone with her condition?

"The only variable I'm worried about is whether Collette has decided to quit smoking. Stick to the immediate. Don't let your mind wander."

Dee made a lowing sound that could have been protest or acceptance.

"Just be ready, okay? That's all you have to worry about."

42

TUESDAY, MAY 7, 1991

BAS DROVE out to Cambridge in the thick of the evening rush hour, a transient in a sea of commuters clocking out for the day, going home to their families, living out their safe routines. He parked a block away from the I, Mine complex, on Elm, making sure to pick a spot where he could leave the car overnight.

He gave the Monza an affectionate pat on the hood before heading down the alleyway, then found his way out to Hampshire, the main road that cut across Norfolk. From the opposite corner he could see all the way into I, Mine's rear lot, including the big wooden door emblazoned with the organization's adinkra emblem, maroon on brown.

Bas leaned back against the brick wall and prepared for a long wait. Only the relative emptiness of the sidewalks made him conspicuous. In the evenings, Norfolk Place was an area to be left behind.

Collette emerged from the compound, alone, only a few minutes after Bas had taken his position. As he watched, she lit a cigarette, then crossed her arms and stared up into the twilight sky.

"Here goes, Dee."

The girl probably wasn't watching yet, but it felt right to kick things off with a formality.

Bas hoofed it across the street and followed the opposite alley to the lot behind I, Mine. As he approached Collette from the side, he realized his hand was back up by his empty pocket.

"You know this is my alone time, Bas." Colette didn't turn, but took a pull from her cigarette as she gazed out over the industrial wasteland.

"Smoking's bad for you," Bas said, sidling up to her.

She looked just as she had when he had last seen her. Just taking a break from another day at work.

"Oh, I try to quit fairly regularly. But it relaxes me, what can I say?"

"Guilt is a stressor." The strained small talk jarred his ears, but he had to give them enough time to activate their surveillance systems, to make sure Dee was locked in.

Collette was studying his face. "I have no guilt."

"Well then I'd say you have deeper issues."

She squinted as she took another puff, then redirected the smoke into the swirling evening air and shook her head. "I think you misunderstand what it is we do here."

Bas's skin tingled as something moved into his peripheral vision. Before he could get a look, a chain of floodlights clicked on, bathing the entire back lot, forcing Bas to shield his eyes. The hum of the transformers overhead seemed to grow tenfold as Bas peeked between his fingers and saw Collette grind out the butt of her cigarette under her toe. Behind her was a man who looked like a bouncer, wearing the traditional black garb. He had a friend with him, standing at the ready only feet away.

This, Bas had not foreseen.

"Oh, come on," he said, squinting through the light's sting. "You really need to resort to muscle?"

"You tell me," she said. "Why did you come back yesterday, and today again? You really think we don't know when you come anywhere near this place?"

"See, now you definitely sound guilty of something." The goons were holding their ground—a bad sign. Any reliance on manpower over magic meant that Dee might not have anything to tune in to.

A second later, the air tore open just to Bas's left, carving through one of the hapless bruisers like a sword through a piñata. Bas reeled, almost backing into Collette before the man's sizzling remains hit the ground.

That hadn't been part of the plan.

"Jesus fuck," said the other man. He backed deeper into the lot, looking like he might flee the scene.

Where was the other half of the body? Maybe vaporized. Or dropped through Dee's magic trap door out by the waterfront. Right into her lap. If she witnessed something that fucked up, this would not end well for anyone.

But the crackling vortex hanging in the air held steady.

Bas grabbed Collette's wrist and wrenched her toward him, pulling her off balance into his arms, but not before the goon, rediscovering his courage, positioned himself in front of the I, Mine door.

"Let *go*," Collette said, her voice controlled.

"Not gonna happen," said Bas, holding her against him, restraining her arms in his. She couldn't overpower him, but he didn't want her taking advantage of his weak points if she was trained in self-defense.

"Sir, you'll need—" The man had stumbled over the leg of his colleague as he moved sideways, but caught himself. He looked like he was going to be sick. Bas didn't blame him. The body on the ground was still smoking where Dee's light portal had lanced through it. "Just let her go, and back away."

By now reinforcements must be on the way. If Bas was going to do something, he had to do it now.

The muscle took two steps forward, moving to within swinging distance. Bas couldn't deal with him and keep Collette by his side. The man knew it, and made like he was going for a tackle.

Only then he stopped.

As Collette struggled to free her arms, her bodyguard's face grew tight, as if he were about to have a seizure. He looked into Bas's eyes. "Take her through *now*," he said through gritted teeth.

"Maurice?" Collette said, squirming.

"I can't hold it, Bas!" the muscle said, standing rigid before them.

Bas hauled Collette back away from the building, pulling her toward the light as she kicked at his shins. Just as the door to I, Mine was thrown open, Bas pushed into the blinding column, sure that he was about to be flayed by white fire.

A bolt of cold tore through his body, making every nerve sing as his muscles seized. Behind his eyes a constellation of silver pinpricks exploded in the darkness as he flew, or fell, and careened into something hard enough to knock the wind from his lungs.

Bas!

A word in his head, pulling him back toward consciousness.

His chest was tight.

There was no air.

He found the ground, but couldn't see straight. Was it his eyes?

I can't control it, Bas!

The words pulled Bas out of his stupor. As his muscles finally released, he pushed himself up from the ground and gulped in the metallic air.

Dee's magic had worked—he had been transported across the city with a single step—but something had gone wrong. Glowing tracers crawled over the inside of the warehouse like captured lightning, warping the walls as they arced.

Dee must be nearby, but what about Collette?

In the flickering light, Bas caught sight of her, writhing on the ground and gasping for air.

He shielded his eyes against the searing tendrils snaking across the walls and ceiling. Stone and steel alike were being eaten away, leaving behind a bubbling sludge that looked cancerous.

As Bas crawled closer to Collette, he scanned for the bodyguard's other half, but saw no sign of it. "Dee, are you okay?" he called over crackling static.

The ozone odor had become fetid, and stung his throat. If those lights kept eating away at the structure, Bas would have to get Dee and Collette out to the lot.

Was the light yellower than it had been before, or was he succumbing to the gases?

Something brushed by his back.

Dee.

She was next to him.

I think I'm okay. Have to stay away from the walls.

"Wait here," Bas rasped. He gathered Collette into his arms and pulled her closer to the center of the space.

The luminous threads working along the inside of the warehouse had grown thin and orange, and white ash drifted down from the rafters like acrid snow. Within a minute they were left in darkness, and the sizzle of disintegrating matter faded to silence, leaving them with only the sound of their own breath in their ears.

Bas finally allowed himself to relax, letting Collette slump against him. He brushed the sweat from his brow and took a deep breath. Was this what a successful plan looked like?

He turned to Dee, just a small pale figure in the gloom. "You, uh, hanging in there?"

Yes, but... Bas, that wasn't me.

43

TUESDAY, MAY 7, 1991

DID you really have to tie her up?

Bas stood over the woman strapped to the recliner as if admiring his work. But to Dee it looked like a magic act gone wrong. He had rushed, and had done a shoddy job.

"We need to keep her secured until we can get her to talk," he whispered. "Hey, it's a Barcalounger at least, not some wooden stool."

I didn't know it was going to be like this.

"Remind me to have that printed up for us on matching t-shirts." Apparently confident that Collette wasn't going anywhere, he returned to Dee's side. "Hey, I want to get this over with too, but you gotta hang in there for a little longer. I can't do this without you."

It was the closest he had come to a compliment, but it was the kind of flattery that came packaged with a certain expectation.

A brushing sound spun Bas's head back around. Dee peered over his shoulder to see Collette stirring. But then... nothing. The jump across town had really taken a lot out of her. Or maybe she was just pretending—and listening in.

Bas wasn't taking any chances. "Come with me," he said quietly, motioning Dee to follow him outside.

Dee was up before she could protest. Apparently her body needed fresh air, and she was just along for the ride.

Outside they hunched in the breezy space between the corrugated skin of the warehouse and the massive blue tarp draped over the front of it.

How long are we planning to be here, Bas?

"It depends," he said. "We need to get her awake and talking."

So why are we out here?

"Because we haven't had time to breathe, and there are some things I want to clear up."

Oh. Okay.

"What was your impression of the bodyguards' reactions to your light tunnel?"

Where had that come from? And who cared anyway?

I guess they acted like people faced with something they've never seen before. What am I supposed to say?

"Whatever, I just wanted..." He rubbed at his neck, but her answer seemed to have satisfied him. "Okay, second thing. Am I right that your words were coming from that goon's mouth?"

I didn't plan that, but yeah. It was like a head-hop, but it turned into more of a head-swap.

"Whatever it was, it bought me some time. So... I appreciate it."

Bas, listen, can we just get this over with? I'm not a kidnapper.

I, Mine might be a dangerous cult, but that didn't justify abducting someone and tying her up. If it did, what else might be allowed?

The expression on Bas's face was hard to read. "This will be over soon, I promise. Have you picked up anything from I, Mine? Any of those remote cameras?"

Other than a vague feeling of mental pressure, there had been no definitive probes—and certainly nothing to pull her from her own head again.

A few little blips maybe, super-weak. It might be my imagination. I'm still jittery from that lightning storm you brought back with you through the light tunnel. Whatever that was, it hurt. In my head. Like I said, that wasn't from me.

"You've never seen that before?"

I mean, the light patterns I make look similar, but they've always been small and controlled. They're stable. But that... two people crossing through must have triggered something.

"Mm." Bas shook his head. "I don't like it."

What?

He looked at Dee. "Whatever that was in the warehouse, I'm having a hard time believing that I, Mine would have done it. Not with Collette there. I'm not even sure they *could*. If you're right that it was some kind of natural reaction, we'll have to be a lot more careful."

Hey, this was your idea.

"Yeah, well..."

He rubbed the back of his neck again. He looked tired, like he hadn't slept in days. And by now Dee knew that he would stay up all night with that woman if that's what it took.

So she would too. Not because she wanted to, but for Gisela.

Right now, she was the only thing that mattered.

"Okay," Bas said, his hand on the door latch. "You ready to get this started?"

Bas took only a single step into the warehouse before his arm was out, blocking her. "Wait here, Dee."

What?

The inside of the warehouse was as dark as a cave. The work lights in the corners had been on just minutes before.

Dee waited by the door as Bas vanished into the darkness. Maybe the electricity had just been turned off. She wanted nothing more than to go back out and wait by the car, but she couldn't leave him here.

All at once the space was flooded with a different kind of light. Dee leapt backward, slamming herself into the door jamb.

Collette was bound to a lone recliner at the center of the cement floor, just as they had left her. But now a dozen ghostly tentacles arced outward from the woman like some horrific bloom, each one sprouting a duplicate of Collette's leering face.

Several of the apparitions converged on Bas at once, and he yelped and dodged, his arms passing through them like smoke.

It was a distraction, that was all. Dee steadied herself and kept her attention on the real Collette. But she was immediately pulled from her body and deluged with a riot of superimposed images.

Bas waving his arms.

Her own body crumpled against the doorway.

Windows and doors and gaps between sheet metal slats.

Dee fought to make sense of it. Was she seeing from every Collette at once?

Distraction!

I, Mine might not have found this place yet, but Collette would definitely lead them here if she kept this up. How long had she been at it already?

"Dee!"

Several of the duplicated Collettes watched from different angles as Bas scrambled to avoid them. He could never have prepared for this.

Dee had to do something.

She remembered the bodyguard from yesterday. She had been watching from a remote viewing point in the air over their heads when the man moved on Bas. Desperate, she had willed herself forward and... squeezed. It was instinctual, but something had happened, and for a moment she had no longer been just a disembodied eye.

She had pushed the man out of his own body. She had felt his chest, heaving. Felt throat, mouth, tongue. Had made her words come out of his mouth as actual sounds.

Now Dee hunted through the maelstrom of shifting views until she found what she needed: a clear view of Collette.

With all of her focus, Dee *squeezed* once more, pouring herself into Collette. As she did, the scramble of warehouse views coalesced into a single ghostly composite. This was how Collette was seeing things. It was like looking into a tornado.

As Dee felt the woman straining outward in all directions, she imagined herself tightening around Collette's mind. The more she strained, the closer Collette's senses felt—lungs raw, muscles tight, cheeks damp—until she had no sense of Collette pushing back.

Something hot was in Collette's hand. Dee lifted the hand, and saw in the stark light a small round stone with a symbol inscribed on it.

Dee turned the hand over, and the stone dropped to the ground.

The multi-headed apparition vanished.

Collette's pulse throbbed in Dee's ears, too fast.

She was pushing back.

Dee relaxed, letting the woman have her body back.

Dee's legs buckled as she returned to her body with a jolt, and she fell to the floor before she could reorient herself.

Bas turned on a work light, rushed to Dee's side, and offered his hand. "You're okay."

Asking or telling, Dee wasn't sure which.

Dee slapped at the ground, which in the moment seemed the most effective way to channel the last of her anxious energy. Bas clearly didn't know how to respond; he just stood there, hands out like he was warming them against a fire.

I think we're okay for now. Don't worry about me. I'm just... that was a lot. I did not expect that.

Collette moaned from her chair.

Bas gave Dee one more glance before retreating to the provisions pile by the door to retrieve a bottle of water. He approached Collette as if she might shatter, bottle extended. But she seemed in and out of consciousness, unaware that Bas was even there.

Dee pulled her legs to her chest and hugged them, bouncing off her toes to rock forward and back.

Bas's voice was quiet. "What did you do?"

Dee peered into the gloom. The stone that Collette had been clutching should be on the floor by the recliner, but she couldn't tell for sure.

Can we get some more light in here?

Bas left the water bottle on the floor by Collette and switched on the work lights. The wide beams crossed, throwing long shadows across the floor.

The stone was there.

Look by the bottle. Do you see it?

Bas returned to Collette's side and squatted down to examine the stone. "I've seen these before."

It was in her hand. She was holding on to it when I jumped into her. I made her drop it.

He looked at Collette. Her eyes were closed, but her face strained with emotion as if she was having bad dreams. Bas reached out and fumbled with something at her waist.

What are you doing?

Was he trying to remove her skirt?

Instead of answering, Bas held up something for Dee to see. If it was a belt, it was a fat one. He came to her with the bundle dangling from one hand.

"She always has this on."

It was a pouch, Dee realized. Bas unzipped it, looked inside, then held it for Dee to see. There must have been several dozen identical stones inside.

"When I was at I, Mine, they told me—Collette and her husband, Fritz—they said these stones were for focus. But they never elaborated."

That stone is what enabled her to do whatever that was. Which means she doesn't get this purse back.

44

WEDNESDAY, MAY 8, 1991

BY THE TIME Collette came around, the moon was high in the sky. Bas had left the door cracked for ventilation, and the only sound from outside was the harbor waters slapping against pylons.

As evening had given way to night Bas checked the restraints on Collette's arms. When she was finally alert enough, he helped her to rehydrate, tipping a water bottle to her lips. She drained nearly half of it before she pulled away.

Now Collette's eyes were on Dee. "Classy, keeping me tied down in front of this girl. It's quite an image she'll have to carry around, not to mention what she did to Victor with her little light trick. I assume that was her, too."

"She's fine," Bas said. He didn't sound sure of that.

What does she mean? Who's Victor?

Bas waved her question away.

Collette was muttering something about a body count when a brief but forceful tug of dizziness forced Dee to steel herself.

The remote viewers.

Someone was trying to spy on them, right now. The open channel threatened to pull her from herself, but their signal was weak.

Dee shut her eyes and willed the remote probes to glide past her, withdrawing from them as they searched for something to latch onto. From the outside it must not have looked like much—it didn't even draw Bas's attention—but she knew it was there. And after a momentary prickling across her skin, the telltale dizziness was gone.

Collette still seemed a little out of it. Was that left over from the transport, or had Dee been too rough with her inside her head?

"Just leave her out of it," Bas said to Collette, circling her chair. He might have been trying to look imposing, but Dee thought it made him look restless.

"She's *your* muscle, is that it? She's very good." Collette attempted a smile, but on a woman tied to a chair it only looked out of place.

"This isn't about her."

Collette called over to Dee. "That was a fancy trick you did to bring me here. Risky, too"—she looked pointedly at Bas—"given you show no signs of knowing what you're doing." She let her head fall back on the headrest. "If you're not more careful, you may both find yourselves—"

"Suddenly believing we're someone else?"

That got her attention.

Collette peered up at Bas as if she might have missed something about him earlier. "You never cease to impress. So you know about the refactors?"

Bas shook his head.

"The persona wipes," Collette said. "Whatever you want to call it."

Bas had been right. This woman knew all about it. This cult really was at the center of everything.

"A friend of ours seems to think she's someone else now, so it's hard to miss."

Collette sighed. "Except that it's not. It's decidedly *easy* to miss. The refactors integrate seamlessly, like a puzzle piece snapped into place from a different set. Yet you—and *only* you—seem to have caught on to this... sleight of hand. I find that almost as inexplicable as the phenomenon itself."

"It's not only us. It's you too."

"Because we've deployed countermeasures that shield us from the effects of that reintegration. What's *your* secret?" Her eyes were on Dee again.

Bas ignored the question. "What the hell are you doing to people? And I'm not just talking about the spying."

Dee got up, moved to within several feet of Collette's recliner, and sat back down on the cool concrete. She didn't want to miss a detail of the woman's explanation.

Collette gave Bas an odd look. "Well, you have it turned around, I'm afraid. We're trying to *prevent* the refactors from happening."

"You've got to be... That's bullshit, lady."

"You've seen it yourself firsthand, Bas. Why do you think we invest so much into our monitoring program? You should be thanking us."

Bas laughed.

What does their spying have to do with anything? We saw what they did to Gisela!

"We've been trying to keep an eye on as many of the lost ones as we can," Collette continued, straining to keep an eye on Bas as he paced around her chair. "You've already met them, you know. Most of them."

Bas stopped where he was. "At I, Mine?"

"Every one of our guests used to be someone else. The day you showed up on our doorstep, we assumed you had been refactored yourself."

"You wiped every single one of those people?"

"The only thing we did for those people was to provide them shelter. We certainly never stooped to *abduction*."

"Oh, come on. The only reason you're here is because something's seriously fucked up, and—"

"I know: desperate times, desperate measures."

By the sound of it, there was a lot more to Bas's stay with that cult than he had let on. Had he really not suspected any of what Collette was now telling him? Even after he had seen one of those "refactors" up close?

Dee steadied herself on the cement floor as a second wave of dizziness swept through her, more intense than before. Someone trying to see what was going on in their warehouse, or trying to locate them. She gritted her teeth and forced them away as easily as if she were shooing away a gnat.

"What about Cynda?" Bas asked, drawing closer to Collette.

Cynda was the woman on Gisela's tape. That tape had eventually made its way to Bas.

Collette looked at him curiously. "What about her?"

"Was she a refactor too?"

"Actually, no. Cynda was... different. More like you, I think."

"Meaning what?"

She squirmed against her restraints. The leather squeaked under her. "Look, I don't know what you think we're up to, but I, Mine is about trying to get these things under control."

"What are *'these things'*?"

"Your friend probably knows more about that than I do."

Dee nearly jumped as Collette looked over at her. From the sound of it, she had it in her head that Dee was some mastermind working behind the scenes. Was that a good thing? Or did it just paint a bull's-eye on her back?

Collette turned back to Bas. "What we seek is to understand."

Bas clearly wasn't buying it. "What does that have to do with a compound full of *refactored* people?"

"If you want to understand bees, you build a hive."

"And what do you do with all the honey?"

Collette's chuckle turned into a cough. Bas helped her with the water again, which she accepted, even as resentment simmered behind her eyes.

"Look," Bas said after she had emptied the bottle, "I know you want to get back to your shenanigans and whatnot. So tell me how we get our friend back into her own head, then I let you go."

"*That's* your proposition?" She shook her head. "You're wasting your time, Bas. As I said, we do *not* refactor people, let alone *un*-refactor them."

She may be telling you the truth, Bas.

Bas came around the chair and faced Dee. "How can you say that?" His voice was quieter now.

Collette watched the two of them, apparently confused.

I didn't even think to question it before. I just assumed the same people were behind all this weird stuff. This woman's cult is behind the remote viewing. We know that now. But when that flash of light happened in the screening room at Gisela's office, it wasn't actually attached to anything.

"Attached how?"

Collette attempted to roll to her side to get a better look at Dee. "Are you talking?"

Dee ignored her. *I don't know how to explain it. It's like, my abilities lead back to me—there's always a kind of connection. And it's like that for them, too. That's how I traced them back to the I, Mine screening room. Even that rock Collette was holding, there's a charge to it that I can track. Think of it like a sound you hear in the dark, and for a moment you know exactly where it came from. But the light ball was different because it didn't connect to anything at all. It didn't... come from anywhere. Or not that I could see, anyway.*

Bas's shoulders slumped. With a heavy sigh, he turned back to their captive.

"Fascinating," Collette said, having seen only the silence between them.

"Tell us where we can find Gisela Andie."

"What did the girl say to you?"

"Do you really want to draw this out?"

Collette shrugged. "Sorry, I'm not familiar with the name. But if your friend has been refactored, she'll find her way to us in time. All of them do."

"You already know where she is!"

"You think we monitor *everyone*? No, we only watch people of interest."

"With your... your invisible cameras."

Collette was silent for a moment, her eyes on Bas as if she was studying him. "You're looking for your wife, aren't you?"

Dee didn't like the look on the woman's face. She had fully snapped out of her torpor and was saying provocative things again. Why? To get Bas to lose his cool? Was it just a dodge?

"And after all this time," she continued, as if drawing from some newfound well of confidence.

Dee tried to push away a pang of guilt. Hadn't she accused Bas of the same thing?

Bas scowled. "Tell us where Gisela is and I let you get back to your creepy shit."

"I think it's sweet, actually. You had to know we'd find out who you were. It was easy enough to find out using public records alone, but once you took that tape... Fritz actually got misty-eyed. He's sentimental, like you."

Bas was silent for nearly a minute, as if he was working something out in his head. Then he spoke, his voice quiet. "Do you know where Lana is? Did she really die?"

Dee got to her feet. Something about Bas's tone made her stomach tighten.

"Honestly? We don't know. We know what you know—you saw the tape yourself. Something happened—something before the Singularity, I mean. That's why the recording started, thanks to a handy little routine that actually predates I, Mine. It was already in place by 1981. In some ways you might say that single tape is the reason we exist." Collette shifted in her seat again, moving her arms to a more comfortable position by her sides. "I suspect your wife wasn't prone to shoving people off balconies prior to that day?"

Bas glared at her.

"So, if something was *compelling* her to do so that day... well, all that remains of her act is that final artifact. Would you happen to have the tape still?"

"It's gone," he said.

"It was worth asking."

Bas's eyes darkened. He reached down and turned Collette's recliner so she was looking at him.

"*Gisela.*"

Collette sighed. "I'm sorry I can't help you."

"You said you track them."

"Well, not me personally."

Bas bit his lip as he considered that. He turned to Dee. "Can you sense any remote viewers?"

They've been trying to get through. I've been stopping them.

"Can you see them now?"

I mean... yes, hypothetically.

Can you follow them back, the way you said you did before?"

I guess, maybe. But why?

"Because I want to tell them something, and you need to tell me how they answer." He turned to Collette. "They can hear us, right?"

Dee hadn't considered that. There had been no sound on Gisela's original tape, nor on the tape Bas had shown to Gisela.

Collette had been following Bas's half of the conversation, and was watching them both intently. "The remote viewers? Sure, if they see you saying something, there is an audio channel."

"Okay. Dee, are you ready to... do whatever you do?"

Yeah, but... you're going to have to break my connection, or I might not be able to return to my body.

"What do I do?"

Just shake me or something, like you're trying to wake me up. That's what's worked in the past.

"Okay."

Dee sat back and waited, her hands flexing and releasing impulsively. She hoped they hadn't given up now that she needed them. Now that she had stopped actively blocking them.

I just have to wait to see if—

Almost immediately she was pulled from her body. She saw the three of them—Collette, Bas, and herself—from overhead, bathed in the beams from the work lights.

Orienting herself toward the source of the intrusion, she forced herself deeper, away from her own body.

And there they were.

The room at the other end of the connection was bright, easy to see in the thick gloom of her tenuous channel. People were packed in tight, all watching the warehouse on a bank of monitors.

The woman closest to the monitors shushed her colleagues. "If they're letting us through," she said, "they can probably see us too."

On the monitors, Dee watched as Bas crossed the floor and grabbed her shoulders. She snapped back to herself, nearly pitching over. The transition was no less disorienting than it had been the first time.

I saw them. They're watching. A whole group of them.

Bas straightened up and addressed the darkness. "To the people watching this from I, Mine: I want to resolve this as much as you do. So I'm asking you just one thing. Tell us where Gisela Andie is." He turned to Dee. "Thirty seconds."

She went still, letting herself drift back across the channel.

She found them.

The woman at the monitor was already repeating Bas's message to the rest of the room. So—she was the viewer. The rest of them could merely see the screen, which, like Gisela's tape, didn't have audio.

"What should we do?" another man asked.

"Can you pinpoint them?" asked a woman.

"If not, we have no choice," said the first man.

"It doesn't matter. Just tell them," the woman said.

Bas's hands were on Dee's shoulders again, and she was back into herself, bracing herself against the concrete.

They're trying to figure out what to do. They want to find out where we are.

"Dammit, I'm trying to make this easy." He turned back to Collette. "*You* tell them. Tell them we want Gisela, then this is all over."

The woman in the chair looked like she was on the verge of exhaustion. As recently as a few minutes ago, she might have preferred to stay here and play games, to talk in circles. But now the idea of getting out of this place seemed to appeal to her.

She squeezed her eyes shut and shouted at the walls. "If you know who they're talking about, just say it out loud. They can hear what you're saying, like our remotes. Tell them where their friend is."

Bas looked at Dee and mouthed *Go*.

Dee returned to the remote viewing room.

"Just say it," said the man sitting next to the woman in front. He looked young, almost as young as Dee herself. How had he gotten involved with these people? "The sooner we can get this over with, the better."

The woman looked over his shoulder, to a man wearing a black robe. "Do you know?"

The man took a step forward and spoke into the monitor, as if that might help. "We have been tracking the woman formerly known as Gisela Andie for the past few days, in Mission Hill. She is Isabel Perreira now, and has an apartment on Stockwell Street." He recited the full address twice while the rest of his cohort looked on.

Dee quickly returned to her body and relayed the information to Bas before her mind could turn the numbers around.

"Okay," Bas said, nodding. He turned to Collette. "Good news. Looks like we're done here."

Collette perked up again. "I know you won't like hearing it, but just because this Gisela may once have been a friend of yours, I, Mine won't be letting a refactor fall through the cracks. We can't afford to."

She looked at Dee. "But who knows, with this young woman here, you might put up some resistance."

"She's not a part of this," Bas said, his voice clipped.

"Oh," said Collette, letting her head fall back again, "I don't think that's for you to decide."

In the stark light, Bas's face was noticeably red. But he only stood there with his fists clenched. After a moment he turned to Dee. "Let's go pick up the car. I have to shuttle her back, and I'm *not* leaving you with her."

45

WEDNESDAY, MAY 8, 1991

BAS WALKED Dee to the Higashi School's main entrance, being mindful not to let her race out in front of a bus. She had been acting erratically since their session with Collette, though she had assured Bas several times that she would be fine.

A young woman not much older than Dee gave them a wave as they ascended the front steps. "Hey, bud-Dee," she said. She looked up at Bas as she offered her hand. "I'm Cathy, Dee's personal aide. You're Mr. Milius?"

Bas shook her hand. He'd phoned the Luckies just after sun-up—not only to reassure them that Dee had been a model houseguest, but to have them call ahead to her special school, so no one would raise an eyebrow when Bas showed up to drop Dee off.

How the girl was going to get by on only three hours of sleep was another matter. But hey, she was young. "Just making sure Dee got here safe."

She looked back at Dee. "You ready? Where's your bag?"

Didn't think about that.

"Oh," Bas said, "yeah, we forgot it... at her parents' place. Sorry about that."

"Not a problem," she said. "You all set?"

Hold on!

Bas almost flinched when Dee grabbed his sleeve. Cathy looked interested, as if unsure whether to step in.

"Uh, could you give us a moment?" Bas asked. "I think she's just a little..." What? The only word that came to mind was unpredictable.

"Big change in routine," Cathy finished for him, with a knowing look.

"Right. That's it, exactly."

Bas watched her leave, then turned back to Dee. "Don't want your schoolmates seeing me out here talking to myself, so better keep it short."

I wish I could go with you to Gisela's new place.

"Come on," he said. "You have a life to get back to, at least until I find out more. Anyway, you saw how Collette's eyes lit up when she saw you do your thing. You've caught their interest enough as it is. Best you just lay low."

Fine. Dee reached into her pocket and pulled something out. *Maybe there's a way for me to stay connected. Take this.*

Bas held out his hand, and she dropped something cool into his palm.

Collette's stone.

"*That's* where it went." He hadn't been able to find it when he was clearing the evidence of the interrogation from the warehouse; he'd thought it might have gotten kicked into the cracks.

Sorry I didn't say anything earlier. I'm a snatcher, and... Anyway, I don't know what Collette did to this rock, but it's still charged with whatever magic her people use, which means I can use it for remote viewing.

"Isn't that dangerous?"

No?

"What if I, Mine are accessing it right now?"

I would know that! They're not attached to it anymore. I am.

"So I just carry this around, like a good luck charm?"

And go about your day as you normally would.
Was that a good idea?
Dee squeezed Bas's hand around the stone. *If you see anything, if you need me to see something, make sure you have that with you.*

Isabel Perreira's address was in Mission Hill, in a sea of duplexes. Her apartment was on the corner of Stockwell and Mission, a sleepy suburban oasis only minutes from Fenway. Bas had followed the flow of afternoon traffic to her neighborhood, and now found a shady spot across the street from the apartment where he could keep an eye on her front door without looking conspicuous.

He removed his seatbelt, cracked his windows, tilted his seat back a few notches, and put the sun visor down to cut the glare. But the sun still glinted off something in the faux-wood tray under the parking brake. Collette's stone.

At the sight of it, Bas's mind went to the image of Collette tied to the recliner. I, Mine would never report the transgression—nor the bifurcated bodyguard in their back lot—but that didn't make those events any less problematic, morally speaking. These were desperate times, as Collette had said. But where would it end? Would Gisela have condoned such extreme methods?

For that matter, would Lana?

And it wasn't just what Bas had done himself. He'd dragged Dee into it. Thanks to him, an eighteen-year-old autistic girl was now a party to abduction. At a minimum, she'd have to carry the psychic baggage of having witnessed it all.

He grunted to himself. "Pull yourself together, man."

He grabbed the stone from the tray and squeezed it in his palm. "I'm probably just talking to myself right now. And if I'm not... I don't actually have anything to report. Except that I feel like an idiot holding a stone and talking to myself in the car."

He opened his hand and looked at the stone as if it might have changed.

"Okay, well. Bas out."

―――

Bas's eyes were half-closed when the man left Gisela's apartment. He immediately sat up straight and batted the sun visor out of his way. When had this visitor gone in? Or had he been inside the whole time? Last night's interrogation, and the lack of sleep afterward, had thrown off Bas's system, and he'd gotten drowsy in the warm car. But he was sure he couldn't have been out for more than an hour.

He grabbed the stone.

"Dee, if you're there, check this out. That man just left Gisela's apartment."

He appeared to be young, but his hair was gray. As he descended the front steps, he was peering down at something in his hand, but by the time Bas had untangled the strap of his binoculars from the handbrake, the man had pocketed it.

The cabin of the car was suddenly flooded with a high-pitched chirping, and Bas jerked forward, flinging his binoculars to the floor as he stabbed the *END* button on his mobile phone. "Dammit, dammit," he said as he rolled up both windows.

Across the street, the gray-haired man didn't seem to have noticed. He was making his way to a black Cadillac with tinted windows idling by the curbside. He got into the back seat, and the car pulled away.

A hired car?

Bas's phone warbled again.

"Bas Milius."

"Hi, Bas Milius, this is Junmo."

That meant Dee.

"Hey, kid."

"Dee has a message for you that I'm supposed to tell you."

"Okay, go ahead."

"She says to say that the gray hair man was holding your business card."

Bas thought back to Gisela's debut as Isabel Perreira last week, outside of the Metro Discovery office. He had handed her his card, never expecting that she would use it. Now, it seemed someone wanted to make sure she never did.

46

THURSDAY, MAY 9, 1991

THE WATER IS RUNNING as Bas stands before his bathroom mirror. Someone has left the sink running again, but only as he goes to turn it off does he realize he has no reflection. He peers at the glass, close enough to see the dirt and dried water droplets encrusting its surface, but there is no face looking back at him. There is only the massive boulder fountain of I, Mine. Turning, he finds Lana standing only feet away, watching him with no hint of the fury she had directed toward him on that last day. Has she come to forgive him?

Bas jerked awake with his ears full of static. His arm flew up from his side, knocking the water glass off the bedside table and onto the floor.

"Ugh," he croaked as he moved his head away from the damp spot on his pillow. He'd been sleeping so erratically over the past weeks that his body had apparently begun to reject sleep altogether.

Bas threw his covers off and sat up, squinting against the light through the window. He blinked his eyes clear and padded out to the kitchen.

His phone rang as he was peering into the fridge.

He picked up the receiver. "Yeah."

The ringing continued. A chirp.

The mobile phone.

He went to the counter, pulled the Motorola from its charging station, flipped it open, and pressed *SND* before pressing the handset to his ear.

"Bas Milius."

He heard only static on the other end of the line.

"Hello?"

"Mr. Bas Milius?" A man's voice.

"That's right," Bas said, covering his other ear to get a better listen. "Who am I speaking to?"

"I'm calling on behalf of Miss Isabel Perreira. She is not interested in in your investigation, nor in having any further contact with you. Please leave her alone."

Bas blinked. Who was this joker? He sat on the arm of his couch. On the coffee table, right next to Collette's magic stone, was a handwritten note.

"Miss Perreira, you said?" His cheeks had grown warm.

"That's right."

"You a friend of hers?"

"Not that it's any business of yours, but yes."

Lying. Bas grabbed the note in his free hand and waved it open.

> Did you find out who that man is? Why did he have your card? Is he part of Isabella's new life? You have to tell me when you find out.

The penmanship was that of a child. Dee must have light-pocketed it into his apartment, using the stone as a locator. He wished she hadn't; her continued involvement only put her in danger. She was still just a kid, after all, and with more challenges than most.

Bas sighed. "Sir, I'd like to ask you to cut the shit."

"I've thrown your card away, so we can just consider this matter settled. Have a pleasant evening, Mr. Milius."

"May I ask who I'm speaking with?"

"Sorry, I'm not taking questions."

Asshole.

"How do I know you speak on behalf of Isabel Perreira? How do I know you didn't just find my card in her purse?"

Bas heard the crackle of an exhaled breath. "I won't be provoked, Mr. Milius. Isabel is a friend, that is all. Goodbye."

Bas spoke quickly. "I happen to know you're lying, sir, because before last week Isabel Perreira didn't exist. Before that, she was Gisela Andie, a woman I've known for two decades."

A calculated risk, to be sure, but putting it all out there might pay off. If the man stayed on the line, it meant Bas was on to something, that the man knew something about Gisela's predicament. If he hung up, Bas would be no worse off.

Bas heard only his own breathing.

"Hello? I said I know—"

"I heard you, Mr. Milius." A crackle of static. "You know, I think perhaps we *should* meet."

"Okay. Where?"

"Are you familiar with Jordan Hall?"

Bas wasn't. "I can find it."

"It's on the campus of the New England Conservatory of Music. Meet me there tomorrow at ten a.m. I'll be sitting in the main auditorium watching rehearsals. I have gray hair."

Bas didn't say anything.

"Does that sound agreeable?"

"Sure, I can do that," Bas said. "I didn't catch your name."

"Call me Clancy."

"Clancy."

"Just Clancy."

47

FRIDAY, MAY 10, 1991

BAS FOUND a parking spot just outside the New England Conservatory campus at exactly ten a.m., then trotted the several blocks to Jordan Hall. He had debated whether to bring Collette's stone with him, but in the end had brought only his phone, leaving the stone in the Monza. Dee didn't have to watch him work.

He nearly missed Jordan Hall. The building was large and rectangular on the outside, looking for all the world like a tan brick office building, save for the posters out front advertising upcoming events.

Affixed to one of the double doors at the front entrance was a sign.

BGMC T<small>ECH</small> R<small>EHEARSAL</small>
9-12

The lobby was nearly empty, and the box office lights were off. Bas followed the muffled strains of vocal harmonics emanating from the auditorium.

Down on the stage a man was soloing something that sounded

contemporary, but was delivered in a classical style. Behind him stood several rows of men in casual attire.

Bas scanned the seats. A dozen or so were occupied, but only one of the attendees—sitting alone at the center of the hall—had that signature shock of gray hair.

Bas tromped down the steep aisle, then cut across. He took the empty seat next to Clancy. It strained under his weight.

"Good lord," Clancy said under his breath as he took Bas in for the first time.

"Mr. Clancy," Bas said.

Despite the gray hair, the man looked young up close—he couldn't have been older than thirty. Something about his face looked familiar, but not enough to jar anything loose.

"Sorry," Clancy said, turning back to the stage and blinking. "You are quite the formidable figure in the flesh."

"I get that sometimes." He eyed the stage. "They sound good."

In his hands, Clancy had a handwritten note—the rehearsal set list, by the look of it—and this morning's *Globe*, which he was just folding up. "I'm glad you could make it," he said, clearing his throat. "It's rare for them to get a rehearsal at the actual venue this far out, but... someone knew someone. The Pride Concert is on June ninth, in case you were interested."

"You know one of the singers?"

"My partner, Pal, sings with the chorus," he said, waiting a beat, in case Bas chose to respond. "I'm here for moral support, mainly. But it's also just a fine way to spend a Friday morning, don't you think?"

It must be nice to have Friday mornings free. But if the man had a car service, maybe he didn't need to hold down a job. Bas had no such excuse.

"Actually, I'm not quite sure why I'm here," Bas said, careful to not be heard over the soloist's balladic delivery.

"Surely that's not true," Clancy said, matching Bas's tone. "If there wasn't something you wanted, I very much doubt we would find you in this part of town."

So this Clancy was a snob.

Bas's phone chirped. He had set it to its lowest volume, so no one on stage should have heard, but Clancy shot him a look as Bas found the *END* button and mashed it.

"So, your partner, does he know about any of this... whatever this is?"

"What exactly do you think *this* is?"

Had he brought Bas all the way out here just to play games?

"I don't know, but you didn't bat an eye when I suggested that people were changing personalities. So why don't you tell me what you know?"

"I doubt I know any more than you do."

Bas nodded. "Fine, I'll start. The first thing I ask myself is what business you have with a person who is effectively four days old. I saw you come out of her apartment."

Clancy looked at him dubiously. "You've been following me?"

"Second, the fact that you invited me here tells me you have some stake in this."

Clancy shrugged, and watched the rehearsal.

"Third, the fact that you're even aware of this phenomenon tells me you're not affected by it. Taken together, I think that describes a person of interest."

Clancy leaned toward him. "Then by your own description, we have a lot in common."

"I told you why this is important to me. A woman I've known for a long time changed in front of my eyes. So what's your excuse? Why is this important to you?"

"Do I need an excuse?"

Bas looked at him blankly.

"Mr. Milius, these people may look convincing from a distance, but up close they're all somewhat lost. So call it a sense of humanity. If you found a wounded bird on your porch every morning, would you not tend to it?"

His choice of words made it sound like he had a knack for finding refactored people. Bas would come back to that.

The music continued, louder now, with the full-throated singing of the entire company.

Bas leaned over to Clancy, who smelled vaguely of cloves. "The way you talk about them—these people who no longer answer to their own names—it's so matter-of-fact."

"Amazing what the mind acclimates to. That doesn't mean I find it any less wondrous or perplexing."

The chorus had reached the thundering finale of their number, and Bas had trouble hearing himself speak.

"Let's just lay it out on the table, because it's making me crazy."

"By all means."

The final note echoed throughout the hall, and Clancy joined the scattered attendees in a round of applause as the chorus members congratulated each other on their performance.

Bas clapped politely as he spoke.

"I've seen two people in as many weeks who no longer recognize who they are. But that's just the start. When a person is refactored, it includes everything around them. Their lives are smoothed over. Their friends and family don't remember them. Their mailing labels show their new names. They have new apartments across town. New jobs. This isn't just amnesia we're talking about. And it's not some kind of elaborate production. From all appearances, these people have disappeared in place. Which is impossible. It would be so much easier to think that I was going insane, or that this was some sort of trick."

Bas's phone chirped again, and he quickly silenced it, but not before he drew some eyes from the stage.

"Maybe you should get that."

Why was Bas doing all the talking? He wasn't getting anywhere.

"Look," he said, "Boston is full of lost, lonely people. So how are you spotting *these* people?"

"I'm not sure how telling you helps me. In fact, my fear is that telling you will only further intertwine our paths, and I'm just trying to live my life, as I said. You should too. I've been seeing these people for a lot longer than you have, so I've seen certain patterns. It often manifests in chains—not just one person, but the people around them, too. It can be like a virus. And a malady this virulent isn't to be trifled with. Why do you think I told you not to contact Isabella?"

Was that the reason why, or was there something more? "I'm not worried about myself—I was in the room when it happened to Gisela, so I think I'm immune."

"Interesting," Clancy said, studying him. "Would you *know* if your personality had been replaced?"

Again with the games. But what would a persona wipe feel like? Most likely nothing at all. Then again, he wouldn't be tracking a refactored friend if he had been refactored himself. It wouldn't make sense.

"And what of the people near you?" Clancy asked. "Are you prepared to risk their safety as well, if you're a carrier? Are you so single-minded?"

Bas looked out over the seats, trying to keep his calm. The man sounded like Dee now. "All I'm trying to do is understand what's going on around me, because it's already hitting too close to home."

Clancy's eyes lingered on Bas for a moment before he spoke. "To answer your question... I see them."

"Seek them?"

"I *see* them, Mr. Milius—I'm not on some crusade. I'm very happy with my life."

"You see them," Bas repeated. "As in literally?"

"As I said. It's hard to describe. There's a kind of... a pearlescence about them. When I find someone who's been... what did you call it?"

"Refactored."

Collette's word. Bas noted that Clancy wasn't familiar with it.

"Refactored. Interesting. When I see one, I check in on them, to make sure all is well."

Which meant Dee wasn't the only one with gifts. It was both

surprising and not surprising at all. That would explain why this man was so secretive, as Dee was with her whispering. She had her struggles, and this man certainly must as well, despite his financial good fortune.

"Have you always seen them?"

Clancy looked down at his set list. "I don't know. It's been a long time."

"So which do you think came first, your seeing them, or their being there to be seen?"

"What are you asking me?"

Bas shifted in his seat. "I'm wondering what all this is about. Refactored people on the one hand, and people with magic abilities on the other. I don't know, you'd think it would make the news."

"I don't think it's as widespread a phenomenon as it may seem to you. I think you're just... caught up in it."

"I'll say."

As the chorus began their next piece, Bas's phone chirped again. He checked the LED display and recognized the number. Luckie Landing. Dammit. It must be Dee.

Bas pressed *END*.

"I want to continue our conversation," Bas said. "Can we do that?"

Clancy looked into his eyes, holding his gaze for longer than Bas was comfortable with. He seemed to be looking for something. But what?

"How about tomorrow, early?"

"I could do that."

"You'll come up to our condo. We're on Arlington Street, overlooking the Public Garden."

Boston's most expensive area. The guy was definitely loaded.

"After breakfast we'll be leaving for a few days, but in the morning I'll be watering my plants. Does before sunrise, at six thirty, sound agreeable?"

Bas didn't have much of a choice.

"Sure, I'll be there."

———

When Bas returned to his car, there was a note on the passenger seat, by Collette's stone.

> I know you have been leaving the stone in your car, Bas. You can not ditch me like that.

48

SATURDAY, MAY 11, 1991

BAS STOOD in the lobby of the posh condominium complex, catching his breath as his jacket dripped on the marble floor from the downpour outside.

"Can I help you?"

The concierge looked like he was made out of uniform, down to his white gloves.

Bas considered using Clancy's name. He'd spotted the man's last name by the front entrance, on the penthouse mailbox: *Puri*. What kind of name was Clancy Puri? It sounded like an alias.

Bas decided to stick with his own name. "Bas Milius."

The concierge didn't even need to consult his monitor. He nodded Bas toward the elevator. "Penthouse suite."

On his ride up to the *P* floor, Bas felt for the stone in his pocket. It was there, along with something extra just for Clancy.

The elevator opened up to a high-ceilinged antechamber, at the end of which was a set of double-doors framed by ferns. Bas knocked, fully prepared for a manservant to answer. But the compact man who pulled the door open was wearing a sauce-spattered chef apron emblazoned with the phrase *"Life Is a Song,"* in fancy lettering.

For a moment the man gaped up at Bas as if in shock, and it took him a moment to find his tongue. "Mr. Milius?"

"That's right."

"I'm Pal," he said, pulling the door wider. Clancy's partner. How much had Clancy told him?

Bas stepped in, removed his jacket, and hung it on a rack on the wall just inside. From within, choral music was playing, and the air smelled of licorice and spice.

"Clancy is expecting you," Pal said, his hands hooked through the front of his apron. He had a slight accent, maybe Indian. "Can I get you anything? Tea or juice?"

"Water would be good. Uh, tap."

"Certainly." He backed toward the kitchen and gestured toward the living room. "Clancy is straight through there, toward the back."

As Bas made his way through the opulent room, Pal returned to the kitchen where, from the sound of it, he was doing lip trills.

The walls of the condo were adorned in bold paintings featuring prowling leopards and sensuous women. Though spacious, the rooms were full of corners, a well-furnished maze of mirrors and glass. Even the awards looked sharp.

He found Clancy in a room that had been converted into a massive built-in greenhouse. Rain clattered against the glass enclosure.

"Pardon the mess," Clancy said, barely looking up from his floral wonderland. "Things are a little bit crazy around here. We have a little getaway planned... anyway, you're catching us before shit really hits the fan, as it were."

"This is some greenhouse," Bas said, approaching slowly, careful not to snag anything.

Clancy tutted. "Oh please, never call it a greenhouse. It is, now and forever, a *'temporary structure.'* As far as the city is concerned, at least."

He smiled as Pal entered with a tall glass of water in one hand and his apron in the other.

"I added a drop of lemon," the small man said, holding the glass up to Bas.

"Thanks."

Pal gave Clancy a peck on the cheek. "Everything should be set here, so I'll meet you after rehearsal, *nuurii*," he said, before turning back to Bas. "It was good to meet you, Mr. Milius."

"Likewise."

Bas sipped his water as Clancy snipped at some tangle of a plant with his pruning scissors.

A few seconds later Bas heard what he thought was the front door clicking shut.

"How long have you been together?"

"Quite a long time indeed," Clancy said, assessing his work before turning to Bas. "You can see I've done quite well for myself. But I can tell you that I would give it up—all of it—for that man. Life has thrown so much at him, and yet I'm the worrier. My concern isn't misplaced—our community faces existential threats daily, from intolerance to AIDS. But these are just the threats you see in the headlines. Other threats though..."

"The refactoring."

"There are threats that most people would never recognize. I'll tell you, I fear it more than anything, not for myself, but for Pal. It's like dream logic, where you may summon something by thinking of it."

"It's not just random though," Bas said. "It's connected to something."

Clancy approached, coming to the edge of the rubberized mat. "Something you said yesterday stuck in my head. You said the refactoring was hitting close to home."

"What?" Bas felt suddenly self-conscious. But maybe that's what Clancy needed before he would spill his guts. To know Bas had a more personal stake in this. "I mean..." What did he have to lose? "I lost my wife, ten years back."

"I'm sorry to hear it." The gray-haired man's pained expression showed that he meant it.

"Yeah, well, a week or so ago I was in..." Bas waved a hand, "wherever people go when they've given up. But I recently found a trace of her—after all this time—that takes a circuitous route all the way back to these personality wipes. A videotape of her, captured just before she died. How could I let that go?"

"I'm not following—related how?"

"Ten years ago, my wife Lana died in the South Station Singularity."

Clancy was silent for a moment, then nodded and moved back to his plants.

"I felt about her the way you do about Pal. Only one day she was gone, and all those feelings I had for her had nowhere to go. In a way that much *nothing*, all at once, is the kind of thing that can make you sick. Even when they sent me her ring."

"Ring?"

"Afterward, the cleanup crews sent out any valuables they'd found, to loved ones, and I got Lana's ring. It was like she took it off before... whatever happened, happened. I carried it around for almost ten years. Clung to it like it might keep me together."

"Do you have it with you now?" Clancy took a sip of his tea, but held the cup in both hands, as if he might drop it.

"I lost it a few weeks ago."

"I'm very sorry to hear it."

"No, it was my fault—call it stupidity tax. But Clancy, my point is, the same people who did what they did to Gisela—to Isabel—did something to my wife just before the Singularity. Now, to me it seems like you know something about all this, but here you are in your penthouse, just... living your life."

"I told you that much on the phone, Bas."

"Right, well, I was just living my life, too, until I lost my wife, and my life has been shit ever since."

Were Clancy's eyes damp? It was hard to tell. "I wish I had something to tell you."

Bas patted his pocket and pulled out the video printout of Lana in the South Station. He held it out for the man to see.

Clancy inhaled sharply and turned away from the photo as if he had seen a ghost.

"I printed this from the surveillance tape of my wife at the South Station. Now, I've seen a lot of strange shit in the past few weeks," Bas said, "from an autistic girl who can speak directly into people's heads to a cult abducting your 'lost people' just to make them dance. But this—"

Clancy turned. "Making them dance, how?"

"I'm talking about my wife, man."

"Tell me about the *dance*."

Bas laid the printout on a work table by Clancy's elbow. But Clancy was no longer even interested in it. Why was the man fixating on the wrong details?

It didn't matter. They could take a detour, as long as Bas could get back to why he had come all the way out here.

"Sure, okay. This group calls it 'the assembly.' It's twenty-some people doing these all-day repetitive routines. Not really a dance, per se, but synchronized. More like a ritual, you know, and they have stones with painted symbols and a scribe transcribing gibberish. Crazy shit. Have you heard of I, Mine?"

Clancy squinted, as if unsure what Bas was asking him.

"They're a secretive bunch. It's actually run by a couple, Fritz and Collette. They're just trying to live their lives, too. You'd like them."

But Clancy had gone pale. Did he know something?

"Mr. Milius, I'm afraid I'm feeling a bit under the weather. If you wouldn't mind collecting your photo—"

A tearing, spitting sound interrupted him, and Clancy backed into a plant holder, making a dozen pots rattle.

The man's face hadn't just gone pale, it was illuminated.

Bas turned to see a ball of light filling the living room he had just walked through, stray beams bouncing from every polished facet. He shielded his eyes as he thought back to the ball of light that had appeared just before Gisela was refactored. This phenomenon was exactly the same.

And then it was gone, without a trace.

"The fuck?" He looked over at his host, who was extricating himself from his plants. "Was that you?"

"It's definitely not—"

The sizzling hiss returned with full force, and Bas instinctively moved to one side. The blinding sphere throbbed with such force that he could feel it in his ribs.

Then it was gone again, just like before.

Bas's heart raced. Had something followed him here? "I swear it's not me."

"*Your photo.*"

Bas turned back to Clancy and peered down at the printout. The image was different. Lana was no longer in the center of the frame, and in fact she was partially turned away. Based on the movement, the shot had taken place several seconds after the moment Bas had captured.

And the image was *still moving*. Like the sheet of paper was a video being played in extremely slow motion.

The malevolent light ball sprang back into existence only feet away, but this time it vanished almost immediately.

Bas's muscles trembled. What was going on?

"You printed this image directly from that video you described, didn't you?" Clancy asked.

"Yeah. Was that... ?" He didn't need to ask if that had been a bad move.

Light filled the room again, making them both jump.

And again it was gone.

"You've been traced," Clancy said. He snatched the printout from the table and tore it into pieces.

"Hey!" Bas reached for the scraps of paper, but Clancy was already around the edge of the planter and into the next row.

His voice was loud. "If you want another Singularity event, you're doing exactly the right thing."

"I didn't do any of this!"

"I'm telling you, you're swatting at a hornet's nest."

But it was done. And with the printout reduced to confetti, Clancy stood stock-still, staring back into his living room.

His heart still racing, Bas watched, and waited.

Whatever the phenomenon had been, it seemed to be done.

Clancy crossed through the living room. Bas followed close behind, crinkling his nose at the smell of ozone. Maybe Clancy was right—maybe that printed image had drawn the attention of I, Mine's refactoring magic. But that didn't give this penthouse-dwelling master of the universe the right to destroy it.

Bas's host held the penthouse door open with one hand, with Bas's raincoat hanging from the other.

"Mr. Milius, I'm going to ask you to please leave."

"You're kidding me. We're just starting to get—"

"And I *implore* you, leave this alone, before things get any worse. You do not know what you're up against."

Clancy wasn't going to talk at all. He was just going to ignore everything and hope it would all go away on its own.

Bas grabbed his jacket. "Do *you* know what I'm up against? What do the rituals and phenomena mean?"

"*No* one knows. Stop looking for conspiracies where there are none."

49

SATURDAY, MAY 11, 1991

DEE WAS IN HER GARDEN, cold and wet, with no idea how she had gotten there. Her body was electric, her nerves coursing with white fire that fed on itself. That was why she was running laps in the mud, slipping sideways, catching herself on the wooden fence, wringing her hands in a desperate attempt to disperse the seething turmoil within.

She had felt something terrible through Bas's stone, the pull from that disconnected energy source—the magic with no conjurer. It was alive, and desperate with hunger. Through its white radiance Dee had glimpsed a room, had seen Bas there with another man. And underlying it all was a desire, insistent and foreign, to fly outward, to expand in all directions until she had consumed everything.

No, not her.

It was that ravenous sun. With each passing second it had grown stronger.

Until Dee had surrounded it and pressed inward.

Until she was blind and numb.

By the time she had regained her senses, Bas's stone had fallen silent.

"You seem to be stuck again, Dee."

She jumped as Junmo touched her shoulder. She was covered in mud to her knees, but the rain had already begun to wash it away.

Residual energy surged up and down her spine, and she flapped as fat drops bathed her cheeks.

Stimming hands, like an intoxicant, taking her away from the buzzing rush.

She peered through her sodden bangs and saw Junmo standing a foot away, his arm still outstretched, wanting to help, but not daring to set her off.

He knew.

He had his meltdowns, too, and understood that she was on the verge.

Say sorry.

She wanted to say sorry, but her mind was going a mile a minute.

Sorry.

She attempted to whisper it, but it didn't feel right.

He didn't hear.

Pushing past him, Dee paced a trench into the mud, marching to and fro until she felt her gears shift.

Her body was winding down, the commotion within finally fading away as Junmo stood watching, loyal.

Dee tried to whisper again, but couldn't articulate. She had to tell him everything would be okay, but her body betrayed her, grabbing his shirt in her right hand and not letting go.

Junmo looked at her closed fist and patted her hand. "It's okay," he said. "Just hang in there, that's all I ask."

Dee might have laughed if she had caught her breath, but the burst of love she felt for her brother right then loosed her hand.

She let go of Junmo's shirt and cooed as a million droplets pelted the ground around them.

"Have you got something you want to say to me, Dee? Because it's getting pretty chilly out here."

Can you hear me, Junmo?

"Yes yes yes I can."

Can you help me with another note?

The boy looked pleased. "I thought you would never ask, actually."

50

SATURDAY, MAY 11, 1991

AFTER CIRCLING the block several times in the rain, Bas noticed a police cruiser making the rounds. He must look like a vagrant, full of nervous energy and soaked to the skin. He dashed across the street, returning to the Monza. But his mind was still going in circles after the encounter in Clancy's penthouse condo, and he dropped the keys twice as he tried to unlock the driver-side door.

Once inside, Bas pulled the door shut and listened to the rain pounding against the windshield. His breath steamed up the glass as he flashed back to the apartment.

The moving photo.

The ball of light.

And Clancy Puri, tending to his penthouse garden and stonewalling at every opportunity, as if Bas were just some magic enthusiast looking to learn the secrets to the act.

A flitting sound was accompanied by a puff of air across Bas's cheek. For a moment he thought a bird had gotten into the car. He flicked on the dome light and saw not a hapless bird, but a slip of paper on the passenger seat—the only dry thing in the car. Bas felt the stone in his pocket, still warm. Dee must have keyed into it again.

He had been so caught up in the commotion that he hadn't thought about her.

He held the note under the orange glow of the streetlight.

Are you okay? I am okay.

I saw you with a gray hair man. I saw inside the energy source. I saw you because it saw you. It wanted everything but I held it down. I made it stop. But it hurt in my head like fire.

That had to explain the on-again, off-again effect. Every time that ball of energy tried to push its way into the condo, Dee smacked it back down.

The note continued.

The light was the same as in Gisela's screening room. It did not have connections. Bas. This magic is unstable. The small things seem safe but the bigger things can set off reactions that get out of control.

I am tired. And now afraid that they may know where I am. Someone may have seen me this time.

But I am not giving up on Gisela. I can figure out the route to Mission Hill, but it would be better if you can drive me. Can we meet? I want to talk about what is happening. And what to do next. I want to get Gisela back before worse thing happens.

Bas put the note down, mulling over Dee's words. She had said before that the sunbursts weren't connected to anything—not even to I, Mine. So who was behind them? If Dee hadn't stepped in this time, would that thing have kept flashing until it found a way through Bas's natural resistance to the refactoring?

Had Collette been telling the truth, that they had nothing to do with the refactors?

Bas made a dismissive sound. Getting the truth out of Fritz or Collette would have been the greatest magic trick of all.

What he needed now was to regroup. Take a shower. Eat something.

He slid his phone out of its car mount and dialed his own apartment. On the third ring someone picked up. He heard only breathing.

"Mo, that better be you."

"Oh, Jesus. Don't do that."

It was good to hear her voice, but the lack of sass was worrisome. "Everything okay?"

"You tell me, old man. Half your living room is gone, and it looks like your landlord abandoned a remodeling job. I mean, I appreciate the minimal thing as much as the next gal, but you could have left the damned TV."

There it was. Just what he needed to take his mind off of the situation up in Clancy's condo. Maybe Mo would even stick around this time.

"I'll explain later," he said, making a note to himself to hatch a plausible explanation. "I was just about to head back. I'll pick us up something for breakfast."

51

SUNDAY, MAY 12, 1991

THE FOOTPATHS of the Arnold Arboretum were swarming with brightly dressed visitors attending the Lilac Festival. Most likely because of the warm, sunny Sunday, the crowds had turned out in droves. Brenda had planned the outing months ago.

As Dee hurried to keep up with Brenda, Walter, and Junmo, she adjusted her brain muffs so they wouldn't pinch her ears quite so much. She was having a hard time losing herself in the floral splendor unfolding around her. She was worried about Gisela. Bas still hadn't responded to her note. If he wasn't going to take this seriously, she would go it alone.

"Look, sweet pea."

Brenda was leaning in close to her and pointing to a row of colorful trees.

Dee could read the concern on her foster mother's face, and she understood why. She took Brenda's hand in hers.

I love it.

She took a deep breath of the honeyed air. She would try to open herself to the momentary distraction, just for a few hours. Strolling the paths of the urban wild might allow her to recharge, as well as put her parents' minds at ease.

Brenda squeezed her hand, and they eased through the crowd toward Walter and Junmo.

The air was thick with the spice of the blooms, the currents so fragrant that Dee could almost see them. Lilacs of every variety were on display, from diminutive shrubs to bush lilacs so tall they resembled trees. They bordered the path like slowly dancing fireworks, exploding with color, though the white ones were always the sweetest. More than once Dee felt herself compelled to get as close to the flowers as possible, lifting her arms through hanging petals and feeling honeybees brush by her cheeks.

Walter and Junmo were moving too quickly, so Dee and Brenda stopped trying to catch up, and instead set their own leisurely pace.

"I love seeing you like this," Brenda said as they followed the path around a pond.

Happy Mother's Day, by the way.

Brenda laughed quietly. "It's funny, but this is the first time I've heard you say that."

Dee had a lot to make up for, now that she had allowed herself to communicate directly. After only a few weeks, the thought of returning to silence felt stifling.

I was thinking the other day, I had just turned eight when I lost my parents. Now I'm eighteen, so I guess we've known each other longer than I knew them.

"Oh, Dee." Brenda inhaled sharply.

She hadn't meant it like that though.

I mean, of course I loved my first parents. But I'm lucky to have second parents like you and Walter.

As they approached the famous gentle spiral of Bussey Hill Road, Dee's attention was drawn to something across the lawn, just through a cluster of torch azaleas. At first she thought something had gotten into her eye, maybe pollen or a gnat. She rubbed her eyelids, then peered more carefully into the gap between two trees, where the foliage formed a welcoming canopy away from the crowd.

At the back of her mind came a single tug, and with that her heart missed a beat.

Would it be okay if I met you back at the Centre Street Gate?

The request took Brenda off guard. "Are you sure?"

Just for a few minutes.

"Of course, you want some quiet. I'll be there. You take your time."

She gave Dee a little wave, then retraced her steps out, clockwise around the spiral path. Dee returned her attention to the back of the park, half expecting the odd mirage to have dissipated. But it remained where she had first seen it.

She left the path and walked carefully across the grass to the space between the lilac trees. There, the crosshatch of branches appeared to merge with each other in a way that wasn't physically possible. Bark and bloom fused together like light bent through a prism. And she was drawn forward by the faintest pull. Not from the trees themselves, but from something raw and foreign.

Something she might be able to decipher if she just looked a little closer.

52

SUNDAY, MAY 12, 1991

BAS HAD MANAGED to avoid the South Station ever since the Singularity. Today he stood close enough to its front entrance to feel the heat reflecting from its refurbished façade.

With equal parts curiosity and revulsion, he allowed his feet to carry him closer. He felt distant from himself, as if he were merely watching it happen, not really experiencing it firsthand. He wiped his palms on his jacket. The weather didn't call for the extra layer, and he shrugged out of the garment and slung it over his shoulder—just another casual traveler—before pushing into the chilly front hall.

Positioned like a chess piece on the marble tile, Bas allowed the Sunday crowd to part around him as he gawked up at the exposed struts along the high ceiling.

Lana was here.

Was he trying to convince himself? Of course she had been here. Just before she disappeared.

After a minute his heart rate evened out, and walking seemed like a good idea, if only to allow the sweat along his brow to air-dry.

If it weren't for Eshe's installation he never would have come.

So: in, then straight back out.

No big deal.

In the meantime, it was good to focus on something other than his case.

Crusade.

Dee had been champing at the bit to pick up where they had left off, to snap Gisela out of it before her new personality became ingrained. But she had been quiet since yesterday's note. Maybe fatigue had finally caught up with her. All that hand waving and rocking couldn't help. Being autistic seemed like a lot of work, even on the best day.

Bas spotted Eshe by a curtained-off section near the stairs up to the second floor. She was speaking with a young man who appeared to be a station staff member, but she broke the conversation off as soon as she saw Bas hanging back.

"Hey, you! I'm so glad you made it." She gave him a one-armed hug, then peered up at his face. "You're looking better than before, I think. Have you been taking care of yourself?"

"Hey, I'm here, aren't I?"

She gave him a nudge. "I know, and I'm glad."

"How's Gaétan?"

Bas felt bad as soon as the words were out.

"He's fine, Bas," she said with a smirk. "You didn't come down here just to ask me about him, I hope."

"I'm sorry. No, I came to see you, and your exhibit, of course. How's it shaping up?"

"Really well. I was just talking to the project manager, and it looks like everyone is happy upstairs. Come see?"

"Yeah, show me."

Her eyes were on Bas as he took in the mosaic of arresting prints along the gallery wall. Her pride was apparent, and she had every right to it.

"It's amazing, Eshe," Bas said.

While he had seen most of the portraits before, on the wall of the station these women's faces had taken on a new gravity. Still, it wasn't the weight of her subjects' captured gazes Bas appreciated most, but the intensity of Eshe's own presence among them. Today the station belonged more to Eshe, and a little less to Bas's memory of the Singularity.

"People are going to see this all the way from the other side of the station," he said. "I'm so happy for you."

"Thank you, Bas. Your opinion means a lot to me."

She looked now much as she had when he had first met her, browsing through art books in the Harvard Book Store. Looking at her face, he could almost pretend he hadn't dragged her through several years of his bullshit.

"Anyway, I need to get back to prep," she said. "I still have some details to get perfect before tomorrow."

"Yeah, go ahead. It's going to be great, sweets."

"*Sweets*," she said, with a grin. "You take care of yourself, okay, Bas? And keep in touch."

"Definitely," he said. "Yeah, definitely."

———

Bas ducked through the curtain on the other side of Eshe's exhibit, at the foot of the stairs. Emboldened by her buoyant mood, he held his ground, his eyes tracing along the railing up to the mezzanine.

"Excuse me," said a short woman hefting a backpack as she made her way past him.

"Yeah, sorry," Bas said, his voice far away.

He couldn't help being curious.

He was already here, after all. He could pay his respects to Lana, instead of just turning the well-worn sorrow around in his head.

He could stand where she had stood.

Taking the stairs, Bas kept his hand on the banister, as if to steady himself. He followed the mezzanine around the perimeter of the open atrium to the point directly opposite the stairs.

In the spot where Lana had once stood, a memorial statue had been installed, a three-faced obelisk. Bas circled the sculpture, examining it as though it might hold clues. Each of its faces depicted, in bas relief, a scene related to the station.

A fleet of buses.

A row of trains.

A crowd of people.

But the three facets ran into each other, as if the monument had been left out in the sun for too long. The result made Bas's hair stand on end. He couldn't help but think of the curious artifact he had seen in the back of I, Mine's display case, the fountain pen and the flip lighter merged in similar fashion.

At the base of the memorial was an inscription that Bas only managed to skim.

... to the fine people ...

... their indomitable spirit ...

... never be forgotten.

Bas's eyes were back on the three scenes, each smearing into the next. Surely that was nothing more than creative license on the part of the artist, a work of impressionism meant to connect three disparate aspects of the station.

Bas turned to face the silver railing. He eyed it as if it might be electrified. Lana had been there, at the very end. But who had she been then?

Realizing he had no desire to relive that particular past, Bas put his jacket back on and retraced his steps to the stairs. The memorial was just an overwrought execution, that was all. To read anything more into it was to indulge in the most self-defeating flight of fancy.

53

SUNDAY, MAY 12, 1991

DEE AWOKE in a strange room with no memory of having gone to sleep.

She sat up on her cot, and suddenly her attention was on herself rather than her surroundings. Something had changed. She looked down at herself, and found she was wearing unfamiliar clothing, some kind of black robe.

As she swung her legs around to the floor, and felt the fabric pull over her skin, Dee realized it wasn't just her clothes that had changed. She *felt* different. The fluidity of her movements. The precision in her limbs. The... focus. It was as if the usual background noise had been dialed all the way down, leaving only a deep silence, with herself at its center.

Vertigo washed over her, but it was gone before she needed to steady herself on the edge of the bed.

Where was she?

The room wasn't like any she had seen before. It was almost empty, with a wooden frame, soft floors, and a small mirror and sink in the corner.

How had she gotten here?

She remembered the Arnold Arboretum.

Lilac Sunday.

The flowers, the crowds, her brain muffs.

Brenda had been with her, and Walter and Junmo. Where they here, too? Had Dee had a catastrophic meltdown, and been brought to this quiet room to recuperate?

But no, she would have remembered something.

Dee remembered the space between the trees.

A light pocket.

No. Why would she have called one there, with so many people around her?

She tried to remember the events leading up to that decision, but her memories were like fallen leaves.

She hadn't opened the light pocket at the Arnold Arboretum.

It had been there already, had been waiting for her. By the time she'd realized that, she had drawn too close to it, and then...

Something.

Something quick.

Now her gravity was off, or the air was too thin. Dee looked at her hands, and didn't recognize them. They didn't just *look* different, they didn't *work* the same way. She rubbed her skin. Was it darker than before? Did her hands feel smoother?

Adrenaline surged through her system as she pushed a flood of thoughts away.

It's not possible.

Dee stood up in a single move, her body obeying her wishes with a newfound grace. As she crossed to the sink, the door to her room slid to the side.

It was a stranger. A man in a black robe like hers. Dee froze as his face broke into a smile. A stranger shouldn't smile that way. She took a step back as he entered.

"Well, Naadiya Khalaji," he said, as if he were meeting a celebrity for the first time. "Am I pronouncing that right?"

Dee's heart pounded in her chest, and she was suddenly all too aware of her dry throat.

"Can I just tell you what a privilege it is to meet you?"

Dee backed up against her cot and put her hands up, though she trusted them about as much as she trusted this man.

"Oh, you have nothing to fear from me. In fact, I *owe* you, let me say. And of course you're absolutely free to go. I just... you know, I'd hope you'd hear me out first."

What do you want? Where's my family?

Her whisper made him blink. "That's a remarkable talent you have. Collette told me about it, but it's something else to experience it firsthand." He retreated to the doorway and leaned against the frame.

Collette. Then this man was with the cult, the one Bas had gotten tangled up with.

The man went on. "Happily, you have no need for this particular skill anymore. You can speak—using your mouth—if you like. Give it a try."

What did you do to me? Why am I here?

The man frowned. "My name is Fritz Frey, and my wife and I run an organization to bring together... well, members of various neurological spectra. Such as yourself."

Skirting around the man, Dee walked to the sink and peered into the mirror.

Only it was a window.

A stranger stared back at her, an Asian woman. Dee reached up and touched the glass with a hand that wasn't hers, and the Asian woman did the same.

Dee's stomach sank.

Where's my body?

She tried to let go, to fall out of herself. But she remained, standing in the middle of the room, in this stranger's body. If her real body was somewhere nearby, she couldn't feel it.

A quick rap sounded at the door. Collette poked her head in behind Fritz.

"Hello, again," she said, her voice far too casual for the circumstances. "I wasn't sure you'd be awake yet."

"We were just getting acquainted," Fritz said, "using the whispering. You were right about that. It'll be useful."

Dee focused on Collette.

You have to let me go. Tell me where my body is.

"She's scared, Fritz," Collette said, her eyes on Dee. "And come on, I don't blame her. Dee, sweetie, I'm sure this is disorienting for you. But we're trying to give you more autonomy. This body you have now is yours, if you like. As an act of good faith on our part."

I didn't ask for this!

Fritz spoke softly to Collette. "I thought she'd be talking."

"Give her time. This a lot all at once."

"Right," he said, nodding. "You're right, of course. Maybe I should go. The assembly has been ingesting the new routines, and I want to be there when they're done."

"Go. We'll check in later, after I get her situated."

Situated. The word struck a chord of fear in Dee as Fritz left and Collette returned her full attention to her.

"Your family is fine, Dee. And your body is safe, too. You're completely safe here. I want you to put that fear out of your thoughts, so you can concentrate on taking advantage of your increased freedom."

What is this? Dee put her arms out in front of her like she was holding something she had found in a field. *Whose body is this?*

"No one who would ever miss it, trust me," Collette said, moving closer, her words out of step with the expression on her face. "This is you, Dee, for as long as you like. And it's thanks to you, after all. You showed us how to do this."

What was she talking about? Had they been watching her when she had *head-swapped* their security man? Had they used her own abilities against her?

"Dee, we owe you so much, because of what you've given us. You really caught Fritz's eye with your transference abilities, calling your routines from such a distance, and without triggers as far as we can tell. I mean, we have similar technology, but nothing quite as elegant as yours. You're a natural. A prodigy. Or... what did they call it? A *savant*. The way you commandeered Anton... well, we've never seen anything quite like that. Fritz was so enamored with your raw abilities that he started to disassemble a sample of it right away."

Why are you doing this? Can't you leave people alone?

Collette's momentary confusion became something duller. Disappointment—that was it.

"Dee, you're young. It's hard for you to imagine the potential of what we've stumbled on to, isn't it?"

Dee felt the body around her, and it was like a suit several sizes too small. Her skin crawled. She eyed the doorway, but Collette was blocking the way. Dee wasn't sure she could control this body well enough to make a run for it anyway. And even if she succeeded, where would she go?

Collette was still talking, more quietly now, as if to herself. "I mean, you discovered it on your own, independently. We're on the same team."

I'm not interested in potential! I only want to get my friend Gisela back.

"So *help* us," Collette said, taking another step forward, her eyes alive. "Work with us to engineer that fix. We can provide any resources you need to patch—"

The floor lurched, and the sound that followed was so loud that Dee felt it in her legs. Collette dropped to a squat reflexively, then turned and leapt for the door, holding the jamb in both hands. She peered out into the hall as a great commotion rose from outside.

Dee leaned against the wall, and she thought she could feel a rhythmic bump reverberating through her hands.

"What the fuck is going on?" Collette called out to someone sprinting by the doorway.

Dee heard no response.

54

SUNDAY, MAY 12, 1991

AFTER WANDERING out of the South Station, Bas drove as if in a trance. He only realized he was on his way to Luckie Landing when he was halfway across town.

He needed to speak with Dee.

His pilgrimage to the site of Lana's death—to the exact location of her death—hadn't helped in the way he'd imagined it would. Standing where his wife had stood should have given him a sense of connection with her—but instead he felt only a great emptiness, as if the void of her absence had marked him.

And there was something else—something more. Something that triggered a seething anger within him. He now felt certain that Lana hadn't been lost, but rather *taken*. And whether or not I, Mine had been behind it, Fritz's and Collette's organization had been there from the start, watching. They had never stopped watching.

One way or another, Bas would bring an end to that. He might not be able to coerce them to reverse the refactoring—Gisela might be lost forever—but stopping their parasitic operation would make for a fine consolation prize.

The question was how to go about it. An anonymous tip to the police would at most ruffle their feathers, and at worst lead to a spate of unnecessary refactors.

Bas exited the freeway and took surface streets toward Dee's neighborhood.

He and Dee were immune to the refactors, and that was the beginning of an answer. And Dee's magic—that was the bigger part. With Dee's help, he could find a way to disrupt I, Mine for good. Break their stones. Disperse their assembly.

Without that, Collette and Fritz would be dead in the water.

Pulling his mobile phone from its holster, Bas dialed Brenda and Walter's number. The line was picked up immediately.

"Did you find her?" It sounded like Brenda, but it was hard to tell. She was panting into the handset.

"Brenda? It's Bas."

"Bas! Dee is missing."

"What?"

"*Missing.* She's *gone.* Tell me she's with you."

Bas nearly sideswiped a car crossing the four-way stop, and got an earful for it as the other driver laid on their horn.

"*Fuck!* No, she's not with me. Where did you last see her?"

"We were at the Arnold Arboretum, all of us. I was with her and she was fine. But I stepped away from her, and she never came out. I thought about calling you, since Dee said you used to be a police officer, but I've been scrambling since the police shut down the park. I just came home to pick up some things, and we're heading back there. Can you help? You still know people from the police, don't you?"

Bas pulled over to the curb. He couldn't concentrate on driving with her yelling in his ear.

"Yes, of course," he said. "Though I'm sure they're already doing everything they can. They take these things very seriously."

Had Dee slipped out to visit Gisela without him? He doubted it. She wouldn't have done something so rash, knowing how it would affect her foster family.

"Brenda, tell me, slowly, what happened. How long ago was this?"

"What time is it?" He heard fumbling on the other end. "Almost two hours."

Something she had said was still bothering Bas. "What did you mean when you said she never came out?"

"I don't understand it. I had only left her for three minutes when I went back in to find her. I left her in the middle of the park, and there was only one way in or out."

A chill crept across Bas's skin.

"Bas?"

"Yeah, can you... do you have the contact number of the officer you talked to?" Bas pulled back into the street. He made a U-turn, nearly dropping the phone as he did so.

"It was a patrol officer," said Brenda. "Uh, Sanni Merilahti. But she passed it to a Detective Bryson Teahan." She read him the number.

"I don't know him, but I'll reach out." Bas pulled back onto the freeway, pressing the gas until the Monza shuddered up the incline.

"Can you come meet us here? We're about to leave."

"I'm sorry, Brenda, I can't right now. But I promise you, we're going to find Dee."

After terminating the call, Bas could think only of the look on Collette's face when she had seen Dee use her abilities. It wasn't just interest, it was something closer to determination. If she and Fritz had found a way to use Dee's light pocket against her, there was nowhere in the world Dee would be safe.

55

SUNDAY, MAY 12, 1991

A SERIES of jolts rocked Dee's room as strangers ran by her open doorway, and a great subterranean zipping sound tickled the hairs of her arms, as if some underlying structure was about to give way.

Amid the clamor, Collette had departed, and Dee's door had been left unguarded. She urged herself toward the doorway, and her donor body complied.

The hallway looked much like her room, with plain wooden walls, soft mat floors, and plants in every nook. Except nothing lined up. Something was pulling this place apart.

A couple ran by, clinging to each other, and Dee ducked back into her room and pressed up against the wall. Every movement felt translated, as if she were working an elaborate marionette. Her captors were crazy to think she could live inside this foreign body, wearing it like a suit.

She squeezed her eyes shut and reached out, imagining her mind expanding into the void in all directions, searching for her own body —her real body. It couldn't be far away, could it? What if it became injured? Or worse?

What if Collette and her husband had gotten rid of it altogether?

A hollow report sucked the air into the hallway, and Dee's ears popped, silencing the din of many shouting voices. She swallowed, and her eardrums clicked back into place, but the muffled groan was now a roar in her ears, loud enough to make her wince. She feared the ceiling might collapse at any moment, trapping her.

She stepped into the hallway and moved in the direction the couple had fled, passing several rooms just like hers, all empty.

A group of strangers appeared from around a corner up ahead, coming her way. All of them wore the same black garb. Dee quickly sidestepped into an abandoned room; she wouldn't make it far going against traffic. Her only option was to go with the flow, and hope no one got close enough to identify her as an interloper.

She checked to be sure no one was around, then sprinted down the hall. A sharp turn took her toward a brightly lit open area, and she saw the source of the commotion.

Several dozen feet away the walls had been shredded, as if torn away by some great beast. The gaping breach offered a view through the underlying structure of the building, to a pristine courtyard beyond. There, a gray-haired man was kneeling in the dirt, his wet clothing hanging heavy in the misty drizzle, his head bowed, as if he was in prayer.

Across the muddy lawn from him, opposite Dee, Collette clung to what remained of the wall with one hand, while the other fluttered at the pouch at her waist. She was grabbing for one of her enchanted stones.

Were they facing off? If so, Dee had a pretty good idea whom she was rooting for.

Dee glanced back at Collette's opponent—and she realized that she had seen him before. This was the man Bas had gone to meet in that fancy apartment.

Clancy.

The man who had known the Isabel version of Gisela.

Had he been working with this cult or not?

Collette's arm-waving caught Dee's attention. At first she thought the woman was waving to her, but then Collette snapped her wrists like she was rolling dice, and something flew from her open hands, too fast for Dee to see.

Clancy flew back across the courtyard, leaving behind a ghostly smudge in the air, as if he had been snatched by an invisible force. He hit the dirt hard enough that Dee could hear it from the edge of the hall. As Collette advanced through Clancy's faded afterimage, smoky tendrils snaked outward from her back, each of them bearing a copy of her face. It was the same nightmarish manifestation she had conjured in the warehouse.

Eyes were suddenly in the air before Dee, empty and leering; one of Collette's rogue tendrils had found her. Dee shrieked, caught her ankle on a potted plant, and spilled backward hard against the wall, drawing the attention of several additional Collettes. The air around Dee was suddenly filled with eyes, drawing closer to her even as the central Collette still stood over Clancy outside.

Dee tried to wave the eyes away, to no avail. Getting her feet back under her, she righted herself and prepared to withdraw. These eyes were on her, but Collette herself was focused on Clancy. She couldn't really monitor everything at the same time, could she?

It didn't matter. Dee didn't have a choice. She had to run.

The main Collette raised her arms. She must have retrieved more of the stones from her pouch. Clancy was propelled back into the courtyard wall, and Dee was nearly knocked off her feet from the resulting shock wave.

Dee turned to flee—only to find nothing behind her but the caved-in wreckage where the corridor had been only moments before. She was trapped where she stood.

I'm never gonna get out.

A tangle of scrap came raining down, missing her by inches.

Dammit!

Against every instinct, Dee faced Collette and Clancy's arena once more. What she saw defied comprehension.

The man, his head lolling and eyes half-lidded, had sprouted a hundred luminous filaments that reached toward his rival like some spectral fungus. At the same time, the anemone of Collettes darted through the air, consuming the glowing threads like some predatory eels taking chunks out of coral.

She was *feeding* on him, or something equally dreadful. And she wasn't finished with her attack. The central Collette was already reaching for her stones again.

The next few seconds were a blur of instinct. With a single practiced hand signal, Dee called up her light pocket as she *head-hopped* to Collette, smearing it across the distance between them. The light formation made Collette lurch back.

Dee snapped back to her borrowed body.

Reached through the light pocket to Collette's side.

Wrenched the pouch of stones from her waist.

And dropped it into the void between them.

As Dee pulled her empty hand from the light pocket, the maelstrom of alternate Collettes dissipated, leaving a single confused Collette spinning around, looking for her thief.

Clancy seized the opportunity. He made a rapid set of gestures with his hands, then shielded his eyes. At first Dee thought he had failed—nothing happened—but a second later a shimmering tornado shot up beneath Collette's feet. It consumed her like locusts bursting from the ground, tiny teeth on the wind.

When the twisting chaos around Collette finally came to a halt, nothing was left of the woman but a vaguely Collette-shaped vortex, like a deeply glowing sand sculpture.

"I should have done that a long time ago."

Clancy's voice was like scissors in a dark room, and stopped Dee where she stood. Clancy had countered Collette's magic, and he'd used no stones as far as Dee could tell. Maybe he was like Dee. Maybe he was actually trying to help. But what if he was worse than the cult leaders he was dispatching? What else was he capable of? What if he was behind the refactors all along?

"What the hell are you doing here?"

It was Bas.

The oversized detective entered the courtyard from the opposite side. He approached Clancy carefully, wary of Collette's residual material. He appeared haggard, like he hadn't slept in days. But seeing a familiar face made Dee's heart race.

Bas!

He glanced up, but showed no sign of recognizing her.

"You have no business being here, Mr. Milius," Clancy said. "I suggest that you go live your life, while it's still yours."

"Not before I get some answers."

Before Dee could explain to Bas who she was, another figure emerged from the ruined passage at the opposite side of the muddy lawn.

"Has it ever occurred to you to ask nicely?" Fritz asked, his arms folded behind his back. "You really did a number on the place, didn't you? Not to mention Collette." He shook his head at the remains of his wife. "I'll get to her later."

Clancy was on his feet. "You couldn't leave it alone, could you?"

Fritz's only response was to stand on his toes, as if he was uncomfortable being the shortest man in the courtyard.

"You two know each other?" Bas asked.

"Sorry," Fritz said to Clancy, "it's just so odd seeing you here, *now*. I guess I'm a little... is it starstruck? I think it is." He looked at Bas. "But I can't figure out why the two of *you* would be on good terms."

Whatever this was, the tension in that open area was thick enough for Dee to feel from the hallway.

Bas, I know you can hear me.

Fritz circled Collette's remains. "I'm going to guess this was you, Clancy. I have to ask, what is it with you and people's wives?"

Clancy moved close enough to Fritz to bite his cheek. *"You're fucking it up for everyone, with no regard for the consequences!"*

"What are you talking about?" Bas asked.

Fritz's eyes were still on what was left of Collette. "You're one to talk, sir. I've been repairing all the damage *you* caused."

"Short-term, myopic..." Clancy scoffed. "You and your wife were easily the worst hires I ever approved."

That made Fritz look up. He stepped gingerly around Collette and peered into Clancy's eyes like he was trying to see what was on the other side.

"Clancy... *Yeats?*"

Bas looked on, his face showing the same confusion that Dee felt.

"Clancy Fucking *Yeats?* I should have... but *how?*"

Dee was focused on Clancy's fingers, and that sinking feeling returned as the man made a series of gesticulations that could only mean one thing. He was about to conjure something, and with Bas not five feet away from him.

Bas, it's Dee! Fritz and Collette body-swapped me.

The detective blinked—he had heard her this time—but his attention was divided.

Bas, we have to get out!

Against her better judgment—and before she lost her nerve—Dee started to make a run for him. She might not be able to drag him out of that courtyard, but she would at least try.

She didn't see Fritz's eyes on her until it was too late. He gave her a kind of casual nod, and with that, Dee's chances of exiting the hallway vanished. The walls and floor stretched backward like rubber sheets, pulling Dee along with them. Even running at full speed, she could make no progress.

As she struggled not to be pulled out of view entirely, Dee shouted, using her body's voice.

"Bas, it's Dee!"

The words didn't sound right, and her effort to keep pace with the sliding ground was starting to make her lightheaded.

But it worked.

Something in Bas's expression changed.

He took a step away from the standoff, finally, only to stop when he had positioned himself between her and the two men. He wasn't coming to her aid; he was blocking her from whatever was about to come next.

"Dee, if that's you, you have to leave!"

As soon as the words were out, Clancy made a gesture with his hands.

Bas, I can't—

Dee's eardrums popped, and for a split second she was in free fall. By the time the ground had caught her in the ribs, knocking the wind from her lungs, the hallway had stopped receding. Out in the courtyard, Fritz had summoned a wall of crawling light to separate him from Clancy, whose hands were already at work on something else.

Bas was on his butt again, and—wisely, Dee thought—he was scooting away from the two other men.

"Please don't," Fritz said, pushing the wall of light toward his opponent like it was a shield. "Clancy, please? I wish we could talk. I don't want to have to do this."

Bas had nearly made it to the hallway.

"Go to hell," Clancy said, raising his arms.

But before he could complete his finger gesture, Fritz's light projection turned into something else. It must have been something like a light pocket, but Fritz had done something different with it. As the light turned blue, it gave off a staticky hiss and leapt the final distance between Fritz and Clancy, consuming the gray-haired man entirely.

Bas shielded his eyes—and for that matter, so did Fritz.

An unfamiliar sound escaped Dee's lips as she stared into the fluttering hole punched through the air where Clancy had been a moment before. Clancy was still visible, but he looked like a hologram, with some other place visible through the place his body had been.

As Dee got back to her feet, only one thought entered her mind.

They had to get out of here.

Bas, let's go!

But Fritz was staring directly at her now. "How about *you* go?" he said. And he brought his hand down as if he was splitting the air.

The last word she heard was Bas's.

"*Dee!*"

56

SUNDAY, MAY 12, 1991

BAS WATCHED—HELPLESS and covered in mud and sweat—as the young Asian woman tumbled to the ground. It wasn't Dee, but it was. And now she was only a body lying on the floor.

"Dee!"

He scrambled to his feet and loped over to her, his knees singing with pain. "No no no..." He gently turned her head to face him. The woman's cheek was warm to the touch, and her chest rose and fell. But was Dee still in there? For all Bas knew this was a trick, a lure Fritz had set up using one of the I, Mine members. But Bas couldn't take the chance. "Dee?" he said, shaking her shoulder.

No answer.

"You *fuck*," Bas said, turning to confront Fritz.

But Fritz was no longer there. The only sign of him in the courtyard was the mist, swirling in the direction of his cowardly flight, like a cartoon.

Bracing his knee, Bas got to his feet once more. He pulled the young woman over to the side of the hall and rested her against the wall.

Then he followed I, Mine's only remaining co-founder.

57

SUNDAY, MAY 12, 1991

EVERY NERVE in Dee's body pulsed with energy. Before she even opened her eyes, she felt sweat break out across her skin, and she knew things had changed. Again.

Changed *back*.

She was on the floor, cheek to mat, her body stuck in a prone position, her head filled with thoughts of failure. She had failed Bas. Failed herself. On top of that, she had provoked Fritz, who was already far more reckless with his abilities than Dee had ever been, an adult with the impulse control of a child.

Now her body was reasserting itself over her, not letting her get up. She would have to calm down before she would have a chance of regaining control.

Where was she?

The floor looked the same as the one in that unfamiliar room. It even smelled good, a little like grass. The walls, too, were the same pale flat panels and wood frames she had seen before. The topmost sections of the walls were translucent, but Dee couldn't tell whether the light flooding in was natural or artificial. It might be daytime, and it might not. Her transfer to this place, this body, had felt instantaneous, but she couldn't know for sure. Especially not where magic was concerned.

Dee sat up without thinking about it.

Immersing herself in the particulars of the room had worked. Now her body was back in operation.

She looked down at her hands.

They were *her* hands. Her old, familiar hands. Already flexing and flapping.

Meaning that whatever "gift" Collette and Fritz had bestowed on her had been officially revoked.

Good riddance.

Dee took a deep breath and squeezed her hands into fists, trying to narrow her attention to a single unwavering point. Until she channeled the free energy bouncing around her system, she wouldn't be able to focus on her escape.

After a moment her efforts began to pay off. The feeling was subtle at first, but something inside her ceded to her will. Had her time in another body granted her finer control over herself? Or maybe it was just luck.

A moment later she was wringing her hands until her fingers tingled, and getting to her feet.

Find the door.

Only there was no door.

Four walls, a floor, and a ceiling. But no doors or windows.

She would have laughed if not for the dire situation she had left Bas in. Fritz hadn't just banished her, he had imprisoned her.

She went to the nearest wall and placed her hands against the parchment-like material. It was neither warm nor cool, and she felt no vibration, heard no sound. She squeezed her eyes shut, but felt no one present near her.

As far as she knew, she might have been transported to a room thousands of miles away.

She backed away from the wall and considered its unbroken surface. Maybe she could make a door of her own. At the thought, her fingers became a blur of movement, calling up the familiar light pattern—but she immediately felt the sensation of being slapped back by some unseen force.

Gulping air, Dee lurched back from the wall.

Something didn't want her poking around outside the room. What had Collette said when they kidnapped her? They had deployed countermeasures. She had been talking about refactoring at the time, but Dee was beginning to realize that these countermeasures meant much more.

58

SUNDAY, MAY 12, 1991

BAS FOLLOWED the muddy footprints Fritz had left on the mat floor. The man had followed a plant-lined corridor that Bas had not seen during his stay in the compound. He couldn't be too far ahead.

But the mud trail eventually ran out, just as Bas was crossing a suspended walkway that led back to one of the two massive boulder fountains. It looked just like the one he had seen outside the residential wing, but that would have been impossible, since he had entered through the back alley and gone the opposite direction from the rooms.

What made even less sense was how the passage leading past the boulder turned left at least ten times without meeting itself. After the fourth turn, Bas even doubled back to the fountain to make sure he was seeing things right. The passage definitely defied traditional architecture.

After turning left until his head spun, Bas finally found himself back at the boulder fountain again. Circling the great sphere monolith, he once more exited into the hall opposite. But it was a different passage now. This one had a low ceiling, forcing Bas to stoop as he followed it.

He'd completely lost Fritz's trail. But the man's fingerprints were all over this place.

"I see you, asshole," Bas said under his breath, pushing deeper into the impossible maze.

59

SUNDAY, MAY 12, 1991

THE AIR in Dee's holding cell had grown noticeably acrid, and she knew why. She had tried several times to use her abilities—the *light pocket* in particular, as it seemed like the best bet for getting out—and each time she'd felt a neck-snapping wrench as if someone had hit the brakes too hard.

Not only did countermeasures hurt, they smelled, too.

Having retreated to a corner, Dee now sat with her back to the wall. She dreaded seeing Fritz's face again. He and Collette had only *body-swapped* her because they thought it would get her on their team. And they wanted her on their team because she had something they wanted.

Given the way they wielded their abilities, she knew what that something was.

Dee sat on her hands and closed her eyes one last time. But instead of reaching out with her mind, which would only draw another retaliatory smackdown, she silenced her thoughts, relaxed her muscles, and imagined herself as transparent as the air around her.

If something was out there, she would feel it.

Anything.

There.

Dee's eyes snapped open.

It had been faint, but she had sensed a single point in the ether, like a beacon on the horizon.

Dee shut her eyes again and imagined herself as empty and open as possible, like a radio tuned to a frequency between stations.

There, again.

The focal point, whatever it was, was unmistakable once she knew what to look for—not just noise, but an active signal.

Resisting the temptation to latch on to it immediately, Dee remained blank, allowing the signal to resolve on its own, like a freshly ejected Polaroid photograph.

Only it was familiar.

She had felt this distinctive signature before.

The stone. Bas must still be carrying it.

But what of the countermeasures? Had she found a way to duck them entirely?

Bas?

No pushback.

Bas, can you hear me?

Still no resistance. But no response either.

Bas, it's Dee. Where are you?

The stone was out there, somewhere—maybe close—but her whispering had a limited range.

Unless.

Tightening her lips, Dee shut her eyes again. She suppressed the urge to stay in control, allowing the tenuous connection to draw her outward. Even as she felt her body back in her doorless room, she sensed motion, insistent yet effortless. She wasn't just adrift—there was a purpose to this sensation, a direction. If she was here, there must be a there.

She saw it then.

Monitors.

The familiar bank of screens danced in her mind's eye like a monochrome glass grid. Before she could get a better look, her view wheeled around to the door opposite the surveillance gear.

Dee braced herself against the wave of dizziness that came from remote viewing; she pressed her palms to the floor as she fought to keep her connection. This was definitely Bas. Was he investigating the cult compound? Why hadn't he left? Maybe he was looking for her.

The thought flooded her system with adrenaline.

She pushed with all her might, whispered into the void.

Bas...

It shouldn't have worked. It never had on previous remote viewing sessions. She could see, but not speak. But this wasn't like the other times. Before, Dee had always latched on to the remote connection like she was gripping the steering wheel of a car; never before had she *let go*, giving herself over to the ache of the stone's attraction.

"Who's there?"

Dee thought she had imagined the voice.

Bas's voice.

Can you hear me?

"Dee? Is that you?"

Yes! I'm here.

He was facing the bank of monitors again, but now he appeared to be looking for something. Looking for her. "Where are you? Are you okay?" Screen after screen showed various locations within the complex, some of which made no sense at all, appearing at odd angles or looking nothing like proper rooms.

I'm okay, I think. And I'm back in my own body. But I'm in a room with no doors.

"Dammit, that's Fritz. He's turned this place into a labyrinth. But you gotta be nearby."

I don't know. I'm connecting through your stone.

He patted his pocket, his hand lingering on the lump.

But Bas, they're using countermeasures to keep me in. To keep me from using magic. I don't know if I can keep the connection. It's fragile.

"Try to stay with me," he said. "I may need you, but for now you're probably safer where you are anyway."

60

SUNDAY, MAY 12, 1991

ON BAS'S first visit to I, Mine's video lab, the cramped room had been all shelves and surveillance equipment. Now the back wall opened up to a precariously descending gangway that had no business being there. It was as if Fritz had brought together a jumble of architectural blocks and mashed them together like an obstacle course.

The path was far too steep for Bas to walk down without assistance. He reached for the nearest support beam connecting the gangway to the ceiling, and tested it for stability.

Careful. Dee's voice.

"That's the plan," Bas said.

The plank seemed rigid enough, which meant he should be able to make it down to the floor below if he used the supports like rungs.

Tightening his grip, he lowered himself down gently. Now was not the time to break a leg.

By the time he made it to the floor below, he was already out of breath. He wrung his hands to loosen up his cramping fingers. "I am too old... for this shit."

What are you even doing here? When I didn't hear from you, I thought maybe you gave up.

"I considered it, more than once," he said, taking a deep breath and considering the path before him, all contorted angles and structures of questionable integrity. "But at this point I've come too far. With how much I've invested..."

You mean your wife?

"Yeah, and everything that came after."

I don't think you're going to find her here.

The note of sorrow in Dee's voice pulled Bas back to the present.

"I'm not here for Lana. And frankly, Gisela may be a lost cause, too. I came for you. I never thought it would come to this. I was gonna meet you at your place, come up with a plan. And it was good I called Brenda when I did, because—"

Do they know?

"I mean, they're pretty freaked out, as you could expect. But they don't know about all this. They have a search team out looking for you out at that park."

Oh no.

"I told Brenda I'd get you back safe, and that's exactly what I'm going to do."

Did you tell anyone you were coming here?

"No. And I'm glad I didn't bring anyone else into it. It's too risky. The best chance you and I have of getting out is by sticking together, not by having a SWAT team storming in through the front door."

You're probably right. So what's the plan?

"The plan." Bas shook his head and pounded the edge of a mismatched wall panel with his fist, testing it for stability. Everything seemed solid, it just didn't line up right. "The plan is to get Fritz to undo all this shit—pardon the *shit*—which will get you out of that room you're in. I'm pretty sure they wanted you as a lab animal, and that's *never* gonna happen."

Okay.

"But that means we've got work to do."

Fritz?

"Fritz."

Up ahead, two opposing corridors came together, intertwined like a helix. Bas saw no way to negotiate that structural muddle. He followed his corridor until the floor listed too much to continue, then he peered out the nearest window—which, given the curve of the hall, was pointing almost straight down. A mere ten feet below, in the shadow of the coiled passages, was the courtyard garden, as pristine as it had ever been. An assembly, in their robes, was going about their motion practice as if this were any other day.

Are those the people you talked about?

Bas jumped. It was easy to forget Dee was seeing everything he saw when he was so immersed in the craziness of it.

Those are the dancers?

"That's them."

Bas's eyes followed the contours of the wall panels.

What are you looking for?

Of course there were no doors. He was going to have to improvise.

"I'm done feeling like a rat in a maze."

He slipped down toward the window and examined the pane. It was fixed, of course. Calculating its weak point, he raised his foot and gave the glass a kick. To his surprise, the pane popped out in a single piece, coming to rest on the moss below with a muffled *thump*.

Several eyes glanced up at him, more glassy than curious. But most of the assembly went about their routine without pause.

Bas straddled the opening, slipped through, then held on to the frame and lowered himself down. It was less than a five-foot drop to the ground, but he was careful not to slip on the glass, planting his feet in a wide stance.

At the other end of the garden, Fritz gawked at Bas. In one hand he had a pencil, in the other a tablet. He had been playing the scribe as the assembly went about their elaborate performance.

"I always wondered what you guys were writing in that notebook," Bas said.

Pencil still poised over paper, as if he had been caught raiding a cookie jar, Fritz only shrugged. "You're looking at it."

"What exactly am I looking at?" Bas asked, dusting himself off. He gave the assembly a wide berth as he approached.

Fritz folded the pencil into the notebook, closed it, and placed it on a table beside him. He clasped his hands in behind him, looking controlled to the point of stiffness.

Bas stopped a dozen feet away. He didn't want Fritz to feel cornered.

"Let's just say that securing permits in Kendall Square for a structure that's larger than the size of its parcel would be impractical without a little..." he waved his hands, "special influence."

"You don't say."

"But look, I could make small talk all day—frankly, that's a big part of my life. But that's not why you're here, is it? You're more of a big-picture guy."

"Right. So let's start by letting Dee go."

For a moment there was only the sound of the assembly, their synchronized breaths, the whisper of silk over skin as they moved in formation.

Fritz stood on his toes. "The one thing I can't wrap my head around is that you're a detective, right? And yet you still don't see it?"

A dodge, to buy time. Which meant he wasn't going to give Dee up so easily.

"We wanted to know what happened to Lana as much as you did."

"Fuck you," Bas said, closing in on the man. "I'll take you out myself in front of your own dancers."

Fritz stumbled back.

Bas, don't. We can get out of here without him.

"I can hear you, you know that, Dee?" Fritz said, looking up toward the open sky. "I tuned into you as soon as we picked you up." He looked Bas up and down. His eyes stopped at Bas's pocket.

A sting of heat on Bas's chest compelled him to pull at his shirt, and he heard something pop. Smoke rose from a singed hole in his pocket, stinging his nostrils.

"What the fuck, man!"

"That was Collette's stone, not yours," Fritz said, holding himself rigid. "But now it is gone. That should give us some privacy."

Bas patted his chest to dull the pain. Without Dee in his ear, what was he supposed to do? Rely on brute strength? That hadn't worked out so well before. And he doubted reason would work much better.

"You're really broken up about your wife, aren't you?" Bas said.

"I can fix this if you'll give me some space," Fritz replied, back up on his toes. "You're just storming around like a bull in a china shop."

"You're not going to do *shit*, Fritz. I've seen what you guys are up to, and it's not helping anyone."

"Fine. You want answers? *That's* why you came here? The answer was staring you in the face, and you *still* didn't see it!"

"Bullshit."

"You never thought to ask Clancy *Yeats* what happened to your wife?"

Bas's muscles tightened. If Fritz was throwing that kind of nonsense at him, he must be getting ready to make a move.

"You should have," Fritz continued. "He was there, after all."

"What the fuck are you talking about?" Bas was letting Fritz get a rise out of him.

"You saw it yourself. Watched it, I should say. More than once, I'm sure."

Bas blinked.

It was the tape Fritz was talking about.

The Lana tape.

Had to be.

In his head, Bas played the scene back.

Lana, planting her hands on the man's shoulders.

Forcing him backward.

"You *never* noticed?" Fritz said.

It could have been anyone standing across from Lana. Anyone with gray hair.

"No, you never saw that it was *Clancy* your wife pushed to his death that day. And I can guarantee you that what came after—and a big part of the reason you're here today—was directly related."

The more Bas tried to push it away, the more insistent the idea became. How could something that made no sense be true?

"There's no way Clancy comes out of that alive," Bas said. "Or anyone."

"Oh, you've profoundly underestimated the man," Fritz said, now almost as close to Bas as they had been when they had spoken at I, Mine's open house that first night. "You ask about the assembly, and the routines they weave. Clancy Yeats was calling these routines before the Singularity ever happened. Granted, he was a much older man back then."

Fritz wasn't just stalling. The man's attention was split between Bas and the assembly, which was dancing more feverishly than ever. Something was going on.

"Just so I don't lose you," Fritz continued, "let me make this clear. If you don't let me patch this, then Collette *and Lana* are truly gone."

"They're both gone already."

"Then you should feel lucky you can even remember them, because not everyone has that luxury. And you should be *thanking* me for what I did to Clancy."

"Which is what? More of the same shit that's been going on for ten years? I should thank you for *that*?"

"A lot of good can come from bad things, Bas."

Bas considered those words, then nodded. "I agree," he said.

And he lunged for Fritz, going for his shoulders the way Lana had gone for Clancy's.

Only Fritz was no longer there.

Bas's own arms reached past his face on either side, as if he were embracing his own reflection. The courtyard garden had been... mirrored, and now the original courtyard and its flipped twin overlapped like a double-exposed photo.

Without Fritz to break his momentum, Bas rolled to the soft ground, getting a mouthful of moss and loam.

He looked up. Fritz was already back at his note-taking, Bas as good as forgotten, a minor interruption now resolved.

Pushing himself back to his knees, Bas saw Fritz's weakness. He would use whatever smoke and mirrors were required to keep Bas at bay, but he *needed* this place. He needed the assembly. Whatever he had them doing now, he needed them to finish it.

A flash shone so bright that it made Bas's eyes sting.

Something in his mind clicked, as if someone had pressed a reset button.

Wet. Cold.

Should stay dry.

Knees and back.

Lana.

Lana and Bas.

When Bas could see clearly again, the mirror-hall effect had gone, and Fritz was collecting something from the ground.

"Dee," Bas managed, his voice like gravel, "did you see that?"

No response.

Gathering his wits, Bas pulled himself toward Fritz, who was the only thing in the courtyard not mirrored by the spell he had cast. As long as the man's attention remained on his assembly, Bas might be able to reach him, to pin him down, to restrain him. Without his gestures, there would be no more of this madness.

Only despite his calm and focused demeanor, Fritz was not so inattentive as that. He noticed Bas before he could make his move, and with a single gesture, he caused the ground to expand outward in all directions, carrying Bas back toward the edge of the courtyard. By the time the ground stopped moving, it had extended into an array of overlapping moss-covered terraces—worse than the mirror effect from before—making Bas feel like he was peering through a kaleidoscope, with Fritz at its center.

Now Bas would have to climb through if he wanted—

Several flashes exploded at once.

Bas's mind clicked off, then on.

Would have to take more time off if he wanted

The carton was open, and the milk inside was thick

Kitten was there, under the crawlspace. Probably feral

Meeting Lana for drinks, which he had been looking forward to all

Lana was late

One of the dancers stopped, an older woman with red hair and green eyes. She turned toward Bas.

"*Get up, now.*"

Bas looked down at himself, his knees planted in the moss, hands full of mud.

Mind full of mud.

He had lost himself for a moment. Something had pushed him away.

Now Fritz was pulling something out of the air. It was like one of Dee's light pockets. Fritz had opened it himself, using Dee's technique. And now he was leaving.

Leaving.

Bas scrambled across the garden, across the infuriating funhouse maze of mirrored courtyards, and launched himself at the singular founder of I, Mine. His fingers closed on the fabric of the man's robe, and he held tight as Fritz waved his hands.

A hundred invisible daggers rained across Bas's back, but it only made him grab tighter as he cringed in pain.

Even through lids squeezed tight he saw the light flashes popping around him like the press of paparazzi at a blockbuster opening.

Action, reaction.

Whatever Fritz was doing was causing the explosions.

Then the flashing stopped, and Fritz twisted out of Bas's grip. The extended courtyard collapsed on itself briefly, giving Bas a sense of vertigo as they plunged back down to the level of the assembly. Then the space expanded yet again, giving Bas that sickening feeling of motion and stillness all at once. Fritz was trying to keep his grip.

"Stop it," the man said, as if imploring the group to cease what they were doing.

But why?

Bas turned. This time he would be smart, and grab the man's arms.

"You don't know what you're doing!" Fritz shouted—not at Bas, but at his own dancers.

From behind, Bas grabbed the man's wrists as he looked out over the assembly.

One of them, a young woman, stopped her cavorting and turned to them. "I think."

Another one of them stopped. A man with a shaved head. "I can."

Another. "Break Fritz's."

Yet another. "Machine."

It was Dee. She had found a way to head-hop to the assembly itself—to all of them.

Fritz pulled frantically against Bas, his panic giving him a strength Bas wasn't prepared for. He wrenched his arms away and nearly knocked Bas over as he reached into the snarl of overlapping courtyards. The nearest instance of his notebook was only feet away, while its reflections unfurled outward like frames of an unspooled movie reel.

At the other end of the garden, the assembly was besieged by a series of light pockets. Bas was unable to look away as a shimmering banner materialized over the head of a man making windmill gestures with his arms. The light formation expanded like a radiant hole and dropped around the man, leaving nothing behind in its wake.

What had Bas just seen? Had Dee just vaporized someone? Would she even realize it if she had?

"Dee!"

But the scenario repeated itself with additional light pockets; by the time each radiant hole hit the moss, nothing was left of each assembly participant but a puff of smoke.

The remaining members scattered, finally terrified enough to flee into the mirror maze.

Bas felt something behind him as much as he heard the telltale flutter of fabric. He spun around just in time to see Fritz coming at him with a rock, still muddy on one edge from being pried up from the ground.

On full automatic, Bas ducked the arc of the stone as it came down. He grabbed the smaller man in a bear hug and took him to the ground. Fritz responded by pummeling him about the neck and shoulder multiple times.

Now the flashes Bas saw were the familiar kind, the result of being beaten to hell.

One more to the base of the skull and he would be out for good.

Bas, let him go!

Dee.

But how?

Let go!

"Let me go!"

Fritz was struggling beneath Bas, his makeshift weapon rolling from his open hand.

Bas's ears rang as he pulled back, but agony lanced down from his shoulder. "Now," Bas said, his chest heaving, "tell me where—"

But something in Fritz's eyes stopped him. Or rather, the absence of something.

There was no recognition in Fritz's eyes.

None at all.

"Get off me!" Fritz said, pushing Bas off. "What are you *doing*?"

Around them, the impossible architecture was already fading, pulling back into itself, receding from the world, and leaving behind nothing but a rusty, grotty warehouse.

The sewer stench of it curled Bas's nostrils.

"What did you do to him, Dee?" Bas said, scooting away from the upset man who looked like Fritz.

Dee didn't answer.

The man regarded Bas with alarm as he struggled to his feet and tried to maintain his balance.

What had just happened? Dee had broken up the assembly, that much was clear. And now that Fritz's illusion had dissolved, Bas saw the vanished members scurrying off into the garbage-strewn depot—not vaporized after all, but light-tunneled.

But what had happened to Fritz? He wouldn't have refactored himself.

Something Collette had said played through Bas's mind. She said I, Mine had been trying to prevent the persona wipes from happening. Had she been telling the truth? And if so, what *was* causing the refactors?

Nothing familiar remained of the I, Mine compound.

Fritz's Japanese-retreat knockoff had yielded to a gutted structure, like the bloated carcass of a rotting whale. Fritz himself wandered off, muttering under his breath as he made his way through the remains of his own creation. There was no telling who he thought he was now. Maybe a High Street tax accountant, or the projector operator at the Zeiterion.

The last trace of anything magical about the place was Clancy—or the Clancy-shaped silhouette that lingered at the rear wall of the warehouse, by the parking lot. Even the Collette-shaped sand sculpture was gone.

Bas's pulse was heavy in his temples as he approached the mirage-like hole that had once been Clancy Yeats.

"Is it true, you son of a bitch? Did you erase Lana?"

Clancy's ghost offered no response.

A crash of metal made Bas jump.

"Dee?"

Rats fled as he ducked under a hanging girder and bounded out from the sagging confines of the industrial office to a more open area at the other end of the warehouse. He found Dee emerging from beneath a tight crawlspace, her hands and knees dripping in mud.

Wrapping his hands under her arms, he pulled her gently from the muck. "That's it." He set her back on her feet. "You okay?"

She didn't answer, but embraced him while he held his arms out to the sides, unsure where to put them.

Did we win?

Bas relaxed then, giving her shoulder a pat as she pulled away. "I don't feel much like a winner."

I was kidding.

Her eyes crawled over the sad wreckage of the building around them.

I think you may be right about Gisela.

"I'm sorry, Dee." And he was. Exactly nothing had gone as planned, and what had they accomplished? "At least we got you out."

Yeah, maybe.

Her hands were already going again. Not conjuring anything this time. Just being autistic.

I know what I did, hopping the dancers and tunneling them away. But those light flashes? That wasn't me.

Bas had never felt anything like that. Had he gotten a glimpse of refactoring himself?

Bas looked around. "Come on, let's get out of here."

Bas's adrenaline had burned off, leaving behind shooting pains, the telltale throb of deep tissue bruises he hadn't felt since his gym days, and a deep, overriding exhaustion.

Are you all right?

Dee put a hand on his forearm. She was a sweet kid, underneath that affliction of hers. Maybe it was because of her whispering. Or maybe it was just who she was.

"I'm fine," he said, ambling toward the alley behind the lot. "Car's this way."

He heard the chirping before he saw the car itself. His mobile phone, still holstered to the Monza's center console.

"Shit, shit, shit," he said, fumbling for his keys as he loped the last few yards to the old jalopy. "That'll be your parents."

As Bas slid into the driver-side seat and picked up the handset, Dee stood at the passenger door, repeatedly trying the handle.

"I've got her," Bas said, all too aware that he sounded predatory. "I found her, I mean. I'm on my way."

"You'd *better* have an explanation," came a familiar woman's voice.

Bas froze. That wasn't Brenda.

It took him a second for the realization to set in.

"Gisela?"

61

SUNDAY, MAY 19, 1991

"I SEE you looking at my potato pieces," Junmo said. "But if you lay a hand on them, Dee, so help me."

"Dee has her own food," said Walter, handing his foster son a napkin.

The days had finally grown warm enough to allow for picnics in the back yard again. And what better way to celebrate? Dee was back with her family, and safe. She knew they were as relieved as she was, after the scare she had given them.

She had convinced her foster parents that her disappearance from the grounds of the Albert Arboretum had simply been the result of her becoming disoriented during a meltdown. The authorities had registered some suspicion over how she could have made it through the park and past hundreds of people in such a state unnoticed, but there was no other explanation, and Dee's assurances had calmed Brenda down enough that she was able to put the minds of the police to rest.

"All good, honeybee?"

Brenda could always tell when Dee was withdrawing into her stim world.

I was just thinking.

"Something on your mind?"

Dee appreciated the extra attention from her foster parents—soon to be her adoptive parents. *Only strategizing how I can get Junmo's potatoes.*

Brenda laughed. "Yeah, that's one thing you want to get right on the first try."

"What's that, hon?" Walter asked his wife, gazing across the table at Dee.

"Girl talk," Brenda said with a wink.

The screen door hissed as Gisela came out onto the deck. Dee couldn't help herself, and stood up as her hands clapped out her glee.

Gisela smiled and touched Dee's arm as she took a seat next to her. "Me too."

Gisela had told Dee that the last thing she remembered was Bas coming into her office. Dee had started to help her fill in some of the blanks, but Gisela stopped her. She didn't want to know, especially now that it was all over.

"Hey, we fixed you a plate," Brenda told her friend. "And there's plenty more. The tomatoes are from Dee's garden."

Dee still wondered about what that thing was that had taken Gisela away. If it wasn't I, Mine, what was it? But she only pondered such things during daylight hours. At night such musing was best pushed away.

Is he coming? she asked Gisela. She meant Bas. She hadn't see him since he dropped her off after the events at I, Mine. Of course he had been through a lot, and had looked like he needed about a decade of rest.

Gisela shook her head. "Bas'll be okay." She piled extra spinach onto her plate with the tongs. "It just takes time, you know? He said to say hi though."

"Hi, Bas," Junmo said. "I like that guy, and not just because he's a giant."

Dee looked over at Gisela. Maybe you guys should do something together.

Was she being too pushy? Maybe. But Junmo was right. Bas could be exasperating, but there was something about him she liked. It would be nice if he had some excuse to stick around.

"We'll see," Gisela said.

That would have to do.

Dee leaned her head on Gisela's shoulder.

I'm glad you're here.

PART 4

EPILOGUE

62

SUNDAY, MAY 19, 1991

RAIN BEADED on the Monza's cracked windshield as Bas sat parked by the curb in front of his apartment. It felt like punishment for passing up Sunday brunch at Luckie Landing. But it was only a week after the I, Mine debacle, Bas's head still wasn't right, and it felt premature to sit around a table chatting about the weather.

He had driven by Norfolk Place a day after his anonymous tip to the cops, and already the authorities had tented the entire plot, like a miniature version of the South Station. What would they make of the Clancy-shaped hole haunting the dried-out husk of I, Mine?

He'd checked up on one other thing too: Mordell Bolden. He'd been thinking a lot about the fate of I, Mine's refactored army. They had scattered to the winds, and he could only guess whether any of them had been "factored back" into their old lives like Gisela had. There was no way of knowing—there would be no news stories about long-lost relatives returning from parts unknown. But if Cynda's father had returned to himself, then maybe others would.

Which meant… maybe Lana would show up, too.

But it hadn't worked out that way. Mordell Bolden had not returned; Alton Griggs still occupied the apartment out in Roxbury.

And Bas had no idea why Gisela was, as far he knew, the sole exception—the only person to return to herself.

Maybe Clancy had done more for her than he'd let on. It was idle speculation.

Bas pressed the phone receiver to his ear. His message service had one message to play for him. Bas pressed 1 on the keypad.

"You have one message. Saturday, 3:05 p.m."

"Hey, Basso Profundo! Mitch. Hey, I just wanted to let you know that the kid didn't work out after all. Had some issues with authority, turns out, so we destaffed his ass, as they say. Anyway, we're one man short, and you're one man tall. So if you're tired of gumshoeing it out in the real world, give me a call. We might have a spot for you. But it'd be cool to catch up either way, man, see how life's treating you. Okay, that's all I got for now. Talk soon. No, you hang up first."

Bas smiled as he pressed *END*.

Maybe he would call his old colleague back this time. Why not? Dee no longer had to worry about I, Mine. Gisela was Gisela again. And Bas would have plenty of time to reminisce about his final case—the case that was never a case—as he guarded art at the Gardner Museum.

At least for a while.

He looked up at his apartment building once more. After the events at I, Mine, he had holed up there for several days, warily regarding his half-living room. The scar I, Mine had left there remained. Or maybe it was a trophy. But at the moment, the sound of a silent apartment was the last thing he wanted.

Twisting the ignition key, he pumped the gas and set out across town.

Harriet Bland flashed Bas a smile as he squeezed between two stools and ordered a High Life. This earned a scowl from the kid on Bas's left, who was nursing an artisanal beer whose label depicted a chimpanzee wearing a space helmet.

"Give us some space?" Harriet asked the kid and his friend. The kid was clearly taken aback, but his more perceptive friend seemed to read the look on the barkeep's face, and convinced the kid to move farther back into the bar.

"Thanks," Bas said once they had gone.

"Be right back," said Harriet. "Got something for you."

As Bas listened to Chris Isaak lowing about wicked games on the jukebox, he traced a symbol on the bar. Cynda's symbol. Half an adinkra. "O God," Bas muttered to himself, "something's in heaven, let it come into my hand."

"What's that?"

Harriet placed a full stein before him, making sure to towel-dry the handle with a rag that was probably dirtier than the floor.

"Nothing," Bas said, shaking his head. "Just babbling."

"Thought you might have found a new joint to haunt. Wasn't sure we'd be seeing you around anymore."

"Don't be all sore. I just had a dry spell is all."

"No, that's *not* all. We need to have words, you and I."

She looked upset, but there was a gleam in her eye.

"Oh yeah?" Bas asked, sitting up.

"I had to learn you were calling it quits from Zelda, and that was almost a month ago. What am I supposed to think?"

"Oh that," Bas said.

"Oh *that*."

"Yeah, I just... You ever have that feeling you've seen all there is to see?"

She rolled her eyes as she whipped the towel back over her shoulder. "Sometimes more than once a night. But that doesn't make us strangers. I hope you won't forget us completely, okay? There, I've said my piece."

"I appreciate it, Harriet. But I'll be around. Promise."

She wasn't the sentimental type, so it meant a lot that his absence hadn't gone unnoticed. But she was right. He could have said something.

"Yeah, well, I shouldn't bother giving you this, seeing as how you're on probation now, but..."

She had pulled out an envelope and was pointing it at him over the counter.

"What's this?" Bas asked, taking it from her and turning it over in his hands. It was heavy, with a bulge in the middle.

"I got x-ray vision?"

Someone at the other end of the bar flagged Harriet down, and she gave Bas a nod as she went to attend to her other customers.

Bas regarded the envelope, which had no markings on the outside. He tore off the short edge, and as he plucked out the slip of paper inside, there was a clatter on the bar. A set of keys had dropped from the envelope, linked by a keychain.

Also on the chain was a wedding band.

Lana's wedding band.

Bas would have known that ring anywhere, even in the dark. It took him only half a second to identify what was wrong with it.

The ring was no longer warped. It shouldn't be possible to untwist metal without leaving a mark. Had Wallace Thaw stolen it, then had a duplicate recast?

Only no, the third garnet was still missing. Bas held it close, examining the inscription along the inner curve.

Svetlana, my heart...

His breath caught in his throat as he saw those words again.

"Guy yesterday just left that sitting on the bar."

Harriet was back.

"Who?"

"No one I know."

Bas bit his lip as a thought occurred to him. Maybe he had been spending too much time around I, Mine, but he had to know.

"Was it a really skinny guy, blond?"

"That's right," Harriet said.

"Built like a grasshopper?"

She laughed. "That's a fair description."

"Wallace Thaw."

Shrug. "Didn't catch his name. So you know him?"

Harriet didn't recognize the name. Yet she had known that name once. Before all this. Which meant Wallace had been refactored. It was still happening. Or had been. Who knew?

And who knew how the man untwisted Lana's ring, or, after going to the trouble, why he would have left it here for Bas?

"Thanks for this, Harriet. Truly."

She took that as her cue and moved back down the bar.

Setting the keys down next to the envelope, Bas unfolded the paper and squinted down at the handwritten note.

> Bas, it's Clancy. I have a proposition for you. The ring is a token of good will, but I can offer you more than that. If you're willing to hear me out, meet me at the address on the key. If not, then we have nothing more to say.

Bas reread the note twice, but it did nothing to answer his main question. How was Clancy writing to him at all? And why was a refactored Wallace running errands for him? None of it made sense. But then, maybe that was how magic was supposed to work.

Bas removed the gold-plated band from the keychain with great care, half expecting it to vanish, just as Clancy had. He dropped the warm ring into his shirt pocket, then brought the keyring close enough to read the yellow paper tag, on which was inscribed an address in plain print.

Berkeley and Beacon.

Not far from Clancy and Pal's penthouse.

Was Clancy there now, waiting? Or maybe it was a setup. The last thing Clancy had told Bas was to forget about I, Mine, to go out and live his life while he still had it.

And Fritz had warned Bas about Clancy. Maybe about that, at least, the co-founder of I, Mine had been right.

But then there was Lana's ring. *A token of good will.*

Bas dropped some cash on the bar, pulled his jacket more tightly around him, and headed back out into the rain.

The townhouse at the corner of Berkeley and Beacon was a monster, a five-story Victorian brownstone just a block from Boston's Public Garden. Bas found a parking spot in the public alley and listened to the Monza sputter. If he was issued a citation for adding to urban blight, he wouldn't protest it.

The evening had brought with it a humid gale that had cleared out the rain clouds. Bas trudged up the front steps, hands in pockets, clutching the keys, ready to show them to anyone contesting his presence.

In the alcove of the front stoop, the mailbox had only a blank metal plate over it where Bas would have expected to see an engraved name. To the side of the double doors was a backlit doorbell buzzer. Bas considered pressing it, but only for only a second.

"Fuck it," he said, pulling out his keys. If Clancy wanted him to let himself in, why disappoint him?

The lock issued a satisfying click, and Bas pushed the door open.

Beyond the entrance, a hall stretched before him. A stairwell rose to one side. Though the place was illuminated with dim lights, it still managed to look abandoned.

Bas stepped over the threshold.

For just a moment, the ground wobbled so slightly that he might have dismissed it as a symptom of his unease had he not felt something similar on the night he had visited the I, Mine compound for the introductory dinner. That first wobble had no doubt been a function of Fritz's trickery. Was something similar happening here?

Bas closed the door behind him and moved toward the stairs, wincing each time the time-worn floor squeaked under his weight.

Why was he sneaking?

"Hello?" he called, projecting his voice up the stairwell. "Mr. Puri?" The echo's hollow ring found its way into every hoary crack and corner, but there came no response. "Mr. *Yeats?*"

What Bas first took to be his pulse in his ears was really the steady thump of slippers on wood beams. An old man emerged from a doorway exactly halfway down the main hall, a mug of something steaming in one hand.

"Mr. Milius," he said, with a voice like desert wind. "I'm glad you came."

Bas was about to ask where Clancy was, but something in the tone of the man's voice stilled his tongue.

The man moved closer, his mug unsteady enough that the brown liquid within sloshed at the edges. Bas scrutinized him. He had never seen this face before.

At least not like this.

"Have we met?" he asked.

That stopped the man's shuffling. He recovered quickly though, nodding as he came forward. "That's right, I forget. This isn't something one ever really gets used to."

Bas gaped as Clancy's voice came from the old man's lips.

Fritz had accused Bas of underestimating the man. Of that much, at least, he had been right.

"How? I saw you—"

"You saw my agent being destroyed, is probably what you saw." He looked distracted. "Look, would you mind if we sat? There's a lot to talk about, and I'm afraid I'm not up to telling you all you'll need to know while standing in the hall."

Bas opened his mouth, then shut it again. If Clancy had aged fifty years in a week, then anything was possible. And that only intensified the questions swirling in his head.

Questions about Lana.

"The parlor, maybe?" Clancy said, already moving down the hall toward the nearest doorway.

The parlor was full of fancy flourishes that reminded Bas of his grandmother's house, if his grandmother's house had been expanded several times over. A cathedral ceiling featured inlaid panels with gold-leaf filigree, and the double-height windows along the east wall rattled against the wind outside.

Clancy set his mug on a table in front of the divan, then lowered himself slowly down. Bas took a seat in a weathered chair that smelled of cigars and old leather. But though they were both now seated, the older man seemed content to relish his tea, sipping it in silence.

Was he waiting for something, or had he simply forgotten?

Bas scooted up to the edge of his chair. "Look, I've seen enough by now to know that weird shit is happening. But you're going to have to explain how it is that you've just aged fifty years."

Clancy looked offended. "Oh, now, I don't look *that* much older, do I?" After a moment's consideration, he added, "Then again, I suppose I do."

"Where did this ring come from?" Bas asked, producing the ring from his pocket.

"You're skipping ahead."

"I'm flying blind. Come on, you summoned me here, so clue me in."

"Summoned." Clancy rolled his eyes. But as he took a deep breath and set his mug down once more, his face took on a grave cast. He settled back into the sofa, looking suddenly smaller. "This is one of those things," he began, "that's as difficult to tell as it will be for you to hear. There are some things in this life that you can only appreciate with some context."

"I've got time."

"I'll begin with a bit of my story, then we'll go from there."

Bas gave him a nod.

Clancy looked out the window as if to get his bearings. Then his eyes were back on Bas. "A couple of decades ago I founded a company called N-Mésa. Our initial focus was adaptive content and dynamic engagement systems." Seeing the look on Bas's face, he waved a hand. "Suffice it to say we found ourselves quite far along the cutting edge, and we left in our wake a string of patents.

"Fast forward almost a decade, and we had on our hands a proprietary technology whose sole purpose was to render fully realized, procedurally scalable virtual environments. Like any business we had to make money, but describing our value proposition only invited mystified looks like the one you're giving me right now."

"Sorry," Bas said. "I'm looking for an in, I really am."

"My point being, how does a company like the one I just described remain commercially viable?"

Bas shook his head. "Not by hitting the money guys across the head with *that* gobbledygook."

"Exactly right. People need to see that gobbledygook in action, with their own eyes. They need to experience it before they can really grasp its potential."

It was a long setup, but it finally seemed like Clancy was leading somewhere.

"So you showed them."

"We did."

"*What* did you show them?"

Clancy pursed his lips. "Imagine Lumière's first public screening of *Arrival of a Train*."

"What?"

"One of the first motion pictures, presented to a paying audience in 1896, in a proper theater. I suspect the crowd response in those early days of cinema was similar to the response we observed when we unveiled our proof of concept, our Infinite Adaptive Resolution technology, applied to a series of simulations. Think of extensible, adaptable microcosms under glass. Like a movie, but interactive, fully responsive to you, and physically accurate. The possibilities for experimentation in controlled virtual environments were so great that we soon found ourselves *buried* in commercial contracts."

"Okay, I get it," Bas said, fibbing only a little bit. "Like a 3D movie, or... like one of those videogames where you can do what you want."

Clancy took a sip of his tea.

The back of Bas's neck felt tight. He had been tensing up without thinking about it. He wiped his palms on his knees and tried to loosen up.

"So that's your setup," Bas said. "Why do I need to know any of that?

"Because this," said Clancy, wiping his mouth, "is a working demonstration of our system. Our masterwork."

Bas looked around the parlor. "This room?"

"And everything beyond it."

Bas's eyes fixed on Clancy. If the man had a tell—a tic of some sort to indicate that he was joking, or lying—Bas couldn't spot it. What did it mean?

"This is your system," Bas said. If he needed to, he was prepared to repeat whatever Clancy told him until the words made sense.

Clancy frowned. "A profoundly powerful hyper-adaptive interconnected system. Everything you see, everything you know, and everything you *are* is part of this system."

"Everything I *am*?" This guy was worse than Fritz and Collette. The founders of I, Mine exploited amnesiacs to build their castle in the sand. But Clancy wanted Bas to believe... what? That Bas was a grain of sand on his beach? "So to boil it down," Bas said, his hands growing colder by the minute, "you're basically telling me that nothing is real?"

"*Nonsense!*" Clancy's ire felt like one of the midair light flashes Bas had seen in the man's own penthouse. "That's a solipsistic way of looking at the world, and maybe sociopathic. It's inaccurate, it's counterproductive, and it's even self-destructive."

"I'm sorry. I'm just trying to wrap my head around it."

"Then I'll try again," Clancy said. "What is matter? What is energy? They're nothing but the manifestations of fields, but it all adds up into the universe. That's the simplest way of saying it. What it comes down to is that you and I are *both* parts of that universe, even if the system that produces you is very different from the one that produces me. The end product is still two men sitting in a room. You see?"

"So I am real."

"You are. You are also a part of a system sampled and modeled from a historic snapshot of 1980. Everything you experience is absolutely real, and essential to this system."

Bas didn't follow. "I bought my Monza in 1979."

"Anything in the system prior to the 1980 inception was imprinted from the source snapshot."

"So it's *not* real?"

"I don't even know how to..."

"We're in a terrarium."

"That's reductive," Clancy croaked. He shielded Bas from the coughing fit that followed with one hand, while waving away Bas's concerns with the other. At the end he cleared his throat, took a sip of tea, and continued. "You are not caged in here," he said, his voice more even. "You could set out for Paris right now, and Paris would be there for you, fully realized."

"Because it's part of the system."

"It is."

"*I'm* part of this system."

"You are."

"But you're not. You're... outside of it."

"That's right. I'm visiting you. Think of it as an elaborate phone call."

"Why though? What's this all about?"

Clancy sat back. "In 2036, Pal got sick."

2036.

Bas didn't have to believe it, as long as he understood it. According to Clancy, there was a time discrepancy on top of everything else. Inside the terrarium it was 1991, but on the outside, where Clancy was, it was much later.

Judging by his appearance, about fifty years later.

"Got it," Bas said, his voice sounding farther away. "You're in the future. And you're spending time in the ant farm... to prove to me that I matter somehow?"

Clancy's cheeks were flushed, and his hands shook. "I would not be here right now if this didn't matter. I have sacrificed my health, my wealth, and my reputation to be here, and to see to it that this system runs for as long as I'm alive. So I think you've got it turned around, Mr. Milius. In some ways this is *all* that matters. If you understand nothing else I've said, I need you to understand that."

Bas nodded. "You were saying that in 2036, Pal got sick."

"Yes. Earlier I spoke of N-Mésa's commercial viability. One of our largest revenue streams came from our life-extension project, wherein we allowed families to integrate their loved ones into this system as fully mapped engrams. Maybe they were terminally ill, or they were enduring any number of ailments. We couldn't help with those things, but we *could* allow the best parts of those individuals to carry on, in a matter of speaking. Call it a vanity project, but it brought joy to many who would otherwise have been lost to despair."

"Did it... bring joy to you?"

The old man raised his eyebrows. "In 2037 I learned that, in addition to his Parkinson's disease, Pal was suffering from the earliest stages of dementia. So I did something that I admit was rash. I incorporated him—a relatively healthy version of him—into this system, along with myself, so he wouldn't be alone. It was a selfish act, but we both knew what was coming, and he was willing to endure the process.

"When he... died, a year later, it was a time of reflection for me. I let N-Mésa languish. I had lost my passion for it, because the most precious thing to me was the time I had with Pal. And now, the only way I could spend time with him was here, in this system. It didn't take me long to decide that I didn't want to leave. I wanted to live my life with Pal again. So I took the place of my own engram, and as a result, I've gotten to spend a wonderful decade of my twilight years with the love of my life."

Bas felt heavy, like he was being pressed down into his chair. He got up, strode to the window, and looked out. The winds had twisted the dusk clouds around themselves, and the leaves flailed as if in desperation.

"A decade ago," Bas said. "April 28, 1981." He focused on Clancy's reflection in the rattling pane of glass.

"The day I resumed my life here."

"The day of the South Station Singularity."

"That was a mistake. Because I couldn't stomach the thought of killing my alter ego, I decided to commandeer someone to do the deed for me."

"Lana."

"It could have been anyone."

"Only it wasn't." Bas blinked the moisture from his eyes before returning to his chair. "It's perverse. And it's all I can do to keep from wrapping my fingers around your neck—"

"*Please* don't do that, Mr. Milius."

"I won't," Bas said, his hand going to his breast pocket. The ring was still there. "I won't, because I need to know what happened."

"What happened is that I overestimated my own system—or underestimated it. The cascade event that followed my assassination was almost catastrophic."

"That's a fancy way of describing my wife's death. You're saying your death caused the South Station Singularity."

"My death *was* the South Station Singularity."

"I don't get it. How did you not see it coming? After you invested so much."

"I assure you I would have found another way if I'd known. In order for me to give you something even approaching an explanation, we'd first need to talk about things like causality models. Suffice it to say that only the most resilient, adaptive system can be self-sustaining, yet an artifact of that dynamic is something called emergent volatility, which is the result of the system adjusting to rectify or justify a paradoxical event. When I had my engram removed, the system interpreted it as... as..."

"It fucked everything up."

Clancy sat up. "I took it at a personal win that the '*Boston 1980*' scenario retained any coherence at all; earlier systems had not. So even though it was severely compromised, it's managed to hold together well past its intended lifespan. The *problem*, as they say, is the people. There are those who have learned to exploit the system's compromised state."

Bas nodded as the winds outside hurled themselves against the parlor windows.

"You knew Fritz and Collette, how?"

"They worked for me. Or, more accurately, they were employees at N-Mésa's front organization, the Mode2 Institute, an entity that existed solely within the system. Mode2's mandate was to observe and experiment on the system's models from the closest possible viewpoint. It included a small core group of my colleagues at N-Mésa, but the rest of the labor pool was drawn from in-system residents, who took on the more menial roles. When I decided to become a permanent resident here, I dissolved Mode2."

"So Fritz and Collette were in on it?"

"Never. No, they knew nothing of the system's existence, nor even of N-Mésa."

Bas shook his head. "They must have figured it out somehow. They must have seen something. Otherwise, how do they get from your front group all the way to I, Mine?"

"You're right, and I don't know the answer. Somewhere along the way they found a way to exploit the underlying system, whether or not they understood *how* their methods worked."

"You mean the assembly?"

Clancy's eyes narrowed.

That's right. He had never made it to I, Mine's courtyard garden.

"Back in your penthouse you got very interested when I mentioned the dancers—the ones Fritz and Collette had doing all the ritualistic stuff. How does that dancing translate into magic?"

Before answering, Clancy sipped his tea. "I have a vague idea, but that's really not my area of expertise."

"That assembly was one of the few things I experienced firsthand. So I'd really like to know."

Clancy set his mug down on the table. When he spoke, it sounded like he knew he was wasting his time. "This system sees everything as data. That includes motion. So in a compromised system, you might produce your own data intentionally, with the goal of inserting it into the fault lines of the existing code. We call this code injection."

"That's what the dancers were doing? Writing software with their bodies?"

"That's actually... yes, in a manner of speaking. But the *real* trick is figuring out a way of triggering your code, which is something we call arbitrary code execution."

"It sounds like planting a bomb in a building."

"Well, but it doesn't have to be a bomb. It could be anything you want to call on repeatedly, like a two-way radio, or a lock. Even a doorway."

"What about Dee? She didn't have any assembly."

"It needn't be intentional. Triggering arbitrary code would be the same for someone with the means, the talent, or the luck. From what you've told me, she must be naturally gifted. But that girl is playing with fire."

Were Dee's special abilities just symptoms of a broken-down system? Bas thought back to the letter she had tunneled directly into his car, just after his meeting with young Clancy in his penthouse. The small acts of magic seemed safe, she had said. But larger acts could set off reactions that could get out of control.

On some level, Dee must have known she was exploiting something volatile.

"Okay," said Bas, his head still somewhat swimming. "You said I needed context. You've given me context. Now tell me why I'm here."

The old man sighed. "As I said in my note, I have a proposition for you. I want you to look after Pal. He is alive here, and real, and he's all that matters to me. But he's also part of a compromised system that I can no longer be a part of. My very presence out there has become too much of a risk. I won't see him die again, not because of me. He must continue to live out his life. So you see, your actions do matter. They matter to me, as much as anything on the outside ever has."

"Why should I help you?"

Clancy left his mug on the table as he got back to his feet, wobbling for a few seconds before finding his balance.

"Follow me," he said.

He shuffled out of the room, and Bas followed him down the hall toward the front door. Bas half expected the old man to throw him out without any further explanation. He wasn't sure what he would do then.

But Clancy turned to the stairwell and, using the banister to steady himself, ascended to the second floor. He took each step with great care, sliding his hand along the wooden rail the entire way up.

Bas followed, his heart pounding, and not just from the exertion.

She was there, lying beneath the covers, her skin nearly as pale as the silk pillow cover itself.

Lana was exactly as Bas remembered her. She had been lost, but she wasn't dead.

Bas froze at the bedroom door, mouth agape. He wanted to rush in, seeing this final confirmation of everything he had hoped was true. And yet, as he looked in on a woman more than ten years his junior, his feet remained planted in the hallway.

This was possible only because they were living inside Clancy's system. The idea left Bas trapped between the desire to deny that any of it was real, and the profound fear that he would break the illusion if he moved an inch.

Clancy was already by the bed. He looked from Lana to Bas.

"Asleep?" Bas barely recognized his own voice.

"Tell me *she* doesn't matter, Bas," Clancy said, speaking quietly. "There's not much I can do for myself, but I can do this, for you."

"Is she asleep?" Bas asked again.

"Not exactly. But she will be awake if you agree to help me. I can do for you what I did for myself, and give you some more time with your partner. With certain limitations."

"Like what?"

Clancy crossed his arms over his chest, as if he was sure he had just made a sale. This was the ace up his sleeve. His sure thing.

"Her presence within this system would normally be dangerous. That is why this house exists. This is the sandbox she may never leave.

"I'll say that again. Lana must remain in this house in perpetuity. So make this an environment she won't *need* to leave. In here she can do as she likes. And you can come and go as you please. She will need your help. She will be confused. But she doesn't have to be alone. You can grow old together. You can do whatever you like within the walls of this house, which is yours."

The keys in Bas's pocket pressed into his thigh.

"So long as Pal is alive and happy," Clancy continued. "That is the single stipulation. And these are the terms of our agreement, in full."

"Yes."

"What's that?"

Bas entered the room and put his hand on Lana's.

Warm.

"I said yes. I'm in."

Who cared if Clancy got his way? If this was losing, Bas was willing to lose. He would figure it out as he went. They could work on it together.

"Then there's just one more thing," Clancy said, "before she wakes."

The old man led Bas back down to the front door. He wrapped his fingers around the handle.

"Your doubt was written across your face, so I just wanted to drive the point home, Mr. Milius. Lana never leaves the house."

"Right."

"Because you know what happens if she does?"

"What's that?"

Clancy pulled the door open, sending a burst of humid air down the great hall. He turned toward Bas, stepped backward onto the front stoop... and dissolved into a million glowing points of dust.

Bas stood staring out the doorway into the night. His mind buzzed, as if a current were moving up through his body from the floor.

Something Clancy had said nagged at the back of his mind. Everything out in that night was a performance playing out on a vast stage, all of it taken from a snapshot of 1980. So didn't that mean there had been a Bas Milius outside of Clancy's system? What had happened to *that* Bas?

Breathing deeply, he caught the edge of the door and pressed it shut until the latch clicked home.

A familiar voice issued from upstairs.

"Bas?"

THANK YOU!

THANK you for reading *The Last Shadow*! If you enjoyed reading this book, I'd be grateful if you'd consider rating it or leaving a brief review to help bring it to the attention of other readers like you!

For info about my upcoming releases, book news, and more, sign up for my newsletter at https://jdrobinson-author.com.

ALSO BY J.D. ROBINSON

The Hole In the World (YA SF)

On the Loop (SF)

Broken Helix (SF)

Songs From the Void (Urban Fantasy)

Whispering Skin (SF)

ACKNOWLEDGMENTS

Many people provided me with invaluable information, obscure details, or inspiration for this book, including family, friends, and complete strangers. I was humbled by their generosity and insight. I must add, however, that I made adjustments and embellishments where necessary in support of the larger story. So any inaccuracies or misrepresentations that arise on the page are mine alone!

The seed for this story was planted when I watched a 2016 video called SNES *Code Injection -- Flappy Bird in SMW* (link), by **Seth "SethBling" Hendrickson**. (Proving that you never know where a good idea will come from.) In that video he demonstrates two concepts that feature heavily in this book: code injection, and arbitrary code execution (wiki).

The idea is that one can inject foreign code into an existing process, then trigger that code to execute the modified process to your own ends. Thus, the video shows our host essentially turning Super Mario World into Flappy Bird just by moving Mario in a certain way. There's more to it than that, of course, but you can see where a writer with an overactive imagination could run with such a concept.

From my notes:

"So, where life is taking place within a simulation, certain incantations or rituals might inject/patch a new routine into an existing area in memory, which could eventually (consciously or unwittingly) be triggered to execute.

"Since every action within a simulation is associated with code behind the scenes, every action is reflected somewhere in the code. Most actions are essentially random, and could never harm the simulation. But rituals and incantations are like small programs in themselves. Even something as subtle as repetitive gesticulation could potentially result in meaningful code on the back end. Such code could also be put in place cumulatively, a little at a time, over a long period of time."

So, in case you were wondering.

Security / CCTV information

Grant Fredericks
Analyst
Forensic Video Solutions

David Witzke
Vice President, Program Management
Foray Technologies

Ryan Newkirk
Security Camera King Sales

Edward M. Robinson (AKA Dad)
Forensic Science Department
George Washington University

Investigation information

Jeff Miller
Detective (ret.)
Fairfax County Police Department

Steven Kerry Brown
Millennial Investigative Agency

Brian Willingham, CFE
President, Diligentia Group Inc.

Trademark information

John J. Devine, Jr.
Reference Librarian II - Research Specialist, Government Information
Research Services Department
Boston Public Library

Social information

Boston Gay Men's Chorus

Beta team

Lorelei Moon · Jake Barlow

Special thanks go to freelance editor extraordinaire **David Gatewood**. Not only did he spit-shine this project, he was also single-handedly responsible for untangling some particularly egregious pacing knots. I was so glad I had this chance to work with him, and I would recommend him to any author out there.

https://lonetrout.com

The cover artwork design is by **Bastien Lecouffe Deharme**, an amazing artist. Check out his portfolio.

https://www.shannonassociates.com/bastienlecouffedeharme

ABOUT THE AUTHOR

J.D. Robinson writes intimate, humanist science fiction, speculating on the human condition as fallible characters face the most exotic existential questions. (The usual stuff.)

He's been a user interface designer for more years than he cares to count, but he's also been everything from a midnight airport custodian, to a cog in the machinery of a spy satellite government contractor, to a designer of the earliest 3D chat spaces.

A reclusive nerd, he loves writing alone at night as far away from everything as possible. He also loves transcribing the weird little movies in his head, with the hope of connecting to his ideal reader. He now lives in Northern California where he's waiting for the big one. The singularity, that is.

- threads.net/@scamper
- facebook.com/jeffrobinson.author
- instagram.com/scamper
- goodreads.com/jdrobinson

Printed in Great Britain
by Amazon